FAIRFIELD ROSE

by
Sue Dyson

Magna Large Print Books
Long Preston, North Yorkshire,
England.

British Library Cataloguing in Publication Data.

Dyson, Sue
    Fairfield Rose.

    A catalogue record for this book is
    available from the British Library

    ISBN 0-7505-1421-3

First published in Great Britain by Headline Book Publishing, 1998

Cover illustration © Gordon Crabb by arrangement with Headline
Book Publishing Ltd.

Published in Large Print 1999 by arrangement with Headline Book
Publishing Ltd.

Magna Large Print is an imprint of
Library Magna Books Ltd.
Printed and bound in Great Britain by
T.J. International Ltd., Cornwall, PL28 8RW.

FAIRFIELD ROSE

Charlie Cartwright left Rose to go and fight in the Spanish Civil War and, pregnant with Charlie's child, Rose married gypsy Luke Barton in revenge for Charlie's desertion of her. Shortly after VE Day, with Rose happy enough and Luke a good father to little Ellie, Charlie returns home with his daughter from a Spanish marriage. Although Charlie is still attracted to Rose, it is not his style to come between husband and wife and Rose decides to honour her vows to Luke. However, Luke's jealousy tears them apart and pushes her towards Charlie's open arms ...

FAIRFIELD ROSE

ACKNOWLEDGEMENTS

With special thanks to everyone who helped and encouraged me in my research, especially Dmytro Bojaniwskyj, and:

Martin Faragher
David Christian
Bernard Moffat, TGWU (Isle of Man branch)
Adrian Cowin, Ronaldsway Meteorological Office
Showmen's Guild of Great Britain
Manx Museum Library
Pam Parkinson

AUTHOR'S NOTE

A permanent amusement park stood on Onchan Head from the early years of this century until its demolition in 1986.

Although Rose's story takes place in a similar location, and draws on the spirit of old White City, 'Funland' is an entirely imaginary place.

PROLOGUE

Birkenhead, June 1937

Rose Dobbs was certain she must be the happiest girl in Birkenhead.

In all her seventeen years she had never once missed a visit to the travelling fair, and this year, to make it perfect, she was here with Charlie Cartwright, walking out with him for everyone to see.

The park was a noisy jumble of happy faces, so packed that it seemed as if the whole town had turned out in force. Rose's mam and dad might mutter about throwing good money down the drain, but even they had been known to fritter away a few bob at the fair on ice creams and pony rides. To Rose it was a magic, romantic world where you could ignore all your troubles for a few hours, forget how ordinary your life was, and go home with a few more trinkets to line the mantelpiece. She wouldn't have missed it for anything.

Rose and Charlie wandered side by side through a kaleidoscope of jostling crowds and thunderous noise, coloured lights winking on and off in the gathering dusk. To the left, an old set of Victorian gallopers was turning round and round to the accompaniment of a steam organ; to the right, the stunt riders on the

Globe of Death were buzzing around their metal cage like angry flies, provoking oohs and aahs of dreadful anticipation from the watching crowd. The sweet aromas of candyfloss and home-made cinder toffee wafted above the acrid stench of diesel.

'Look, Charlie.' Rose pointed to the rifle range. 'You'd be good at that. Go on, have a go.' She slipped her hand through the crook of Charlie Cartwright's arm and fixed him with her green-flecked eyes. She knew he could never resist her when she'd set her heart on something; maybe that was why she loved him so much.

Then again, he was easy to love. With his broad shoulders, wavy blond hair and heart-melting hazel-gold eyes, there were plenty of other girls in Birkenhead who'd have set their caps at the young shipyard worker given half a chance. Not that they were going to get one: Rose knew that Charlie belonged to her.

'Come on, mate,' coaxed the man on the rifle range. 'Six shots for ninepence, win the lady a prize.'

'Well ... I dunno. I'm not much for fair-grounds an' that.'

Rose wondered why Charlie looked so ill at ease. He'd not been himself all afternoon, quiet and uncommunicative, as though he was secretly brooding on something.

'What's up, Charlie love?'

'Nothin'.' He gave Rose a smile and bent to kiss the tip of her nose.

'Go on then, win us a prize.' She giggled and hugged his arm, hoping to jolly him back to the

Charlie she knew. 'Look, that lad's just won a goldfish.'

'Oh, all right.' Charlie smiled ruefully, fetched out ninepence and shouldered a rifle. 'Dunno what you want with a goldfish, though.'

She watched him line up the sight with the moving targets, the little tin ducks leaping up and snapping back with a metallic ping as the bullet struck home. One, two, three ... that lad had got five, she was sure Charlie could hit six in a row.

'That's it, mate,' said the stallholder, hands in the pockets of his brown coat. 'Two more gets the goldfish.'

The fourth and fifth shots went wide of the mark, and Rose bit her lower lip with disappointment.

'Bad luck, mate,' commiserated the lad with the fishbowl.

The sixth shot hit the bull's-eye and a whole stack of tin cans went tumbling over.

'Good shot,' conceded the stallholder. Stretching up on tiptoe, he took something small and silvery from the back of the stall. 'Here y'are, mate. Consolation prize.'

'Oh. Ta very much.' Charlie took it and held it out to Rose. He grinned. 'Sorry it's not a goldfish.'

She smiled back and kissed him, looking down at the trinket in his hand, curious to see what it might be. It was what her dad Stan would call a worthless bit of tat, a little brooch stamped out of tin plate, shaped like a bouquet of pink enamelled flowers with the words 'FORGET

ME NOT' inscribed underneath.

'It's better than a goldfish. Go on, pin it on.'

He pinned the brooch to the lapel of her jacket and stood back, suddenly taking her hands and looking into her eyes with such intensity that she was astonished and ever so slightly afraid.

'Charlie? What is it?'

'You won't, will you, Rosie?'

'Won't what?'

'Won't forget me.'

Rose's brow wrinkled in puzzlement. 'How can I forget you if you're here? You only live three streets away.'

Charlie turned away without replying, grabbing her by the hand and towing her through the crowd.

'Where are we goin'?'

'Somewhere quiet. I've got somethin' to tell you.'

She struggled to keep up with his long strides, mumbling ' 'Scuse me' as she wriggled and dodged her way through the crowd and finally reached a bench at the edge of the park.

'What's all this about, Charlie?'

He sat down beside her on the bench and slid his arm round her waist, pulling her close. In the distance, the fairground lights seemed to grow brighter as darkness closed in around the rides.

'You know I've been in a bit of bother at work?'

Rose nodded. She knew. In fact her dad had

hardly stopped all week, going on about how Charlie had stood up for this other bloke at the shipyard and got himself into hot water with the bosses. Charlie's communist principles were always getting him into trouble, and to Rose's mind Stan only made things worse by encouraging him. Rose's dad was so besotted with Charlie that she sometimes joked that he ought to marry him himself.

She looked at Charlie's face now, and felt a horrible sense of foreboding. 'I thought that was all sorted out.'

'It was.' Charlie looked down at his boots. 'But then yesterday I had this barney with Sam Kenney ...'

'Kenney? The foreman? Oh, Charlie ...'

'I know, I know. I should've kept me mouth shut, but the way he was treatin' old Danny Mac ...' He blew out his breath in a short, sharp sigh. 'He sacked me on the spot, told me to get me cards an' not bother comin' back on Monday.'

Rose stared at him in horror. 'Sacked! Oh God, no Charlie ... What are you goin' to do? What about the weddin'?'

He silenced her gently, laying a hand on her arm. 'It's not just the job, Rosie. There's somethin' else. You ... you remember Manny Green?'

'Manny? What about him?'

'He's goin' to Spain. So's Phil from the Fox an' Grapes. Enlistin' in the International Brigade. The thing is ...' He raised his head and looked straight into Rose's eyes. 'I've been thinkin'.'

She felt her heart contract as though icy fingers were squeezing at it. Suddenly and horribly it was all starting to make sense. Spain. The Civil War. Charlie and those hotheaded communist mates of his. No, not that. He wouldn't do that to her. Not this man she loved to distraction, this man who'd sworn he'd marry her and take care of her for ever and ever.

'I'm goin' with them, Rosie.'

She clapped her hands to her face, her lips icy cold against her fingers.

'No!'

'I've got to do it, Rosie, you know I have. There's people dyin' out there, our innocent brothers an' sisters. An' now there's no job for me here ... it's like there's no reason *not* to go—'

'No reason!' Shock turned swiftly to pain and anger. 'So that's all I'm worth to you, is it?'

'Please, Rosie, listen to me. We'll still get married ... we'll just have to wait a bit, a few months, till I come home.' He tried to touch her but she sprang away.

'Don't touch me!'

'Rose ... You mean the world to me, Rose. I thought you knew that.'

She looked into those sad, golden eyes and realised that yes, she did know it; but sometimes the world wasn't enough. Sometimes there were things that meant more, and she could not bear the thought of being less than everything to Charlie. Tears prickled the corners of her eyes, tears of anger and betrayal. 'All I know is, you've been plannin' this for God knows how long an' never said one word to me. Not one word. How could you do that to me, Charlie Cartwright? How could you?'

The words seemed to echo on the evening air. A couple walking by hand in hand turned and gave them a curious look, then laughed and hurried on towards the funfair.

Charlie got slowly to his feet, holding out his arms. 'I *love* you, Rose, I swear I do. I'd never let you down. Just a few months till it's all over an' I'll come home ... I suppose we could even get married before I go—'

'A few months? An' what if you come home in a wooden box, what do I do then? Marry you, Charlie?' With awkward fingers she wrenched the forget-me-not pin from her jacket and flung it to the ground at his feet. 'I wouldn't marry you if you were the last man in the world!' She ran away from him, blundering towards the park gates, not really seeing where she was going because of the tears brimming in her eyes.

'Rosie! Rosie, come back!'

Charlie grabbed the brooch from the ground and ran after her, catching her, holding her still and kissing her though she struggled and fought to push him away. All she could do was blurt out her pain in hacking sobs that soaked the shoulder of his best shirt.

'I hate you, Charlie Cartwright, I hate you. I do, I do.'

'Don't say that Rosie, please don't say that.'

She felt him press the forget-me-not brooch back into her hand and curl her fingers over it. His voice was a tender, loving whisper in her ear.

'Please wait for me. You mean the world to me ...'

But that was Charlie's world. And Rose's was tumbling down around her ears.

CHAPTER 1

Birkenhead, March 1946

Sofia Barton stood in the doorway of the terraced house, brawny arms folded, her muscular bulk barring the way. 'Why you brought *her* with you?' she demanded, glaring first at Rose and then at her son.

'Because she's my wife, Mam,' said Luke, weary of trying to pacify his mother.

'Wife!' snorted Sofia. 'She's nothin' but a *gorgio looverni.*'

'Mam!' hissed Luke, but Sofia's leathery brown face was fixed in a smile of triumph.

Looverni. Rose didn't know Romany, only the few words she'd picked up from Luke, but she knew what that word meant: whore. She felt a hot rush of blood to her cheeks as the anger of humiliation reared up inside her. Why did it have to be like this every time she and her mother-in-law crossed swords? She opened her mouth to give as good as she'd got, then saw Luke glance at her imploringly, and for his sake closed it again.

'Are you goin' to let us in, Sofia?' she asked quietly. 'Or shall we just stay out here an' have a row on the doorstep?'

Sofia's lips clamped into a tight, thin line, but she turned round and stomped back into the house, allowing Luke and Rose to step inside. He gave her hand a reassuring squeeze.

'Take no notice,' he said. 'You know what she's like.'

I ought to by now, thought Rose, still smarting from Sofia's insult. Why should she be ashamed that she'd borne another man's child, years before she'd ever set eyes on Luke? Charlie was dead and gone, killed in the Spanish Civil War, never knowing he'd left Rose expecting Ellie. Nearly nine long years had passed since that day, three happy ones since she'd married Luke, but Rose knew that however many years went by she'd never be good enough. According to Sofia, only Romany girls were fit to marry her sons. Which was why Rose was so determined to prove her wrong.

'Come on,' she said. 'Let's find out what this is all about.'

Rose was certainly curious. It wasn't every day that Manfri Barton summoned his younger son to 'talk family business'. Wild speculations ran through her mind. Perhaps this was something to do with the car repair business Manfri ran from a bomb-site at the other end of Ferry Street. Yes, that might be it. Manfri wasn't as spry as he used to be, what with the rheumatism so bad in his hands; and Luke was just about the best car mechanic in Birkenhead. Maybe his dad was going to make him a partner in the business.

She and Luke followed Sofia down the passage and into the front parlour, which was kept for special occasions. Rose had seen inside it just once before, and then only because it was her wedding day. Sofia and Manfri might have given up their vardo for a simple terraced house, but Sofia had never lost her Romany pride in her home. She kept it immaculate, with hand-made lace antimacassars on the chair-backs, and sills and shelves lined with the very best quality china. Minton, Doulton, Dresden, Spode, a cluster of Staffordshire spaniels on the table, a row of porcelain horses wending their way across the mantelpiece in descending order of size. Shiny copper kettles on the hearth, and a square of carpet that was gaudy but expensive. Rose found it dazzling, not a bit like her and Luke's two-up-two-down, with its Utility wardrobes and second-hand bed, or her mam and dad's green distemper and worn-out lino.

Manfri's favourite chair sat empty by the hearth, his pipe and tobacco pouch balanced on the arm. Rose and Luke sat down on the sofa, Rose perching uncomfortably on the corner, edging herself as near as possible to the warmth from the crackling fire.

'Where's Dad?' demanded Luke.

'He come, he come.' Sofia picked up a cushion and punched it into shape before dropping it back down on to the chair.

Luke glanced at the hands on the big gilt-cased clock. 'Ellie'll be back from school soon, Rose'll have to go.'

'Good,' snapped Sofia. 'She has no place here.' She muttered something in Romany, just loud enough for Luke to get the gist.

'Daia ...'

23

Luke raked long, oil-smeared fingers through his mop of black wavy hair, pushing it back from his forehead and the long scar which ran from his left temple to the corner of his mouth. The deep white furrow was partly covered by the leather patch he always wore to cover his missing eye, legacy of the terrible motor-cycle accident which had ended his career as a stunt rider. 'Ma, Rose is part of the family, she's a right to be here.'

Sofia's expression shifted to disdain. 'Who's the master in your house, boy? You or that *juvi?*'

Rose saw the suppressed anger in him, making the muscles in his lean, hawkish face tense like wires. Poor Luke. Twenty-five years old and his mam treated him like a kid.

The sound of the back door opening and closing brought a smile to Sofia's face. 'Manfri. He will tell you your duty.'

'Duty!' Rose exchanged looks with Luke. 'What's goin' on?'

Luke shrugged. The door opened and in came Manfri. Though his blue-black hair was streaked with grey he was still a handsome man at fifty, but his finger-joints were gnarled and his movements jerky and stiff. It was rheumatism that had forced him off the road to become a house-dweller, and Sofia had never quite forgiven him for it.

'Luke,' he acknowledged his younger son with a nod and a grunt. 'Rose,' he added, not unkindly.

'I tell her she should not stay,' said Sofia.

24

Manfri waved her aside. 'Stay? Course she should, she's family.'

'*Dadrus,* what's all this about?' demanded Luke as Manfri took off his overcoat. 'There's work wants doin' on that car—'

'The car can wait.' Manfri sat himself down in his chair, filled his pipe slowly and lovingly from the tobacco pouch, and lit it. 'I've had a letter.' He sucked on his pipe and blew out the smoke. 'From Dan.'

Luke's face darkened as though a storm cloud were passing over it. There had never been any love lost between Luke and his elder brother. They might look alike, but that was where the similarity ended. Dan Barton was as devious and unreliable as Luke was honest. A spiv and a loser who cared for nobody but himself.

'He's bein' demobbed?' asked Rose.

Manfri shook his head. 'Nope. They're keepin' him in.'

'Keepin' him in! But why?'

'The army wants him for a special job,' interjected Sofia. 'Special,' she repeated, in case they hadn't heard the first time.

'How long for?' demanded Luke. Rose could tell he was hoping it would be a very long time.

Manfri blew out a long curl of tobacco smoke. 'Two years, maybe three.'

Three years! A thought suddenly occurred to Rose. 'But if he's stayin' in the army, what about his fairground rides? The ones on the Isle of Man?'

'*My* fairground rides,' Sofia corrected her

with a self-important toss of her head. 'My uncle Walleye's rides. Dan runs them for me. He look after them before the war.'

'He can't run them if he's in the army,' pointed out Luke. 'What are you goin' to do, sell them?'

Sofia looked at him as though he had just suggested murder. 'Sell! I would never sell, never! The fairground, it is opening again in April, the Barton rides they will be there.'

'But, Ma ...' Luke looked baffled. 'If there's nobody to run them, then who ...?'

Rose saw Manfri and Sofia's eyes fix on Luke, and realisation hit her like a punch in the stomach.

'You'll pick it up quick enough,' said Manfri. 'You're a bright lad.'

Luke looked thunderstruck. 'Me! You're askin' *me* to go to the Isle of Man an' run Dan's rides for him!'

'Course they're not,' said Rose, praying she'd got the wrong end of the stick. 'That's not what you mean, is it Manfri?'

'Your mother reckons you'll do a fair enough job of it,' he replied. 'It's only for a year or two; you're young an' strong—'

'There is no one else,' added Sofia, making it quite clear that she wished there were. 'I have no other sons.'

'Beggars can't be choosers,' agreed Manfri. 'This is the first season Funland's opened since the war. If we don't take up the pitch next month we'll lose it to someone else.'

'Next month!' Luke froze in horror. Rose

stared in shocked silence at him, willing him to tell his parents how crazy this scheme was. 'I won't do it,' he blurted out.

'You'll do your duty.' Sofia's dark, unforgiving eyes dared her son to defy her.

'His duty!' exclaimed Rose, unable to keep silent any longer. 'This is Dan's duty, not Luke's. Get somebody else, pay somebody!'

'There is no one else,' repeated Sofia.

'You expect my Luke to give up his job an' ... an' go off an' leave me an' Ellie ...'

There was a horrible sarcastic smile on Sofia's face as she replied. 'It is *your* duty to go with him, Rose. You are his *wife.*'

'Me! Go there?'

Luke laid his hand on hers. 'It's all right, Rose love. We're not goin'.'

Sofia fumed. 'Tell him, Manfri. Tell him he must go!'

Manfri looked weary and worn down. 'Luke, lad, there's no other way. I'd do it myself, only ...' He held up his hands, the fingers bent into gnarled claws. 'Look at me, I can hardly hold a spanner any more.'

'That's why you need me here!' pleaded Luke. 'With you, in the business. I'm a good mechanic; you need me.'

'There's other mechanics,' pointed out Manfri. 'An' plenty of 'em demobbed from the army, lookin' for work.'

'Then send one of *them* to the Isle of Man!' Rose cried out, exasperated beyond the point of endurance. This wasn't happening; she couldn't let it happen. All that she and Luke had worked

27

for, the money they'd scrimped and saved so they could rent a little house and give Ellie a proper home ... she couldn't let Sofia wave it all away, as if it didn't matter.

'*Hush kacker!*' growled Sofia.

'No, I won't shut up!' retorted Rose. 'This is our life, you can't just tell us to drop everythin'—'

'Hush love,' said Luke quietly. He looked grim, grey-faced beneath the natural olive of his skin. 'Look, Dad, this ... it's not right.'

'I'm sorry, lad,' said Manfri. At least he sounded sympathetic, thought Rose. Perhaps he was coming round. 'But you'll have to go an' that's that. Look at it this way; it's a job, it pays money—'

'I've *got* a job,' protested Luke.

But Sofia wouldn't listen. 'You will go,' she insisted. 'You will do this thing, or you will have no job.' She looked at Manfri and her expression hardened. 'Tell them, Manfri. Tell them this is true.'

'Damn,' muttered Rose as she stopped half-way down Florizel Street and rummaged in her shopping basket. As if these last couple of days hadn't been bad enough, she'd forgotten the veg for tea.

'What is it, Mam?' demanded Ellie, pirouetting on one clumpy shoe as she drew the other foot up behind her back, ballerina-style. Ellie Barton couldn't abide standing still.

Fishing in the small change at the bottom of her purse, Rose popped half a crown into

Ellie's palm. 'Run down to Wilson's, there's a good girl. Get two pound of spuds.'

'Spuds.' Ellie nodded energetically.

'Don't let him palm you off with the green ones, mind. An' some greens ...'

'Greens.' Ellie shifted from one foot to the other, eager to be gone.

'... if he's got any. Oh, an' two ounces of ...'

As usual, Rose was talking to herself. Ellie was already on the other side of the street, golden pigtails streaming out behind her as she skipped along the pavement towards the corner shop. Rose watched her with amusement. Her daughter was just like a coiled spring. I used to be like that, she thought. Everything was one great big adventure.

'An' mind you hurry back home!' she called out after Ellie, then turned down the alley and walked towards the back gate of number forty-seven.

There was nothing remarkable about Rose and Luke Barton's house. It was just another rented two-up-two-down in a row of identical red-brick houses, blackened by a century of industrial grime. But inside it was clean as a new pin, there was always food on the table, and spotless white washing flapped on the line every Monday morning. Rose was proud of the home she'd made for Luke and Ellie, proud of the cheap knick-knacks on the mantelpiece and the walnut-cased wireless set she'd bought with what she'd saved from the housekeeping money. What they had, they'd worked for, she and Luke. They might not share a glamorous life, but their love had grown deep and loyal and enduring. And they made a winning team, no matter what her father might say.

Pushing open the back door, she wiped the mud from her shoes on the iron scraper and went in. To her surprise, she found Luke in the kitchen, elbows on the table and chin propped on his hands. Something about the slump of his shoulders told her that things had not gone well.

'You're back early,' she hazarded, her mouth dry with apprehension. 'Did you speak to Manfri?'

Luke nodded dejectedly. His spine uncoiled as he sat back in his chair. 'I tried, Rose. I really tried, I swear I did.'

A cold tingle scurried up Rose's back. Setting the shopping basket on the table she sat down next to Luke, not even bothering to take her coat off. 'What did he say?'

'He said he's made his mind up. If we don't go an' open up them rides, I'll be out of a job.'

'He'd sack you!' Rose could hardly believe what she was hearing. 'Sack his own son!'

'It's Ma, she's put him up to it.' Luke turned to look at Rose. 'He doesn't want to, but what else can he do?'

'What else? He could try standin' up to her for once!'

'It's no good, love,' said Luke. 'We'll have to go.'

'But if we go we'll lose everythin'—our home, everythin'! Oh, Luke, there's got to be somethin' we can do ... You could get another job.'

Luke shook his head. 'I'll have to go. You an' Ellie could stay here.'

'Stay behind!'

'There'd be no money to keep on the house, but you could stay at your mam an' dad's—'

'Stop right there, Luke Barton.' Rose peeled off her gloves and threw them on the table. 'D'you really think I'd let you go off there all on your own? Well, do you?'

Luke looked sheepish. 'I dunno ...'

'If you're goin' anywhere, we're comin' with you. We're family, remember?' And I'm not letting your mother tear us apart, she added silently. There's nothing she'd like better than to see us at each other's throats. 'We'll get by. Somehow.'

Luke reached into the pocket of his overalls and took out a couple of crumpled sheets of paper.

'What's that?' asked Rose.

'It's what Dan sent Dad. A list of instructions. There's not much here, mind. How to get to Funland, a couple of names ...'

Rose peered at the list.

'Who's Eddie Kneale?'

'The bloke who used to maintain the rides, I think. He's got a workshop or somethin'. Sean Rourke ... he used to work with Dan. Doreen Kneale ... s'pose she must be Eddie's wife. Somebody called Cec, God knows who he is.'

31

'An' Percy Sayle?' Rose read off the last name.

'Oh, he's the one with the keys. You know, to Walleye's vardo.'

'Vardo? You're not tellin' me we're supposed to live in a caravan?'

Luke shook his head. 'There's a cottage as well, somewhere close. Walleye used to live there in the winter. I s'pose this Sayle bloke has the keys to that an' all.'

Rose gazed down at the rumpled paper. Their whole future, scribbled down on a tatty page torn from a notebook. It just didn't seem right somehow.

'It's not for ever,' said Luke. He sounded as if he was trying to persuade himself.

'But ... the Isle of Man.' Rose tried hard to imagine it, but all she knew was that it was a place where posh people went for their holidays. Posher than the Bartons, anyhow. And now they were going to live there. It was silly to be afraid, and yet Rose was. She'd never lived anywhere but Birkenhead. 'Oh, Luke, I just don't know ...'

A small voice piped up in the silence, making Rose start. 'Mam? Mam, are we goin' to the Isle of Man?'

Rose stood up, hands on hips. 'Ellie Barton, how many times have I told you not to listen at doors?'

'Are we *really* goin' to the Isle of Man?'

Rose looked at Luke, folded her arms and sighed. 'We'll have to see about that,' she said.

CHAPTER 2

Horace Spence, owner of Funland, stuck his thumbs into the pockets of his ample waistcoat and surveyed his domain. Acres of busy fairground stretched out in front of him, bustling with showmen scurrying about putting their rides in order in these last few weeks before the grand reopening. The tober was bordered to the left by hills and to the right by Douglas Bay, scooping round to cup the wild March sea as though determined not to let it escape: just as determined as Horace was to lure every one of this season's trippers to Funland.

Frankly, the place had seen better days. Six years of war had replaced laughter and multi-coloured lights with boarded-up sideshows and ripped awnings. The parts of the tober that weren't concreted over were rutted and waterlogged from the toings and froings of army vehicles, which had been using the ground as a car park and general-purpose rubbish tip. Still, nothing that a coat or two of paint and a bit of elbow-grease couldn't put right. Pity the alien internees had gone home—he could've got the job done on the cheap. Anyhow, Horace would make sure the showmen who leased pitches from him had their rides in tip-top condition before Funland opened its gates on Easter Monday.

Percy Sayle came across from his living

wagon, boots squelching in the mud, cap pulled down against the wind and rain. Two small children and a dog wove in and out of his legs. Widowed with six kids, numerous chickens, ducks, a pig and sundry other domestic animals, Percy seemed surrounded by a permanent aroma of livestock.

'Electrics is on the blink again, Misther Spence.'

Horace distanced himself from the smell by a couple of steps. 'Then sort 'em out, man,' he boomed in his rich Pennine burr. 'I don't pay you sit around on your backside all day.'

'No, Misther Spence.' A big raindrop ran down Percy's nose and splashed to the ground. 'I'll see to it meself.'

Percy squelched off across the muddy tober. That was what Horace liked to see: other people working. Sheltering in the doorway of his office, he rubbed his hands together with glee. Things were going well, even better than he'd hoped. Showmen were clamouring to get back into Funland after six years of nothing but black-out fairs; they'd pay anything to get a pitch.

The only bad news was the losers. People like that dead loss Dan Barton, who as yet hadn't even bothered making an appearance. The job of getting his clapped-out rides into commission seemed to have been left to Sean Rourke and Doreen Kneale, who never stopped arguing long enough to get anything done.

Spence laughed to himself. It was perfect, really. Doreen and Sean would never pool forces long enough to prevent Dan Barton defaulting on his lease. And when he did that, the Bartons would be off that pitch faster than Paddy Cooill's racing pig. This would leave Horace free to move the Darwells on to part of the pitch at an exorbitant rent, and use the free space for his own rides.

Horace's fat jowls wobbled with mirth as he thought of all the money he was going to make. Provided Dan Barton didn't suddenly pop up like a genie out of a bottle, absolutely nothing could go wrong.

Rose's parents did not take the news well. Edie made pint after pint of over-sugared tea; Stan glowered from the depths of his armchair and wouldn't say two words to Luke. And all the time, Ellie was careering up and down Mersey Row like a miniature tornado, telling anyone who would listen that 'I'm goin' ter live in the Isle of Man! I'm goin' ter live on a *fairground!*'

Rose felt a stab of pain as she gazed over her mother's shoulder, through the ancient net curtains to the street. She'd lived round here ever since she was a baby, had played hopscotch on every paving-slab from here to Woodside. She just couldn't imagine being somewhere else. But the choice had been made and now she must make the best of it.

Edie pushed a plate of sandwiches under Rose's nose. 'Those are spam and the others are paste.'

Rose knew she was upset, but Edie would never show it. After supporting the family for years because Stan was usually malingering when he wasn't on strike, there wasn't much Edie couldn't cope with.

'Go on, Rose love, you've got to keep your strength up.'

Rose shook her head. 'Maybe later. Luke?'

But Luke's eyes were on Stan. And Stan was pretending to read the paper.

'Luke?'

'What's that?'

'Another butty,' said Edie. 'Do you want one?'

'Oh. No thanks, Mrs Dobbs. Actually I'd best be off. Da's got this baby Austin what wants lookin' at.' He grabbed his jacket and threw it over his arm. 'It's kind of you to give us tea Mrs Dobbs. Stan,' he added, offering him a last chance to be civil. But Stan didn't take it.

'I'll only be a minute, Mam,' said Rose, getting up and trailing Luke down the passage to the back kitchen.

'Luke, wait. I'll come with you.'

Luke shrugged his arms into the sleeves of his jacket, put his arm round Rose and kissed her on the brow. 'You stay here, love. It's you they want to talk to, not me.'

'That's not true,' protested Rose.

' 'Course it is. They've never liked me—well, your dad hasn't, anyroad. 'Sides, they won't be seein' so much of you for a while, will they?' He kissed her again, very tenderly. 'I might be late home, there's things to sort out down the garage.'

When he was gone, Rose went back into the parlour.

'What was all that whisperin' about?' demanded Stan suspiciously.

'Oh, so you've got a tongue in your head have you?' retorted Edie, coming back into the room with a tray of cake baked from the rations she'd saved up for a special occasion. She put the tray on the table. 'What do you think it was about, you great lump? They've been here an hour, an' you've not said one word to Luke.'

'What's there to say?' snorted Stan. 'Givin' up a good job to drag you all that way.'

'He had no choice, Dad. His family's got no one else to run the rides.'

'Bloody gyppos.'

'Dad!' warned Rose, but Stan was on his high horse.

'He'll have you sellin' clothes pegs out of a basket, you mark my words.'

'Don't be ridiculous!'

'That what you want, is it? You an' Ellie livin' in a van like tinkers?'

'Give over, Stan,' said Edie, raising her voice to get a word in edgeways. 'There's a nice little cottage, Rose told you—'

'Didn't I tell you his sort were no good? Didn't I?'

Rose could see where things were heading. It was like this every time Stan failed to get his own way. And Stan's way of dealing with any situation he couldn't control was always to take it out on his nearest and dearest.

'Calm down, Dad. We'll be fine.' She'd just about convinced herself that it was true, that Ellie was right and it was going to be like a big

37

long holiday. 'Think about Ellie—she'll love it at the seaside.'

'I *am* thinkin' of her.' Stan thumped the arm of his chair. 'Leave 'im, Rose. Come back an' live here with your mam and dad. He's no good for you.'

Rose sighed. Getting up from her seat, she went across to her father's chair, perched on the arm and stroked his cheek the way she used to do when she was a little girl.

'Don't think you can get round me like that, girl ...'

'Luke loves us, Dad. And he's a good father to Ellie. He wants the best for us, just like you do.'

'How can you say that? When he's takin' you away to ... to God knows what!'

Rose laughed. Suddenly this all seemed very silly and overdramatic. 'Dad, it's the Isle of Man, not Timbuctoo! Half of Birkenhead goes there for its holidays!'

'The toffee-nosed half,' sniffed Stan.

'P'raps me an' Ellie'll come back posh then.' She stood up and planted a cheeky kiss right in the middle of Stan's bald head. 'Just give Luke a chance, Dad. You owe him that.'

Almost two weeks later, Rose found herself standing next to Luke on the deck of the old *Manx Maid*, watching the Liverpool waterfront sliding slowly into the distance. It was a blustery, damp March day, but Ellie wouldn't hear of going below to the saloon. She'd never been on a boat before, if you didn't count the Woodside ferry, and she kept running from one side of the deck to the other, staring at everything in wide-eyed fascination.

'Mam, Mam, how much further?'

'Dad, what's that?'

'Mam, I'm hungry!'

'Mam, I feel sick!'

Rose felt Luke squeeze her hand and she squeezed back, glad of the warm strength of his grip. After Charlie, it had taken a long time to learn to love again, but now Rose couldn't imagine being without Luke. They'd come so far together.

'I'm goin' down to get a drink. Comin'?'

She shook her head. 'Soon, love. I'll wait for Ellie.'

Face to the offshore wind, she leaned over the rail and gazed at the grey, smudged line of the faraway quayside. Nine years ago she'd stood at Woodside and watched Charlie sail away on the Liverpool ferry, never to return. They'd been hardly more than kids. Neither of them had the faintest idea that Rose was in the family way. Would things have been different if they had? She remembered how Charlie's face had got smaller and smaller, his features blurring to uniform grey until he had dwindled to a distant blob, and then ... nothing. It was strange how he had just faded from her life like that, vanished without a trace, leaving only Ellie to remind her that he had ever existed. That day she'd been so wrapped up in her own misery that she'd never paused to wonder how Charlie had felt, leaving everything he'd ever known, and not knowing if he'd ever come home. Had he wondered what the future held in store? Had he thought about little Rose Dobbs in the moments before he died—wherever and whenever that might have been?

How could somebody just vanish like that?

Well, if there was one lesson Rose had learned, it was that you could never be sure what lay round the next corner; and whether life dealt you aces or jokers, you just had to set to and make the best hand you could.

Ellie came running up, flinging her arms around Rose's waist. 'Mam, Mam, I'm cold.'

Rose opened her coat, snuggled Ellie against her body and wrapped the front around her daughter's shivering form. 'Shall we go and find your dad then?'

Ellie screwed her head round and peered at the horizon, afraid that she might miss something. 'I want to see the Island.'

'We'll see it soon enough,' smiled Rose and, hugging Ellie close, she headed down the companionway to the saloon.

CHAPTER 3

Rose couldn't believe that anywhere in the world could be so quiet.

The Island wasn't anything like she'd imagined. For a start you could hardly make out its famous hills for sea-mist, and a fine drizzle was filtering down through a sky the colour of gunmetal. This was not at all like the sunshiny advertising posters she'd seen at Lime Street Station: 'COME ABROAD TO THE ISLE OF MAN'. Where were the toast-rack horse trams, the happy people in summer frocks? Did people really come here for their holidays? Abroad! This was deader than Birkenhead on a Sunday morning.

At least the locals seemed friendly enough, helping them and their battered old suitcases off the boat and showing them where to find the bus station. But Rose had never felt so much like a stranger in a foreign land. And when she found out that the buses only ran to Funland in the summer, she felt like sitting down in the nearest puddle and sobbing her heart out.

Yet by the time the yellow single-decker bus deposited them at Port Jack the drizzle had stopped and the mist was clearing. A faint, watery sunshine was even beginning to filter through the clouds, revealing hilltops and patches of blue sky.

'It's a sign,' grinned Luke. 'Everything's goin' to be fine, just you wait an' see. Soon as we've got the keys to the cottage ...'

Painted arrows, half washed-out by six wartime winters, pointed up a steep hill. 'THIS WAY TO THE FUNFAIR!' read the faded posters. 'FOLLOW THE CROWD TO FUNLAND!' 'MANXLAND'S BIGGEST ATTRACTION!' The cliff lift, which had carried so many holidaymakers up the hillside before the war, was closed and deserted; they would have to make the climb on foot.

As they trailed up the hill, footsore and wet, Rose prayed that Funland would be everything that Manfri Barton had promised. She remembered the funfairs of her childhood, the rare day-trips to New Brighton, the annual treat when the travelling fair came to Birkenhead, so noisy and brash and exciting.

She watched Ellie, determinedly 'helping' Luke to carry one of the suitcases, even though it was five times too heavy for her and she was really just getting in the way. It made Rose smile, seeing how well they got on together. Whatever else might happen, she knew that Luke Barton would stand by them and see them right.

'Almost there,' called out Luke. 'I can see the gates.'

Rose felt her heart skip a beat. She turned and looked back over her shoulder at the town clustered around the sweep of the bay. It all seemed so alien—beautiful, but nothing like the world she knew. Could she really learn to be a part of it?

Luke reached the top of the hill and stopped in his tracks, gazing ahead of him. Ellie scampered about his feet like a spaniel pup, one wet braid escaping from its sodden blue ribbon.

'Rose. We're here.'

She caught him up, eager to see what he could see. Before her stood a huge gated arch bearing the words 'WELCOME TO UNLAND' in tall blue letters, the missing F swinging crazily upside down from its one remaining screw.

Beyond lay the tober, a chaos of half-assembled rides, trucks, children, and men in overalls running about. It looked to Rose for all the world as if someone had taken a beehive and turned it upside down. She scanned the scene, half-excited, half-afraid, making out the names of some of the attractions: Ghost Train, Fun House, Dodgems.

'Are our rides here, Luke?' she asked.

'Somewhere,' shrugged Luke.

'Where, Dad, where, where?' demanded Ellie, jumping up and down.

Luke laughed. 'I don't know where, love. We'll find out tomorrow, eh?'

'You goin' to show us our new home then?' asked Rose, picking up her suitcase.

'Course I am. Best find Spence first, tell him we're here.' Luke called out to a shabbily dressed middle-aged man who was crossing the fairground, a live chicken tucked under one arm and a small boy under the other. 'You seen Horace Spence anywhere?'

The man stopped in his tracks, turned and came tramping across to meet them. Despite the fact that she was cold, wet and miserable, it was all Rose could do not to burst out laughing.

'What's that you said?'

'Spence. Horace Spence. He around, is he?'

'Misther Spence? He's down the harbour, yessir. Got a new ride comin' in on the *Tynwald*, see.'

'But he'll be back later?'

'Later? Oh aye, later.'

'When?'

'Oh, I couldn't rightly say, yessir. He's a law unto himself is Misther Spence.'

Seeing that the conversation was going nowhere, Rose cut in. 'Can you help us? We're the Bartons, we've come to take over Dan Barton's rides.'

This news produced an almost magical effect. Setting down the uncomplaining toddler, the Manxman spat on his palm and wiped it on the seat of his grimy pants, extending it in welcome. 'Sayle's the name. Percy Sayle. This here's my youngest, Percy junior.'

Luke accepted Percy's handshake. Percy junior chuckled and sucked his thumb.

'Luke Barton, I'm Dan's brother. This is Rose, my wife, and Ellie.'

'Say hello, Ellie.' Rose nudged her daughter forward.

'Hello, Mr Sayle,' said Ellie brightly. 'Is that a *real* chicken?'

Percy Sayle laughed. 'Oh aye, she's real enough. Lays real eggs an' all.'

Ellie's eyes lit up at this; there'd been dried egg at best for as long as she could remember, sometimes not even that.

'Now then,' said Percy, 'you'll be wantin' the keys to Dan's wagon?'

Luke scratched his head. 'The old vardo? Not really. Leastways, not yet.'

'It's the keys to the cottage we've come for,' explained Rose. 'You know, Dan's cottage.'

Percy blinked. *'Dan's* cottage, you say?'

'The cottage, that's right,' repeated Luke, slightly impatient now. 'If you could just give us the keys an' tell us where it is ...'

Percy looked mortified. 'Misther Dan's not told you then?'

'Told us what?' demanded Rose.

'The cottage, Missus Rose. There ain't no cottage. It don't belong to him no more, see. Likes his gamblin', does Misther Dan.'

'Gamblin'!' exclaimed Rose; and she had a premonition of what Percy was going to say even before he'd opened his mouth.

'Lost it to Misther Spence in a card game he did,' Percy went on. 'Oh, must've been seven year or more since. There's just Walleye's old vardo now. Shall I be after gettin' you the key?'

Percy Sayle returned from his wagon with a bunch of keys, sorting through them for the right one. Rose watched him in dismay. No cottage, after everything they'd been promised? How could Dan have deceived them like this?

Luke seemed to read her thoughts. 'Don't worry, love,' he reassured her. 'I saw Walleye's vardo once, when I was a kid. Kept it like a little palace, he did. Proper cookin' stove, carpets, feather beds ...'

'There, that'll be the one,' announced Percy, releasing a heavy key from the ring. 'Misther Dan's wagon's over yonder, by the hedge.'

Rose followed the pointing finger to a scattering of vans arranged in a straggly line along the far perimeter of the site, marked by a thick hedge of hawthorn and gorse.

Percy dropped the key into Luke's palm.

45

'Furthest one it is, yessir, that one set a little ways apart, near the water tap.' And with a touch of his cap, he trudged off towards the roller-coaster, Little Percy chattering in his wake.

The living-wagon stood by the communal tap, just as Percy had said. A traditional horse-drawn Romany vardo, it had once been the finest van on the Island, its sloping walls intricately carved and picked out with touches of red and yellow. It sat high upon iron-shod wheels that were almost as tall as Rose herself; a six-rung wooden ladder at the front led up to double doors, and the canopy's sides were so beautifully carved that they looked like lace when the sun shone through them.

This was how Luke remembered his grand-father's van—and perhaps that was how it had been, all those years ago when Luke was a boy. But the memory could play tricks, and now ... now it broke Rose's heart just to look at it.

'Luke ... Luke, just *look* at the state of it!'

Rose stared at the weathered carcass of the van, speechless with horror, blinking back sudden tears of despair. In all her worst nightmares she had never imagined things could be so bad. One of the windows was broken and the curtains hung in dripping-wet tatters, plastered to the frame. The painted decorations had long since flaked away, and in places the wooden structure looked cracked and rotten. Part of the chimney had snapped off and lay on the ground amid the debris of broken china which had slid out of one of the underboxes, now occupied by a robin's nest. Some of the tarred felt which once covered the roof had torn and hung now in flaccid ribbons, and when she walked round to take a look at the back, Rose found herself wading knee-deep in rubbish.

Tears threatened to break through and she had to hold them back. Had she really given up her neat little terraced house for this?

'It's not as bad as it looks,' said Luke. 'It can't be.'

The two of them stood there, paralysed, while Ellie ran round and round, chattering and laughing as though this was the most wonderful thing she had ever seen.

'Give me the key,' said Rose, steeling herself for whatever else she might find. She took it and very gingerly climbed the wooden steps to the front door. They groaned under her slight weight, but did not give way. The key turned sluggishly in the lock then the door swung outward, and Rose was swamped with the stench of mildew and neglect.

She took a deep breath, stooped, and stepped inside. Think positive, girl, she told herself. You have to, it's the only way to bear it. But it was hard—very, very hard.

She took a mental inventory. The floor was puddled with water where the rain had got in, and every bit of bedding was mildewed and ruined, but that could be put right. They could put glass in the windows and mend the roof, clean out the Hostess stove and scrub away the thick layer of filth which covered everything. It was just a question of getting down on her hands and knees and doing it, and Rose Barton had never been afraid of hard work.

She heard Luke's voice behind her and knew how deeply he was feeling this new disappointment. He had been so proud of his grandfather.

'I just don't understand,' he said. 'How could it get like this?' Angrily he picked up a sodden feather pillow and flung it down the steps. 'Ma was right, they should've burned the bloody thing when Walleye died. It's the bad spirits ...'

Rose turned round and forced herself to smile. After all, what was the use of long faces? 'Chin up,' she said. 'It could be worse.'

'Oh yeah?' he said ruefully, picking up a headless china ornament and letting it fall with a dull clunk.

'Yeah,' she replied softly, snuggling up to Luke and laying her face against his shirt-front. It was warm and damp, and she could hear the reassuringly regular thump of his heartbeat just underneath. 'I might never have met you.'

Luke chuckled darkly. 'Maybe you'd have been better off if you'd not!'

She punched him playfully. 'Don't talk rubbish!'

Ellie came bouncing up the steps with an energy that set the whole van juddering on its axles. 'It's a real caravan!' she squealed, breathless with excitement. 'We're goin' to live in a proper gypsy caravan! Isn't it just the wonderfullest thing in the whole world?'

Wonderful was not the first word which sprang to Horace Spence's lips when Percy Sayle gave him the news.

'Barton's brother? He's here—at Funland?'

'Took him over to the van meself, Misther Spence. Him an' the missus—an' the kiddie, o' course.'

Horace raised a bushy eyebrow. 'Well, well. Married, is he? I wonder what his wife makes of old Walleye's van. Not quite Buckingham Palace is it?' He considered this new development for a moment. Perhaps Luke Barton's presence on the Island might work in his favour after all. A couple of weeks' earache from the missus and Luke would be begging to sell up and get out.

'And he's met Sean and Doreen, has he?'

'Not yet, Misther Spence. Least, I don't reckon so.'

'Good.' Horace cracked a smile, leaned back in his chair and gave a comfortable belch. With a bit of luck, all he had to do now was sit back and wait.

Rose was alone, crouching on her hands and knees and scrubbing the vardo floor, when she heard raised voices, getting louder and louder as they came closer to the vardo.

'... you stupid woman!'

'Oh, so *I'm* stupid now, am I?' snapped back a young woman's voice. 'What does that make *you*, Sean Rourke?'

Rose's ears pricked up. Sean Rourke? Wasn't

that the name of the bloke who'd worked with Dan?

'Don't look at me,' growled the Irishman. *I never snapped the bloody thing in half!'*

'It was rusted through, you great oaf! If you'd taken a look at it once in a while—'

'Now look here Doreen. You're the mechanic, I'm the showman, I thought we'd got that straight.'

'Oh, you mean I do all the work and you take all the money?'

'Right! Now he's back, let's get this sorted out once an' for all!'

The argument came to an abrupt halt with a loud rapping on the vardo door. Rose eased herself upright, cursing her aching knees.

'You in there, Barton? Get your lazy backside out here!'

When Rose finally opened the vardo door the looks of astonishment that greeted her were a sight to see. There were two people standing outside: a young man with gingery hair and sharp, slightly weasely features, and a tall young woman dressed in a man's oily overalls. That must be Doreen, surmised Rose. Doreen Kneale. She was handsome in a jolly sort of way, with brown curly hair and expressive eyes the colour of chocolate drops. Mind you, she didn't look so pretty with her mouth hanging open.

'Who the hell are you?' demanded Sean Rourke.

'Missus Barton,' replied Rose, squeezing out her floor cloth on to the muddy ground below.

'I ... er ...' Doreen's quizzical gaze seemed

to travel up from Rose's shabby shoes to her turbaned hair. '*Missus* Barton?' She looked as if she couldn't quite believe it.

'That's right. Why?'

'We're looking for Mister Barton.'

'I'm Mister Barton,' said Luke, arriving back at the vardo with Ellie and a loaf of bread.

If Doreen had looked surprised before, she now looked flabbergasted. 'You're ... Mister Barton?'

'Luke Barton. Who are you?'

The confusion dissolved from Doreen's face and she burst out laughing. '*Luke* Barton? Dan's brother? Percy just told me *Mister* Barton was back.' She extended a hand. 'Doreen Kneale. My dad and I used to maintain Dan's rides. For our sins,' she added, pulling a face.

'Sean Rourke.' Sean shook hands with Luke and Rose. 'Me an' Dan, we're sort of ... business partners if you like.'

'So,' said Doreen cheerily. 'Where's Dan?'

'It's a long story,' said Rose. 'I think you'd better come inside.'

CHAPTER 4

Luke and Rose followed Sean and Doreen across the tober to take a look at the Barton rides.

'So you an' Dan are partners then?' ventured Rose.

51

'Me an' Doreen's dad get five per cent each,' nodded Sean.

Doreen laughed and tossed her short brown curls. 'What he means is, we get five per cent of the money and Dan does five per cent of the work,' she joked. 'Or at least, that's how it used to be.' She looked thoughtful. 'So ... he's really not coming back then?'

'No chance,' replied Luke. 'He's got it cushy in the army. So you know him well then, do you?'

Sean threw Doreen a meaningful wink. 'Oh, our Doreen knows Dan *very* well,' he grinned. 'Don't you, Dor?'

Doreen aimed a kick at his ankle.

'Ow!'

'Shut up, Sean, or next time it won't be the ankle. Yes,' she sighed. 'I do know Dan. Sometimes I think it'd be better if I didn't.' She darted a glance at Luke. 'Sorry, I didn't mean to be rude about your brother.'

'Don't apologise,' said Luke. 'You can say what you like about him, it won't be any worse than what I'm thinkin'. Now, where's these rides then?'

Rose and Doreen chatted as they walked towards the rides. Doreen was a real tomboy and a fully-qualified mechanic, had her own motorbike too—nothing like the average twenty-four-year-old you'd meet down Florizel Street. But she was friendly, funny and Rose liked her instantly.

'I'll introduce you to Cec later,' said Doreen.

'Cec? Who's Cec?'

'He's one of the gaff workers—you know, a labourer. He's been with the Barton rides for years.'

Sean snorted contemptuously. 'Labourer? Pig-headed gorilla more like.'

'Don't take any notice,' said Doreen. 'It's six of one and half a dozen of the other. Sean hates people who don't agree with every word he says.'

'I do not!'

Doreen grinned. 'See? I told you.'

'Well, here they are,' announced Sean, indicating two half-assembled rides. The rounding boards on the nearer one proclaimed in peeling paint: 'BARTON'S MODERN CHAIROPLANES.'

'They don't look very modern,' remarked Rose, walking round to take a look at the ride from the other side.

'That's because they're out of the ark,' replied Doreen. 'Used to be a set of old steam gallopers years ago, then Walleye had them converted.'

'Should've had 'em scrapped years ago,' said Sean, picking up a length of iron pipe. It had corroded right through. 'See this? Useless. It'll all have to be replaced.'

Luke's face was falling further with every word that Sean and Doreen said, and Rose was worried for him. Sometimes he had such black moods, and she knew that for him to return to fairground life was a real ordeal. After all, it was riding in the Globe of Death that had robbed him of his sight in one eye. What terrible thoughts must be passing through his mind now?

'Less than four weeks to go,' he murmured, running his fingers over the roughened metal. 'An' it's nothin' but a heap of rust.'

'It's not that bad,' said Rose, slipping her arm through his. 'We'll manage. Won't we, Doreen?'

Doreen managed a smile. 'The TT Racer's in pretty good condition anyway,' she conceded.

'Considerin' it's just spent six years with nothin' but a tarpaulin over it,' grunted Sean Rourke.

Luke looked up sharply. 'A tarpaulin! But I thought Spence—'

'You get what you pay for, mate,' commiserated Sean. 'An' Dan was never much good at payin' for anythin'.'

'Anyhow,' said Doreen. 'Me and Sean reckoned it wouldn't be long before Dan showed up, what with the season about to start—and we thought we'd better start getting the rides up and running, so they'd be ready for him.'

'Good thing you did,' said Luke. 'I'm grateful to you.'

'Don't thank us,' replied Sean. 'How're we goin' to get back the money Dan owes us if the rides don't run?'

Rose felt a sinking sensation in her stomach. 'Dan owes you money?'

'He owes *everybody* money.'

Rose glanced to her right and saw a huge, red-bearded man standing on the half-built staging of the Wiggley-Waggley. He seemed to be watching her. At first she thought she was mistaken, but when she looked a second time he was still glaring in her direction. She nudged Doreen.

'Who's that?'

Doreen looked where she was pointing. 'That? Oh, that's Ranty Darwell, his vardo's the nearest one to yours. Funny family,' she confided. 'Bit rough and ready, if you know what I mean. Loads and loads of kids and none of them ever go to school.'

'He doesn't look very friendly,' said Luke.

'Well he wouldn't, would he?' said Sean. 'He's wanted this pitch for years, an' Dan ...'

'Dan diddled him out of it,' said Doreen bluntly.

'An' Horace Spence was that sure Dan wasn't goin' to turn up this year he almost promised it to them. Then you turn up out of the blue like this—'

'Hang on a minute,' said Luke. 'Spence *promised* it to them? He can't do that!'

Doreen and Sean looked at each other, and Rose got the feeling that Horace Spence generally did whatever he damn well liked.

The next day was blustery but dry. Rose took advantage and threw open the doors and windows of the wagon, chucked out the rest of the mouldy old bedding and curtains, and gave the whole van a good airing. Ellie helped, fetching water from the tap and running down to the shops in Onchan for milk and bread. Even two of Percy Sayle's many children dropped by with half a dozen eggs.

Luke sat apart, deep in thought. Six years of neglect had done few favours to the TT Racer, and as for the Chairoplanes, they were more rust than anything else. Only the boarded-up sideshows had escaped relatively unscathed and, as Luke pointed out, no one had ever got rich running a coconut shy. Rose retorted that in that case they would just have to be the first people ever to manage it. She wasn't going to let him sit around for ever, doing nothing. Somehow, between now and Easter Monday, they had to do the impossible and get the two big rides up and running. They both knew it was a tall order, but Rose was already thinking of ways to achieve the impossible.

She was beating dust and grime out of the rugs when she saw the fat man in the tight suit walking across to the van. Nobody in their right mind would wear a pale grey suit on a muddy fairground; there was only one person it could be.

'Luke!'

Luke snapped out of his reverie and looked up.

'Luke, I think it's Mr Spence, come for his rent money.'

'I'll get it.' Luke got to his feet and went into the van for the cash box.

Spence rolled beachball-like over the muddy turf, a smile all over his big round face. An insincere smile, thought Rose, disliking him instantly.

'Well, well, you must be the lovely Rose.'

'Luke's wife, yes.' She escaped from the handshake as quickly as possible. Spence's palm was unpleasantly moist with perspiration. 'He'll be out in a minute, Mr Spence, he's just gone to fetch the rent money.'

'Ah yes. The money for the pitch.' Horace Spence leant against the side of the wagon. 'I must say, I did think the Bartons might not be back this season.'

'Why's that, Mr Spence?' enquired Luke, appearing at the top of the steps. 'Thought we couldn't pay our way, did you?'

'Luke!' Rose felt her cheeks burn, but it was obvious Luke wasn't going to put out the red carpet for Horace Spence, even if he was their landlord.

'S'pose you thought I'd take one look at the state of them rides, give up an' go home, did you?' demanded Luke. 'Funny how all the other rides are fine an' it's just ours what's rusted to buggery.'

The smug smile turned to a scowl. 'Now listen, Barton—'

'It's *Mister* Barton to you.'

'Now just you listen, Barton, there's no call for that. I stored your rides same as everyone else's. You can't hold me responsible if your brother didn't look after 'em proper in the first place.'

'Are you suggestin' that—'

'Luke, *stop* it!'

This time, Rose got through to her husband. Banging the cash box down on the steps, he disappeared back inside the van.

'I'm sorry, Mr Spence, he's a bit upset about the rides.'

Spence turned on his most ingratiating smirk. It made Rose's flesh creep but she smiled back at him, determined that she'd do her best to keep the peace.

'You seem like a sensible young woman, Rose,' he said, edging fractionally closer. 'Why don't you have a quiet word with your husband, eh?'

'A word? What about?'

Spence glanced at the van, then round at the site. 'This place. The future. You could sell your rides to me; I'd give you a good price. You could set up somewhere else.'

'Why? Why would Luke want to do that?' And why are you so keen to get us out? she wondered silently.

Spence shrugged, as if he didn't much care either way. 'Suit yourself,' he said.

Rose fumbled with the cash box, opened it and took out the bundle of notes Manfri had given them. 'Here you are, Mr Spence. The first quarter's rent—it's all there.'

Horace flicked through the money and stuffed it in his inside pocket. 'And the rest?'

'The rest of what? I don't understand.'

'If your husband's intending to take on his brother's business, he'll have to take on his debts an' all.'

'Debts!'

Horace shook his head sorrowfully. 'Don't say Dan never told you about the two hundred quid loan he had off me?'

58

Rose's heart stopped in her chest, then started pounding at twice its normal rate.

'T-two ... h-hundred?'

'Well I never, that's a right disgrace. P'raps you'd better send Luke over to see me when he's cooled down, Mrs B. It looks like we've got a few things what want sortin' out.'

Horace Spence jammed his hat on his head and went off whistling. Ellie emerged from behind the van, the loaf of bread and bottle of milk clutched tightly to her chest.

'I don't like that man, Mam,' she announced.

No, thought Rose. Neither do I. And that goes for Dan Barton, too.

CHAPTER 5

'Right. That's bloody that then, ain't it?' Luke appeared in the doorway of the living wagon. His gaze followed the rolling figure of Horace Spence until he was no more than a distant speck. It was murderous.

'Luke,' said Rose quietly, praying she could pour oil on troubled waters. 'Luke, it's not as bad as all that—'

'Not bad! I'm tellin' you, Rose, we might as well pack up an' go home right now.' Luke stared down at the wrench in his hand, then raised his arm and flung it away from him. It landed in the earth with a soft thud and he leapt down after it, sitting down heavily on the bottom step. Rose had never seen him look so angry. His chest was heaving with rage, his face crimson beneath its weathered sheen. His fingers clenched and unclenched as though they longed for revenge. 'Bloody Dan. No wonder you're in no hurry to get demobbed, you lyin' bastard. I'll kill yer, I will ... This is the last time you make a monkey out of me.'

'Luke, listen.' Rose laid a hand gently on his arm. 'Please.'

He started, as though seeing her for the first time. Then shook his head. 'It's no use, we're as good as done for. Two hundred quid he owes Spence. If we work flat-out all season we'll hardly do more'n cover Dan's bloody debt. I've had enough, Rose, I've just had enough.'

'I know, Luke, but ...' She sat down on the step next to him and edged closer, slipping an arm about his shoulders. His body was hard and tense, but at her touch she felt it relax a little. 'Shouldn't we at least give it a try? I know you don't really want to give up, do you?'

He looked at her, surprised. 'You'd give it a go? After all *this*?' His gaze swept the churned-up fairfield, the rickety wagon, the boarded-up kiosks.

'Course I would. If you wanted to.'

'But you never wanted to come here in the first place! I know you never.'

'That don't matter. We're here now, aren't we? What's the point of goin' home without even tryin' to make it work?'

'I don't know, Rose.' Luke stared at the scuffed toe-caps of his boots. 'I just don't know.

Two hundred quid ... Ma an' Da should've told me, Rose, they should have told me.'

'I don't think they knew.'

'They must've done! They just reckoned if they told me about the two hundred quid I'd tell them where to stick their bloody fairground rides. An' they reckoned right. Why should I saddle myself with Dan's bad debts?'

'I know. It's not right.' Rose considered. 'Would Dan send you the money, if you asked for it?'

'Fat chance!' snorted Luke. 'Any money he's got'll go straight on women an' horses.'

'All right, then, maybe your dad'll give it you.'

'What? It was hard enough gettin' the first quarter's rent out of him.'

'Still, you don't know till you ask, do you? An' maybe we can manage without.' She could hardly believe she was saying this—she, Rose Barton, who'd cried herself to sleep the night Luke told her they were coming to the Island.

'How? The rides are shot to bits, you've seen 'em.'

'No they're not, they're just a bit rusty, that's all. Look, all we have to do is get down to it an' work hard. Doreen'll help, she said so. An' you're a good mechanic, Luke, the best.'

Luke managed a weak smile. 'Not bad,' he conceded. 'But it's bikes an' cars with me, not clapped-out trucks an' roundabouts. An' there's parts on them rides that's rusted so bad they'll want replacin'. There's more'n I can manage

on me own, Rose, a lot more—you an' I both
know it.'

'You don't *have* to manage on your own,'
persisted Rose, determined now that they weren't
going to give in, at least not without a fight.
'You've got me an' Ellie, an' Doreen an' Sean.
An' Percy Sayle said he'd lend a hand ...'

Luke laughed, but it was good-humoured
laughter. 'Oh aye, we've got it made! A wife,
a mechanic and a spieler who never stop rowin,'
an' a bloke what talks to chickens.' But he slid a
hand round her waist and drew her close, kissing
her long and slow on the lips, like he had when
they were courting.

Giggling and red-faced as a schoolgirl, she
pulled away, eyes darting around her in case
Ellie or the Sayle kids were nearby. She fiddled
the pins back into her hair, resecuring it into
neat red-brown rolls. 'What's that for?'

'For bein' bloody pig-headed, when anyone
else would've give up first time they saw them
rides.'

Rose laughed and snuggled into the crook of
his shoulder. 'You know me, Luke. Stubborn as
a mule.'

'Must be, to stick with me. I'm not good for
much, am I?'

'Rubbish! You're the best catch on the Isle
of Man, Luke Barton!' Rose closed her eyes,
enjoying the faint warmth of the sun as it filtered
hesitantly between puffy white clouds. 'It'll all
work out, you'll see. This'll be the best season
for years, even better than before the war!'

'Oh yeah? Why's that then?'

'Cause everyone's sick of the war, that's why. It's over now, they want some fun ... an' just think of all them demob gratuities waitin' to be spent! All we've got to do is make sure there's somethin' worth spendin' them on.'

Luke grinned. 'I don't know what I'd do without you, Rose Barton.'

'Good job you'll never have to find out then,' retorted Rose. 'Come on, love, there's work wants doin'.'

Three days later, Doreen's dad Eddie Kneale came out to Funland and looked over the Barton rides with much tutting and shaking of his head. Rose watched Luke showing him round, feeling every hurt with him, willing him not to take it to heart. She needed him to be strong right now, especially since Manfri Barton had made it clear that business was bad at the car-repair business and they were going to have to stand on their own two feet.

Of course, times were bad for everybody, not just the Bartons. People had lost loved ones. Soldiers were coming home to the Island to find they had no jobs and nowhere to live. Food rations were getting smaller and smaller, beer was running out, you couldn't get decent coal for love nor money, and in Douglas the landladies were wondering how on earth they were going to feed their summer guests on a meat ration of one-and-six. Come to that, thought Rose, it might be a struggle to feed Ellie and Luke if things didn't go the way they planned.

At least Ellie, galumphing about in the spring sunshine with Percy Sayle's half-wild brood of urchins, was too young to understand just how bad things really were. At that age, even living in a leaky caravan could be an adventure.

Doreen Kneale seemed to understand Rose's mood.

'How about a cuppa? We could both do with a sit down.'

Rose was relieved to climb back into the living wagon, the place she'd been so sure she could never call home. Now that she'd cleaned up the Hostess range, evicted the mice and patched the biggest holes in the roof, it was at least less damp and draughty.

She heaved the kettle on to the top of the stove. 'It's good of your dad to come,' she said, measuring two very small spoonfuls of tea into the pot.

Doreen shrugged. 'He knows you're up against the clock. We both do.'

'It's good of you, all the same. I mean, there's people round here wouldn't give us the time of day, what with Luke bein' ...' She wondered why she fought shy of the word. 'Some folk don't like gypsies.'

Doreen sighed. 'You know what people are like, always afraid of what they don't understand. And Dan ... well, he wasn't always popular round here, if you know what I mean. It was nothing to do with being a gypsy, he just made a lot of enemies, got up everybody's nose.' She glanced out of the window at Luke, bare-armed and glistening with sweat from his exertions. A lively sea-breeze whipped his longish hair back from his face, emphasising the strong lines of his profile. Her gaze lingered, then returned to Rose. 'You're not Romany though, are you?'

Rose shook her head. 'No, I'm from Birkenhead. Me dad's a docker.' She laughed. 'When he's not on strike, that is.'

'So how did you meet Luke?'

'His family aren't travellers any more, they live in Birkenhead. Luke used to be a fairground stunt-rider though, years ago ... before he had his accident.'

'Oh.' Doreen looked out of the window again. Ellie was squealing with laughter as she and the Sayle children raced across the tober, a piglet and a dog in hot pursuit. 'Ellie's a pretty girl, isn't she? Lovely golden hair.'

'Yes.'

Doreen yawned. 'Funny, isn't it—how kids sometimes look nothing like their parents?'

Rose opened her mouth, almost blurting out the whole story, then closed it again. No point in going over old ground, she reminded herself. Besides, she might like Doreen Kneale, but she hardly knew her. 'It is, yeah.' She reached up and opened the top cupboard. 'Do you want a biscuit?'

'Er, no. No thanks.' Doreen sat back on the cushioned locker-seat and surveyed the inside of the van. With the gleaming tiles and brass rail round the stove, the carved and polished doors of the cupboards and the clean cloth on the fold-down table, it looked very different to the wreck it had been only a week ago. 'You've worked wonders with this van, Rose.'

'You reckon?' Rose looked over her shoulder at Doreen, pleased that she had noticed.

'Good Lord, yes. I don't know how you've managed it. If we can do as well with the rides, you'll have nothing to worry about.'

Rose took out five mugs and dabbed milk into each. 'To be honest,' she admitted, 'I think Luke still reckons we're wastin' our time. But I keep tellin' him we have to give it a go, don't we? If we don't we'll never know ...' She flopped down on the bench to wait for the kettle to boil. 'Don't mind me, Doreen, my head's goin' round in circles, I don't know if I'm comin' or goin'. There's so much wants doin', an' hardly any time to do it in.'

Doreen leaned forward. Her voice was gentle, understanding. 'Lots of people used to work for Dan; I'm sure they'll come back and work for you. And Dad'll help you if he can, I know he will. He always did have a weak spot where Dan was concerned.' She gave a throaty chuckle. 'So did I, God help me.' Her soft brown eyes made contact with Rose's. 'I used to think I was in love with him, can you believe that?'

Yes, thought Rose. Funnily enough, I can.

'Really?' she said.

'Really. Course, it was all animal attraction. That rat had me wrapped round his little finger for months, even had me working for nothing on his damned rides—till I found out what he'd been getting up to behind my back.'

Rose had a suspicion she could guess what was coming next. She was right.

66

'Turned out he'd been sowing his wild oats from here to Ramsey,' said Doreen, a half-smile on her lips. 'The cheating swine. Mind you, he was careful, I'll say that for him. He never got any of them in the family way. Still, you can see why a lot of people round here aren't too fond of him.'

'So you gave him the push then?'

'Sort of. Once I could see him for what he was. I just kind of lost interest in him. Strange thing was, the less I wanted Dan, the more he wanted me. It was quite funny, really.' She chuckled at the memory. 'He ended up that desperate, he asked me to marry him!'

'He did all this to you, an' you're still offerin' to help us?' joked Rose, pouring boiling water into the teapot.

Doreen threw back her short, neat hair. 'Guess I've still got that soft spot for him,' she said softly. 'Come on, Rose, let's take that tea out, shall we? Dad and Luke must be parched.'

Work? It was endless. If it wasn't painting up the coconut shy or the Knock the Lady out of Bed stall, it was trying to figure out how Rose, Luke, Cec and Sean were going to run two rides and three stalls. There was nothing for it but to find summer workers, and fast.

What with the Island grapevine, it didn't take long for word to get round that the Bartons might be looking to take on gaff-lads for the summer season. There were plenty of willing folk looking for work, too; the trouble was, the Bartons couldn't afford to pay top rates like Horace Spence or Jack Verney, with his spectacular Wild Australia Show, all the way from the posh end of Wigan. And, as Sean Rourke never tired of pointing out, you got what you paid for.

Which was how they came to be interviewing the most motley band of misfits Rose had ever seen. Cec and Old Peg, a distant cousin of Luke's who'd had a fortune-telling booth on Douglas Head before the war, were soon joined by a gawky youth called Terry, and then by Mario, an Italian ex-internee who spoke hardly any English but claimed he had once sold ice-cream in Blackpool. Still, beggars couldn't be choosers. They needed half a dozen people, and so far nobody better had turned up.

Barton's Knock the Lady out of Bed had been one of the most popular sideshows in Funland before the war. For years, schoolboys had queued three-deep to throw beanbags at a target. Hit the bull's-eye and the bed tipped up, throwing out a pretty girl. Rose and Luke were checking over the mechanism one chill and misty morning when two young girls came teetering across the field towards them.

'Duveleste!' gasped Luke, oil-can poised over a rusted bolt. 'Will you take a look at that!'

Rose clapped a hand over her mouth. It was a hilarious sight, all right. Two young girls dressed up to the nines in their mothers' best summer frocks, high heels and ridiculous pillbox hats. They couldn't have been more than sixteen, and they must have been frozen to the skin.

The taller girl picked her way gingerly across the frost-hardened turf. 'This must be it then, Gracie,' she announced disdainfully. 'Not up to much, is it?'

Gracie, a small, fluffy brunette with huge grey eyes, hung back eyeing up Rose. She could be quite pretty, thought Rose, if she scrubbed off all that make-up.

The grey eyes moved on to Luke. 'You Mister Barton, are you?'

Luke nodded. 'What can I do for you ... er, ladies?'

The two girls exchanged looks and dissolved into fits of laughter. They looked, thought Rose, like the silly schoolgirls they were.

Gracie took out a lacy hanky and dabbed her eyes. 'Don't take any notice of Dot, you can't take her anywhere.'

Dot feigned outrage. 'You what?'

'You heard!'

Dot flicked a stray strand of blonde hair out of her eyes. 'We've come for the job.'

Luke looked resolutely stone-faced at Rose. Rose had to glance away or she'd have burst out laughing too.

'What job?' she managed to ask.

'Knock the Lady out of Bed,' said Gracie. 'Dot's mam used to do it before the war, but she reckons she's too old for it now.'

Dot nudged Gracie in the ribs. 'Too old to show her knickers, you mean!'

'Nobody'd want to see 'em!' screeched Gracie.

Luke scratched his head. 'You're a bit young, ain't you?'

69

'We're seventeen,' retorted Dot. 'Does it matter?'

'It does if your mam and dad don't like you workin' in a place like this,' replied Luke.

'But my mam used to work here,' protested Dot. Bouncing up on to the wooden platform which served as a bed, she lay down. 'Like this, is it? Then what happens?'

'I'll show you,' giggled Gracie. And before Rose had a chance to intervene she had grabbed an armful of beanbags to chuck at the target above Dot's head.

'Can't throw for toffee,' jeered Dot, a split second before Gracie hit the bull's-eye and Dot was tipped unceremoniously into a puddle, her skirts billowing over her head to reveal navy-blue school knickers.

She was on her feet in moments. 'Gracie, you cow! Me bum's all wet!'

'Serves you right,' retorted Gracie.

Dot wriggled down her damp skirts and turned her brown eyes on Luke.

'So. Get the job, do we?'

'Thirty quid. Another lousy debt.' Luke kicked the wheel of the aged Leyland truck that provided the centre engine for the Chairoplanes. 'How much more of Dan's whorin' is there that we don't even know about?'

Rose put her arm about his shoulders. 'I know it seems bad ...'

Luke turned round, his back to the truck. 'What are we goin' to do? Two hundred quid to Spence, another thirty to this tart at the Albion,

God knows how much Eddie Kneale will need to put the Chairoplanes to rights ... Where are we goin' to find it from, Rose? Where?'

She pressed herself against him, trying to envelop him in her warmth as she would a hurt child. 'Your dad,' she replied simply. 'He'll have to pay up, whether he likes it or not.'

'Da? But he's already said he can't afford to help us.'

'I don't care what he's said, Luke; either he helps us or we go bust before we start. Someone's goin' to have to go to Birkenhead an' talk to him.'

'Oh aye? An' who's goin' to do that? I'm stuck here with this lot, we're up against it as it is ...'

'I know,' said Rose. 'Which is why I'm goin' to have to do it.'

'You!' Luke's eyebrows shot up into an astonished arch. 'But you an' my folks ... you don't exactly get on, do you?'

'No,' sighed Rose. And her heart sank to her boots at the very thought of Sofia Barton's icy welcome.

CHAPTER 6

Rose walked very slowly down Ferry Street. She was in no hurry to see Manfri and Sofia again, and she didn't suppose they'd be any more overjoyed to have her land on their doorstep

71

unannounced. Head down, hands in pockets, she walked past the bomb-site where Manfri ran his used-car and scrap metal business from a makeshift shed, skirting a group of kids kicking a football up against the back wall of the Maypole Dairy. Just another quiet Sunday morning.

Ferry Street had what Stan Dobbs called 'big ideas'. It might be only a five-minute walk from Mersey Row, but it was definitely a cut above. Never mind the weed-strewn gaps where bombed-out houses had been cleared, or the patchwork of windows boarded up because it was impossible to get the glass to mend them; the nets were all whiter than white, every front step was immaculately scrubbed and donkey-stoned. Even the mongrel dogs had collars. Yes, if you moved to Ferry Street, you knew you were going up in the world.

The Bartons lived at number forty-six, on the corner of Gladstone Street. Rose hesitated, thought about going round the back, then walked up to the front door and knocked. Back door was for family, she reminded herself, and Sofia Barton had never thought that way of her daughter-in-law.

The door opened and a red face appeared, haloed by curling-pins. Far from looking surprised, Sofia Barton's face merely set into a mask of cold hostility.

'You.'

Rose took a deep breath. 'All right if I come in?'

For a minute, she thought Sofia was actually going to turn her away; then the woman relented and stepped back, just far enough for Rose to squeeze past her vast bulk.

Manfri Barton was sitting in his favourite chair, listening to the wireless. The long line of china horses on the mantelpiece seemed to be listening with him. He, at least, had the good grace to look taken aback when Rose walked in.

'Well I'll be ... What you doin' here, girl?'

Sofia snorted. 'What you think? Sent the *gorgio juvi* to do his dirty work for him.'

Rose held on to her temper with both hands.

'If you mean Luke has sent me—no, he hasn't. I've come of my own accord.'

'She's run off an' left him,' sniffed Sofia.

'Left him!' gasped Rose, almost speechless with indignation.

'Come runnin' back with her tail between her legs,' commented Sofia with relish.

'Be quiet, woman,' commanded Manfri, and for once the thin red lips clamped shut. 'Rose, sit yourself down. What's brought you back here?'

Rose perched herself on the edge of one of the big old chairs. 'You got Luke's letter?'

Manfri's expression changed to discomfort.

'Aye. What about it?'

'Things are bad over there, Mr Barton, real bad. You should see the state of them rides, more rust than anythin' else.'

Manfri shrugged. ' 'Tis seven year since them rides was used, a *dinilo* could see they'd want some mendin'.'

'It's worse than that, Mr Barton,' insisted

73

Rose, desperate to make him understand. 'Much worse ...'

'My family are not afraid of hard work,' snapped Sofia.

'I never said they were. And nor am I,' Rose added, anticipating Sofia's next accusation. 'But there's only so much we can do with no money.'

'I gave you the money for the first quarter's rent,' Manfri pointed out, reaching down his pipe and tobacco jar from the mantelpiece.

'An' we're grateful, Mr Barton,' said Rose, 'really we are. But there's food to buy, an' paint an' prizes, an' men to pay, an' ... an' ...' She dried up, suddenly catching sight of Sofia's favourite photo of Dan, hanging above the statuette of St Sara like a holy icon.

'An' what?' demanded Sofia.

Rose looked her square in the eye. 'An' all Dan's gamblin' debts to pay off.'

A horrible silence fell for a few seconds. Rose heard Manfri draw in breath, then the regular *clunk, clunk, clunk* of the ormolu clock that had come from Manfri and Sofia's old living-wagon.

'Lies,' said Sofia—but she was quieter now, Rose noted, some of the wind taken out of her sails.

'These debts ...' began Manfri slowly and painfully, staring straight ahead of him as though he could hardly bear to look at Rose. He swallowed. 'How much?'

'It's worse than we thought. There's the two

hundred he owes Spence, ten he borrowed off Doreen Kneale, thirty he owes to a bookie, an' a lot more besides ...'

'No. No, this is not true.' Sofia shook her head, refusing to listen. 'Dan's not like that, he's a good boy.'

'It *is* true,' insisted Rose, pulling a sheaf of IOUs out of her bag. 'See? All this money ... Every day someone comes up to Luke an' says, "Are you Dan Barton's brother?" An' when he says yes, they say. "Right then, you can pay me back that money he owes me." ' Rose laid the IOUs on Manfri's lap. 'Where are we goin' to find money like that, Mr Barton? You've got to help us.'

Manfri let out a long, heavy sigh. 'I'd like to. But—'

'Please, Manfri. We'll go under otherwise. Luke's always been a good son to you, he's only doin' this 'cause you asked him to—why won't you help him?'

Sofia remained tight-lipped.

Manfri leant forward and took Rose's hand. 'I said I'd like to, Rose. An' I would. But business is bad.'

'Let her help herself, Manfri. Little *gorgio chovihanni*. Spinning her lies. If she want money she can *jess to booti* like the rest of us. Bone idle, that's what she is.'

Rose felt her eyes prickle with the beginnings of tears. All this way she'd come—God knows, they couldn't afford the fare—and she'd been so sure she could bring them round. She blinked back the tears, but they came anyway, a couple of wet trickles which she smeared quickly from her cheeks.

'*Hush kacker*, woman,' Manfri growled at his wife. 'Can't you see you're upsetting the girl?'

Rose guessed that Sofia could see that very well indeed; upsetting her son's wife was one of the few activities Sofia actually seemed to enjoy. Well, Sofia Barton might be able to hurt her, but if she thought she could drive a wedge between Rose and Luke she had another think coming.

'I'll go then,' said Rose dully, getting to her feet. 'If ... if you've made up your mind.'

Suddenly all she wanted was to get out of this stifling room, away from these people, from the woman who resented her so much, for no good reason she could think of.

'I wish I could help,' murmured Manfri. 'But I can't, not right now. Unless I could ...'

Rose looked at him, her heart momentarily stopping in its tracks. 'Unless what?'

'Nothin',' said Manfri. But maybe there is a way, he thought, a way to get more money from the business.

Just maybe ... if he was willing to bend the rules.

'Well?' demanded Stan as Rose walked back into the Dobbs' back kitchen. 'Did you get the money?'

Rose slid her arms out of her coat and hung it on a peg by the door. She shook her head.

'No, Dad.'

'I told you so!' Stan thumped the table with

his fist. 'Didn't I tell you, Edie? Them gyppos, all they care about is their own.'

'Stan!' snapped Edie, banging a plate of sausage and mash in front of him. 'Eat your tea an' shut up. Rose, love,' she said more softly, 'sit down an' have a bite to eat.'

'Sorry, Mam, I'm not very hungry.'

'A cup of tea then.'

Rose couldn't help smiling at her mother's insistence. 'All right then. I'll make it, shall I?'

'No need, there's a cup left in the pot. You sit down, you look all in.'

Rose sat down at the table, trying to ignore her father's grim face, and Edie squeezed the last cup of tea out of the big brown pot.

'There y'are, love. I've put two sugars in it—you need the energy.'

'But Mam!' protested Rose, thinking of her mother's tiny sugar ration.

'It's all right, love, your dad's givin' up sugar in his tea. Aren't you, Stan?'

Stan shoved his plate away from him with a grunt of anger. 'Bloody Bartons,' he seethed. 'Look what they've done to our Rose. Look, woman!'

'It's not Manfri's fault,' said Rose, wishing her father would stop making things worse. 'He's not got much money comin' in at the moment.'

'Not his fault! Did you hear that, Edie? Not his fault! He's bloody rollin' in it, is Manfri Barton. An' as for that useless husband of yours—'

'Dad! You know there's nothin' Luke can do.'

77

'He could have come over himself,' growled Stan. 'Didn't have to send you over to do his beggin' for him, did he?'

'Oh for God's sake pipe down, Stan,' urged Edie.

'I'll not shut up till I've said me piece.' Stan punctuated his words with thumps on the table-top. 'That gyppo's bad for you, Rose. I won't have him sendin' you out to beg—'

'It's not like that!' exclaimed Rose, her head aching with tension. First Sofia, now Stan. Would the bullying never stop?

'Open your eyes, girl! Leave that loser, get out while you can.'

'Shut up, Dad! Shut *up!*'

Stan's face turned white at the sight of his own daughter standing up to him. 'Right,' he said coldly. 'I can see I'm not wanted.' He got to his feet and took his cap from the peg by the door.

'Where are you goin'?' demanded Edie.

'Out.'

The door banged shut behind him. Rose launched herself after her father, but Edie held her back.

'Let him go. He's only gone to his allotment to sulk.'

'Oh, Mam.' Rose deflated on to her chair, head in hands. 'I never meant ...'

'I know.' Edie laid a hand on her shoulder. 'It's not your fault. God knows, none of this is your fault. Your dad just worries about you.'

Rose gazed down at her father's abandoned dinner plate, untouched except for a single bite of mashed potato. 'He's wrong about Luke, Mam.'

Edie sat down opposite her. 'Luke's a good man, I know that. Your dad would too if he wasn't so pig-headed. He'll come round.' She pushed the teacup nearer to Rose. 'Drink your tea before it gets cold.'

Rose took a couple of sips, for her mother's sake. It tasted like warm treacle. 'Thanks, Mam.'

'Rose ...'

'What, Mam?'

'Are things really bad with you an' Luke? The money, I mean?'

Rose hesitated. She didn't want to worry her mother; on the other hand Edie was no fool and she always knew when Rose was lying to her.

'Money's short, Mam. But we'll get by.'

Edie paused. 'I've not got much, love, but there's your granny's ring. I could pawn it.'

Rose looked at her mother in horror. 'Granny Peters's ring? No, Mam!'

'The money might tide you over—'

'No!' This time, Rose was firm. 'No, Mam, I won't have it. Luke an' I will manage on our own, you'll see.'

She prayed that she was right.

Her mother's kitchen was shabby but cosy, filled with the reassuring smells of cooking and floor polish. For a fleeting moment Rose imagined leaving Funland behind, coming back here, moving in with her mam and dad ... But how could she think that, even for a moment? She loved Luke, and she certainly wasn't going to let him down just because things had got a bit difficult. She'd stick it out and they'd get by.

Together.

CHAPTER 7

Luke took a big swig of tea and leaned back, his eyelid closed.

'Guess what,' said Rose. 'We've 'ad some money from your mam and dad.'

Luke sat up straight.

'Don't get too excited.' Rose produced the envelope and dangled a single one-pound note between finger and thumb.

'That's it?'

'Guilt money. It'll pay the boat fare an' not much else. I tried, Luke, I really tried.'

He took her hand and squeezed it. 'I know you did. I'm proud of you, Rose. None of this is your fault, it's mine.'

'If you ask me it's Dan's. But he's well out of it, so we'll just 'ave to manage, won't we? Right—what about the Chairoplanes? Will they be ready for next Monday?'

'You want the honest answer?'

'Course I do.'

'Don't look like it. It's mad busy at Kneale's yard. Eddie can't get the bolts made till Wednesday.'

Rose's face screwed up with frustration. 'Well,

at least the TT Racer's in good nick. That'll get us by.'

'Guess so. An' Sean Rourke's got the gift of the gab, he'll bring the punters in.'

'You bet he will.' Question is, can we trust him? thought Rose. Let alone Cec, who looked like an escaped convict, or the terrible twosome of Dot and Gracie.

'Knock the Lady out of Bed's bound to do well—an' the fortune-tellin's always popular.'

Luke munched on his butty. 'Only other problem is the coconut shy. You can't have a coconut shy without coconuts, can you?'

'You think we'll have to close it down if we can't get any?' Rose searched her brain for a solution. 'There must be some way round it.'

'Matter of fact there is,' replied Luke, tapping the side of his nose. 'Leave it to me.'

At eight o'clock on Easter Monday morning, Percy Sayle was sticking up a fly-poster, shamelessly pasting it right on top of an advertisement for the Crescent Pavilion. Setting down his bucket and brush, he stepped back to take a look:

FOLLOW THE CROWD TO FUNLAND!
GRAND REOPENING TODAY!

MANXLAND'S ONLY ROLLER-COASTER! * BIG WHEEL * DODGEMS * WILD AUSTRALIA SHOW * DAREDEVIL DIVER * HOUSE OF WONDERS * GHOST TRAIN * SWING BOATS * RIFLE RANGE

81

A WHOLE MILE OF SIDESHOWS!
AND ALL YOUR FAVOURITE RIDES!

Well, that was the last of 'em, mused Percy. Nothing to do now but wait for the punters to roll in.

He turned round, yawning, and surveyed the scene. In the distance he could see the *Lady of Mann* steaming into harbour with her cargo of day-trippers from Liverpool. Half of 'em would spend the whole day boozing before being dumped back on the Prince's Landing Stage at two in the morning to sleep it off. Question was, would the other half find their way to Funland?

They certainly couldn't miss it. In the last two hours Percy had put up posters right along the prom, from the Pier Arcade to Derby Castle. They screamed 'GRAND OPENING TODAY!', 'THIS WAY TO FUNLAND!' and 'RIDE THE AMERICAN ROLLER-COASTER!', interspersed with big red arrows pointing the way. Horace Spence had even bought advertising space on the horse trams; the new roller-coaster he'd brought over from America had cost him a fortune, and he wasn't taking any chances.

As the first toast-rack of the day clip-clopped past, its iron wheels making the tramlines sing, a few lazy seagulls rode the air-currents overhead. The faint smell of fresh paint hung on the salty air, and boarding-house landladies stood out on their front steps, beating the dust out of doormats not cleaned since 1939. Nothing much moved.

It was as if the whole world was waiting for

something to happen.

By half-past nine Funland was in chaos. No one talked any more, they just shouted and ran about. There was so much to do, how could they possibly get everything ready for the Grand Opening at ten o'clock?

'Boogie Woogie Bugle Boy' blared out over the fairfield as Archie Crellin's Waltzers took a final practice spin. The swing-boats lurched up and down, stopped, then started again. Jack Verney, otherwise known as Ned Kelly, cursed loudly into his dustbin-sized helmet as a skittish Palomino trod on his foot. The Darwell kids stopped terrorising all the other children and fought each other instead, vying for first go on the Wiggley-Waggley. Over everything floated the aroma of hot, stale dripping. The Luxury Fish & Chip Saloon, at least, was ready for anything.

The Bartons had no time to bother much with what the rest of the world was up to. From now on until the end of September, all these showmen and their families would be their deadly rivals. It was a question of survival. Somehow, thought Rose, they had to get that through to the likes of tarty Dot and scatterbrained Gracie, granite-faced Cec and poor, baffled Mario, who had enough trouble understanding 'hello' and 'goodbye'. Not to mention Terry, a nervy lad of sixteen with a tendency to blush crimson if a girl so much as looked at him.

Rose stood, hands on hips, surveying the coconut shy.

'*Wooden* coconuts?'

Luke nodded. 'An' we'll use them trinkets we found up at Spence's barn for prizes. It was Sean's idea—he knows a man who knows a man.'

'Let's just say I've a very accommodating friend, Mrs B,' grinned Sean. 'Made me these special, he did.' Picking up a coconut, he juggled it deftly in one hand and winked. 'Very special.'

'Special?' Suspicious, Rose picked up one of the other coconuts, shifting it from one hand to the other. It was made of very light wood, but there was something peculiar about it. 'These are weighted!'

'Course they are, Mrs B. Don't want the punters winning too often, do you?'

'So we cheat?'

Sean plonked the coconut back on its stand. 'Just tricks o' the trade, Mrs B. Ain't that right now, Luke?'

Luke didn't reply.

'You ask Dessie Randall.' Gracie nodded towards the Hoop-La stall three booths down the line.

'Yeah,' cut in Dot, pulling a long strand of American chewing-gum out of her mouth and trawling it back in with her long pink tongue. 'He makes his hoops too small so they won't fit over the big prizes. Everybody knows that.'

It didn't seem right to Rose, but as Luke had pointed out they had to make money somehow—a fact brought home by the sight of Horace Spence, whose fat, expensively suited body was heading straight for them. Rose nudged Luke. The muscles in his jaw tensed slightly. Gracie giggled nervously. Dot pulled a face.

'Course,' wheezed Old Peg, taking no notice of anything around her. 'There's them as says the dukkerin' is all made up ... but I'm the seventh daughter of a seventh daughter, I got the second sight—'

'Shush, Peg,' said Rose. 'Not now.'

Spence elbowed his way past Gracie and Dot, who threw him filthy looks.

'What's all this about then, Barton?'

Luke stepped forward. 'All what?'

'Them Chairoplanes.' Spence jabbed a fat finger at the ride, glittering with new paint but listing slightly in the middle where the wheel axle leant to one side. 'What's this I hear about you not running them?'

Luke folded his arms and leant against the side of the booth.

'It's only for a couple of days.' The look of pure animosity on his face matched the look of contempt on Spence's. 'I can't do nothin' till I get the parts.'

'Parts, Barton?' Spence's voice rose half an octave. 'We're opening in ten minutes and you're waiting for parts?'

'What am I supposed to do, Spence? Magic the bloody things out of thin air? If you'd looked after them rides properly—'

'That's right, Barton, blame someone else for your own incompetence.'

Rose stepped between them, uncomfortably aware of Gracie and Dot's fascinated stares. 'Mr Spence, please. There's nothin' Luke can do. It's not his fault, it's the shortages see—'

'I can fight my own battles, Rose,' snapped Luke.

Taken aback, she shrank away. This wasn't like Luke; normally he was so quiet, so unassuming. 'I ... I was only ...'

Luke's face was set in a scowl. His fist tapped against his right thigh, threatening at any moment to spring up and fetch Horace Spence a well-deserved thump.

'It's my ride, Spence, I'll do as I see fit.'

'Oh, it's your ride, Barton, for what it's worth. But this is my fairground and I'm not runnin' a charity.'

'You'll get your two hundred back. An' your five per cent.'

'Five per cent of nowt is nowt, Barton. I want that ride up an' running by next week, got that? Or I'll know the reason why.'

Luke and Spence stood glowering at each other like two prize bulls. They might have stayed like that for ages if a brass band hadn't struck up the strains of 'Ellan Vannin'. Across the tober, Douglas Town Band came marching in through the big arched gateway, brass buttons glinting in the sunlight as they tramped in formation past the roller-coaster and the ghost train. Rose made out other figures behind them, following the band into the fairground. Men, women and children: their very first punters. Her stomach turned over; her legs felt like jelly.

Suddenly she wanted desperately to go to the lavatory.

'Oh, Luke,' she whispered. And he gripped her hand briefly then let it go.

'Can't stand around all day,' barked Horace Spence, bringing Percy Sayle to heel with a snap of his fingers. 'Some of us 'ave money to make.'

As dusk began to close in over Douglas, lights began to sparkle in the semi-darkness. Strings of bulbs that had lain in storage since 1939 burst into multi-coloured life. Laughter and screams of excitement mingled with the cacophony of music and the rumble of machinery. And the showmen's patter rose above it all, shouts competing with each other for attention.

'Roll up, roll up, a prize every time!'

'Two rides a shillin'—can't say fairer'n that, can I?'

'Come on, lady, try your luck.'

Sean Rourke was standing by the Knock the Lady out of Bed booth, just across from the coconut shy where Rose was working. He was good, thought Rose grudgingly, watching him play the punters, wheedling them into parting with their money. Better than she was, that was for sure. She'd hardly made three bob all afternoon.

'Four goes for sixpence, sonny. Knock the lady out of bed. Pretty girl, ain't she?' And Dot giggled on the bed, pulling the covers up over the lacy pink nightie she'd borrowed off her mum, one toe wriggling provocatively in

87

the air. Sean grabbed an airman by the arm and practically magicked the money from his pocket. 'How about you, sir? Like a pretty girl, do you, sir? Bet you're a fine shot ...'

Rose digested the messages Terry had passed her from all round the tober. Darwell's Wiggley-Waggley was doing well enough, and there was a big crowd of airmen from RAF Jurby queueing up for the roller-coaster. The Wild Australia Show was pulling them in too, and you couldn't go wrong with waltzers. But what about the TT Racer? She strained to make it out through the Easter crowds milling about in the dusk, and just made out Luke's tall, lean silhouette, now in view, now hidden as the ride spun round and round. And there was Ellie, standing on the staging with her dad, determined to help though it would soon be well past her bedtime. Rose made a swift mental calculation. Half full, that's all the TT Racer was at best, half full on Easter Monday. And all these people to pay ...

'How much?' demanded a voice at her elbow.

'What? Oh, twopence. Three balls for twopence.'

'Go on, Gary.' The redhead tugged at the young man's sleeve, and Rose saw the very new wedding ring gleaming on her finger. 'Go on, win me a coconut.'

Across the way, a cheer went up as Dot fell out of bed for the umpteenth time and Gracie jumped up to take her place, treating the audience to a good few inches of bare leg in the process.

'We've just got married,' beamed the redhead.

'We're on our honeymoon. Go on, Gary, show me how clever you are.'

'Oh, all right then.' Gary fished in his pocket and brought out four pennies. 'I'll have six goes.'

Rose dropped the money into the deep pocket at the front of her apron and fished six wooden balls out of the bucket.

'It's a china dog if you win,' she said apologetically. 'Can't get the coconuts, see.'

The redhead tossed her curls and laughed. 'Tell you the truth, I don't like the bloomin' things anyway. Hang on, here's another twopence. I'll have a go an' all.'

All at once, it seemed as if the whole world and his wife wanted a go on the coconut shy. The twopences were coming so fast, Rose could scarcely keep up with them. As the money-pouch grew heavy with copper and silver, Rose allowed herself a smile of relief.

Everything was going to be fine.

CHAPTER 8

It was a fine morning towards the end of May when the lorry dropped its two passengers in the centre of Birkenhead.

'Have to leave you 'ere mate. You an' the kiddie'll be all right now?'

'Right as rain, ta very much. Come on, Lola, jump down—we're goin' home.'

The tall, blond-haired man and the dark, skinny little girl made a curious pair, drawing glances from passers-by as they crossed Grange Road and walked past the double row of shops. The girl clung to the man's hand, but seemed to be doing so as much from fear as affection. She scarcely glanced at him, the bright black beads of her eyes darting about her as if she expected something terrible to happen.

The sudden leap of a playful dog sent her cowering against the man's thigh, her fingers scrabbling, her mouth open in a silent whimper of terror. The man patted her dark hair and prised open her fingers with weary patience.

'Only a dog, Lola, nothin' to be frightened of. Look ... nice bow-wow.' He tried stroking the dog to show that it was friendly, but the girl just shrank away and hid her face.

'Bloody funny kid,' commented the dog's owner. 'Scared of 'er own shadow.'

The look in the golden eyes hardened. 'Mind yer own business, mate.'

They continued on their way. The man walked with slow, measured strides, one broad shoulder weighed down by the heavy, naval-style kitbag. Under his arm he carried a bulky parcel wrapped in brown paper and string. He was dressed very much like any other merchant seaman, but there was something about him that made him stand out—perhaps the cut of his clothes, or the look of sorrow etched into the fine lines around his eyes.

Things had changed around here, he mused, and not necessarily for the better. It wasn't just that Hitler's bombers had made a right mess of the docks, everything just seemed drabber somehow. There was nothing in the shops, yet people would queue for two hours just on the off-chance of an extra scrap of mouldy cheese. If this was the brave new world they'd all been promised, it still had a long way to go.

They passed a baker's shop and Lola pulled free, running to the window and pawing at the glass. Her mouth made wordless sounds.

He crouched down beside her and tried to make her look at him. 'Hungry, Lola? You're hungry?'

The same, desperate, incomprehensible sounds —more like animal grunts than words.

He dug deep in his pocket, drew out half a crown and, taking Lola firmly by the hand, propelled her inside the shop.

'Two meat pies, please.'

'Sorry, luv, pies are all gone.'

'Give us a couple o' them buns then.'

The baker's assistant bagged up the order and took the money. As she turned to drop the half-crown into the till, Lola suddenly broke free, snatched a rock-cake from the stand in the window and made a run for the door.

'Well! Did you see that!' sniffed a middle-aged woman in a black coat. 'The thievin' little ...'

If he hadn't made a swift grab for the back of her dress Lola would have been away down the road like a greyhound pup. He hauled her back into the shop and took the cake from her fingers. 'Sorry, miss.'

The baker's girl regarded the rock cake with distaste. 'I don't want it back like that, she's bitten it! You'll have to pay fer it.'

He stumped up the extra coppers and ignored the whisperings going on behind his back.

'An' if I was you, I'd give 'er a good hidin' when you get 'er home,' commented the baker, setting down another tray of greyish 'national' loaves.

'Oh you would, would you?' muttered the blond man under his breath. He pocketed his change. 'Know the Dobbses, do yer?'

The baker pondered for a moment, then shook his head. 'Can't say I do.'

'Stan an' Edie Dobbs?' cut in the black-coated woman who had tutted at Lola.

'That's right. Still live in Mersey Row do they?'

The woman looked him up and down, then cast a disgusted glance at Lola, who was cramming the remains of the rock cake into her mouth as if she hadn't eaten in days. 'Who wants to know?' she demanded.

The blond man drew himself up to his full height and looked her straight in the eye.

'Charlie,' he said. 'Charlie Cartwright.'

Rose was humming to herself as she got on with making the breakfast. With Whit weekend coming up and the fairground so busy six days a week—from ten in the morning till eleven at night—this was the only really quiet time of the day, and she cherished it.

Little by little, she was getting used to life

on the fairground. There were plenty of bits she didn't enjoy—the long, exhausting days, the rude punters, the snide comments from the envious Darwells, and, not least, worrying about where Ellie's next pair of shoes was coming from—but there were worse places to be than a showman's van on a sunny late-spring day.

'Got the milk, Mam,' announced Ellie, bouncing up the steps so energetically that the whole wagon shook. 'An' bread, an' a penny-halfpenny change.'

'Good girl. Put it on the table. Oh, an' slice us some bread, will you? No doorsteps mind, it's got to last.' She dropped a precious rasher of bacon into the frying pan and watched it sizzle. Only Luke would actually get any bacon with his breakfast; the rest of them would make do with fried bread, but at least with Percy Sayle they could always be sure of an egg or two off the ration. 'Go on, you can keep the change.'

'Thanks, Mam.' Ellie gave her mother a hug round her middle. 'Mam ...'

'What?' Rose knew that tone of voice. She wondered what was coming next.

'Mam ... if Dad's not my dad, who is?'

Rose flipped over the bacon. 'I've told you, he went to Spain an' he got killed.'

'Yes, but ... who *was* he, Mam?'

Rose gave a little soft sigh and left the bacon to its own devices for a few moments. She sat down on the edge of the locker-seat, watching Ellie cutting wobbly slices off the new loaf. 'Just you be careful with that knife. I don't want you cuttin' your fingers off.'

'I won't, Mam, I'm a big girl.'

'I know. Just be careful.' Big enough to know all about your dad? wondered Rose. Someday she'd tell her daughter everything. But not right now. It was ancient history, and she couldn't bear the thought of raking it all over; it would be like a betrayal of her love for Luke. 'Ellie ... you love Luke, don't you?'

'Course I do, Mam.'

'An' you like callin' him Dad?'

Ellie nodded vigorously.

'An' Luke loves you too.'

'Lots?'

'Lots an' lots. So what do you want another dad for, eh?' She put her arm round Ellie's shoulders and kissed her lightly on the forehead. 'Now, finish off that bread an' go an' tell your dad his breakfast's nearly ready.'

Ellie cut the last slice of bread and went off to find Luke. She at least seemed perfectly happy, thought Rose, and she'd settled in fine at the local school, so that was one less thing to worry about. And it was wonderful to see how Ellie's uncomplicated happiness rubbed itself off on Luke. When they were working the rides together Luke was almost his old self again, the way he'd been when he and Rose had first met. He really adored that kid, loved her just as much as he could have loved any kid of his own.

Rose smoothed a hand over the front of her shabby pinafore. She'd hoped that this month, at last, she'd be able to tell Luke that she was having another baby—*their* baby. She knew how much it would mean to him, though if she was honest she couldn't imagine how they'd manage with another mouth to feed. But in any case it wasn't to be, not this month. Maybe next month ...

She was dropping slices of bread into the frying pan when the wagon door opened.

'Mmm. Something smells good! Can I come in? I'm a bit oily.'

Rose's spirits lifted at the sound of Doreen Kneale's cheerful voice and the sight of her inextinguishable grin. 'Course you can. Come in an' pour yourself a cuppa. What are you doin' here?'

Doreen made space for herself and spread out an old newspaper to protect the upholstered seat from her oily overalls.

'Drove over with the spare bolts for the Chairoplanes.' She poured herself a mug of strong tea, made to add her usual spoonful of sugar then thought better of it. 'Don't want to get caught out again.'

'No,' agreed Rose. 'I couldn't face goin' through all that again. Don't reckon Luke could neither.'

'Shall we drink a toast then?'

'A toast? What with?'

'Tea, of course!' Doreen filled another mug and put it into Rose's hand. 'To the Bartons.'

'To the Bartons,' smiled Rose. 'No. To you.' She drank a second toast.

'Me? What've I done?' laughed Doreen.

'You've kept me an' Luke from goin' round the bend, that's what. You an' your dad. D'you want some breakfast?' she asked, fetching plates out of the overhead cupboard.

Doreen scanned the single rasher of bacon, the two eggs and the three slices of fried bread. 'No. I'm fine, thanks. Had something before I came. I'll have a bit more tea though.' She topped up her mug from the pot. 'So, how's business? Any better this week?'

Rose forked a slice of fried bread on to a plate and set it on the table. There seemed little point in lying to Doreen, not now they'd become so close. 'Takings have hardly gone up at all, an' we're almost into June! What are we goin' to do, Doreen?'

Doreen put down her mug. 'It's not the proper season yet, Rose. You wait till the wakes weeks—and think of all those demobbed soldiers with money burning holes in their pockets. They'll all come to Funland, there's nothing else like it on the Island.'

'But will they come to *us?* What if they don't?'

'You know they will. They are already. I mean, the TT Racer's doing well ...' She saw Rose's face fall. 'Isn't it?'

Rose remembered the figures she'd totted up in the accounts book. She was no office girl, but they'd made uneasy reading. 'Not ... not as well as I thought it was.'

'But all those punters you've been getting ... I don't understand. The takings should be well up. What does Luke say?'

'He says what he always says. That things are all right an' I mustn't get myself in a state. He doesn't want me to worry, see.'

'But you do anyway?'

Rose nodded. 'The thing is, if things don't get better soon ...'

She had no chance to go on. Through the tiny side window of the wagon she made out two figures coming across the tober: Luke, long and lean and dark, and Ellie by his side, a tomboy with perpetually scraped knees and golden hair that refused to be neatly plaited. For the first time in as long as Rose could remember, Luke looked relaxed and completely happy, laughing and joking with Ellie as they came towards the living-wagon.

Doreen followed her gaze. 'Luke's coming?'

'You ... you won't say anythin' to him? About the takin's, I mean?'

'Not if you don't want me to. But Rose, if something's wrong you should talk to him about it.'

'I know.' Rose watched Luke, happy Luke, striding along like he hadn't a care in the world. 'But not today, he looks so happy.'

Stan and Edie Dobbs could not have been more stunned if George Formby had turned up on their doorstep. Stan kept beaming and pumping Charlie's hand up and down, while Edie just stared and kept saying the same thing over and over again:

'Charlie? Sweet Jesus, Charlie, is it really you?'

'Come in, lad. Come in off the street for God's sake,' said Stan, at last finding his voice.

'Come in, come in,' echoed Edie, her hands all a-tremble as she took Charlie's coat and hung it on a hook in the passage.

Charlie stepped into the Dobbses' front parlour. It hadn't been opened since VE Day and it smelt of floor polish and mothballs. Charlie couldn't suppress a faint smile at the memory of all the uncomfortable hours he'd spent in here talking politics with Stan when he and Rose had longed to sneak off somewhere and do what came naturally.

'Come on, Lola,' he said, refusing to let go of the child's hand though she tried with all her might to tug herself free. 'This is Lola,' he told Stan and Edie. They stared at her, aghast. 'It's a long story.'

'Then you'd best sit down an' tell us it. Edie, love ...'

But Edie was already on her way to the kitchen for the best china and the tin of chocolate biscuits she'd been saving, she'd never been quite sure what for.

Charlie sat. Lola crouched beside him, every muscle in her body tensed and ready to spring, her dark eyes full of mistrust.

'Charlie, lad.' Stan shook his head. 'I just can't credit it. All these years an' not a word, Rose was half out of her mind ...'

'I know, Stan. It ... couldn't be helped.'

'Could you not've sent a letter or somethin'? All this time we've been thinkin' you was dead.'

Charlie hung his head. Now that he was here it was so hard to explain, and the weight of guilt was so heavy to bear that he almost wished he'd stayed away. But he was here now, it was too late to change his mind; besides, where else was he to turn?

'I'm sorry, Stan, really I am.' He cleared his throat. 'Fact is, things was pretty bad in Spain—men dyin' like flies. Then I fetched up in a fascist jail—'

'That's where you've been all these years? In a Spanish jail?'

Charlie avoided Stan's gaze. 'Let's just say there was one or two times I almost wished I *was* dead.'

He was grateful for the arrival of Edie Dobbs and her tea-tray. It gave him valuable moments to pull himself together, marshal his thoughts. To his relief, Lola accepted a biscuit without trying to steal the whole lot or grab the plate and fling it at somebody's head.

'You're lookin' well, Charlie,' commented Edie, handing round the teacups.

'Thanks, Mrs D.'

'Course he's lookin' well, Edie,' blustered Stan. 'He's a bloody hero, ain't you Charlie? Hero of the bleedin' proletariat, that's what he is.'

Charlie looked away, suddenly uncomfortable with the reminder of what he had once hoped to be.

Stan rested his teacup on the shabby arm of his chair and leaned forward, hands on knees. 'Tell us what happened, lad. With the fascists an' that.'

'There's not much to tell. They caught me,

they put me in jail.' He stared at a spot on the dingy brown wallpaper. 'It wasn't pleasant.'

Edie glared at her husband. 'Can't you see he don't want to talk about it? Leave him alone, Stan. After all the lad's been through ...'

'It's all right, Mrs D, I don't mind.' Charlie looked at Lola, who was staring unblinkingly at Edie Dobbs. 'While I was in prison I palled up with this bloke—Miguel, he was called. Anyhow, some of the guards weren't what you'd call friendly an' Miguel, well, he gets himself roughed up by one of 'em. Course, I can't just let this bloke beat him to a pulp, can I? He's me mate ...'

'Course not,' nodded Stan, biting into another biscuit. 'So what happens?'

'Some more guards come along, pull me off this guard an' he lets go of Miguel. I get thrown in solitary for a week ...'

'And Miguel?'

'By the time I come out of solitary I find out he's dead. The thing is, me an' Miguel were mates, we'd made each other promises, the way you do when you're up against it. You know, to take care of each other's families an' that. An' it turns out Miguel's got this kid ...' He let his gaze travel to Lola.

Stan blinked. 'You mean Lola ... she's this Spanish bloke's daughter?'

'I promised I'd look after her if anythin' happened to him—an' it did, didn't it? Next thing I know I'm bein' deported from Spain with this little Spanish girl.'

'Bloody hell,' observed Stan flatly. Charlie

100

could feel his heart thumping in his chest. Edie made shocked, sympathetic murmurings. Only Lola seemed completely unmoved, staring stolidly into space, her lower lip jutting in defiance of a world she didn't understand. 'So you've got yourself landed with this little Spanish kid who don't speak a word of English ...'

'The thing is,' went on Charlie, 'Lola doesn't speak at all. She can't—she's deaf an' dumb.'

Edie gave a little gasp. 'Oh, Charlie! The poor little kid ...'

Colour drained from Stan's normally ruddy cheeks. 'Well I'll be ... So what you goin' to do with her then? I mean, you can't keep her, can you? You'll have to put her in one o' them homes for kids nobody wants.'

Stan's matter-of-fact callousness made Charlie's blood freeze. He stretched out his hand and stroked the wild black tangle of Lola's hair, feeling her quiver at his touch. 'I'm not havin' her go into some institution,' he said firmly.

'But, Charlie,' protested Stan. 'It's not as if she's yours ...'

'I promised Miguel I'd look after her an' that's what I'm goin' to do.' The golden eyes blazed. 'I'll find a way. Somehow.'

'Have some more tea, Charlie.' Edie was already on her feet with the big brown teapot in her hands.

Charlie let her top up his cup and accepted another biscuit, though his throat was so tight he could hardly swallow. 'Ta, Mrs D.' He took a sip then set down his cup on the floor, next to a dog-eared pamphlet entitled *Why Be A Communist?* It was a question he'd asked himself more than once over the last nine years. 'I meant to ask before, but ... Rose—is she all right?'

The minute he mentioned Rose's name, he felt the atmosphere grow heavy with tension.

'She's ...' began Edie, but Stan threw her one of his looks, and uncharacteristically she fell silent.

'She's what?'

'She's not here,' said Stan. 'Got herself a new job, she has. I'n't that right, Edie?' He jogged his wife's arm and she nodded like an automaton.

'Oh. Yes. Yes, she has.'

'At a fairground ...'

'A *fairground?* But ... but she used to work down the laundry at St Catherine's—'

'... in the Isle of Man.'

Working at a fairground in the Isle of Man! Charlie was stunned. It was impossible to imagine sweet, loyal, unadventurous Rose anywhere other than at twenty-seven, Mersey Row. And perhaps, with a kind of unthinking arrogance, he'd half-expected her to be sitting there waiting for him, in her mam and dad's front parlour.

He wasn't normally at a loss for words, but all he managed to get out was a shocked, 'Oh.'

'You should go an' see her,' said Stan eagerly.

'You think she'd want to see me? After me goin' off an' leavin' her like that?'

Edie opened her mouth as if to contribute

102

something, but Stan got in first. 'Course she would, lad. All these years, I've never heard her say one bad word about you. But don't take my word for it. Why don't you go over there an' find out for yourself?'

CHAPTER 9

By the middle of June, Rose was so busy she hardly knew whether she was coming or going. Trippers were pouring into the Isle of Man now that the double daily sailings from Liverpool had started up again, and best of all the trippers had money in their pockets.

Saturday nights were the busiest—and naturally Gracie had to choose a Saturday to go sick and leave them one person short. If it hadn't been for Doreen offering to take Gracie's place in the pay booth, and young Terry cheerfully doing two people's jobs, the Bartons would have been in a right old pickle. Sean Rourke was more than pulling his weight too; Rose might not care for him over-much, but he had a showman's natural gift of the gab and, with him at the helm, the TT Racer was never short of customers. The fact that he and Doreen had called a truce made life easier too.

On her break, Doreen came bounding over to the coconut shy for a chinwag.

'How's it going?'

Rose handed over another dozen wooden

balls and fished in her apron pocket for change. 'Amazin'! ... An' thruppence, that makes sixpence. Ta very much, sir. Another three? That's tuppence. Ta.' She wiped the back of her hand over her brow. It was sticky with perspiration. 'I can hardly keep up! Not that I'm complainin',' she added, dodging out of the way to retrieve a stray ball from under the guy-ropes of Peg's dukkering tent.

As she bent to pick it up, she spotted Billy Darwell, Lissa and Ranty's youngest, hovering by the toffee apples on Sid Christian's stall. It was obvious from the look on his face that, as usual, he was up to no good.

'Billy Darwell, what you up to?' Rose demanded.

The grubby-faced urchin stuck his tongue out at her, snatched an apple from the pile and legged it across the fairfield, zigzagging between the crowds of punters, Sid's curses ringing in his ears.

'Cheeky little bugger,' commented Doreen, who had a very colourful vocabulary for such a nicely brought-up girl. Rose wondered if she'd picked it up from Dan. 'Did you *see* that?'

Rose handed over a hideous china poodle to a freckly soldier-boy. 'There y'are, love. Real china that is.'

The soldier promptly presented it to the pretty Manx girl on his arm. She accepted it with as much excitement as if it had been a diamond tiara.

'Ooh thanks very much, Lou, it's lovely.'

Rose turned back to Doreen. 'Them Darwell

kids are nothin' but trouble. You know what Luke caught Billy up to this mornin'?'

'He never let Jack Verney's ponies loose again?'

'Worse. He were in the House of Wonders, pokin' a stick at the bleedin' lion!'

Doreen chuckled. 'Serve his mother right if it'd eaten the little monster.'

'Don't suppose she'd give a damn if it had. Six balls, sir? That's fourpence, ta. She lets them kids run wild; I doubt they've had a day's schoolin' in the last month. If that Billy was mine ...' She conjured up an appealing mental picture of her hand making contact with his raggy little backside, then relented. 'Well, I s'pose it's not his fault, not really. If his mam can't be bothered with him what can you expect?'

'His father's no better,' commented Doreen, helping to collect up the used balls and put them back into the big barrel.

Rose rolled her eyes. 'The way he chases the girls, at his age! Well done, miss. Fancy another go? Two coconuts down an' it's one of them lovely plaster dogs.'

'Ellie's lucky,' said Doreen.

'Lucky? Livin' here?' Rose reached up for the plaster dog. The punters were getting lucky tonight as well—hopefully not too lucky though, or the Bartons wouldn't be making any money out of them.

'She's got you and Luke.'

'We're hardly Mr an' Mrs Rockefeller! All we've got are the rides an' the old van, an' they're not even ours.'

'But you're happy. And you love Ellie to bits. She's tucked up in the van now, isn't she? Not running around getting herself into trouble like the Darwells.' Doreen shook her head. 'Mind you, I feel sorry for those Darwell kids.'

Rose raised an eyebrow. 'Why's that then?'

'What with their mother the way she is, running around after sailors all the time. I bet those poor little brats don't even know who their dad is.'

It was a close, stickily warm evening, and Luke sweated as he worked the big centre engine on the Chairoplanes, nursing it gently to full throttle then leaning back against the centre truck to watch the cars fly up and outwards like captive bluebottles.

The coloured lights in the fairground had turned dusk to a kind of artificial day. Excited faces in the crowd flashed red, blue and green as the rides turned. In the distance, gunshots rang out at the Wild Australia Show as Ned Kelly was captured and shot for the fourth time that day; flames flared briefly as the world-famous one-legged diver plunged a hundred feet into a small, round pool through a hoop of fire. Screams of delight cut through the air as Horace's roller-coaster cars reached the summit of the incline, hesitated for a brief, heart-stopping moment, then went hurtling down the curving slope on the seaward side. Sean Rourke's voice could just be heard over the blare of 'Zip-a-dee-doo-dah' and the 'Hokey-Cokey': 'Come on now, ladies, don't be shy, give yerselves a thrill. How about you, sir? Hop on a bike and win the TT Races, just like the real thing!'

As the music cracked and grated to its end, Luke wound down the Chairoplanes and watched the cars slowly descend to the staging. The engine stopped with a satisfying clunk. Two girls fell about giggling as they got out of their car, tripping over each other with dizziness, their high-heeled shoes getting caught between the planks of the staging. A young man stumbled out, green-faced, one hand over his mouth and no doubt regretting that second visit to the Fish & Chip Saloon.

Luke smiled and took a deep breath. 'Barton's Modern Chairoplanes—just like flying over the Irish Sea! That's right sir, only a shillin'. How about you, lady?' He knew he didn't do it as well as Sean Rourke, but he got by. Even though he was no born showman, he'd not forgotten the patter he'd learned in his days with the Globe of Death. 'Only a shillin', just a few places left. Hurry up now, she's about to start ...'

Something caught his eye as he was speaking. A small, raggy-trousered figure messing about round the base of Wilcock's Electric Swing Boats. Billy. Billy flippin' Darwell, what was he up to now? Whatever it was, Luke would lay money he was up to no good. He strained his eyes against the flicker of many-coloured lights. Billy was crouching down by the engine, and there was something in the kid's hand.

Oh God, no. Not that.

'Billy! Billy Darwell!' he shouted across the

tober, but the kid didn't hear him or he ignored him. Either way, he just went on with what he was doing.

Luke looked around him. Where the hell was Darwell? Some blonde girl was minding the Wiggley-Waggley and as usual there was no sign of Lissa. Wilcock was on the far side of the Swing Boats; he'd never cotton on to what Billy was doing to the mechanism right under his nose. The Chairoplane cars were filling up with punters, but they'd have to wait.

A tall, thin-faced man in shirt-sleeves came up to him. 'How much is it, sonny? A shilling?'

Luke waved away the money and jumped down from the staging. 'Sorry, mate ...' But the punter pursued him, cash in hand.

'Look, sonny, are you going to take my money or what?'

'Will you get out the bloody way!'

He had practically to push the bloke out of his way as he sprinted the fifty yards or so to the Swing Boats. Surely somebody else had noticed ... But the big gondolas just kept swinging up and down, oohs and aahs getting louder and louder—and Jesus, if that kid did what Luke thought he was going to do ... Somebody had to stop him, and quick.

'Billy! Billy, for God's sake no!'

Rose, trying to find change for fourpence out of a half-crown, noticed nothing of all this until she heard the loud, sickening crunch of machinery grinding to a premature halt. And then the single, high-pitched scream of a woman, filled with anguish: 'Billy!'

Rose's blood ran cold. She felt the coins slip between her fingers and roll on to the trodden turf. For a split second, everything on the tober seemed to stand still. Voices were silenced; even the cacophony of the music seemed muted. Then somebody shouted out, 'It's the Swing Boats. There's somebody trapped underneath!'

'Get a policeman, for God's sake ... Get a doctor!'

Sid Christian, white as a sheet, turned and shouted across to Rose.

'I reckon it's your Luke ...'

And then Rose was running, coins jingling and spilling out of her apron pocket, people staring at her as she hurtled towards the Swing Boats. One gondola was resting on the staging, the other stuck high in the air, its cargo of young men and girls and little kids clinging to the sides.

'What's going on? Get us down!'

'Why's it stopped? Mam, I wanna get down!'

Rose paid no heed to their grumbles and cries; they were safe. All she cared about was Luke, crouching by the side of the ride, and the child in his arms, no longer defiant but sobbing, his legs caught underneath the staging and an iron bar lying half-in, half-out of the workings. So that's what the kid had been doing: poking a crowbar into the engine, making mischief as usual, never thinking what the consequences might be. A toffee apple lay on the ground a few feet away, a single bite exposing the creamy-white flesh under the sweet gold glaze.

A semi-circle of gawping punters had gathered round the two figures, and at the front of them stood Lissa Darwell, her face chalk-white save for two lurid spots of rouge in the centres of her cheeks. Her fist was clutched against her lipsticked mouth as though to stifle her weeping.

'Billy! What's 'appened to my Billy?'

'It's all right, Billy lad,' said Luke softly. 'It's all right, we'll soon 'ave you out.'

'I've ... 'urt me leg, I've 'urt me leg,' Billy kept sobbing over and over again.

'I know, lad. Be brave, soon sort you out.' Hands under the boy's arms, Luke drew him as gently as he could from underneath the ride. The reddish sheen of blood made Rose's heart miss a beat.

'Billy ...' wailed Mrs Darwell. And, in spite of every foul-mouthed insult she'd had to put up with from the Darwells over the last few months, Rose went and put her arm around her.

'Here, take this hanky. He'll be all right.' She prayed that it was true as she watched the sobbing child being wrapped up in a blanket.

'What's all this? What you done to my boy, Barton?' It was the gruff roar of Ranty Darwell, pushing and shoving his way through the onlookers, as usual putting two and two together and making five. 'I'll kill you if you've 'urt my boy!'

'He never touched him.' Rose clutched his arm but he shook her off.

'Get your hands off me, woman.' He caught

110

sight of Billy, shivering in an old army blanket, a smear of blood on his cheek. 'Jesus, Mary an' Joseph,' he muttered. 'What's that *chikly joob* done to you, son?'

Luke did not reply. He simply got to his feet. A thin trickle of dark blood made its way down his arm from a long, shallow cut above his elbow, but he paid it no heed. 'Doctor'll be here soon, Billy lad. Chin up.'

Darwell seized him by the shoulder, spinning him round and shouting into his face. 'You'll answer me, Luke Barton! I'll have the gavvers on you, I swear I will ...'

Jack Verney stepped forward. He was even bigger than Ranty Darwell, built like a prize-fighter and afraid of no one.

'Leave him be, Darwell. He's done nowt.'

'He's 'urt my boy!'

'He's saved him, that's what he's done. Billy was messing about with a crowbar, poking it in the engine. It would've had his arms and legs off if Barton hadn't come along when he did.'

This took some of the wind out of Darwell's sails. 'You're sayin' ...'

'I'm saying Luke's a hero, Darwell. You should be thanking him, not making yourself look like a fool.'

'Aye,' piped up Sid Christian, who had followed Rose across to the Swing Boats. 'An' why wasn't that kiddie in bed? That's what I'm askin' myself—'stead of runnin' about half the night makin' trouble for 'isself. You don't give a damn about them kiddies, Ranty Darwell—'

'Now just you watch your mouth.'

111

'You don't give a damn, an' it's time you put your own house in order, 'stead of goin' on about other folks all the time.'

The doctor came and took Billy away to the hospital in an ambulance, the police arriving shortly afterwards and asking a lot of awkward questions about safety and responsibility, while Percy Sayle brought a ladder and helped the punters out of the stranded Swing Boat. Horace Spence turned up with a face like thunder and made out that the whole thing was Wilcock's fault for not having eyes in the back of his head. When the police said that some of the rides might have to be closed down if the inspector said they weren't safe, Rose thought Spence was going to hit poor weeping Lissa Darwell.

And all the time, Luke stood quietly to one side, not speaking except when he was spoken to, not even rising to the bait when Horace Spence tried to pick a fight. Rose saw that, despite the warmth of the evening, he was shivering, beads of cold perspiration standing out on his tanned skin.

She touched his hand and drew him away, gently directing him back towards the wagon. 'You all right, love?'

He nodded and managed a smile. 'Right as rain.'

Her fingertip traced the line of the shallow cut which ran down the underside of his upper arm. He flinched slightly.

'Best get that cleaned up, eh?'

'Yeah. Yeah, s'pose.'

'Tell me what's wrong, Luke.'

'Nothin's wrong. Nothin'.' His voice trailed off. 'I thought he were a goner, you know. Billy. An' I thought, what if it was Ellie lyin' under there?'

'Billy's all right. The doctor said he'll be fine. Everythin's all right. Come on back to the wagon. I'll make you a cup of tea.'

'This inspector they're sendin' to look at the Swing Boats ...'

'Don't you worry about him.'

'He'll want to go over all the rides.'

'I told you, don't worry.' She kissed him and that shut him up, his arms curling gratefully around her and pulling her close.

When they got back to the wagon they found Ellie sitting on the top step, sleepy-eyed in her nightie.

'What's goin' on, Mam?' The eyes widened. 'Dad, what've you done to your arm?'

'Just a scratch,' Luke reassured her with a smile. 'Back to bed now.'

'But—'

'Back to bed. I'll tell you all about it in the mornin'.'

Morning brought the news that Billy Darwell was in Noble's Hospital with nothing worse than bruised pride and a broken ankle. As far as the other showmen and their families were concerned, Luke Barton had gone from outcast to hero in one night. But any relief was short-lived. By nine o'clock the safety inspector was at work on the rides, going through every one of them with a fine-tooth comb. Nobody was spared, not even Horace Spence. If there was anything even slightly amiss, the inspector wasn't going to miss it. And since Funland was going to have to stay shut until the following day, every single showman on the park was going to lose out on a whole day's takings, just when the season was really starting to pick up.

Rose watched Luke pacing up and down like the lion from the House of Wonders, wishing there were something she could do to reassure him but knowing that nothing would help. The inspector had already shut down the Swing Boats and the Waltzers, pending repairs, and now it was the turn of the Chairoplanes. All they could do was wait.

'Luke's a good mechanic,' said Doreen, helping Rose to unpack cheap trinkets and set them out on the stall. 'He wouldn't run the ride if he didn't think it was safe.'

'I know.' Rose polished a china cat on her skirt and plonked it on the shelf between an elephant and a pig. 'But just look at his face, you can tell he's worried sick.'

It wasn't just Luke's expression, either. It was the inspector's. There was something about the hunch of his shoulders, the way he poked and prodded and shook his head, that did not bode at all well. A few moments later they knew why, as Luke came across with the inspector in his wake. The expression on Luke's face said it all.

'Non-standard parts, Mrs Barton,' announced the safety inspector, jotting something down in his notebook.

'You what?'

'Non-standard. There are certain regulations laid down, you see, and regulations are established for a reason. We must keep to them for everybody's sake.'

Rose was aghast. 'You're not ... you're not closing the Chairoplanes down?'

'That remains to be seen.'

Doreen intervened. 'Those parts are perfectly safe, you know they are! They're the best available. And with all these shortages it's impossible to obtain the standard parts, people have to make do ...'

'Indeed. But I have public safety to consider, Miss ....?'

'Kneale. Doreen Kneale. My father's garage helps with the maintenance.'

'Well, Miss Kneale, I'm sure your father does his best, but we have to be sure that his best is good enough, don't we? I'll be in touch, Mrs Barton, Mr Barton.' He touched his cap.

'But when—'

'I'll be in touch.'

Rose watched him head off towards the House of Wonders, no doubt to inspect the toothless lion and the two-headed baby, pickled in a bottle. A small figure in a long raincoat and drab tweed cap, it was hard to believe that he controlled the fortunes of so many people.

'Damn,' said Doreen, kicking the earth with the toe of her motorcycle boot. 'Look, if this is any of my fault, I'm truly sorry.'

'Your fault!' exclaimed Luke. 'If it wasn't for you an' your da, God knows how we'd ever have got them Chairoplanes workin' in the first place. It'll be all right,' he said firmly. 'Won't it, Rose?'

'Course it will,' she smiled, trying to be brave and positive though inside she was cursing Dan Barton and his blasted Chairoplanes. All the time, all the sweat and tears and cash they'd spent on them, and now they might be closed down again. She was beginning to wonder if the damn things carried some kind of jinx.

Later, sitting on the steps of the wagon, Luke tinkered with the carburettor out of Dan's old Leyland truck. He was never happy unless he was doing something, thought Rose; taking things to bits and putting them back together was his way of coping with the terrible restlessness that never seemed to leave him. With Ellie out playing with the Sayle kids, Rose took the chance to talk to Luke about the thing that was bothering her more than anything else.

'Luke, love ...'

'Mmm?' He looked up, wiping the end of his nose with an oily hand.

'It's about the takin's.'

'Oh.' The gaze focused once again on the carburettor.

'We've bin gettin' loads more punters these last couple of weeks, haven't we?'

'I reckon.'

'But the money's hardly up at all. I've counted it over an' over again, an' I can't make any sense of it. You know what I'm thinkin', Luke, don't you?'

He looked up at her. 'You reckon someone's got sticky fingers? But Rose—'

'I know, I know. I just can't think what else it could be.'

'But showmen don't steal from each other. They ... they just don't. Who'd steal from us, Rose? Who'd do a thing like that?'

'I wish I knew, love. An' the question is, how're we goin' to find out?'

It was 30 June 1946, and the British Legion parade was marching proudly along Douglas promenade, uniform buttons glinting in the warm sunlight, banners fluttering in the lively sea breeze. Happy crowds lined the seafront, waving miniature Manx flags and Union Jacks, cheering the veterans on their way past the Gaiety Theatre and the Villa Marina. It was a day to celebrate ... and remember.

Charlie Cartwright was remembering too, only his memories were not of the Dunkirk landings or the Blitz. As he stood apart from the crowd, Lola's small hand gripped firmly in his own, he fought those memories and prayed that one day he might be allowed to forget.

'Poor buggers,' he muttered, shaking his head.

Lola cowered at his side, clearly terrified by the sight of so many men in uniform. Little wonder, thought Charlie, wishing he were not so powerless to take her fear away.

'It's all right, Lola,' he mouthed at her and smiled, but her eyes were not on him, they were fixed on the men and women in uniform

117

as she felt the *thump, thump, thump* of the big drum and the tramp of their big shiny boots, vibrating through the metalled roadway beneath her feet.

'Come on, let's be goin' now, eh?'

Charlie knew the kid couldn't hear a word he was saying, and even if she could she'd not have understood his language; but even so he felt he had to try. Maybe something would get through to her in the end, somehow. You couldn't just give up on a child, could you? No matter how hopeless it might seem. He tried to pull her away from the parade but she stood firm, rooted to the spot, refusing to budge an inch until the last of the marchers was far in the distance, heading up towards Derby Castle and the electric railway.

At last she allowed herself to be coaxed away from the parade and the two of them walked slowly down the promenade, not really heading anywhere in particular because in his heart of hearts Charlie was putting off the moment when he'd have to face Rose again. No matter what Stan might say, Charlie was beginning to have second thoughts. It was one hell of a long time since he'd kissed her goodbye, all those years ago at the Woodside ferry. What if she wasn't pleased to see him? What if she sent him away with a flea in his ear? In all honesty he could hardly blame her if she did.

The parade over, the holidaymakers got back to the business of enjoying themselves. Rowdy groups of lads and lasses exchanged good-natured banter as they skipped along, arms linked, the sunshine colours of the girls' summer frocks contrasting with the sprinkling of khaki and Air Force blue. Charlie's rough working clothes and Lola's shabby hand-me-down skirt and blouse drew a few curious glances, but on this rare, perfect day the Villa Marina gardens and the shingly sands held more interest than a couple of waifs and strays.

'Come on, we've got to find this place ... What's it called?' He talked more to himself than Lola as he fetched out the crumpled fag packet Stan Dobbs had scrawled the address on. 'Funland', that was the name of it. Funland. It wasn't a lot to go on, but surely someone would know where it was.

A tug on his hand broke his concentration. Lola was straining to pull away from him, towards one of the horse-drawn trams which had drawn to a halt a few yards away.

'Lola ...'

'Aaah ... aaah.'

She might not be able to utter more than inarticulate grunts, but Lola had ways of expressing what she wanted. Charlie gave in and let her drag him towards the tram-horse, a huge, gentle-faced grey Percheron with broad shoulders and hairy feet that ended in giant, plate-sized hooves. The age-smoothed leather collar around the horse's neck bore a metal plate engraved with his name: 'BADGER'.

Despite Badger's immense bulk, Lola broke free and flung her skinny arms round his chest, nuzzling against the bristly skin, eyes closed in silent pleasure. It was just about the first time

119

Charlie had ever seen her smile. He hadn't the heart to drag her away, though it was obvious the tram-driver was waiting to set off up the prom with his cargo of trippers.

Charlie touched the child lightly on the shoulder. 'Lola ...' He glanced up at the tram driver. Behind him, a whole tramload of passengers were hanging out of the open sides, trying to see what was holding things up. 'Sorry, mate ...'

The tram driver, reins in hand, smiled benignly and leant back in his seat. 'Let the littl'un take 'er time, boy. Badger's a good ol' fella, gentle as a lamb. Loves the kiddies, he does. Takin' a ride, are you?'

Charlie produced the old Woodbines packet. 'We're lookin' for this place. Do you know it?'

The driver guffawed and pointed to the painted advertising hoarding running around the top of the tram. It read: 'FOLLOW THE CROWD TO FUNLAND!'

'Know it, boy? Hop on an' I'll take you there!'

Percy Sayle hitched up his braces and rubbed his stubbly chin. 'So what is it you're lookin' for again?'

Charlie raised his voice above the churning mechanical din of the fairground. With every step he had taken into Funland, he could feel the muscles in his stomach tightening with nervous anticipation; and this idiot wasn't helping.

'Miss Dobbs. Rose Dobbs. She works here.'

Sayle looked blank. 'Dobbs, you say?'

'You know her?'

'Dobbs? Can't say as I do ...'

Charlie felt close to desperation. 'Well, just tell me where to find the Barton rides, will you?'

'Bartons? Over there, past the Wiggley-Waggley, turn right at the Swing Boats ... but—*Dobbs*, did you say?'

Charlie didn't stop to listen to Percy Sayle drone on. He had to find Rose, if she was still here. And she surely was; Stan had been certain she would be.

Lola dragged her feet reluctantly at his side, staring at the ghoulish painted heads on the Ghost Train as though afraid they might leap out and bite her. Charlie sensed that if he let go of her for one moment she'd be off again, determined to put as much distance as she could between herself and this horrible man who'd taken her away from everything she'd ever known. He knew he'd never find her if she got herself lost in these crowds, and he held on to her so tightly he was afraid he'd hurt her small, fragile fingers.

Rounding the corner of the Swing Boats, Charlie caught the elbow of a man on the darts stall. ' 'Scuse me, mate. I'm lookin' for Barton's.'

'Over there.' He nodded towards two rides, one stationary and oddly silent, the other spinning rapidly about its centre truck, kids laughing as they crouched over the handlebars of the motorbikes, two abreast. The gilded capitals on the rounding boards spelled out: 'BARTON'S FAMOUS TT RACER'.

As the ride wound down, a rough-looking gypsy bloke jumped down from the staging and went to talk to a girl in the pay booth. Charlie noticed the leather patch he wore over one eye. He looked like a real rogue, with collar-length black hair and a gold earring—the kind you'd rather not trust with your wallet. The girl in the pay booth didn't look any better, with make-up plastered over her face, and her hardly more than a kid. Charlie wasn't sure he liked the idea of Rose working with people like this. As he crossed to the pay booth, he wondered what on earth had possessed her to want to come and live on a fairground.

'I'm starvin', Luke.' The girl spat out a wad of chewing-gum, rolled it up and stuck it to the underside of the pay desk. 'Can't I go for my dinner now?'

'You can go soon as Terry gets back.'

'But I'm starvin'! Dot went for hers ages ago ...'

'Mr Barton?'

The rough bloke turned round and looked Charlie up and down. 'Luke Barton, yeah.'

'I'm lookin' for Miss Dobbs.'

'Miss Dobbs? Oh! You mean Rose?'

'Rose Dobbs, that's right. Is she here? Only I'm an old friend of hers. From Birkenhead.'

Luke's gaze lingered for a few moments on Lola, perhaps trying to work out the precise relationship between the scowling little urchin and the blond giant holding her hand. 'She's

122

here. Bin away a while have you, mate?'

'Yeah ... in Spain. Why?'

'It's Rose Barton now. We're married, see. Have been these past three year.' Luke nodded across the tober to the living-wagons lined up against the perimeter fence. If he saw the look on Charlie's face, he did not comment on it. 'You'll find her in the wagon, last but one on the right. Birkenhead, eh? I reckon she'll be pleased as punch to see you.'

CHAPTER 10

'Gracie?'

The grey eyes snapped away from their fascinated contemplation of the stranger and returned to gaze uninterestedly at Luke Barton. 'What?'

'Take Mister ...?'

'Cartwright.' Charlie just managed to get the word out. His throat was dry as dust. For two pins he'd have turned tail and fled. 'Charlie Cartwright.'

Luke nodded affably, pleased for Rose. It would do her good to see an old friend.

'Take Mister Cartwright over to the van. An' Gracie ...'

The head cocked on one side, accompanied by a dramatic sigh. *'What?'*

'I want you back here in five minutes, you got that? No slopin' off for a crafty fag.'

123

'Yeah, yeah, I know.' Gracie threw Charlie a come-hither smile. 'You comin' then?'

Charlie followed her past the Wiggley-Waggley and the Swing Boats, the House of Wonders and the Ghost Train. Gracie was dodging in and out of the crowd so fast he and Lola could scarcely keep up—not that there was much danger of losing her in the crowd, not in that garish polka-dot frock.

It didn't matter to Gracie that Charlie might not be in the mood for conversation; she just kept babbling nineteen to the dozen. 'You on holiday then, are you?'

'What?'

'On holiday. You on holiday?'

'Oh. No, not really.' Every yard closer to the Bartons' living-wagon made the icy hand clench more tightly about Charlie's heart. He said the first thing that came into his head. 'I'm ... lookin' for work.'

'Yeah?' Gracie's gaze lingered appreciatively on Charlie's strong, muscular shoulders, the smooth, masculine angle of his square jaw, the softness of the golden-blond hair that kept slipping boyishly across one amber eye. 'Where you stayin' then?'

'With a mate. This bloke I used to know, keeps a hardware shop up Mount Havelock ... Is it far? The van?'

'Not much further, just over there.' Gracie pointed to a row of wagons parked beyond the furthermost stalls and rides. There were perhaps ten or fifteen there, a motley mixture of everything from ancient to modern. Then

Gracie turned her attention to Lola, who was trailing her fingers along the painted edge of a ride. 'Hey, don't do that kid, you'll have your fingers off ... Kid ... Are you listening?' She touched Lola on the shoulder and the child jumped away with a squeak of alarm. Charlie pulled her gently but firmly away from the ride.

'What's up with you then?' demanded Gracie, stooping to look Lola in the face. 'Daft or something?

Charlie's strong arm drew Lola towards him, the gesture not so much tender as aggressive. 'She's deaf, all right?'

'Oh.' Gracie reddened. 'Sorry, I never meant—'

'Where's the Bartons' van then?' Charlie's hand moved instinctively to the breast-pocket of his shirt and the folded-up envelope inside. It was there, safe; at least there was still one reason for being here.

'Over here. See that old one, second from the end?'

It was a hot day, the air unusually still and muggy, but Charlie felt cold fingers of sweat creeping down over his skin, collecting in a clammy pool at the base of his spine. The hairs on the back of his neck stood to attention.

The van was the oldest one there, that much was obvious. A real old-style gypsy showman's vardo, with walls of carved oak that sloped outwards and upwards to meet a curved roof topped with a metal chimney. From a distance it looked not too bad, quite romantic even.

125

But with every step nearer that Charlie took he noticed another thing wrong with it: the rust on the chimney, the window-pane obscured by a sheet of plywood, the patched roof and sagging front steps. No. This couldn't be right, she couldn't have made her home in a place like this. Not Rose. Not his Rosie Dobbs ...

'I'll get her for you.' Gracie marched up to the van. Charlie hung back, suddenly afraid of what he had done. He wanted to turn and leave, to lose himself and Lola in the crowd and simply melt away. But all he could do was stand rooted to the spot.

'Mrs B?' Gracie climbed the steps and rapped on the closed door of the wagon. 'Mrs B, someone to see you.' After a moment she jumped down. 'She'll be out in a minute. Got to go now, or Mr B'll tan my hide.' She winked at Charlie. 'I'll be on the TT Racer if you fancy a go.' Then she was gone.

Charlie took a slow, halting step towards the wagon. Behind him the fairground was in full swing, but all he could hear was the sloosh and thump of his own heart, pumping so violently in his chest that he felt dizzy and sick.

Then the door of the wagon opened and he saw her, standing at the top of the steps. She wasn't quite as he remembered her: the red-brown hair wasn't braided any more, it was pinned up in rolls; and she was thinner, her shabby short-sleeved blouse revealing lean, wiry arms lightly tanned from the sun; older too, the fierce light a little fainter in those green-flecked eyes. But it was her all right, it couldn't be anyone else.

In the split second before Rose saw him, time seemed to move impossibly slowly. He couldn't breathe, he couldn't move. A weird sense of unreality overwhelmed him, as if he knew he was in a dream but couldn't wake up.

Then their eyes met. He saw the colour drain from her face, leaving it livid white. The metal bucket slipped from her fingers and went crashing and bouncing down the wagon steps, splashing its contents everywhere. Dirty water spattered over her feet, leaving dark stains all over her thick stockings. Her mouth opened in a shocked gasp, her lips moving though Charlie could not hear her voice above the din from the fairground rides. But he didn't need to hear. He knew what Rose was saying.

'Charlie ...'

Gracie took the long way back to the TT Racer; she was in no hurry to get back to work. Why should she have to starve to death in that stuffy pay booth when Dot was off somewhere stuffing her face and not giving a damn about anybody else?

As she walked along the line of vardos, she heard laughter coming from Jack Verney's smart new living-wagon. It was a gleaming monster of a thing, brand new and shiny white, the size of two ordinary wagons stuck end to end, and it was Mrs Verney's pride and joy. The laughter came a second time. Gracie paused in mid-stride, frowning. There oughtn't to be anybody in the van, not at this time of day. Jack and Lou were doing their Ned Kelly routine, Mrs Verney was running the pony rides, and any kids that weren't at school were busy taking the money. What's more, Gracie knew that laugh ...

Standing on tiptoe, she pressed her face up against one of the windows. Sure enough, through a gap in the curtains she could just make out the outline of two figures, clearly enjoying themselves. And whatever it was they were enjoying, it definitely wasn't afternoon tea.

'Dot Matthews, you dirty little cow!'

The two figures sprang apart as Gracie burst into the van. The lad, who couldn't have been more than eighteen, blushed redder than his carroty hair as he scrambled off the bed and fumbled desperately to pull up his trousers. 'Bloody hell, Dot, bloody hell! I told you it wasn't safe here!'

Dot slid off the bed with a look of weary contempt. 'Relax, Andy. It's only Gracie.' With a deft wriggle of her hips she shrugged her skirt down over her bare legs. 'No one ever tell you it's rude to interrupt?'

Gracie's mouth dropped open. 'Rude? What d'you call *this* then? You go off and leave me running that flippin' ride, an' all the time you're ... you're ...' She stared from Gracie to Andy and back again, for once in her life completely speechless.

'Keep your hair on, Gracie.' Dot picked up her knickers from the floor, stuffed them into her handbag and took out a small powder compact.

128

'I'm only a few minutes late.' She grinned at the hapless youth. 'Everyone's entitled to a dinner break, i'n't that right, Andy?'

Andy was fiddling nervously with the top button of his shirt. He grabbed his jacket off the back of a chair and ran a shaking hand through his tousled hair.

'I ... I think I'd best be off now.'

Dot blew him a kiss. 'See you tonight then. If you're good I might bring Gracie too!' She giggled as the door of the van closed behind him, and went back to preening herself in the mirror of her powder compact.

Gracie seized her elbow. 'You mad or something?'

'Dunno what you're on about.'

'Bringing a bloke here? This is Jack Verney's van. If he catches you in here, doing *that* ...'

Dot smiled and shook her head. 'Sometimes you're just like a little kid, d'you know that? You scared or something?' Her eyes narrowed and she tossed her curly blonde hair. 'Nah, you're *jealous!*'

'I am *not!*'

'Yes you are. Jealous just 'cause I've got a bloke and you haven't.' She snapped shut the compact and put it back in her bag. 'We going back to the rides then, or are you just going to stand there gaping all afternoon?'

'Two adults and one child? That's two an' six, ta very much.'

Pocketing the last of the money, Luke cursed under his breath. First Dot had disappeared, now Gracie. They worked hard enough when they put their minds to it, but let them off the leash for five minutes and you'd not see them for the rest of the afternoon. The trick was keeping them apart, otherwise you'd end up doing their jobs as well as your own.

As the TT Racer wound down and the punters got off, Luke saw Sean Rourke coming across the tober. Thank God for that. At least you could rely on him to turn up when he said he would. And he was a good worker too, willing to have a go at anything short of doing Old Peg's fortune-telling for her.

'Take over for ten minutes will you, Sean?' Luke jumped down and unfastened the money-pouch from round his waist.

'I thought you wanted me on Knock the Lady out of Bed?'

'I do, but first I've got to find the "lady". I sent Gracie off to the van with a bloke ten minutes ago, an' she's still not back.'

Sean gave a dirty chuckle. 'Gracie an' a bloke! God man, the poor fella'll never get out alive.' He tied on the money-pouch and started taking fares. 'Three bob, an' there's your change ... Tell you what, Luke, if she's not back at the booth by two I'll put on a frock an' do it meself.'

'Yeah, well, it might just come to that. Anyhow, I've got some news for you. Good news.'

'What's that then?'

'The safety inspector. Come round this mornin' he did, an' passed the Chairoplanes safe to run. We can start again tomorrow.'

Sean whistled. 'Well if that ain't the best news I've heard all week. Maybe I'll start makin' some money out of you Bartons at last, eh? 'Bout time I got some return on that five per cent ...'

At that moment Dot and Gracie rounded the corner of the Electric Swing Boats.

'Well, well,' commented Sean, jumping up on to the centre truck and setting it running. 'The prodigals return. Wonder what excuse they'll come up with.'

'Whatever it is,' replied Luke, 'it had better be good.'

'Please, Rose, please listen. I'm so sorry, I didn't know ...' Charlie took another step into the wagon but Rose backed away from him, shaking violently, hands in front of her face as though warding off a ghost.

'No,' she whispered, slowly shaking her head. 'No, no, it can't be you. It can't.'

Lola stood very still in the doorway where Charlie had let go of her. Only her large, dark eyes moved, following every inexplicable thing that was happening before her.

'Listen to me, please. Rosie!'

Rosie. The name that only Charlie had called her. A cold shaft of light entered Rose's soul and suddenly she felt strangely calm, almost detached from what was happening. 'It can't be you,' she said softly, sinking down on to one of the bench-seats that doubled as a bed. 'You're dead.'

Charlie stood stock-still, towering over her.

131

Part of him wanted to take her in his arms and hold her again, to rediscover the softness of her body, speak to her with kisses, for words would never suffice. But the greater part knew that there could be no possibility of that—not now, not ever. For she was another man's wife and that was nobody's fault but his own.

'I'm truly sorry, Rose. I ... I wouldn't have come if I'd known. It was Stan, see. He never said you was married ...'

Rose stared at Charlie, hardly believing her ears. 'Dad? You've seen my mam and dad?'

'Yes, but—'

'An' you never even thought to write to me?'

'I should've, I know I should, but ...'

A cold, still anger was spreading slowly through Rose's whole being. How could he do this to her? How could he have let her believe him dead, all these years, then suddenly walk back into her life and make her relive all that hurt?

'Should've? There's a lot of things you *should've* done.' She almost spat the words in his face. 'It's been nine years, Charlie. *Nine years.*'

Charlie hung his head, unable to look Rose in the face. 'I know,' he said softly.

'You know? I don't believe I'm hearin' you say that! How can you know anythin' about me?' She tried to collect her thoughts, to take hold of her anger and pain and turn them into words that made sense. 'Why are you here, Charlie? Why have you come back? Why now?'

Charlie reached into the breast pocket of his shirt and took out the folded envelope. 'I've got somethin' for you. From your mam.'

He held it out. Rose stared at it, for a moment unable to move or to think. The writing on the envelope was her mam's all right: 'Rose', picked out in the painstaking hand she'd learned at school many years before.

'What is it?'

'It's your grandma's ring.'

'What?'

'The one she always wanted you to have. Your mam says ... she says you can sell it if you're ever short of a bob or two.'

Rose didn't take it; she couldn't. Couldn't bear to touch it. This was the ring she'd refused to take from her mam, and now her mam and dad had gone behind her back.

'I don't want it.'

Charlie laid the ring on the table, still in its folded packet. 'I'll put it there then.' He stepped away.

Rose got to her feet. 'Get out,' she said, very quietly.

'Rosie, please—'

'Get out!' Her fingers scrabbled for the nearest thing they could find: the heavy, old-fashioned flat iron she kept beside the stove. They curled around it and she raised her arm. 'Leave me alone, Charlie Cartwright, get out! *Get out!*'

The flat iron hit the doorframe just above his head, leaving a shallow dent before clattering to the floor. Charlie stood there for a few seconds, his golden eyes pleading with her in wounded silence; then he turned away from her, pushing open the door and bustling the thin, dark child ahead of him.

A moment later, both were gone.

Rose slammed the door behind them and leant her back against it, trying desperately to catch her breath. She was shaking all over now, delayed shock taking hold of her in great chilling waves and leaving her helpless. 'No,' she whispered, her hands clenching into fists as she slid slowly down to her knees. 'Please God, no.'

It was almost dusk, but Charlie had lost all track of time. He sat cross-legged on the shingly beach, staring out to sea while Lola splashed about in the shallows, barefoot and tangle-haired. She at least seemed content at last; perhaps this place reminded her of the beaches she'd left behind in southern Spain, or perhaps it was simply that all children loved the seaside.

Charlie wished it could be that simple for him. He took up a handful of pebbly sand and watched it filter between his fingers, the way his own life had done.

Gone.

How could he have been so stupid? Or was it sheer, pig-headed arrogance that had made him believe, somewhere at the back of his mind, that Rose would still be waiting for him, ready to welcome him back with open arms—and Lola with him?

But that didn't matter now. What did matter

was how he was going to put the past behind him and get to grips with the future. Even if he cared little for himself, he had Lola to think about now, and she was by far the biggest responsibility he had ever had to face up to.

He watched her playing, lost in her own silent world; and the pain of his own guilt was almost too much to bear. All he had in the world was a few pounds and a return boat ticket to Birkenhead. No family to help him, no work, no proper place to live—he certainly couldn't impose on John Gorry for much longer. Foolishly, he'd banked everything on Rose being able—and willing—to help him.

And without her, whatever was he going to do?

CHAPTER 11

When Funland closed that night, Rose was dreading the difficult questions Luke might ask about her unexpected visitor. Sitting outside on the van steps, they drank mugs of tea while Ellie slept, watching the coloured lights going out as the last rides were put to bed.

'Old friend of yours, was he?'

Rose was grateful that the darkness hid her face. 'From Birkenhead. We knew each other when we were kids.'

' 'Spect you had plenty to talk about then.'

Rose watched a string of red and yellow lights

click off. Somewhere in the distance she could hear Jack Verney's ponies whinnying as they were led back to their stable. 'Not really.' Her heart was pounding, but she fought to keep her voice steady. 'It was a long time ago. Luke ...'

'Hmm?'

'About this money that's goin' missing.'

'What about it?'

She had heard the edge come back into his voice. It was the same every time they tried to talk about anything practical, he simply wanted to switch off and run away, like he thought the thing would sort itself out if they ignored it for long enough.

'I think we ought to tell Sean.'

'Sean! Why?'

'He owns five per cent. Besides, we've already told Eddie an' Doreen.'

'That's different.'

'Why?'

'It just is.' Luke glared down at his feet, stubborn as a child.

Rose slid closer to him and laid her head on his shoulder. 'I'm not that keen on him either. But he wouldn't steal from us, would he? It'd be like stealin' from himself.'

'I s'pose,' conceded Luke.

'An' he's a good worker; we really need him on our side. You'll tell him then?'

'All right. I just hope he don't take it the wrong way.'

'He won't.' She kissed him lightly on the cheek.

He laughed. 'What's that for?'

A tiny arrow of guilt sped through Rose's heart and then was gone.

'Nothin'. I just love you, that's all.'

Early the next morning, Rose and Luke went to find Sean. He was with Terry and Mario at the Chairoplanes, giving them a final once-over before the fairground opened.

'Mornin', Luke. Rose,' he added, with a smile that stopped just short of a leer. Rose wished he wouldn't look at her like that. She hated the way his eyes ran all over her as though he were appraising horseflesh. She reminded herself that it was nothing personal; after all he looked that way at Doreen too—*especially* Doreen—plus half the young women who came to the fairground. But almost instinctively she folded her arms over her breasts.

'Luke wants a word with you,' she said. 'A private word.'

'Private, eh?' Sean's gingery eyebrows knitted in puzzlement. He nodded to Mario and Terry. 'All right, boys, go get yerselves a bevvy—an' you can bring me one back while you're at it.' He sat down on the edge of the staging, hands resting on his knees. 'What's all this about then?'

Luke thrust his hands into his pockets, awkward as he always was when he had to deal with people. 'We've got a bit of a problem.'

'Problem?'

'It was Rose as noticed it first. There's some

137

money gone missin' ...'

'From the takin's,' cut in Rose.

'Oh yes?' Sean's smile faded, the normally genial grey eyes taking on a hard, defensive glitter.

'Far as I can tell,' said Luke, 'it's been goin' on for weeks. We're down a good ten pound ...'

Sean Rourke fixed Luke with an unforgiving stare. 'So what exactly are you sayin'? That I might have a notion where these ten pounds have gone?'

'No, not that,' said Rose.

'No? So why are you tellin' me then? For the good of me health?'

'I thought you'd want to know,' said Luke lamely.

'Oh you did, did you?' Sean's resentment curdled into open contempt. Rose felt the anger sparking out of him like forked lightning. 'An' this wouldn't have nothin' to do with you thinkin' it's me what's been puttin' my hand in the till?'

'No!' snorted Luke. 'But—'

Rourke laughed humourlessly. 'Do me a favour! If you're callin' me a thief, at least come out an' give it to me straight. Even Dan was man enough to do that.' He stood up. 'Is that what you're callin' me—a common thief?'

'Of course bloody not,' muttered Luke, but he didn't sound much like he meant it. Rose felt her cheeks burn, aware that several people had stopped work and were staring. To make matters worse one of them was Horace Spence, pausing at the Waltzers on his way to the office.

'Sean,' pleaded Rose, 'nobody's accusing you of anythin'.'

But there was no getting through to him now. 'I was willin' to give you a chance,' he raged. 'D'you know that? But you Bartons are all the same. Greedy, graspin', always thinkin' the worst of people—I don't know why I bloody bother. I tell you, I don't.'

'Then bloody don't!' snapped back Luke, his short fuse sizzling.

Rose looked on in horror. 'Luke!'

'If you're so sick of workin' for me, why don't you just get lost?'

Sean blazed back at him. 'Yeah. Why not? Know somethin', Luke? I reckon I'll do just that.'

For a brief moment they were eyeball to eyeball, Luke too angry and too proud to back down, Sean so certain he was being victimised that he didn't even want to listen. Then Sean threw down his oil-can and stalked away without a word.

'Luke, do somethin'?' pleaded Rose. 'Go after him.'

'Why?' Luke glared after the retreating figure. 'Why should I? I reckon we're better off without him.'

Later, he will regret this, thought Rose. Later, when it will be too late.

And she thought of what she'd said to Charlie, how she'd refused to listen to his excuses and screamed at him to go away, to get out of her life, never to come back. There were so many

139

questions buzzing around in her head, questions that had tormented her for nine long years.

Was it too late to hope there might be answers?

No matter how much Luke might secretly regret what had happened, there was no persuading him to seek Sean out and try to change his mind.

'I don't know what we're goin' to do,' Rose confided to Doreen as they set up the coconut shy. 'I really don't.'

'He really won't talk to Sean then?' Doreen looked down in the mouth as she polished a wooden coconut on the seat of her corduroy pants and plonked it into its cup. Rose guessed that Sean's sudden departure had hit her harder than she was willing to admit.

'Talk to him? He won't have anythin' to do with him—not that Sean's been anywhere near us since. An' I don't blame him neither,' Rose added, huffing and puffing as the two women struggled to drag out the tub full of coloured balls. 'There, that don't look too bad, does it?'

Doreen straightened up, hands on hips. 'It'll do fine.' She drew an invisible pattern on the concrete floor with the toe of her boot, thinking. 'Tell you what, why don't I find Sean and have a word with him? It might not do any good, but what've you got to lose?'

Rose toyed with the idea then cast it aside. She glanced across at Luke, stone-faced and monosyllabic as he handed out orders to Cec

140

and Mario. 'Not in the mood Luke's in right now. Even if you got through to Sean, Luke wouldn't have him on the site.'

'He really thinks Sean's been stealing from the takings? But Rose ...'

Rose raised her hands and let them fall to her sides. 'I know, I know. I don't believe it either. But Luke's got this idea in his head an' now he can't bear the thought of bein' wrong.' She tied on the blue apron with the big money-pouch on the front. 'Pig-headed, that's my Luke. There's no shiftin' him once he's made his mind up.'

'But you wouldn't have him any other way?'

Rose gave Doreen a rueful smile. 'Right now I'm not so sure. Anyhow ...' She patted her hair, easing out a stray hairpin and jabbing it back into place. Her mind might be in turmoil but she was darned if anyone was going to see her looking a mess. 'No use cryin' over spilt milk.'

'You'll manage,' said Doreen. 'You're strong, you and Luke.'

Surprised, Rose looked up. 'Strong? You reckon?'

'I'll say! It's not every woman who'd take on Dan Barton's mess and sort it out for him.'

'I'm not doin' it for Dan, I'm doin' it for Luke.'

'I know. And that's why you'll get by.' Doreen gave her friend a reassuring hug, and for two pins Rose would have burst into tears. She so desperately needed someone to talk to, someone she could tell about Charlie and the terrible hurt inside her, and this was one thing she could never bring herself to share with Luke. But something was holding her back from telling Doreen. Maybe she didn't want to burden her with her problems; maybe it was stupid pride ... or shame. She turned her face away, hoping that Doreen wouldn't notice she was upset. But Doreen wasn't stupid.

'What's wrong, Rose?'

'Oh, just this business with Sean, you know.' She fumbled in her apron pocket and took out a handkerchief, swiftly dabbing her eyes. 'Nothin' really.'

'There's something else, isn't there?'

Rose looked into Doreen's kind brown eyes. She knew she could trust her, and for a split second she almost told her everything: about Ellie, about Charlie, about the awful gnawing fears and regrets. Then she shook her head and forced herself to smile.

'Nothin' for you to worry about. Just somethin' I've got to work out for myself.'

It wasn't as difficult as expected to work out where Charlie was staying: Gorry's was the only ironmonger's shop on Mount Havelock. The hard part had been getting the information out of Gracie without arousing her suspicions—and having rumours spread all over the fairfield. There was nothing Dot and Gracie liked better than to gossip at other people's expense.

Rose kept telling herself that she was doing nothing wrong, that she was only seeking out Charlie because she had to protect the family life she and Ellie had built for themselves with Luke;

but she hated having to do it behind Luke's back. As the bus rumbled towards the centre of Douglas she kept hearing her old granny, scolding her when she was a little kid: 'Big troubles start with one little lie.' But surely this wasn't a lie. She was only going to see Charlie because they both needed to know the truth.

Getting off the bus, she walked very slowly up the hill towards the little parade of shops. All last night she'd lain awake, going over and over the same thoughts and fears as she listened to Luke's slow, steady, exhausted breathing and Ellie's snuffly wheeze as she tossed and turned, trying to shake off a summer cold. She'd taken Ellie a glass of water and slipped into the narrow bed beside her, cradling her in her arms until the little girl finally fell asleep. You're a good man, Luke Barton, she'd thought to herself as she lay there in the stuffy warmth, waiting for morning to come. You've been a fine husband to me, and Ellie couldn't wish for a better father. You're her dad, not Charlie Cartwright, and you always will be.

But doesn't Charlie have a right to know ... and if he sees Ellie won't he work it out for himself? That was the thought that had kept coming back, again and again, to torment her. What if she told him and he wanted to take over their lives? What if he refused to go away and leave them all in peace? What if ...?

She was still asking herself the same, unanswerable questions when she'd fallen asleep just before dawn.

And now here she was, walking towards the

display of dustbins and broom handles outside Gorry's store, scared half out of her wits and still wondering if she was about to make a terrible mistake. But she'd made her decision and she'd stick to it. She'd tell Charlie, and make it clear he wasn't welcome any more. He'd understand. Whatever else he might be, Charlie had never been a vindictive man. But in nine long years, who could say how much he might have changed?

Rose caught sight of her reflection in the butcher's window. It didn't flatter her. The tall young woman who gazed back was lean to the point of boniness, her red-brown hair austerely rolled and pinned and her unfashionable clothes washed-out and patched. Even the thin slick of red lipstick did little more than highlight the dark shadows under her eyes. *The years have changed you too,* she thought, *and not for the better.*

But she drew herself up, threw back her shoulders and walked towards the ironmonger's, telling herself that it didn't matter a damn what Charlie might think of the way she looked. She'd get this over with and then they could both get on with living their lives.

As she approached the shop door, she heard a man shouting, 'Stop that! Will you *stop* that?' and then a great clattering sound, like a suit of armour falling down a flight of stairs. She stopped in her tracks, then took a step forward and peered in. Inside the shop, a small, skinny, black-haired child was running about, overturning the stands and sending the

144

pots and bins and saucepans crashing to the ground. There couldn't be two kids like that one, thought Rose. It was the little girl Charlie had brought with him to Funland, the one Gracie had said was deaf and dumb.

The middle-aged shopkeeper, frantic with frustration, was leaning on a walking stick, and moving far too slowly to catch the little urchin. He made a grab but she darted out of his reach and let fly with a colander before making a rush for the door.

'Stop her will you?'

Rose grabbed for her and just managed to seize a handful of sleeve. The child spun round with a kind of muted snarl, and as she did so Rose caught the look in her eyes, a look she hadn't seen since Jerry bombed Florizel Street: a look of pure, naked terror. She was so astonished that she relaxed her grip, and in that split second the kid was gone, racing out of the door and shoving over a pile of paint tins as she went.

But she didn't get far. Through the shop window, Rose saw her run straight into the arms of a blond, broad-shouldered man, almost knocking him over as he dropped the package he was carrying and grabbed hold of her.

'Lola! Lola, what's all this about?'

Charlie.

Rose's heart stopped in its tracks, restarting with a huge thump that made her dizzy. Given a chance she'd have turned tail and fled, but she was stuck inside the shop, watching Charlie and the child walking towards her.

'Are you all right?' asked the shopkeeper.

'Yes. Yes, I'm fine.'

John Gorry passed his hand over his balding scalp, shaking his head in sorrowful disbelief. 'That child ... I've tried, I swear I have, but she's got the devil in her.'

He stooped awkwardly to pick up a dented saucepan. Not knowing what else to do, Rose crouched down and started helping him, her hands automatically picking up the tins of paint and stacking them, though her eyes were fixed on the door. At any moment now he would step through it ...

'There's no need to do that,' protested Gorry.

'It's all right, I don't mind.'

Charlie came through the door, his face falling at the sight of the mess. 'God, John, she's not done it again ... Hell, I'm sorry. You sit down an' let me ... Oh!' His eyes lighted on Rose.

She stood up slowly, wiping her dusty hands. 'Charlie.' She wondered if he had caught the slight tremble in her voice.

'I ... I thought ...'

'We need to talk.'

'Yes.' Charlie looked at Gorry. 'John, this is really important, would you mind if ...?'

Gorry picked up a stack of sieves and set them on the counter. 'Go in the back room, we can clear this up later.'

Rose looked at the devastation around her. They could hardly leave the poor man to clear it up on his own. She took off her jacket and rolled up her sleeves. 'Let's do it now,' she said.

146

'I've waited nine years to talk to you, Charlie, I can wait a bit longer.'

John Gorry's sitting room was small and sparse, a real bachelor's room. There was little in it beyond a square of faded carpet, a standard lamp, a wireless set and a few old photographs. The only thing to sit on was a two-seater settee, one cushion worn threadbare and the other as good as new. Nine years ago Charlie and Rose would have snuggled down on it together; now they were standing at opposite ends of it, using it as a barrier, trying to maintain as much distance between them as the tiny room would allow.

'D'you want to sit down?' asked Charlie. He sounded nervous, Rose thought, almost as nervous as she felt.

She shook her head. 'I'm not stoppin'.'

Charlie perched on the arm of the settee, his fingers picking at the worn moquette.

'I thought ... I thought I wasn't going to see you again. You said—'

'I know what I said an' I meant it.'

'Then why—'

'There's unfinished business between us, Charlie. Things what want sortin' out.' She felt her throat tighten, her resolve wavering, but she knew she had to go through with this. 'There's somethin' I have to tell you.'

Charlie looked up at her, then looked away, shamefaced. 'There's things I ought to tell you an' all. God knows, you've a right to know what I've been up to these last nine years.'

Rose was about to tell him that frankly she

147

was no longer interested in what he'd been doing—because if he'd ever cared tuppence for her he'd not have left her in limbo, not even bothering to let her know he wasn't dead. But her attention was drawn by the door-handle turning slowly. The door clicked open and a mop of tousled hair and two eyes, black and bright as a demon's, appeared in the doorway.

Charlie got up as the child walked in. Stooping, he took her by the shoulders and shook his head. 'No, Lola, not now.'

But the child shook him off and stalked across the room towards Rose, sat herself down on the settee with her legs curled under her and tugged at Rose's dress. Rose looked down into her face. The look in those eyes both chilled and disturbed her. There was such pain, such anger, such pleading.

'I'm sorry, Rose,' said Charlie. 'She's ... difficult.'

Rose gently detached her dress from Lola's fingers but the child simply latched on again, and this time Rose didn't bother dissuading her.

'Who is she, Charlie?'

Charlie stood up and walked across to the fireplace. He took one of the framed photographs from the mantelpiece. It showed five men in uniform, sitting cross-legged on the ground, cleaning their rifles.

'That one there, that's John Gorry, see? When we was in Spain.' He pointed to the second man from the right. 'Same brigade as me. It was hell, Rose ...'

148

'What's this got to do with anythin'? If you're expectin' me to feel sorry for you or somethin'—'

'No, no, not that, I'm just ... just tryin' to explain. It's hard.' He took the photo and placed it back on the mantelpiece. His back to Rose, he went on talking. She could see his face reflected in the mirror, the muscles of his jaw visible like strings of tension beneath the tanned skin.

'When I saw your mam an' dad—'

'Without botherin' to see me first. Without even botherin' to let me know you were alive.'

'Please, Rose ... When I saw them I had Lola with me. I told them ... I told them she was the daughter of this Spanish bloke I was in jail with. He got killed an' I said I'd take care of her. An' when I come over here to see you, that was what I was goin' to tell you an' all. Only ...'

'Only what?'

'Only it were a lie.' Charlie turned slowly round to face her. She saw his throat clench as he swallowed. 'Lola's ... She's mine. She's my daughter.'

'She's ...' Rose stared down at the olive-skinned child, the dark eyes, the glossy black hair, in every respect as different from Charlie as it was possible for a child to be. As different, in fact, as Ellie was from Rose. How old would Lola be? Seven years, eight? No younger than seven, that was for sure. Probably no more than a few months younger than Ellie.

The fact that Charlie might be her father as well as Ellie's was something that Rose did not want to believe. 'No. No. Charlie. That's ... that's not true!'

'It is true, Rose. An' God I've wished it wasn't; but how can you wish a kid wasn't yours? I'm sorry for what I did, but I'm not sorry I've got her. Can you understand that, Rose?'

'Understand?' Rose felt the cold rush of shock turn to an avalanche of burning fury within her. 'Understand, Charlie? You expect me to *understand* that you cheated on me? You leave me high an' dry with a bunch of worthless promises, you bugger off to Spain an' set yourself up with some tart, an' all the time I'm sittin' at home thinkin' the reason you've stopped writin' to me is 'cause you've been blown up or shot or somethin'.' She stopped in mid-flow. 'You bastard, Charlie Cartwright,' she hissed. 'You lyin', cheatin' bastard. Why did I ever waste my tears on you?'

Charlie's golden eyes narrowed with pain, but this time he did not look away. 'I'm sorry, Rose. I really am. I just thought ... I thought you ought to know the truth.'

She knew he was willing her to forgive him, but Rose felt as if the last shred of love she had felt for Charlie had been wrenched out of her heart. All she was capable of feeling right now was anger, pain, betrayal.

'It's a bit late for that, Charlie. Nine years too late. Perhaps you should've thought of that before you bedded your Spanish tart.'

Charlie took a deep breath and let it out slowly as if trying to control his emotions.

'She's dead. Lola's mother.'

'So?' Rose spat the word at Charlie, daring him to make her feel pity.

'So the kid's eight years old, Rose. She's deaf. She's got nobody but me. So I've got to look after her somehow. What am I supposed to do—leave her to rot in some Spanish orphanage an' pretend she doesn't exist?'

The question hung in the air. Rose felt a tug at her sleeve and looked down. Lola was smiling at her.

Rose tore her gaze away and took a step back. 'You never came back for my sake, did you, Charlie? Not to see me; you couldn't care less about me. No, you came back 'cause you thought I'd take pity on you for the child's sake. My God, Charlie, you were even goin' to let me think she was some other man's kid, so you wouldn't look such a two-timin' bastard!'

'I know it sounds bad—'

'It *is* bad.'

'But if you'd just let me try to explain ...'

Rose picked up her jacket and put it on, grabbing her handbag from the settee. 'I've heard all I want to hear. Goodbye, Charlie, I'm goin' home. To my *husband.*'

She headed for the door but Charlie got there first and barred her way. 'Don't go.'

'Get out of my way, Charlie.'

Their eyes met, and for a fleeting moment she recalled the way she had felt when she was seventeen, when he had kissed her one last time before stepping on to the boat that carried him far, far away. Then Charlie stepped aside and

151

she pushed past him, hurrying out through the shop and slamming the door so hard behind her that it rattled in its frame.

Outside, she took a few moments to calm herself before she walked slowly down the hill towards the bus stop. Had she really intended to tell Charlie Cartwright that Ellie was his daughter? Had she really been stupid enough to care about him? Well he could rot in Hell before she'd tell him now; and if she ever saw him again it would be a hundred years too soon.

CHAPTER 12

It was late July. Almost a month had passed, and in all that time Rose had not heard a word from Charlie. That, at least, was something to be grateful for—and with each new day that went by Rose began to feel a little more certain that she had heard the last of Charlie Cartwright.

She would have died rather than admit that somewhere, in a very deep and forgotten corner of her heart, she felt the faintest twinge of regret.

But there was nothing to be gained by dwelling on the past. And there were plenty of other things to occupy Rose's mind. The summer season was going well enough for the Island, with thousands of visitors pouring off the boats every Saturday. But it wasn't such a good season for everyone at Funland. The safety inspector had closed down the Swing Boats and the ancient Razzle-Dazzle, and the Wilcocks and the Millers had sold out, in despair, to Horace Spence.

As Rose stepped down from the vardo very early one Sunday morning she saw the Millers dismantling the Razzle-Dazzle for the last time. They hadn't even bothered trying to get it repaired; it was old and worn out and had hardly been making any money anyway. The only ones making much of a profit were people like Spence and the Verneys, the big showmen whose brand new attractions dwarfed anything the Darwells or the Millers or the Bartons could afford.

Rose thought of going over to say goodbye, but the Millers and the Bartons had never really exchanged more than a few words; and what could she say to a family whose entire way of life was coming to an end? There was a kind of superstitious fear inside her too, an irrational feeling that, while today ill fortune had touched the Millers and the Wilcocks, tomorrow it might call on the Bartons. Her heart heavy, she turned and headed in the opposite direction, towards Spence's little whitewashed office on the far side of the tober.

Luke came out on to the top step of the wagon, drying his hands, and called after her, 'Don't take any stick from him, Rose. An' don't let him—'

She turned and smiled with more confidence than she felt. 'Don't you worry, love. I'll just give him the money an' go.'

As she walked past the Wiggley-Waggley and the bare patch of concrete where the Swing Boats had stood, Sid Christian called out to her from behind his stall.

'Mornin', Rose.'

'How're you doin', Sid?'

'Oh, not so bad. Can't get the sugar for me toffee apples, mind, an' Lord knows where the next lot of ice cream's comin' from. Still, can't complain. At least we're still in business, eh?'

'For the time bein'.' Rose wrinkled her nose. 'If him over there doesn't get us out.'

Sid followed the direction of her gaze to the square building. Percy Sayle was standing outside, a pot of black paint in his hand, touching up the sign that read, 'MANAGER'.

'Ah—off to see the Big Fella are you?'

Rose couldn't help smiling. Horace must have known that everyone on the fairfield called him the Big Fella, but apparently he had no idea that it was a Manx way of calling him a rat. 'No choice, is there? We've got the next quarter's rent to pay.' And a bit extra we can't afford, she added to herself, cursing Dan Barton's fondness for spending other people's money.

'Oh aye? Rather you than me. He's an old skinflint, an' if you don't mind me sayin' ...'

'What?'

'I'd watch yerself if I was you. He's a bit of an eye for the ladies, has our Horace.'

Rose pulled a face. 'Don't I just know it?'

She walked the last hundred yards to the office. Percy touched his cap with painty fingers. 'Mornin', Missus Rose.'

'Mornin', Percy. In, is he?'

'Aye. Best knock, though—he's very particular is Misther Spence.'

She knocked, waited a couple of seconds then walked straight in. Horace Spence was sitting behind his big desk trying to look like a fat tycoon out of an American movie, a big cigar clamped between his teeth, his wiry grey hair slicked back with half a pot of brilliantine and his left thumb stuck through his braces. With his other hand he held the telephone receiver to his ear. '... Well bloody get it sorted out ... No, I'm not interested in your flamin' excuses, just do it. Got that? An' tell Wainwright ...' He looked up and saw Rose hovering by the door, not sure whether to come in or go back out. He beckoned her in with a pudgy finger. 'Get back to me by five. Or the deal's off.'

Crashing the receiver back on to the hook, Spence took a draw on his cigar. 'Rose Barton, well well.'

The piggy eyes took a good long look at her and she shifted from one foot to the other, discomfited by his obvious interest. It was almost as if Horace Spence had X-ray eyes.

'Take a seat.'

Rose ignored the invitation. Reaching into the pocket of her apron she took out the rent money and laid the bundle of notes on the desk.

'Next quarter's rent.'

'You're a day late.'

She felt her pulse quicken. 'Surely ... surely that doesn't make any difference? The Darwells

155

are always weeks late, an' you never complain about them.'

'What about the next payment on the debt?'

'Count it if you want, it's all there. Every brass farthin'.'

'I don't doubt it.' Horace smiled like the cat who'd stolen the cream and sold it on at a profit. He picked up the notes, put them to his ear and flicked through them with an almost sensual pleasure; and Rose noticed with disgust that there were big wet circles under the arms of his expensive shirt. 'You're an honest lass.' The piggy eyes appraised her a second time. 'Fine-lookin' one an' all, though I'll bet it's not easy lookin' nice.'

Rose fell right into the trap. 'Not easy? Why?'

'On that pittance your 'usband gets from them clapped-out rides. Thought a bit more about my generous offer, 'as 'e?'

Irritation kindled, but Rose refused to let it burn. 'If you mean are we sellin' out to you, then the answer's still no,' she said coolly.

Horace Spence shrugged. The smile did not dim. 'Give it time,' he said serenely. 'You'll see reason. Gets cold 'ere in the winter, not much work neither. Fixed up, are you?'

That hit a raw nerve, and Rose kicked herself for letting it show. 'We'll get by. Luke'll find somethin'.'

'Mebbe. Mebbe not.' Horace stubbed out his cigar. ' 'Eard you 'ad a bit of trouble. With the takin's.'

'What! Who told you that?' Damn the

fairground gossips, thought Rose. Did everyone in the world know why Sean Rourke had walked out on them?

'Careless, that.' Horace shook his head reprovingly. 'Shouldn't never employ people you can't trust. They'll rob you blind, first chance they get.' He got up from his chair and his fat body undulated, the huge sphere of his paunch straining the shirt-buttons across his chest. 'You're a fool to yourself, Rose, stickin' with that idiot Luke Barton.'

'Luke's a good man!'

'He's nothin', Rose. A loser. Believe me, stick with 'im an' you'll 'ave nowt but bad luck. Know what folk round here reckon? There's a curse on Luke Barton, an' one day it'll catch up with him ...'

For all that she'd promised herself—and Luke—that she'd keep her temper, this was too much for Rose to stand. She squared up to Spence like a prizefighter, eyes blazing. 'How dare you! How dare you talk to me like that! My Luke's ten times the man you are, Horace Spence.'

To her dismay, Horace's response was a guffaw of delighted laughter. 'By God, you're a sparky little woman.' The self-satisfied smile turned into a leer. 'Don't think to watch your tongue, do you?'

'I'm not goin' to stand here an' listen to you insultin' my Luke when he's not even here to defend himself—'

'Passionate an' all, just the way I like 'em.' Spence moved in closer, his sweaty odour warm and obtrusive in the confined space. Rose stepped back but he followed her, plucking at the shabby pinafore she wore over her washed-out summer dress. 'Pretty woman like you should 'ave nice frocks, not these old rags. I can be a generous man, Rose.'

'Get your disgustin' hands off me!' With a shove to his middle she pushed him away. For a moment she thought he was going to rage at her, strike her even—but no, he just chuckled as if it was the funniest thing in the world.

'Right little wildcat. Not scared of owt, are you?'

Oh yes I am, thought Rose. But I'm darned if I'm letting you see it. She stared right into his fat face. 'Well I'm not bloody scared of *you*.'

Still chuckling, Spence turned to the pile of money on the table. He peeled off a ten-bob note and, seizing Rose's hand, closed her fingers over it before she knew what he was doing. 'Like I said, Rose, I can be a generous man. I'm sure the two of us could come to an ... understandin'. Take this an' buy yourself summat nice.'

She stared down at her closed fist, dumbstruck, then slowly uncurled the fingers. The brown ten-shilling note lay there, crumpled up like an old dried-up leaf. Then disgust overwhelmed her and, dropping the money to the floor, she turned on her heel and stalked out without a word.

Spence didn't follow her. Outside, in the early morning sunshine, Rose wondered what had possessed her to let fly at him like that. But why should she put up with his lecherous attentions or his vile insinuations? She'd never wanted to come here anyway, to give up her ordinary, comfortable life for this unreal, hand-to-mouth existence.

But right now, more than anything, she wanted the Bartons to win through, if only to spite Horace Spence. The question was, could they do it?

As she walked back to the vardo, she reminded herself that things were by no means all bad. Since Sean Rourke had left the takings had risen steadily; so it seemed that Luke had been right all along, and Sean really had been on the take. Funny, that. She'd never cared much for Sean but she'd not have had him marked down as a thief.

Sean Rourke, Horace Spence, Charlie ... If it hadn't been for Luke and Doreen, Rose would have wondered if there was anyone left she could really trust.

It was two o'clock on a hot August night, but Manfri Barton was not sleeping. He hauled open the back gates of the big wooden shed with painstaking slowness, anxious to make as little noise as possible. He was sweating profusely, but the oppressive heat had nothing to do with it. This was a dangerous game.

He peered into the darkness. Thankfully there were no streetlamps round the back of the bomb-site, and at this time of night there shouldn't be anyone around to poke a prying nose into things that didn't concern them.

Something stirred down by his foot and he

jumped half out of his skin. Then a glimmer of moonlight illuminated two small amber discs and he saw that it was just a scrawny black cat, on the lookout for prey. He whistled softly. A few moments later two cars emerged from nowhere, gliding almost soundlessly past him and into the workshop. Following them inside, he took a final look round then locked the doors.

It was time to get down to work. And he would have to work fast.

Rose pulled her cardigan more closely around her goose-pimpled arms. It might be August, but she was frozen stiff. In the distance, beyond the looming skeleton of Spence's roller-coaster, she could just make out the thin grey line of the sea, chopped by the wind into peaks like the spines on a hedgehog's back.

This Manx weather took some getting used to; one minute it might be warm and sunny, the next it was chill and gusty, or so blanketed in damp sea-mist that you couldn't see your hand in front of your face. Not that the holidaymakers seemed to mind much if the weather wasn't as kind as it might be. The minute Funland's gates opened at ten-thirty, they started pouring through in their hundreds. After all, they had six years of fun to cram into one precious week's holiday.

'Are you still cold, Mam?' asked Ellie. They were working the coconut shy together, sheltering behind the thin plywood wall of the booth as the canopy flapped above their heads.

'I'm all right love,' smiled Rose, taking another fourpence and nodding to Ellie to hand over three wooden balls.

'You can have my cardi as well if you want,' said Ellie. And she meant it too, bless her, thought Rose, though the poor child was shivering under that cotton frock.

'Like I said, I'm right as rain. I can manage here—why don't you go back to the van an' have a bit of a rest?'

'But I'm not tired! An' I want to stay here an' help you!'

Rose cursed silently as a girl in a straw coolie hat scored a direct hit on one of the wooden coconuts, making it capsize and topple off its red stalk. The girl's face flushed bright pink with triumph, and her friend threw her arms round her.

'You did it! You won, you won!'

'Well done miss, get the lady her prize, Ellie.'

Ellie took one of the china poodles off the bottom shelf. It was one of the last they had left, and if Luke didn't manage to buy up some more soon, at the right price, they might find themselves with no prizes at all, save for the ornate biscuit barrel which sat in splendid isolation on the top shelf, as it had sat since 1936. Nobody ever won the 'star' prize; it was only there to entice the punters in.

'Tell you what,' said Rose as the two girls went off giggling into the swarm of passers-by. She couldn't bear to see Ellie shifting from one foot to the other like that, trying to keep warm. 'Why don't you go an' make us a nice cuppa?'

Ellie pouted thoughtfully. 'Well ...'

'Go on. You can make an extra one for your dad; he'll be back soon. Nine balls, sir? That'll be sixpence ...'

Ellie would have set off for the vardo, but at that moment the heaving mass of people parted and two familiar figures emerged, heading straight for the coconut shy.

'Mam—Mam look, it's Billy Darwell an' his dad. Why are they comin' here?'

Rose counted out two thrupenny bits. Why indeed? she wondered. It wasn't as if the Bartons and the Darwells were bosom friends, though relations had been less frosty since Luke rescued Billy.

Ranty Darwell had Billy's earlobe in a vice-like grip between forefinger and thumb, and a look on his face that spelt trouble. Rose steeled herself. What now?

She gave him a cautious nod. 'Mister Darwell.'

Ranty Darwell gave Billy's ear a fierce tweak and pulled him forward.

'Dad! Aw, Dad, you're hurtin'! Let go me ear!'

'I'll let you go when I'm good an' ready.'

'Daaad ...'

'Go on. Say yer piece.'

Billy Darwell glowered under his mop of tangled, ginger-brown hair. He was a right little urchin, thought Rose: his clothes filthy, his socks concertinaed round his ankles, and

162

the bandage on his leg more grey than white.

'Me dad says I've to say I'm sorry,' he grunted.

'Sorry?' Rose folded her arms and returned the child's gaze. 'Sorry for what?'

Ranty tweaked the ear a little harder. 'Give it 'er.'

It was then that Rose noticed Billy Darwell's right hand, closed in a tight fist half behind his back. Very slowly and reluctantly he brought up the hand and opened it. In his palm lay one of the china poodles from the coconut shy.

Ellie's golden eyes opened to wide circles of outrage. 'Billy Darwell! You rotten—'

'Hush, Ellie.' Rose took the china dog. 'Where did you get this, Billy?'

'Its tail's all broke,' grunted Billy. 'It were no good—I reckoned you'd never miss it.'

'He nicked it,' Ellie piped up. 'You flippin' nicked it! You're a thief, Billy Darwell!'

'I said be quiet,' said Rose firmly. 'You see to those punters, they're waitin' to pay.'

'The lass is right,' said Ranty Darwell grimly. 'He's a little thief an' I won't 'ave it. No son of mine nicks stuff from other showfolk.' There was real fury in his eyes. 'Now say you're sorry.'

Billy scrabbled at his twisted ear, trying to free himself from the discomfort. Rose suddenly felt a vague sympathy for the kid, brought up with brutality instead of love.

'Let go of him, Mr Darwell. Let him speak for himself.'

Ranty Darwell looked at Rose as if she was

163

mad, but shrugged and let go of Billy's ear. It was obvious he expected Billy to take the opportunity to leg it, but the boy stood his ground and stared down at his feet.

'Sorry,' he grunted almost inaudibly.

'It don't count if you don't mean it,' said Ellie.

Billy raised his head, glanced at Ellie and stuck his tongue out. Then he looked at Rose. 'Sorry, Missus.'

Rose set the china poodle back on the shelf with the others. It was true what Billy had said, the tail was broken off, but that was no excuse. All the same, it was hardly the crime of the century and it was probably punishment enough having to have Ranty for a father.

A fleeting thought crossed her mind. 'Have you nicked anythin' from us before, Billy?'

Billy's brow knotted. He looked defensive, thought Rose, angry even—but not guilty.

'No!'

'Nothin'? You're tellin' me the truth?'

'Nothin', I told you ... only toffee apples an' that, off Sid Christian.'

'An' you'll not do it again?'

'Too bloody right he won't,' growled Ranty, taking a swipe at Billy's head with the flat of his hand.

'No, Missus. Can I go now, Missus?'

Rose sighed. 'Go on, then.'

The child disappeared into the crowd like a will-o'-the-wisp.

'I'll give 'im a good hidin' later,' said Ranty Darwell. 'Taste of the strap, that's what he wants. Your Luke not 'ere then?'

'He's gone buyin' prizes for the stall.'

Ranty grunted. 'Runnin' out, are ye?' He watched Rose handing out balls to a group of young lads and lowered his voice. 'You're makin' it too easy for 'em to win. Let me 'ave a look at them coconuts, I'll get 'em weighted proper for ye.'

'Thanks ... thanks, Mister Darwell, but we'll manage.' Rose wished Ranty would go away; having him standing there, scowling like a bogeyman, was putting off the punters.

'Well ...' Ranty turned to leave. It was obvious from the look on his face that there was something difficult he thought he ought to say. 'When you see your Luke, tell 'im ... tell 'im I'm much obliged for what he did for my Billy. An' ... if he's in the Manx Arms tomorrer dinnertime I'll buy 'im a pint.'

Rose could hardly believe her ears. Maybe Ranty was going to sweet-talk Luke into giving him his pitch back.

'I'll tell him,' she promised.

She went back to trying to make a living, wondering how Mario and Gracie were getting on, running the TT Racer while Luke was away. Really they could have done with Doreen pitching in, but things were getting pretty hectic over at Kneale's yard, what with the first Manx Grand Prix since the war only a few weeks away and so many bikes to get ready. Rose and Luke were lucky that the Kneales could spare them any time at all. At any rate, she could see the brightly painted rounding boards

165

of the TT Racer and the Chairoplanes turning with reassuring regularity over the heads of the punters, and Old Peg seemed to have a pretty steady stream of takers at her dukkering tent. All in all they were managing OK, even without Luke at the helm.

If Rose thought she'd seen the last of Billy Darwell for one day, she was mistaken. He came hurtling through the middle of a group of mill-girls as if the Devil himself were on his tail.

'Missus, Missus!'

Rose looked at the breathless child with suspicion. 'What is it now, Billy?'

'It's that Dot, Missus.'

'Dot? What do you mean, it's Dot?' Rose felt a frisson of unease. 'What's happened?'

'It were this bloke, you know, one o' them religious blokes from off the prom ...'

'What about him?'

'He were shoutin' at Dot an' tellin' folk it wasn't decent an' makin' trouble an' that, an' then Dot got angry an' told him to go away, only he just kept on shoutin', an' then ...' Billy stopped, either because he had run out of breath or because he was enjoying the suspense.

'Then what?' demanded Rose.

'Come an' see for yerself, Missus!'

Rose tore the money-pouch from round her waist and pushed it into Ellie's hands. 'Can you manage on your own for a mo, love?'

'Yes, Mam.'

Rose seized Billy Darwell by the shoulder. 'You'd better show me. An' if you're havin' me on, Billy Darwell, I'll have your guts for garters.'

Showbusiness was in Dot Matthews's blood; she liked nothing better than hogging the limelight. And on Knock the Lady out of Bed, she was guaranteed a permanent audience from ten in the morning till eleven at night. Lazing around and getting paid for it—that was the kind of work that appealed to Dot. Today she'd been having the time of her life, lounging under the bedcovers like Lady Muck and giving the nice-looking blokes the eye while Terry rounded up the punters.

'Come on sir, try your luck. How about you, sir? Six goes an' you'll still have change from a bob ...'

Dot knew it wasn't Terry's amateurish patter that had them coming back for more. He wasn't a patch on Sean Rourke when it came to the spiel. No, it was the hope of hitting the bull's-eye and sending a pretty girl tumbling out of bed on to the pile of mattresses underneath, knowing that when she fell, Dot always gave excellent value for money. A flash of leg, a glimpse of white silk knickers ... Decent underwear wasn't easy to come by, of course, but you could get parachute silk if you knew the right people to ask—and Dot knew plenty of airmen.

Whack! The bean-bags pounded into the board behind her head but hit wide of the target. Shame, really. She quite fancied that sporty-looking lad with the dark hair and the muscular arms.

'Come on, boys!' she coaxed, giving Terry a little extra help. 'Knock the lady out of bed ...'

'You're no lady!' some wag called out from the back.

Dot stuck her tongue out at him. She encouraged the onlookers by sliding her right leg out from underneath the covers and wriggling the toes. 'Come on, don't you want to see some more?'

She acknowledged the wolf-whistles by blowing a kiss to the dark-haired lad who, much to her delight, bought another four bean-bags and started pelting the target with them. A few seconds later the bed tipped sideways and she plunged through the air on to the mattresses.

It was as she was getting to her feet, assisted by Terry, that things went wrong. Someone pushed his way to the front of the crowd and started shouting, 'Mother of harlots and abominations of the earth!'

'Who the heck ...?' Startled, Dot swung round to confront the heckler. She knew him instantly from his drab black suit and Homburg. He was one of those religious fanatics who'd set up camp on the beach, the ones who reckoned Funland ought to be closed down so everyone could be as miserable as they were. 'What d'you think you're playing at?'

A gust of laughter ran round the crowd.

'That's it girl, give it him straight.'

'The wages of sin, young woman, the wages of sin!'

Dot turned to Terry for help. 'Terry, tell this idiot to get lost.'

'On your way, mate, you're upsettin' the lady.' Terry tried to usher the man away but he just shoved him to one side and stepped between him and Dot, wild-eyed and ranting.

'I saw a woman sit upon a scarlet coloured beast, full of names of blasphemy ...'

Dot took a step back. This lunatic was beginning to unnerve her with his biblical quotations and staring eyes. The crowd stopped laughing and went quite silent. Behind them, the rides thundered on, girls squealing with delight as they skidded down the helter-skelter, courting couples cuddling close on the Ghost Train, rifles cracking at the shooting gallery.

'Terry ...'

'Have you no shame, woman? Have you no modesty?' The lunatic in the black suit grabbed a blanket from the bed and tried to wrap it round her. 'Cover yourself, you painted Jezebel!'

It might almost have been funny if it hadn't made her so angry—and Dot Matthews had a temper you trifled with at your peril. This bloke could be an escaped madman for all anyone knew, and all these people were just standing and staring, doing nothing at all to help her. Terry was less than useless, with his embarrassed babbling and his polite 'Please, mate, if you wouldn't mind movin' along'.

It was more than Dot could stand to have everything ruined like this. And to add insult to injury, the sporty young lad with the dark eyes was laughing at her. She stopped backing away and stood her ground, tearing the blanket out of the man's weedy grasp and throwing it away from her. 'Will you get *off* me an' *leave* me *alone!*' Each word was accompanied by a shove. The third shove, more violent than the last, caught the man off balance and—much to Dot's surprise—he stumbled and fell backwards, fetching up on his backside right up against the Hook a Duck stall.

'That'll teach you, you stupid—'

Dot might have gone in for the kill if Billy Darwell hadn't come pushing to the front of the crowd at that very moment, Rose two steps behind.

'See, I told you!' he said with a broad grin.

But Rose Barton wasn't smiling.

Rose stared at the scene before her. A man in a black suit was sprawled on the ground, Dot standing over him, eyes blazing, looking as if she was about to tear him to ribbons with her varnished fingernails, be he twice her size or not. A semicircle of onlookers had gathered round like the crowd at a boxing match, hoping for blood. Oh, Luke, she thought. Why does this have to happen when you're not here?

'Dot! What on earth ...?'

Dot blanched. 'I ... he was botherin' me, wasn't he Terry?'

'You *hit* him?'

'Not hit. He just sort of ... fell over.'

Rose bent down to help the man up. He seemed unhurt but shaken.

'Are you all right?'

'She ... she pushed me.' He grabbed his hat and jammed it back on his head. His finger trembled as he pointed it at Dot. 'Th-that girl. Sh-she ... *pushed* me.'

'Is that so?' said a voice behind Rose's shoulder. 'Well perhaps you'd best calm down and tell me all about it.'

How the police constable happened to be passing at that very moment, Rose could only wonder. But one thing was for sure: before they could get rid of him there was a lot of explaining to be done.

CHAPTER 13

It was just after six on a clear August morning when Charlie got up and went downstairs for a strip-wash at John Gorry's kitchen sink. Lola was still sleeping peacefully and he didn't want to risk waking her. The shaving water was icy-cold but that didn't bother him; he'd got used to going without luxuries. The problem right now was not luxuries but necessities—finding some way of keeping body and soul together for himself and Lola.

As he drew the safety razor across his skin he wondered if he'd done the right thing, staying on the Island. It wasn't as if he belonged here, and Rose had made it very clear he was to get out of her life and stay out—a wish he had no choice but to respect. Charlie Cartwright was not the kind of man who'd come between a wife and her husband.

But Lola seemed happier here, less troubled than she'd been on the mainland. She loved the sea and the sand and the open spaces. What's more, it wasn't as if there was anything to go back home for. Charlie had no one and nothing left in Birkenhead: no parents, no brothers or sisters, nowhere to live. Not even a realistic chance of a job, since the shipyard still had him blacklisted as a communist agitator.

Today, at least, he was working for a few hours. Hauling scrap metal for pennies, just enough to keep the wolf from the door. How John managed to turn up these odd jobs for him he had no idea, but he was more grateful than John Gorry could ever know.

But he couldn't stay on here indefinitely, could he? He rinsed the blade and towelled his face dry. What would happen when the winter came, and there were no more odd jobs to be done? He wasn't a Manxman, so he couldn't expect any help from the Island government. If he chose to stay on here, somehow he was going to have to find himself a proper job.

A job. The thought filled him with a mixture of hope and despair. How was he ever going to manage that? There were so few jobs to be had, and so many men going after them. And if he did somehow achieve the impossible, he couldn't keep relying on John to step into the breach ...

So who was going to take care of Lola?

It was nine in the morning when the green Norton motor bike came roaring into Funland, its wheels bouncing over the bumpy earth as it headed towards the line of vardos.

'Morning troops,' said Doreen cheerily, taking off her helmet as she hopped off and shook out her brown curls. She looked from Luke to Rose. 'Why the long faces?'

'You'd have a long face if you'd seen this,' commented Luke, picking up the discarded newspaper.

Doreen's expression unclouded. 'Oh, the *Examiner?* I wouldn't worry about that, something and nothing.'

'Nothin'!' exclaimed Rose, gazing in horror at the photo of the Knock the Lady out of Bed stall and the caption underneath: 'BREACH OF PEACE AT FUNLAND'. 'We're lucky the bloke didn't take us to court after what Dot did to him.'

Doreen scanned the page. 'I thought she said he fell over.'

'Oh she did,' said Luke. 'That's what she swore blind to the copper, an' God knows why but that's what the punters told him an' all. But Terry saw her, an' he said she pushed him an' he went arse over tip.'

'Ah well, no harm done. I expect you gave Dot her marching orders though?'

Rose exchanged a dark look with Luke. It wasn't often that they disagreed, but Rose had had doubts about Dot Matthews from the first time she'd teetered into Funland on her mother's high heels.

'Well, no,' Luke said, 'not exactly.'

Doreen looked surprised—as well she might, thought Rose.

'Luke thought we should give her another chance.'

'I don't see as we've got much choice,' Luke retorted, picking up his toolbag. 'What with Sean gone we're already one short. If we lose another we'll have to close down a ride. 'Sides, it's not as if Dot actually *did* anythin' ...'

'But what about next time she loses her temper?' demanded Rose, anxiety resurfacing as exasperation.

'There won't be a next time. I've had a word with her, I told you.' Luke heaved his toolbag up under his arm. 'Anyhow, I'm off. Cec an' me've got the Chairoplanes to check over.'

'Shall I come over and give you a hand later?' asked Doreen.

'Please yourself,' shrugged Luke, and trudged off towards the rides.

'I'm sorry, Doreen, he's a bit miserable today. To be honest we both are. If it's not one thing it's another ...'

Doreen buckled the strap on her helmet and hung it over the handlebars of her bike. She sighed. 'If I could help more I would ...'

'I know you would,' said Rose, sitting down heavily on the front steps of the wagon. 'But you've got your dad's garage to think about; this isn't your problem.'

'Oh yes it is. And I don't mean 'cause my

dad's got a stake in your rides. We're friends, aren't we?'

Rose almost laughed at Doreen's combative stance, hands on hips, chin out. 'Yeah. At least, I hope so.'

'Well then. What I can, I'll do. I'll start now if you want.'

'Now?'

'Dad says he can spare me today, so just tell me what wants doing and I'll do it. I'm all yours!'

Doreen was good as her word. All day long she worked without complaint, running the TT Racer while the gaff-lads nursed along the ailing Chairoplanes, taking the money in the pay booth, even doing a stint in the bed when Dot went off on her break. Doreen isn't just a friend, thought Rose, she's a good friend. If I can't trust her, then who else can I trust?

When six o'clock came and the new men came on, Rose sent Ellie off to the shop for some milk and invited Doreen into the van.

'It's going well,' said Doreen, plonking herself on one of the benches and lying back against the wooden panelling. 'I'm bushed. Bet you've taken plenty today.'

That struck an unpleasant chord for Rose. 'I wondered if ...' She fiddled with the stove, taking an age to set the kettle on the boil.

'If what?'

'Nothin'.' Rose cut some bread and spread it thinly with jam. 'Sorry there's no marge.'

'Jam's fine. What's up, Rose?'

'Oh, you know ...' She sat down next to Doreen. 'Things. I had a letter from my mam today, you know?'

'That's nice.'

Rose gave a hollow laugh. 'Not really.'

'But I thought you and your mother got on well.'

'We do ... We *did.* Till all that business about ...' She stopped short, not wanting to think about Charlie but unable to stop herself. Why had Mam not told her he was coming? Lies she could expect from her dad, but not Mam. Why hadn't Edie told Charlie straight off, and saved Rose all that pain? Pain over a man who'd turned out to be worthless, a betrayal of her memories.

'About what, Rose?'

'We had a bit of a misunderstandin', see. About someone I used to know. Turns out Dad told lies an' Mam covered up for him. He's never been worth much, my Dad. Bit of a skiver really. Works on the docks when he can be bothered to work. Used to nick stuff off the boats in the war, you know ...'

'Oh,' said Doreen. Rose could see she was shocked.

'It's all right, I'm not proud of him. You can say what you like about Stan Dobbs, I won't defend him. But Mam ... All these years she's been workin' her fingers to the bone just to keep a roof over their heads. She knows how bone-idle an' useless he is.' Rose waved Edie's letter at Doreen. 'An' still she writes to me tellin' me it's not his fault, an' that he's a good man really.'

'I suppose it's loyalty,' said Doreen, getting up. 'You stay there, I'll make the tea. You know, she knows the truth about him but she can't admit it to anyone else.'

'I s'pose. An' she keeps sendin' me money. I tell her not to, but she won't listen!' Rose looked at the two ten-shilling notes sticking out of the envelope.

Doreen poured hot water into the teapot and popped on the cosy. 'Maybe she knows things haven't been easy. She wants to help.'

'But she can't afford it!'

Doreen sat down again. 'I don't know her, Rose, but she sounds nice. Like a proper mum. Mine died years ago, you know. That's why I'm the way I am. Dad didn't know how to bring up girls, so he brought me up like a boy!'

Rose felt sorry now for complaining. She'd forgotten, in her preoccupation with her own troubles, that Doreen didn't have a mother. 'Oh, Doreen, I didn't think. I'm sorry.'

'Don't be. It sounds like your dad's ... well, not the best dad in the world.'

'He isn't. I do love him, I suppose, but he's so ... unreliable. I think that's why I fell for Luke, I knew he'd never let me down.'

'No,' said Doreen softly. 'Not like Dan.'

They sat in thoughtful silence for a few minutes, then Rose made up her mind. She had to confide in someone, and that someone should be Doreen.

'You know I said about wantin' your advice?'

'Mmm?'

'It's about the takin's.'

'But I thought ... since you got rid of Sean ...'

'Money's started goin' missin' again. Just a bit to start off with, then a bit more.'

'And what does Luke say?'

'He won't listen. Keeps tellin' me I've made a mistake, an' it can't be missin' 'cause it was Sean what had his hand in the till. An' now ... I've been countin' up yesterday's takin's. We're nearly three pound down.'

Doreen whistled. 'That much? You're sure?'

'I thought Luke was right an' I'd made a mistake, so I counted it again.'

'And you got the same amount?'

Rose nodded. She got up and took the bag of money from old Walleye's secret cupboard behind the dresser, and emptied it out on the table. 'I wondered ... would you help me count it again? I thought if you was to tell Luke as well, this time he might believe me.'

Horace Spence was not pleased. Then again, Horace was seldom the sunniest of individuals. But today he was barely keeping the lid on his temper.

He slapped the *Isle of Man Examiner* down on the desk, pudgy forefinger jabbing at the headline.

'See what it says? "Breach of peace at Funland." Bloody shambles at Funland, more like.' His red-rimmed eyes contracted to malevolent pinpricks in the pink dough of

178

his face as he glared at Luke and Rose. 'An' you know what else? Folk'll be sayin' it's all down to me, that Horace Spence can't even control his own tenants.'

Without so much as touching him, Rose could feel the explosive charge of anger building up inside Luke. The set of his jaw, the whiplash tautness of his spine, the shallowness of his breathing ... Any moment now he might blurt out something they'd all regret.

'We're very sorry, Mr Spence,' she said for the umpteenth time. 'Really we are.'

Spence's gaze mellowed very slightly as it lighted on Rose, then turned to granite again. 'Sorry? Sorry's not good enough. You realise that bible-bashin' lunatic could've pressed charges?'

'But he didn't, did he?' muttered Luke between clenched teeth.

This seemed only to antagonise Spence. 'That's not the point! Do you know how hot the Onchan Commissioners are on this kind of thing? First the safety scare, now this all over the papers. D'you *want* 'em to close us down?' He let out an explosive blast of stale breath. 'God, Barton, I thought your brother was a feckless waster, but you ...!'

'You'd better mind your mouth, Spence,' growled Luke.

Spence glared back at him from the other side of his desk. 'An' you'd better see sense, boy, 'cause you'll not get another chance.'

'Meanin'?'

'Meanin', you Bartons are nowt but trouble-makers, an' I want rid of you.'

179

Luke's lip curled into a sneer. 'Too bad we've got a permanent lease then, ain't it? You can want all you like, we're not goin'.'

'Like I said, Barton,' Spence went on, apparently unmoved. 'I want rid of you, and 'cause of that I'm willin' to make you a generous offer.'

'We're not interested,' snapped Luke.

'What kind of offer?' asked Rose. All this time the two men had almost forgotten she was there; now suddenly they were both looking at her.

'I've told him, Rose, we're not interested,' said Luke.

'What kind of offer?' Rose repeated, folding her arms and confronting Spence with a confidence she did not feel.

Spence smiled. 'See, Barton? Your wife's got her head screwed on right, even if you 'aven't.' He scribbled some figures on a scrap of paper and shoved it across the desk. '*That* kind of offer.'

Rose stared at the figures on the paper. At first they didn't seem to make any sense, there were so many of them, interspersed with dots and dashes and commas.

'*How* much?' Rose blinked. Surely it must be a mistake ...

'Enough to pay off all your debts an' a bit more besides.' Horace slid open the top drawer of his desk and took out a sheet of paper. He took the top off his gold-nibbed fountain pen and offered it to Luke. 'I've 'ad an agreement drawn up, all legal an' proper. All you 'ave to do is sign 'ere an' clear off within seven days.'

Luke seized the paper from Rose's hands, screwed it up and threw it on the floor. 'Like I said, Spence, we're not interested.'

'Luke ...' protested Rose. 'Don't you think we ought to—'

'Ought to what, Rose? Give in to him? Give up an' go home? My God, Rose, you're quick to take his side—'

'No, Luke, it's not that, only—'

'Only nothin'. The answer's no. An' you're forgettin' somethin', Spence. The rides belong to Dan, me an' Rose are just takin' care of 'em for him till he comes home.'

'Come off it, Barton, your brother's no interest in the business, he never had an' he never will. Listen to your wife. Sell up, pay him off, an' get out.'

Luke wrenched open the door. 'We're not the Millers or the Wilcocks, Spence, you can't just stamp on us an' expect us to play dead.' He jabbed a finger at the open door. 'Rose, out.'

'Just listen,' she pleaded. 'What's the harm in listenin'?'

'You're making a big mistake,' commented Spence, shoe-horning his bulk between the mirror-smooth leather arms of his chair. 'She knows, don't you, Rose? A very big mistake.'

'No, Spence, it's you who's makin' the mistake. Come on, Rose, we're goin'.'

He strode out of the door, punching it as he went so that it juddered on its hinges. Rose hung back just for one second, torn between love and loyalty for her husband, and the dreadful fear that this time he was wrong.

'Told you,' said Spence, clipping the end off a new cigar. 'That boy's a loser. Ditch 'im while you still can.'

Rose didn't even bother closing the door behind her. She turned and went after Luke, running to catch up with him as he strode along, head down, hands thrust in his trouser pockets.

'Listen to me, Luke,' she begged. At her touch on his arm he stopped but didn't look at her.

'Listen to you? An' have you tell me I should sell up to Horace Spence?'

'No, Luke ... I just think you ought to listen to what he has to say.'

'God, Rose, you've changed your tune.' Luke's one dark eye fixed her accusingly. 'After all that talk about us pullin' together an' seein' it through—an' now you want to give up and sell out!'

'I never said that,' said Rose wearily. 'Please, Luke, can't we just sit down an' talk about this?' She sat herself down on the grass, her back to the perimeter fence, and reached out her hand to Luke. 'Come on, sit down, just for a minute.'

'Can't see the point,' he grunted, but relented and sat down beside her, stretching out his long legs. In the distance, hundreds of happy holidaymakers were enjoying a carefree afternoon at the fairground, never dreaming for a moment that the people who ran the rides might have cares of their own. 'But go on—I'm listenin'.'

Rose took a deep breath. 'Nobody hates

Horace Spence more than I do. An' I want us to keep on fightin' him, really I do. It's just ...'

'Just what?'

'We might need to take his offer.'

'Never!'

'We mightn't have a choice. It's the takin's, see. I didn't want to bother you till I was sure, but I am now. Money's started disappearin' again, Luke, an' this time it's worse than before. A lot worse.'

The shop was long closed by the time Charlie got back that night, but the lights were on and John Gorry was busy inside, pricing up the stock.

'Sorry I'm so late, John. Had to walk back from Union Mills.' Charlie glanced up at the ceiling. 'She's not been runnin' rings round you again, has she?'

The shopkeeper put down a box of hammers and stretched his aching back. 'Quiet as a mouse all day. No trouble at all.'

This came as a welcome surprise to Charlie. He'd had a back-breaking day and had dreaded coming home to another tale of temper tantrums and broken china.

'Upstairs then, is she?'

'Tucked her in myself, 'bout an hour ago.'

Charlie didn't want to disturb Lola if she was asleep, but he'd got into the habit of looking in on her when he got home, just to check she was all right. He didn't like to admit to himself that it was probably more to assuage his own conscience than anything else; he felt guilty about leaving her so much on her own. He tiptoed up the back stairs to the bedroom. She couldn't hear him, of course, but he'd read somewhere that deaf people could sense vibrations and he didn't want to frighten her. Very softly he turned the door handle and peeped inside.

And then his heart missed a beat.

'Lola?'

The room was empty, the bedclothes barely disturbed, Lola's nightdress draped over the back of the chair where her clothes and shoes ought to be. Panic gripped him. She was gone, leaving not a sign.

Nothing but a half-open window, letting in a breeze that nudged around a litter of old paper bags covered with Lola's childish scribbles. He picked one up and then another. They were all the same, covered with crude drawings of roundabouts and roller-coasters and clown faces.

So that was where Lola had gone.

CHAPTER 14

'Watch where you're goin', mate!'

'Sorry ... sorry, can I just get past?'

Frantic with worry, Charlie shouldered his way through the swarming crowd at Funland. This was the very last place in the world he would have chosen to come back to, the place he had sworn to keep away from—but what choice did he have? He was certain that Lola was here somewhere, if only he could find her.

He'd been to the fairground only once before, and that had been in broad daylight. Now it looked completely different, a weird, unearthly world of flashing coloured lights, continual noise and ever-moving crowds. Sometimes he thought he recognised something—a face, or the name of a ride—but most of the time he felt lost and intimidated. The place reminded him too much of the noise and chaos of war. He shuddered at the thought of Lola in the middle of this Saturday-night mêlée, lost, alone, not even able to speak to anyone to ask them for help. Whatever had possessed her to want to come here?

He had to find her.

Was that her? That dark-haired child by the baked potato stand? His heart lurched with disappointment as she turned round and walked away, hand in hand with her mother. Nothing like her, nothing like her at all. But in his panic every child looked like Lola.

Humanity seethed around him like the high tide round Conister Rock. Voices and music roared and babbled in his ears.

'Sixpence a go, only sixpence a go ...'

'Roll up, see the House of Wonders!'

' 'Ow about you, miss, guess yer weight?'

'Go two rounds with the Champ! Come on, gents, try yer luck ...'

Charlie peered into the middle distance,

praying for a sight of Lola. If he just kept calm he would be sure to find her, that's what he told himself. But with every moment he remained on the fairfield he felt more anxious for Lola—and for himself. For another thought kept entering his mind.

What was he going to say if he saw Rose?

Ellie Barton loved it when her mam and dad let her stay up late. It was nearly half-past nine and she still wasn't in bed, and that made her feel grown-up and important.

'Can I help, Dad?'

Luke waved her away. 'No need, Cec an' me can manage. Ask your mam, eh?'

But Rose didn't have many punters on the coconut shy tonight, and she told Ellie to be a good girl and go off and play for a bit.

'But mind you don't get under people's feet ...'

'No, Mam.'

'An' don't go too far!'

'I won't.'

Ellie nibbled at the apple Sid Christian had given her and wandered a little further from the Barton rides, in search of somebody else to help. Sometimes Micky on the Ghost Train give her the money bag to hold, or Mona on the Wheel 'Em In would let her dole out the prizes. She liked helping.

She liked watching the people, too. Some of them had nice new clothes that they'd bought for their holidays, and sometimes Ellie wished she could have nice clothes too; but she knew it wasn't Mam and Dad's fault they didn't have much money. When she was older and left school, she'd buy a ride of her own and make loads of money, so she could buy Mam a new frock.

One figure among the crowds caught Ellie's eye. It was a little girl, about her own age but sort of foreign-looking, standing all on her own, watching the Waltzers whirl round and round. She really stood out from the other holidaymakers—not just because of her dark hair and olive complexion, nor the drab clothes that were even more threadbare than Ellie's, but there was something else about her, something that Ellie found irresistibly fascinating. She had to find out more about this odd-looking little girl.

'What's your name then?'

The girl didn't turn round, so Ellie touched her arm. She sprang away like a startled faun, her dark eyes round with fear, and shrank back against the side wall of the ride.

Puzzled, Ellie tried again. 'My name's Ellie. What's yours?' The girl didn't reply, but the expression in those strange, fathomless eyes began to turn from animosity and fear to curiosity. 'What's up? Why won't you talk to me?'

Again, the child did not reply, but her eyes roamed Ellie's face, as though discovering something there that she could recognise and understand. And then, quite unexpectedly, she smiled.

'Aah. Aa-aah.'

'I don't understand ... Are you foreign or somethin'?'

Quite suddenly it dawned on Ellie that the little girl couldn't tell her anything, that she couldn't speak at all, simply because she couldn't hear. This strange, lost, frightened little girl was deaf. That realisation threw Ellie for a moment. She'd never met anyone deaf before, if you didn't count Great-Grandpa Dobbs, and he was ever so old. But Ellie was a resourceful child and it was obvious the little girl was lost, so she knew she had to do something.

She held out the apple.

'Want a bite?'

That much, at least, the little girl understood. A brown hand snatched at the half-eaten apple and crammed some of it into her mouth.

Ellie stuck out her hand and, to her relief, the strange little girl took it. 'Come on, let's go an' find Mam. She'll know what to do with you.'

Charlie was at his wits' end. He'd tried to be systematic, but how could one man on his own find a child in a place like this—a child who probably didn't even want to be found?

He hesitated outside the entrance to the Wild Australia Show, watching the crowds ebb and flow. What next? It was no use letting his pride get in the way. Without help he might never find her.

A massively built man in a checked shirt and buckskin trousers walked past him, barking out orders. He handed an over-sized metal helmet to one of the lads.

'Polish this up and feed the ponies, Albert.'

'Yes, Mister Verney.'

'And make it snappy, it's only half an hour till the next show. Tom?'

'Yes, boss?'

'That lassooing trick falls flat every time, I want it moved back to the first half and we'll finish with Ned Kelly and the boxing kangaroo. That way we'll get more tips off the punters on their way out. Got that?'

He turned to go back inside the show but Charlie stepped ahead of him.

' 'Scuse me, mate.'

The man turned slowly to look at him. 'Pay box is over there, sir, just behind the sign.'

'I don't want to see the show, I need your help.'

Jack Verney scratched his chin. 'What kind of help?'

'To find my little girl. She's deaf, see, an' she's run away. I know she's here somewhere.'

Verney frowned. 'Deaf, you say?'

'If you could help somehow, get people to look out for her ... Her name's Lola an' she's eight years old.' He stuck out his hand, the palm greasy with sweat. 'I'm Charlie, Charlie Cartwright.'

Verney accepted the handshake with a nod. 'Jack Verney. Well, Charlie, I'll do what I can. Jock, Tom? Run round the rides and tell them there's a little girl gone missing. We'll get some kind of search going. Paddy? Fetch Sid Christian and Percy Sayle—oh, and the Bartons, they'll lend a hand.'

The Bartons? Charlie was so disorientated that he hadn't realised he was so close to the Barton rides. But there they were, just across to the right; he could make out the rounding boards of the Chairoplanes and something called 'Barton's Famous TT Racer'.

For two pins he would have told Paddy not to bother, it was all right, he'd manage on his own. But now was not the time to be wondering what Rose might say if she found him here. It was his negligence that had driven Lola to run away, and it was his job to make sure she was safe. That was all that mattered.

'We'll find her,' said Jack Verney. 'Don't you worry.'

'Thanks. It's good of you ...'

Verney clapped Charlie on the back. 'I know kids, always getting into mischief. You turn your back for two seconds and they're gone.'

A man in a flat cap and boiler suit came loping over the tober.

'What's all this 'bout a little girl, Misther Verney?'

'Ah, Percy—try looking by the roller-coaster will you? There's a little deaf girl gone missing.'

'Lola,' cut in Charlie. 'Her name's Lola. About eight years old, dark hair ...'

'Right y'are, Misther, she'll not have gone far ...'

Percy Sayle's voice seemed to fade suddenly into silence in Charlie's head, squeezed out by a single word.

Rose.

He caught his breath as he saw her. She

190

was walking quickly towards him, one step in front of her husband, that tall, lean gypsy bloke with the eyepatch. Wisps of red-brown hair had escaped from their pins to frame the pale, tired oval of her face, and the pinafore she wore over her dress had seen better days. Yet there was a kind of dignity in the way she held herself, a defiant energy he had never encountered in anyone else. He couldn't help but admire her, even if she did loathe his guts.

Did she hesitate briefly as she looked up and saw him? Did a look of horror cross her face? If so it was hardly perceptible; and a split second later he was face to face with her again.

Rose felt the blood freeze in her veins as she looked up and saw the man standing next to Jack Verney. It was Charlie. Every impulse in her body screamed to her to turn and walk away, but how could she, without having to rake up the past and tell Luke everything?

'Isn't that that friend of yours who came to see you?' commented Luke. 'What was his name? Charlie?'

'Charlie Cartwright,' said Rose quietly.

'That's the one. I thought he was off the Island now.'

So did I, thought Rose bitterly. So did I, Charlie Cartwright. So what are you doing here? Why have you come back to torment me?

'What's all this then, Jack?' demanded Luke when they got to the Wild Australia Show.

'Feller here's lost his little girl,' explained Verney. 'Poor kid's deaf.'

'That so?'

'I thought you'd not mind helping him look for her.'

'Course not, Charlie.' Luke offered his hand. Rose saw how Charlie hesitated, just for an instant, then took it with a forced smile.

'Thanks, Luke. I'm much obliged.' His eyes met Rose's for the briefest of fleeting moments, then darted away. 'An' ... an' to you, Rose.'

'You've nothin' to thank me for.'

Could everyone hear the bitterness in her voice, or had they really not noticed the dreadful awkwardness between her and Charlie? At this moment Rose really believed she hated him, lost child or no lost child. He'd sworn to keep out of her life and here he was, back again like a bad penny. Couldn't he even keep one promise?

'Right,' said Jack Verney. 'Best get started. I've sent Percy Sayle to do the eastern side of the site. Luke, if you could take ...'

Rose tried to listen but she was watching Charlie. Typical Charlie, getting everyone on his side, stirring them all up, making them like him the way he'd made her fall in love with him all those years ago when she was no more than a kid. Good old honest, reliable, lovable Charlie. How could such an honest face hide such a deceitful heart?

'Lola!' Charlie cried out suddenly. 'It's all right, Mr Verney, it's her!'

Two small figures were rounding the corner of the Wiggley-Waggley, hand in hand. The smaller girl, dark-haired and skinny, was gnawing on the remains of an apple, the taller one leading her like a recalcitrant puppy.

'Mam! Mam, I found this little girl. I think she's lost.'

Charlie dropped to his knees and held out his arms; and Rose felt a knife enter her heart as the child broke away and ran to him, burying her head in his shoulder. Charlie, she thought. Charlie Cartwright, the perfect father.

'Oh, Lola, you gave me a right old scare you did ... Thanks for findin' her, kid.' He looked up at Ellie and the knife stabbed home a second time as Rose saw the look that passed between them. A look of instant recognition, the look she had feared ever since Charlie had come back to seek her out. Father and daughter, so very alike with their blonde hair and golden eyes.

'Who ...?'

Jack Verney laid his hand on Ellie's shoulder and gave an avuncular smile. 'This is Ellie Barton, Charlie. Rose and Luke's daughter.'

In the noise and bustle of the fairground at night, it was easy to move around without being noticed.

He took a quick glance about him, then slipped inside. As he'd expected, the tent was deserted and the evening's takings were just sitting there in the old tobacco jar behind the curtain. There for the taking.

Quickly he turned the jar upside down and started counting out sixpences and shillings. Not a large sum, but enough to cover his needs, and not so much that it would be missed.

He scooped the rest of the money back into

the jar and was just sliding it back behind the blue velvet curtain when he heard a noise behind him and spun round.

It was Old Peg.

'You!' she hissed. And she drew down the curtain and stepped inside.

CHAPTER 15

'There's your thief!' snarled Old Peg, slapping Mario's face so hard that he stumbled against the side of the wagon. 'I knew it was 'im all along, dirty little Itie.'

It was almost more than Rose could bear in one night. First Charlie, turning up out of the blue and going off again without a word of explanation; and now the news that Mario had been caught stealing from Old Peg's tent.

'Is no true, is no true,' whimpered Mario, cringing in anticipation of another slap from Peg.

'Course it's true!' spat Peg. 'Caught you red-handed I did, you two-faced thievin' little—'

'Please, please no hit me! Signora Rosa, is no true that I thief!'

He cut a pretty pathetic figure, thought Rose, cowering like a beaten child, his hands over his head. But a thief was a thief, and if it really was true ...

'Peg caught you with your hand in the takin's,' growled Luke. 'How can you say

194

you're not a thief? An' after me givin' you a job like you was an honest mush? You no-good mongrel.'

'That's what you get when you go trustin' flatties,' opined Peg. 'Go on, hand 'im over to the gavvers, let them deal with 'im. What 'e wants is a proper weltin'.'

Rose was more than surprised to hear Old Peg talking about handing Mario over to the police. She'd been married to a Romany long enough to know that gypsies and coppers didn't mix; and in her time Peg had had enough run-ins with the law to steer well clear of any bloke in uniform. There was something not quite right about Peg's sudden enthusiasm for the due processes of law.

Luke shook his head. 'The gavvers?'

'Go on, he's bin robbin' you blind for months. Get 'im arrested—it's no more'n he deserves.'

'No.' Luke's brow furrowed. 'There's other ways. We'll deal with this ourselves, our way. We don't need gavvers.'

He raised his fist and Mario shrank away, all his usual bravado completely gone.

'Please, no, Signor Luke. It is true, I take Peg's money, I very sorry ... but I no do this other thing.'

'Sorry? You'll be sorrier before Luke Barton's done wi' you,' snarled Peg with relish.

Luke lunged at Mario, but Rose stepped in front of him.

'Don't.'

He looked at her in astonishment.

'Please, Luke, don't hit him. It's not right.'

195

'Oh? An' it's right for him to rob us, is it? All these months?'

'Course not. But hear him out, let him say his piece.'

Maybe she was being too soft on Mario; by his own admission he was a thief. But there was something going on here that didn't quite square. Why was Peg dead set on calling the police? Why wouldn't she let Mario get a word in edgeways?

'Why did you do it, Mario? Why?'

Mario flicked the tip of his tongue over his dry lips.

'I ... I take from Peg because I ... I have nothing. No money for food, nothing.'

'Nothin'?' Luke snorted in disbelief. 'I pay you a wage.'

'Yes, Signor Luke. And I very grateful, very sorry. But it is hard for me ... The people in my house, they no like me because I am Italian. They say I *fascisto.*'

'I don't see what this has to do with anythin',' retorted Luke.

'Two days ago, they break into my room, they steal all my money, my watch, everything. That night Signor Kelly, my landlord, he tell me I am big trouble and I must leave, but where I go? I have no friends, no money ...'

Rose looked closely at Mario. His hair was greasy and lank, his normally spotless shirt collar ringed with dirt.

'You stole from Peg because your landlord threw you out?'

Mario nodded vigorously. 'Si, Signora Rosa.'

196

'Then where are you livin'?'

'When everybody go home I sleep under tilt on Chairoplanes, Signora Rosa. Tonight I very hungry, I take from Peg ... I steal a few shillings only, to buy food. I pay back when Signor Luke he pay me on Friday. This is first time in my whole life I ever steal, I swear it!'

'An' if you believe that you'll believe anythin',' commented Old Peg sourly.

'If this is true, why didn't you say somethin'?' demanded Luke.

Mario's head sank to his chest. 'I tell everyone I happy, I doing well, saving plenty money for my sister in Napoli ... I very ashamed.'

Luke let out a hiss of exasperation, his fist falling to his side. 'Thievin' bastard. I should break your bleedin' neck for you.'

'Don't listen to 'im,' said Peg. 'He's lyin', spinnin' you a yarn. They're all like that.'

But Rose wasn't convinced. In fact, the more she looked at Mario's downcast face, the more certain she was that they still hadn't found their thief.

The following afternoon, with the fairground in full swing, Luke and Rose did the rounds of the rides.

'God knows why I agreed to keep him on,' muttered Luke as they passed a row of knock-'em-downs. 'I must want my head examinin'.'

'All we're doin' is givin' him a second chance,' Rose pointed out. 'I mean, if what Mario says is true—'

'Yeah. An' what if he's just a good liar?'

'Then he'll start thievin' again, won't he? But I don't reckon he will.' She squeezed Luke's hand, willing him to share her feelings about Mario. 'It's not him, Luke, he's not our thief.'

'I wish I could be so sure.'

'I can't be *sure,* but ...' Rose struggled to find the right words to explain how she felt. 'Look, if he'd been nickin' all that money off us all these months, he'd be rollin' in it by now, wouldn't he? Not wanderin' round in boots with the soles hangin' off.'

Luke shrugged. 'He might be stashin' the dosh somewhere.'

'He might. But you know how vain Mario is; if he could afford it he'd be walkin' round dressed like Rudolf flippin' Valentino. Besides, you know what the other blokes are always sayin' about him.'

'What?'

'You know, the light's on but there's nobody in. He's no master criminal, Luke, he can hardly tie his own bootlaces. How'd he figure out how to cream off all that money? No, Luke, the more I think about it the more I reckon he's tellin' the truth.'

'Then who the hell's doin' this to us, Rose? It can't be Sean, surely?'

'I dunno, I'm not sure. Can't see how ...' Something stirred at the back of her brain as they passed Peg's tented booth, then it slipped away again. If she could just think what it was ... 'We'll work it out somehow.'

They reached the Knock the Lady out of Bed

stall to find the canvas curtain drawn down and a 'Closed' sign pinned to it. They pushed through half a dozen disgruntled punters to find Terry looking flustered and Gracie clutching Dot's powder-blue nightdress.

'What the 'ell's goin' on?' demanded Luke. 'Where's Dot?'

Terry looked like he wished the ground would swallow him up. 'She went off for her break an hour ago an' she's not back yet. I had to send your Ellie to go and fetch Gracie. We were going to open up again in a minute.'

Gracie shuffled from one foot to the other. Rose sensed that there was more to this than met the eye.

'Where's Dot gone, Gracie?'

Gracie tried to avoid meeting her gaze. 'Don't know.'

'Are you sure you don't know?'

A blush of discomfort spread out under the pancake make-up. 'Don't know.'

'Come on, Gracie.' Rose took her by the shoulders. 'Come on, spit it out.'

'I can't. You'll be angry.'

Rose counted silently to ten and tried to keep her patience. 'I won't be angry with *you*.' Dot, on the other hand, was a different matter.

Gracie half-opened her mouth and for a second Rose thought she was going to spill the beans, but before she could get one syllable out a commotion of shouting and wolf-whistles erupted outside the booth. Men's voices, coarse and ribald, rang out over gusts of laughter.

'Well, will you take a look at that!'

'Cor, what an eyeful!'

Then a girl's voice, shrill and furious as a fishwife's: 'Get off me! Get *off* me, you bastard, let me *go!*'

Pushing back the canvas, Rose and Luke hurried outside. Jack Verney was striding towards them, his face set in an expression of cold fury. His massive bulk dwarfed the girl who trailed on the end of his arm, her feet lashing out, one hand scratching and flailing as she struggled to pull free, the other trying to pull the two unbuttoned halves of her blouse together.

Rose felt a horrible sense of inevitability settle on her shoulders like a black cloud. Who else could it be but Dot?

No wonder the men were whistling and cat-calling. Dot was hardly what you'd call decent. Her blouse was half off, her lipstick was smudged and she wasn't wearing a skirt at all, just her underslip. One stocking hung at half-mast, crinkling as it dangled sluttishly from a single suspender. 'Let go!' she squealed, aiming a vicious kick at Jack Verney's knee. 'You've got no right, I'll have the coppers on you!'

Verney, unmoved, swung Dot round in front of him. 'Barton,' he growled, 'this is yours, I believe.'

'What the hell's goin' on?' demanded Luke, his face drained white beneath the deep tan.

'Caught her in my living-wagon,' said Verney. 'With some lad.'

A ripple of interest ran round the crowd. Finally wriggling free of Jack Verney's bear's-paw grasp, Dot rounded on him. 'How dare you? How *dare* you do this to me!' She spun round and confronted Rose, blazing mad and spoiling for a fight in spite of her humiliation. 'Tell him, Mrs B.'

Rose regarded her with amazement. The girl was utterly shameless, playing to the gallery. 'Shut up an' get in there, Dot Matthews.' She held open the canvas curtain and shoved Dot inside. Her eyes swept the jostling throng of sightseers. 'Show's over. You might as well go, you'll see nothin' else.'

Behind the canvas Dot turned on Gracie. 'You said you'd cover for me!'

Gracie's big grey eyes moistened with indignant tears. 'That's not fair! I thought you'd be back in half an hour!'

'Yeah, and I thought you were my *friend.*'

Rose, near the end of her tether, raised her voice above the childish bickering. 'Shut up, both of you! Gracie, Terry—go an' help on the coconut shy till Luke sends for you.'

Gracie trailed reluctantly out of the booth, casting Dot a backward glance which was met with a stony glare. Luke waited till the canvas had twitched back into place before he spoke.

'Right, Jack, what's this all about?'

Verney treated Dot to a long, slow, murderous stare before he spoke. 'Went back to my living-wagon to fetch a knife. Caught the little tart doing what comes naturally with some spotty lad she'd picked up on the tober. On *my* bed.'

Dot had the grace to pale slightly, but said nothing.

'Well?' said Luke.

Dot's elfin chin jutted defiance. By God she's a cool one, thought Rose.

'Well what?'

'What've you got to say for yourself?' demanded Rose. In spite of her suspicions she was prepared to give the girl one last chance to explain.

'You'd better speak up now,' said Luke coldly. ' 'Cause the way things look ...'

'You can take it from me,' said Jack Verney. 'The two of 'em weren't shelling peas. And you can bet it's not the first time they've done it, neither. If you ask me she's been taking money for it.'

'Is that true?' Rose fixed Dot with a look that could freeze a volcano. It was all she could do to keep herself from slapping the little vixen's face. 'Is it?'

'Oh, what's the point?' snapped Dot. 'So what if we were in his stupid van? Who cares?'

'I think you'd better take her somewhere and get her decent,' Jack commented drily, observing Dot tugging up her sagging stocking. 'Wouldn't want any more people seeing her like that, would you?'

As he spoke he threw a meaningful glance at Luke, and Rose sensed that there was something he wasn't saying.

'Luke ...?' she began, but Luke tossed her the coverlet from the bed.

'Here, take this. An' get that girl out of my sight, 'fore I forget meself an' give her a good hidin'. Go on.'

'You might as well, Rose,' urged Verney.

202

'There's a few things I want to talk to Luke about. You know, man to man.'

Rose hesitated. She wanted to stay and find out exactly what those 'few things' might be. It angered her when the menfolk excluded her from their conversations. Wasn't she supposed to be part of all this? Didn't she work just as hard as anyone? But she could tell from the look on Verney's face that she wasn't welcome.

She picked up the blanket and threw it round Dot's shoulders. 'Right, you. Back to the wagon an' no messin'.'

'Good woman you've got there,' commented Verney, watching the canvas flap drop down behind Rose's back.

'One of a kind,' said Luke. 'But that's not what you want to talk about, is it?'

Verney conceded with a nod. 'Now that Dot Matthews, she's big trouble. I could have told you that from the start. How old is she, d'you reckon?'

Luke frowned. 'Sixteen, seventeen? I dunno, why?'

'Rising fifteen's what I've heard.'

'Fifteen!' Luke's face registered incredulity and horror.

'You're right, Luke. Folk on the island ... well, they're decent people, the Manx, don't like any hint of shenanigans—and you know what some of 'em are like about this place. You'd reckon it's Satan's front parlour to hear 'em talk.'

'What are you gettin' at, Verney?'

203

Jack Verney sat down on the edge of the barrel filled with bean-bags. 'You Bartons have had a few troubles lately, haven't you? And if the local paper was to hear about Dot and what she's been getting up to ... well, it might not go down too well, and then there's Horace ...'

Luke's jaw tensed. 'Spence? I don't see why he'd get to hear about this, unless ... unless *you* made sure he found out.' His eyes narrowed. 'An' I never took you for that kind of lowlife, Jack Verney.'

Verney scraped the bowl of his pipe with his penknife. 'I'll not beat about the bush, Luke. I'll be straight with you; I'm not the one for dirty tricks and double-dealing. But business is business, and if that's what it takes to get what I want ...'

'Want? What've I got that you could want?'

Verney leaned forward. 'The TT Racer. I'll give you one and a half for it.'

'The TT Racer? But ... why?'

'It's like this. The Wild Australia Show's finished. It's old hat. I want something new for next season, and seeing as they're going to restart the TT races next year, I'm going for a TT Extravaganza. I want the TT Racer as part of it.'

'But why should I want to sell?' Luke's mind whirled. 'An' for one an' a half? Spence has offered me more than that!'

'Ah, but has he offered you a job an' all?' Verney lit his pipe and puffed reflectively. 'Look, it's no secret times are hard for you what with debts to pay off, the Chairoplanes are broken

204

more than they're running, the coconut shy's a washout, you've been losing money hand over fist—'

'Yeah, an' it's the TT Racer that's been makin' money for us. How'd we manage without that?'

'I'm gettin' to that. In this TT Extravaganza, I'm going to have a stunt riding show.'

'Bikes?'

'Bikes. Real spectacular stuff. The thing is, Luke, I've got a couple of riders lined up, and they're not bad, but they're not ... not crowd-pleasers, if you get my drift.' Verney's eyes met Luke's. 'Not like you.'

Luke felt electricity prickle up his spine. 'Me? Now just hold on—'

'I remember you the way you were, Luke. Working the old Globe of Death. There wasn't better on the Lancashire circuit. Aye, you used to be the best ...'

'I used to be a lot of things,' retorted Luke. 'An' one of 'em was stupid.'

'Think about it, that's all I'm askin'.'

'I've already thought. I'm not interested.'

Verney got to his feet. 'Then think about it some more. Take your time. But make no mistake, Luke, I'm havin' that TT Racer of yours.'

Alone in the booth, Luke closed his eyes and tried to control his breathing. His hands were trembling and he was getting the shakes, like an alcoholic remembering the taste of his last drink. He couldn't let himself feel this way. He'd put it all behind him long ago: the thrill, the desperate need for danger. He remembered how, even as he lay in hospital with the bandages wrapped tightly over the empty eye-socket, he'd wanted so badly to get back on that motor bike that he'd cried out loud in his sleep. He'd been so sure, so stone-cold certain that he'd put the love of danger far behind him.

But perhaps he hadn't after all. Perhaps he never could.

CHAPTER 16

Gracie Cubbon walked slowly down Douglas Promenade. It was a beautiful August day and the town was packed with happy smiling faces, from Derby Castle all the way down to the Pier Arcade. On the beach, small children squealed as patient donkeys were coaxed into a trot and they held on for dear life. A string of yellow Corporation buses crawled past Broadway, threading between gangs of laughing girls on their way to the bathing beauty contest at the Villa Marina. Everybody in the whole world was happy—or that was how it seemed.

But in the distance, just across the way from Greensill's Cafe, Gracie could make out a solitary figure, slumped on a bench and staring out to sea. *Their* bench, hers and Dot's; the one they always sat on to watch the lads go by. It wasn't difficult to tell that it was Dot sitting there, nobody else would have dared wear that sunburst-yellow frock, and that red hat with the feather that danced whenever she moved her head.

Very timorously, Gracie approached the bench. The figure did not move.

'Hello.'

Dot didn't answer. Gracie noticed she was clutching a damp hanky, screwed up in her right hand.

'I'll go away again if you want.'

This time Dot sniffed and dabbed the end of her nose with the handkerchief. Gracie couldn't help noticing how the make-up had worn off her nose with all the blowing, and how very pink her eyes looked, like a rabbit's.

'You can stop if you want, I don't care.'

'All right then. Just for a bit.' Gracie perched herself on the other end of the bench. 'You're angry with me, aren't you?' Without waiting for a reply she gabbled out, 'I'm sorry, I really am.'

'Sorry?'

' 'Bout you losin' your job an' that. But I never said anythin', not to Rose or Jack Verney or nobody.'

'I know you never.' Dot sat up, blew her nose again, hitched up her skirt and tucked the hanky into the top of her stocking. 'It's not your fault.'

Gracie felt a wave of relief wash over her. She edged a little nearer to Dot on the bench. 'I'll leave as well if you like. Tell 'em I don't want to work there any more if you're not.'

Dot shook her head. 'No need for that. 'Sides,

I'll get another job quick enough, you see if I don't.' She managed a half-smile. 'Tell you what, though, I gave that Rose Barton a few surprises before she kicked me out.'

'Surprises? What surprises?'

Dot tapped the side of her nose. 'Told her a few things she ought to know, didn't I? Honest to God, Gracie, them Bartons don't know what's happenin' under their flippin' noses.' She laughed. 'Wiped that look right off her smug face. Serves 'em flippin' well right if you ask me.'

Gracie didn't ask Dot to explain. All she cared about was that Dot wasn't angry with her. 'We still friends then or what?'

Dot looked at her, surprised. 'Course we are. Didn't want their rotten job anyway.'

They sat in companionable silence for a few minutes, watching the world go by.

'What do you reckon to him then?' Dot perked up suddenly and nudged Gracie in the ribs as a young lad in uniform swaggered past. 'Bit of all right or what? Look, he's givin' you the eye!'

'He's not!' giggled Gracie, flushing scarlet.

'He is! Hey, you're blushing, you fancy him!'

'I do not, Dot Matthews!'

'Yes you do. Hey, you! My friend fancies you!'

The two girls fell about laughing as the sailor winked and walked on by.

'What shall we do tonight then?' said Gracie.

'Let's go to the pictures. That new Jenny

Fisher film's on at the Strand.'

'Ooh, Jenny Fisher, I like her,' mused Gracie. 'Is it that new one with Tommy Handley?'

'That's the one.' Dot half-closed her eyes as if conjuring up some wonderful image. 'She used to be a shop-girl, you know. From St Helens. She's nothin' special. *I'm* goin' to be a big star like Jenny Fisher, what do you reckon?'

'Better than Jenny Fisher,' beamed Gracie. And arm in arm the two girls paraded down the prom to Strand Street like they owned the whole of Douglas.

'No!' screamed Sofia Barton, picking up a saucepan and flinging it at her husband's head. He dodged it with a scant inch to spare.

'Listen to reason, woman!' snapped Manfri. But Sofia Barton was incandescent with rage.

'No, I won't have it, I won't! Some *gorgio gajikano* buyin' up my Dan's rides—'

'Only one ride, Sofia,' pleaded Manfri. How come he, who was supposed to be the head of the household, was having to go cap in hand to his own shrewish wife? It wouldn't have been like this in the old days, their travelling days. Sofia had had some respect for him then. 'You'll drive us all to the grave ...'

'Those rides belonged to *my* family, not yours,' spat Sofia. 'You Bartons, you had nothing. They are not yours to sell, they were mine and now they are Dan's. My son's. *My* son's!'

209

A china plate slammed into the wall and smashed into fragments which flew in a dozen different directions. Another followed it, then a teacup and a saucer.

'Listen to me, Sofia, you're my *monisha* and what I say goes.'

'You?' Sofia's face twisted into a mask of utter contempt. 'You're nothing but a *dinilo!*'

'A *dinilo?* If there's anyone stupid round here it's you. If Luke can't come up with the money to pay back Spence and all the others, how d'you think he and Rose are going to survive? Tell me that?'

Sofia glared at him but at least she didn't shout or throw anything. The teapot in her hand stayed there, a missile poised for launch. Manfri took the opportunity to get a word in edgeways.

'If he can't pay Dan's debts, then Spence gets the rides for nothin'. Is that what you want, woman? Well? Is it?'

Sofia banged the teapot down on the draining-board. 'I tell you I won't have it! I won't have him give my Dan's rides to that man!'

'For God's sake, woman!'

But Manfri could see from the gleam in her eye that it was no use. Grabbing his jacket from the back of a chair he pushed past her and out of the house, slamming the yard door behind him.

Outside, in the alley, he offered up a silent prayer for patience. Luke was worth ten of Dan—no, a hundred. And all the time Dan had been constantly indulged and forgiven, they'd treated Luke worse than a dog. However boneheaded Sofia might be, Manfri vowed he'd find a way to help his younger son.

Whatever it took, he'd not let Luke down.

'Here y'are, Ellie love.'

Old Peg fished into the deep apron pocket and took out a shiny sixpence. Ellie could hardly believe her good fortune.

'All that? For me?'

Peg's crinkly old mouth arranged itself into a kindly smile. 'You're a good girl. Now you take it an' buy yourself an ice cream or somethin'.' She leaned closer and squeezed Ellie's hand with her bony, leathery fingers. 'It'll be our little secret though. No need to tell your mam an' dad.'

'Well ...' Ellie looked at the sixpence, so silvery and inviting in Old Peg's palm. She remembered what her Mam was always telling her about not taking money from strangers; but Granny Peg wasn't a stranger, was she?

'Go on, take it. Run along now.'

'Thank you, Granny Peg!' Ellie gave Old Peg a hug and pocketed the sixpence, silently deciding that she would spend just tuppence on herself, and slip the other four pennies into her mam's purse when she wasn't looking.

Peg watched the child race off across the tober, her two golden plaits bouncing behind her, and breathed a sigh of relief. Ellie was a bright child; it hadn't been easy to get rid of her. And the last thing Old Peg needed right now was a kid snooping around.

On her own at last, Peg climbed the steps to the Bartons' living-wagon. She knocked, just to be on the safe side, waited a couple of seconds, then slipped inside, fastening the door behind her. Going straight to the cupboard above the stove, she felt round behind it for the secret drawer—no great secret to her, she'd known the vardo when it was Walleye's and it held no surprises. The drawer clicked open and she withdrew it, her old eyes glittering with pleasure at the sight of the money inside. Now to take her regular cut.

Normally she preferred to take her share before the takings found their way back to the Bartons' van, but that idiot Mario had almost ruined everything. Luke and Rose had been far more careful since then, and Peg was having to be more resourceful than ever.

She picked out two ten-shilling notes and was about to slide back the drawer when she heard a voice behind her.

'So Dot was right.'

Peg turned slowly. Rose Barton was standing in the doorway, her arms folded, her face set hard. And Old Peg knew her goose was well and truly cooked.

Rose's stomach lurched with the sickness of betrayal, knowing the terrible hurt that would tear Luke apart when he knew the truth. All this money stolen from them, driving them to the edge of ruin, and all the time the thief was one of their own.

'Why?' she demanded, slamming the door of

the vardo and standing with her back against it, ensuring that there was no escape. Now that she had uncovered the unpalatable truth, she was determined that Old Peg was not going to get away without telling her everything. 'Why have you been doin' this to us?'

Peg shrugged unconcernedly.

' 'Cause it was owed me.'

'*Owed* you? We don't owe you nothin'.'

'No? Well Walleye did, an' by my reckonin' that means you owe me now, since you've taken on Dan's debts.' Old Peg laughed at the look of bafflement on Rose's face. 'He stitched you up good an' proper, didn't he, that Dan Barton? Never told you nothin' 'bout how he stole what was rightfully mine.'

Rose saw the mocking, loathing sneer on Old Peg's face and wondered how she could ever have been stupid enough not to see through her. 'He ... stole from you? But what?'

'This.' Peg indicated the vardo. 'This was goin' to be mine, Walleye promised it to me when he was gone.'

'The vardo!' Rose remembered all the times Peg had admired it, the times she'd hinted that it might have been her home 'if things had worked out different'.

'Course, in the old days they'd have burned it to keep away the bad spirits, but Walleye reckoned that'd be a criminal waste of a good vardo. Then he went, an' your Dan took it, didn't he? Had nowhere else to live once the cottage had gone an' he'd pissed away all the money. Took the vardo off me, told me if it wasn't written down he didn't have to give it me. That's when I reckoned, if I wasn't goin' to get my share that way, I'd have to get it some other way.'

'So you decided to steal—from your own family?'

Peg laughed. 'Family? You lot? A one-eyed loser an' a *gorgio* wife who can't even give him a son? You're no family of mine. Besides, you're finished here. Everyone knows that, I've made sure. I'm just takin' what I can before there's nothin' left to take.'

Rose stared at Peg, for a moment speechless with anger. 'You old bitch,' she gasped finally. 'You cheatin', lyin' old bitch.'

Peg just smiled. 'You want to watch your mouth, my girl. I might just walk out an' leave you flat.'

Rose could hardly believe her ears. 'You think I'd let you go on workin' this pitch after what you've done to us?'

'You can't get rid of me, girl. Dukkerin' pays; you can't close me down. You *need* me.'

'Need you?' It was Rose's turn to laugh. 'Oh no we bloody well don't.' She stepped aside and flung open the door of the wagon. 'Get out, Peg.'

'You'll be sorry if you do this.' The smile twisted to cold, vicious malevolence. 'There's a curse on you Bartons, nothin' good'll ever come of you. A curse, do you hear?'

Rose glowered back, resolved never to let Luke hear such superstitious rubbish.

214

'I said get out, an' don't bother comin' back.'

Luke couldn't get Jack Verney's offer out of his mind. Or was it an offer? That was what he kept asking himself: an offer or a threat?

As he walked through the back-streets of Douglas, heading for the Labour Exchange, he thought of Rose and how much he loved her. She was so happy when he gave up stunt-riding, so dead set against anything that might bring him into danger. He could understand that, knew that she was right. But Rose could never understand the feelings of guilty excitement that coursed through him whenever he let himself remember the electrifying thrill of terror as he'd rev up the bike for another show.

And that was why he couldn't tell her about it. He just couldn't.

There was a huddle of blokes smoking and chatting, hanging around the door to the Labour Exchange. Luke gave them a quick nod, acknowledging the hopeful looks on their faces. So many blokes without work. Well, maybe he could make one of them happy—for a few weeks at least. Without Sean, and now Dot as well, the Barton rides were desperately short-handed. Besides, the effort of finding the right bloke for the job took Luke's mind off other things. Like Jack Verney ...

The funny thing was that he never actually made it to the desk to tell the clerk about the job. Just as Luke stepped inside the gloomy hall he spotted a familiar figure standing dejectedly by the door. It was the tall, muscular frame and honey-blond hair that caught his eye—so different from the typical compact, dark Manx physique.

'Charlie? Charlie Cartwright?'

The man looked up. A shadow seemed to cross his face, then he smiled, a little crookedly.

'Luke.'

'You still lookin' for work then?'

Charlie shrugged. 'There's nothin' for me here; I've just about given up. Couple more days then me an' Lola'll be off back to Birkenhead, I reckon.'

There was something about Charlie that Luke liked. The bloke seemed honest, straight, and there was no doubt he had the physical stamina to work the rides. Besides, he was a friend of Rose's, and that was a good enough reference in Luke's book.

Luke wasn't by nature impulsive, but he made his mind up there and then. 'I might have a job for you, if you're interested.'

'You?' Astonishment registered on Charlie's face. 'What—at the fairground?'

'Only temporary, mind. Till the season's over, maybe a bit longer. An' I couldn't pay you much.'

'I ...' Charlie swallowed. Luke wondered what was going through his mind. Maybe he just couldn't believe his good luck.

'Think about it, eh? But don't take too long. There's plenty other blokes here'll have the job if you don't want it.'

CHAPTER 17

Rose sat in the wagon, trying to make sense of the books and wishing she'd paid more attention at school. It was so hard to concentrate on the figures as they swam in and out of focus. The late summer heat didn't help, and the wagon door stood open to let in a little light and air. The distant din from the fairground might once have distracted her, but over the months since the season had opened she had learned to blank it out. It was an ever-present, nagging anxiety that stopped her concentrating on her additions and subtractions. No matter how many times she totted up the numbers, she came up with the same answer: the Bartons didn't have enough money to pay off Horace Spence, let alone survive the winter.

But it was pointless sitting here and worrying. There were more immediate problems that had to be sorted out. Despite Rose's show of angry bravado she knew that Old Peg had been right: they *did* need the money that came in from the dukkering tent—and if Peg wasn't going to be there to tell fortunes for sixpences, then somebody else would have to do it instead. Peg, Sean, Dot ... Sometimes it felt as if, one by one, everyone was going to turn out bad; until finally she and Luke would be left with no one but each other. But, God willing, Luke would come back from the Labour Exchange with good news—there must be hundreds of men, down on their luck, who'd be glad of a few weeks' work, however hard and however badly paid.

She heard Luke's voice, shouting across the tober. 'Tell him he'll have it Friday. Gave him my word didn't I?'

Then Percy Sayle's long, lugubrious drawl. 'Friday? Yessir. I'll tell him that then, Misther Luke.'

It wasn't hard to work out what that conversation was about. Money. Rose put down her pencil and rested her hot, clammy forehead on her folded hands. Why did everything have to be about money?

'You all right, love?'

Luke's voice broke into her thoughts. She mustn't let him see how tired and worried she was. Fixing on a smile, she turned to face him.

'Just dozin'. Must be the heat.'

'Wears you down, don't it?' agreed Luke, flopping down on a bench and tossing his cap on to the table. 'Brings in the punters, though. Where's Ellie?'

'Off with that Billy Darwell. God knows what they're up to.'

'I wouldn't worry 'bout Ellie. She's got an old head on her shoulders, that kid. You know that sixpence I let her keep from Old Peg?'

'What about it?'

'Only caught her puttin' it in the takin's, didn't I? Said she wanted to help, bless her.'

It's not right, thought Rose. She ought to

218

be out spending her money on comics and ice cream, not giving it back to her mam and dad because they were too poor to manage without it.

'How'd you get on down the Labour? Did you take someone on?'

Luke scratched his head. 'I'm not sure,' he said. He leaned forward, hands on his knees. 'But you'll never guess what happened. I met that old friend of yours—you know, Charlie Cartwright.'

A lightning bolt seared through Rose. Her mind whirled. What had happened? What had Charlie said to Luke—and what had Luke guessed? And then came the next thought, more dreadful still.

'You didn't ...?'

'Offer him the job? Course I did, knowin' he were a friend of yours. An' seein' he was on his uppers—God but he's in a state, hardly a penny to his name, an' that deaf kid's a real handful—'

'Ch-Charlie's ... goin' to work for you?' Rose stared ahead of her at the paper on the table, not daring to look Luke in the face in case he saw the fear inside her. This couldn't be true, it must be a bad dream. 'Charlie?'

'That's the funny thing,' said Luke. 'I don't know. Wouldn't say yes or no, just stood there with his mouth hangin' open like he couldn't believe his ears.' He got up. 'I'd best go an' check on Terry, see how he's gettin' on with the Chairoplanes.'

'B-but the job.' Rose could hardly speak, her

mouth was so dry. 'Charlie. What about him?'

'Oh, in the end I got him to say he'd come up here on Sunday before the park opens an' take a look at the rides. You know, see if that makes up his mind for him. Told him we can't wait long for his answer, though ...'

'No,' said Rose quietly, hope daring to blossom. 'No, we can't.'

There was still time for Charlie to keep his promise, to turn round and walk right out of her life.

'Still.' Luke put his arm round Rose's shoulders and gave her a brief hug. 'I said you'd have a word with him when he comes. Maybe you can change his mind for him, eh? Make him see sense?'

'I'm sorry,' said Charlie flatly.

Rose glared at him, beyond anger, beyond pain. But he didn't return her gaze, he didn't even look at her. He just went on staring at the empty TT Racer, watching it turn endlessly round and round with no destination and no end.

'It's a bit late to be sorry,' she said acidly.

This time Charlie did look at her. 'I didn't mean ... about what happened. I meant about this. About bein' here now.'

'Yes,' said Rose. 'Why *are* you here?'

'Luke asked me ... I didn't know what to say ...'

'How about "No thanks"? You made me a promise, Charlie. Mind you, you made me

220

another promise an' you never kept that one neither.'

'Oh, Rose.' Charlie let out a long, slow exhalation of breath. The little girl clung to his side like a limpet to a rock, her dark, knowing eyes fixed on his face as though it and it alone held the answers to everything. Rose thought she read despair written on that face, but she couldn't allow herself to feel sympathy for Charlie, not after all that had passed between them.

'Go home, Charlie. Leave us alone.' She said it quite softly, not that there was anybody around to overhear, not this early on a Sunday morning; but somehow all her strength seemed to be ebbing away. 'Please, Charlie.'

He seemed to make up his mind, straightening up and turning to face her. 'I'll go away an' never come back, if that's what you want. But don't ask me to go home, Rose—there's no home left for me.'

'Go back to Birkenhead. That's where you belong.'

'Is it?' Charlie gave a softly mocking laugh. 'I've no family there; you know that. My mates are all dead or married or gone away, even the old house isn't there any more. There'll be no job either, I'm blacklisted. That's why I've stayed over here this long.'

'I don't understand.'

'While John Gorry was findin' odd jobs for me, at least I was workin', bringin' in money for me an' Lola. It's the kid I care about, Rose, she's the only thing I've got left.'

Rose looked at Charlie and the child beside him. Something tore at her heart as she saw the tenderness in him, that same tenderness that had united father and daughter on the night when Lola had run away to the fairground. Jealousy bubbled up inside her, dark and poisonous.

'Is that so?'

'It's difficult, Rose.'

'Difficult!' This time the jealous anger sparked out of Rose, as she thought of all those long years of having nothing and never daring to hope that things might get better. 'It's been *difficult* for me, Charlie—my God, you don't know the meanin' of *difficult.*'

She felt a tug at her hand and looked down at Lola, her two small hands clasped tightly around her wrist. A tear escaped and rolled silently down the child's cheek, leaving a lighter track on the grubby skin. For a fleeting moment Rose saw Charlie in those dark eyes, and it was more pain than she could bear.

'When did this poor kid last have a bath, Charlie?'

Charlie blinked at her, completely thrown by this sudden change of tack.

'A ...?'

'A bath, Charlie. A wash.' She looked him up and down with a critical eye. Shabby, down-at-heel, his blond hair dull with grease, he looked like a man who was well past caring—which might have been none of Rose's concern if it hadn't been for the child, the innocent result of a long-dead betrayal. Whatever punishment

222

Charlie might deserve, Lola didn't deserve to suffer with him.

'Come to mention it, you could do with one yourself. An' when did you last change your clothes?'

'I ...' Charlie looked down sheepishly at his old, grubby trousers and torn shirt. 'I can't remember. Tuesday?'

Rose thought about Charlie and Lola heading back to Birkenhead with nothing but the clothes they stood up in. With nothing to look forward to, nowhere to live, no one to help them, destitution staring them in the face. And nothing for Lola but the prospect of growing up in yet another terrible, bleak institution.

For the child's sake, Rose pulled herself together and said the only thing she could. 'If you're goin' to work here you'll have to smarten yourself up. My Luke's very particular.'

The look on Charlie's face was almost worth the pain in Rose's heart.

'Me? Work here? But you said—'

'I know what I said. I can change my mind, can't I?' She defied him to say otherwise. 'Anyhow, it's not for your sake, Charlie, it's for Lola's. Five weeks you've got, till the end of the season, then you're gone from here an' you don't come back. Right?'

'Anythin' you say. You know ... you know I'd never do anythin' to hurt you.'

'You'd better not try,' she replied. 'Because if you do—'

'Never, Rose, I swear. An' Rose ...'

'What?'

'Thanks.'

'Don't thank me, thank Luke. If it was up to me you'd never have come here in the first place.'

Their eyes met, a distant spark of the old closeness passing between them; then it was gone, leaving Rose feeling suddenly cold and a little afraid. Behind Charlie the TT Racer spun round and round to the sound of a crackly old record.

'This kid needs proper lookin' after. Come on, Lola.' On impulse Rose took the Spanish child's hand in hers; to her surprise she didn't try to pull away or run back to her father. 'I've still got some of Ellie's old clothes. Let's go an' find you somethin' decent to wear.'

Charlie called after her as she led the child back to the vardo. She paused and looked back at him over her shoulder.

'What?'

'I'll be gone soon, I promise.'

'You'd better be.'

I know you will, Charlie, she thought to herself. Leaving people's what you do best. And this time she truly believed that she was glad.

There was still an hour or so to go before dawn, but Manfri was as nervous as a lad on his first poaching expedition.

The resprayed Bentley slid out of the wooden shed and disappeared down the lane into the darkened back streets of Birkenhead. Gone. Manfri breathed a sigh of relief. He beckoned to the man in the raincoat and they disappeared back into the shed. Manfri fastened the doors behind them.

'Nice job, Barton.' The big brown trilby shadowed the top half of the man's face, so that it was impossible to make out his expression. 'The boss is pleased with you. Keep this up and he'll be putting plenty more work your way.'

Manfri knew he ought by rights to be delighted; so why did he feel so uneasy? Maybe because he'd got out of the habit of being on the wrong side of the law.

'An' the money?'

'Like I said, he's very pleased. Good to have you on the firm.'

Manfri felt a cold shiver of apprehension run between his shoulder-blades. 'If you could just 'and over the cash ...'

The man in the trilby gave a low, throaty laugh. 'The boss always pays up, you know that. Always settles his debts.' He thrust a hand into his inside pocket and drew out a thin envelope. 'Here.' He tossed the envelope, but Manfri's arthritic fingers fumbled the catch and he had to scrabble on the oily floor to pick it up.

'It's not all here,' he protested.

'Half now, half later,' said the stranger. 'That was the deal. You'll get the rest when we sell the motors on.'

'But ...' A twinge of doubt nagged at Manfri. 'How will I know if you've sold 'em or not?'

The stranger laughed again, throwing back his head so that the light from the single fly-specked lightbulb caught the hard glitter in his eyes.

'How? You'll just have to trust me, won't you?'

CHAPTER 18

'Dressed crabs, only two an' six, missus ...'

'Lovely Manx kippers, post some home today!'

'Roll up ladies an' gents, take a ride on the TT Racer. Two for a shillin'.'

It was cold for late August, and the crowds at Funland were thinner today—a lot thinner than Rose would have liked. There was a lot of money to be earned between now and the end of September if the Bartons were to meet their obligations. Surviving the coming winter was something Rose didn't even like thinking about.

Through a gap in the crowd she watched the TT Racer and the Chairoplanes. Luke was working the old ride, nursing it along, understanding its cranky old mechanism better than anyone, while Gracie sat in the pay booth, taking the money for the rides. Charlie worked the TT Racer.

Much to Rose's relief, her fears about Charlie seemed groundless; he had given his word, and for once he seemed to be keeping it. She had dreaded seeing him everywhere she turned, horribly certain that everyone would guess what they had once been to each other, but either luck was with her or Charlie had made up his mind to keep well out of her way. At any rate, their paths scarcely crossed except when Rose went round the rides to collect the takings. For that, she was grateful.

He was a hard worker too, uncomplaining and reliable. Not that that was any great surprise to Rose; all those years ago he'd been the best worker in the whole shipyard ... when he wasn't calling the men out on yet another wildcat strike. Whatever had happened to Charlie in the intervening years—and Rose sensed there was plenty he hadn't told her—it seemed to have knocked that reckless streak out of him. Now, all he cared about was Lola.

The skinny, dark-haired child flitted between the punters in Ellie's wake, laughing silently with her new friend, dodging in and out of the canopied stalls as though she had known and loved them all her life. People had remarked on how the two kids had taken to each other, a smile and a hug from Ellie calming the most furious of Lola's frustrated rages. What was it Percy Sayle had said? 'Chalk an' cheese, them two, missus—chalk an' cheese Gaw' bless 'em.' And it was true; the two girls couldn't have been more different. Lola capricious, dark and stormy, Ellie blonde and playful as a Labrador pup.

But Rose knew why they got on so well together—it was only natural. Half-sisters was what they were, though no one would ever

227

guess it to look at them. Not even Lola and Ellie themselves, thank God.

But what about Charlie? Her eyes drifted back to the TT Racer. She watched him reach down to help a girl up on to one of the motor bikes, then heave the centre engine back into life and disappear as the ride slowly revolved.

You've worked it all out, haven't you? she thought. You know all about Ellie, you guessed the truth the first time you saw her. But don't you dare try to steal her away from Luke, she's his little girl now, you've got Lola.

Oh, Charlie, don't ever ask me about Ellie. I don't want to have to lie to you.

Rose was finding out about fortune-telling the hard way.

It had looked so easy when Old Peg did it, but Rose was coming to see that there was a lot more to this dukkering business than putting on a red shawl and sitting behind a beaded curtain.

'And what about children?' asked the earnest youth in the blue demob suit. 'We want *lots* of children.'

The girl on his arm flushed beetroot red and hid her face in his sleeve. 'Oh, Dickie! Dickie, you're *terrible*, you are!'

'Well we do!' retorted the youth, dotting a kiss on the girl's forehead. It wasn't difficult to work out that they'd just got engaged; you had only to look at the brand-new ring with its tiny diamond glittering on the girl's finger. 'Dozens. Don't we, Louie? Go on, miss, tell us what we're going to have.'

Louie emerged from the security of her fiancé's sleeve. 'Will it be twins? Twins run in the family, see.'

Rose searched the girl's face, well aware that the trick was to tell the punters what they wanted to hear. The difficult bit was working out what that might be. 'Well ...' she began, passing her hands over the crystal ball to give herself time to think.

'Louie's auntie had triplets. Didn't she, Louie?'

'Oh, Dickie, she was ever so poorly. She nearly died! It was awful. Oh I hope it's not triplets ...'

That made up Rose's mind for her. She gave Louie her most reassuring smile. 'I see no triplets in the crystal.' That bit, at least, was no lie. She couldn't see anything but her own reflection.

'Oh thank goodness for that!' Louie looked radiant with relief.

'But it does tell me that you will be very happy, and you will have many healthy children.'

'Did you hear that, Dickie?'

'See, Louie? We're going to be the happiest couple ever, didn't I tell you we would?'

They kissed and hugged. Two more happy customers, Rose thought as the courting couple left the booth, arms linked and giggling again. If the best she could do was stop folk worrying about things they couldn't change—well, that was better than nothing. It was hard enough keeping track of today without trying to work out what would happen tomorrow.

Luke cycled slowly along the Peel Road, the bag of money hanging heavily against his thigh. He was acutely aware of the looks of amusement he attracted from the occasional Highlander coach as it rumbled by, but kept reminding himself that he ought to be grateful for the loan of Percy Sayle's old boneshaker. Even if the rusty frame did creak and squeak with every push of the pedals, it was saving him a bus fare he and Rose could ill afford.

He heard Kneale's yard long before he saw it. For Luke there could be no mistaking the seductive thunder of motor-bike engines revving, the acrid scent of two-stroke that caught at the back of his throat and evoked a thousand bitter-sweet memories.

Dismounting from the bike, Luke wheeled it towards Eddie Kneale's garage. With the Manx Grand Prix only a week away, it was organised chaos. The forecourt was crowded with bikes: Nortons, an AJS Porcupine parallel twin, Vincents, even a Moto Guzzi. Overalled mechanics swarmed over the vehicles, stripping down engines, tightening chains, tweaking and coaxing the last degree of perfection from the gleaming machines.

Luke felt his chest tighten, his legs more leaden with every step he took. He might well have turned tail had it not been for the money he had to deliver to Eddie—and the fact that at that moment, Doreen spotted him and beckoned him over.

At first he didn't recognise her. She had her back to him and was almost indistinguishable from the other mechanics in her dirty blue overalls and clumpy boots, her curly brown hair hidden under a man's cap. As she turned to him and grinned, she wiped the back of her hand across her face and left a long black smear of oil. 'Hello, stranger!' she shouted merrily over the sound of an Excelsior zooming out of the yard on to the open road. 'Come to trade that thing in for a proper bike?'

It was an innocent remark, but all the same it cut deep. Luke propped the bicycle up against the gatepost and pointed to the money-bag. 'Bit of business to sort out. Eddie around, is he?'

Doreen shook her head. Behind her, the engine noise faded as two of the Nortons followed the Excelsior and headed off towards St John's. 'Gone to check over the Grand Prix course.' She looked down at the canvas bag in Luke's hand. 'What's that?'

'Your cut of the takin's for last month.' Luke swung it up and Doreen caught it. 'It's a bit short ... Things is a bit tight, see. But tell Eddie I'll bring him the rest next week.'

Doreen's face registered more exasperation than gratitude. 'What are we going to do with you, Luke Barton? How many times does Dad have to tell you? You don't have to pay us a penny till the business takes off properly. Wait till next season, Dad doesn't mind.'

Luke's stubborn chin jutted. 'I'm not Dan. I pay me way.'

'I know.' Doreen rested her hand on his arm,

just for a moment. It felt cool in the muggy afternoon heat. 'But I know how difficult it is for you too.'

'What's Rose been sayin'?' demanded Luke defensively.

Doreen laughed. 'Don't you go blaming Rose. She doesn't have to say anything, I just know. I'm not daft, Luke.'

'I never thought you was.' Luke stared moodily at the ground. 'I s'pose us Bartons are a laughin' stock all over Douglas.'

The laughter in Doreen's jolly, dark eyes turned to earnestness. 'You're wrong, Luke. Nobody's laughing at you. You'd be surprised how many people admire you and Rose, the way you've kept going in spite of everything.' She weighed the bag in her hands, grimacing at the weight of so many thrupenny bits and halfpennies. 'What've you got in here, pebbles off Douglas beach? Hang on, I'll just go and put this in the office so Dad sees it when he gets back.'

Luke watched Doreen bounce off into the office, radiating energy and optimism. It was obvious what Dan had seen in her, though why he'd been stupid enough to two-time her was beyond Luke. Still, a lot of things about Dan Barton were impossible to fathom. Luke often wished he could face up to life the way Eddie's girl did, seeing a bit of good in everything instead of half-expecting that everything he tried to do would turn out bad.

'Like bikes do you, boy?' enquired the mechanic working on the Moto Guzzi.

232

'I like this one,' replied Luke, running his fingers along the smooth black chassis.

'Aye, she's a beauty.' The Manxman winked towards Percy Sayle's ancient boneshaker. 'Bit faster'n yours an' all! Ride, do you?'

'Used to.'

If the mechanic said anything more to him, Luke didn't hear it. He was still gazing at the bike, lost in thought, when Doreen skipped up behind him.

'Talk about the little boy and the sweet-shop window!'

'What?' He swivelled round. 'Oh. Didn't see you there.'

Doreen was watching him, her head cocked on one side. 'You miss riding, don't you?'

'Well ... sometimes.' There was no way he was going to admit how much, not even to himself.

'I knew you loved bikes, I've seen the way you look at my Norton. Once they're in your system ...'

'Yeah, well, missin' it's one thing an' doin' it's another.' Luke tore his gaze away from the Moto Guzzi. 'I'd best be off then.'

'Already?'

'We've got this new bloke, an' he don't quite know the ropes yet.' It wasn't really true; Charlie was picking up the job fast, and Luke knew he could trust him to run things for a few hours. But something told him if he didn't go right now he might not want to.

'But you could spare half an hour, couldn't you? Tell you what ...' Doreen's gaze drifted across the forecourt to her own Norton. 'Why don't you take my bike out for a quick spin—you know, put her through her paces? She's been playing me up a bit lately.'

'Me?' Luke felt sweat pool in the small of his back.

'You're such a good mechanic. I'd appreciate your opinion. Really, you'd be doing me a favour.'

Luke took a few steps closer to the bike. The whole world seemed to fade around him, contracting until it enclosed only himself, Doreen and the bike. 'I don't know. I haven't ridden since ... since the accident. An' Rose ... I sort of promised her ...'

He'd promised Rose he'd never get on a bike again. But after all, it was just a short run as a favour to Doreen. There was no need for Rose even to know ...

'Oh, I'm sorry, Luke. I didn't think,' apologised Doreen. 'That's me all over. If you'd rather not—'

'No,' Luke said hastily. 'I ... I'd like to.'

He laid his hand on the handlebars, drew open the throttle and let it snap back, slid his leg over the seat and felt the sun-warmed leather yield under his weight. He shivered, hot and cold, utterly terrified and exhilarated all at once.

'Luke? Luke, are you sure about this?'

He forced a relaxed smile as he pulled on the gauntlets and buckled on the helmet. Could he do this? Could he—after such a long time and so many terrible nightmares? Nightmares in which

234

he could still feel the metal slicing into his face as the bike stalled and turned over and over and over, hurling him against the slatted walls of the Globe of Death, could still taste the sudden hot spurt of blood before the pain began ...

'Course I am. Why shouldn't I be?'

He lifted the bike off the stand and jumped on the kick-start. At the third attempt it grumbled into life. His heart racing, he pulled the goggles down over his eyes.

'Ease her along, Luke, she can be temperamental sometimes. Don't go too far.'

'Just to St John's and back,' he promised; but it felt like flying to the moon.

Coming to a corner, Luke boy. Change down. Steady now, not too fast.

Luke leant into the bend and the bike hugged the corner tightly, righting itself with a satisfied roar as they hit the straight. He patted the petrol tank as though it were the neck of a favourite horse. 'Good girl, good girl, that's it, easy now.'

Luke leant over the handlebars, feeling the wind rip at his clothes, the engine gently vibrating between his knees. His heart was pounding but he had gone beyond fear now into sheer joy, had broken through the barrier with the first bite of tyre-rubber on the metalled road.

Hedgerows flashed past on either side, the stone walls buffered in places with sandbags and straw bales in readiness for the races. A stray sheep scuttled off the grass verge into his path but he swerved the bike to the right and avoided it with ease. Although it was a little tricky getting the hang of judging distances with only one eye, the old skills were coming back, and the old reflexes were as swift as ever, he was sure they were.

It was a perfect day to be riding, a perfect day to be free. And that was how Luke felt: as if all these years he'd been in self-imposed exile, separated from the thing he loved most in all the world save Rose and Ellie. He had been so afraid of trying.

And now it was almost frightening, how quickly he was getting the hang of it again.

Just after eight, Rose hung the 'Closed' sign on the dukkering booth and took the takings back to the vardo. Business had been dead slow all day, her head ached from making up two-bob fairytales, and it was hours since Luke had left for Kneale's yard. Had something happened to him? Had Eddie cut up rough about the missing money?

There were times when Rose wished she didn't have quite such an active imagination.

As she was climbing the wagon steps she saw a van driving out through the gates, a familiar figure waving at someone through the window. Doreen Kneale. As the van moved away Rose saw who Doreen was waving at: it was Luke, Percy's old bike propped up by his side.

'Thanks for the lift, Doreen.'

'Don't mention it. See you soon.'

Rose jumped down the steps and marched across to Luke. 'What's happened? Did you have a puncture or somethin'?'

'No, nothin' like that.'

'What then?' All Rose's anxieties poured out as anger. 'You should've been back hours ago.'

'I know, I'm sorry. Somethin' ... came up.'

A frisson of fear made Rose's skin prickle. 'Eddie wasn't angry, was he? About his money?'

'No, no.' Luke laid his hand on Rose's shoulder as they walked back towards the living-wagon. He looked tired, but more than that; he seemed distant, distracted. 'Look, Eddie wasn't there—but Doreen was fine about the money, she said take as long as we like.'

Rose breathed again. 'Thank God for that.' She put her foot on the bottom step. 'That gives us a bit of breathin' space, anyhow.'

Luke took her hand and drew her round to face him. 'I told Doreen Eddie'd have the rest of his money next week.'

'You *what?*' Rose gaped at him, caught between disbelief and fury.

'It's only right,' said Luke. 'We pay what we owe.'

'We pay what we *can*, Luke! It's all very well you goin' round makin' all these promises, but what are we goin' to use for money? Tell me that.' All Rose's worst fears seemed to crowd in around her like black-eyed demons—fears of destitution, the terror of having even less than nothing—and she blurted out the first thing that came into her head. 'Or are you

237

plannin' on takin' the food out of your own daughter's mouth?'

How long Charlie had been standing there, neither Rose nor Luke had the faintest idea. The first Rose saw of him, he was hesitating by the perimeter fence, a money-bag in his hand.

'What do you want?' snapped Luke, uncharacteristically sharply.

'I ... er, brought the afternoon takin's, like you told me to,' said Charlie. He avoided looking at Rose. How much have you heard, Charlie, she wondered to herself. How much have you heard, and how much have you worked out for yourself?

'Not now,' growled Luke.

Charlie held out the money-bag, looking profoundly uncomfortable. 'What about the ... er ...'

'I said, not now!'

Charlie turned and walked smartly away, head down, shoulders slightly bent. Rose might have felt sorry for him if she hadn't been out of her mind with worry.

'Luke ... Luke, we *can't* pay back Eddie Kneale, not next week. Not the week after neither ...'

'I know.' Luke trudged up the wagon steps, threw open the door and sat down. Rose followed him, not sure whether to be angry or puzzled.

'But if you *know* we can't pay, then why did you—'

'I've been thinkin',' said Luke. 'Thinkin' a

238

lot, these last few days. An' I've made up me mind. We're sellin' the TT Racer.'

'Oh.' The feelings that flooded Rose were confused and contradictory, a peculiar mixture of relief and remorse. She sank down on to the bench next to Luke, the money-bag slumping to the wooden floor with a muted clunk. Part of her was still defiant, wanting to go on fighting even when the battle was lost. But she knew in her heart that there was no choice, not any more. 'So, Spence has won then.'

'I'm not sellin' to Spence,' replied Luke.

'Not Spence?' Rose struggled to make sense of what Luke was saying. 'Then who?'

'Jack Verney.'

This came like a bolt out of the blue. It was madness, sheer madness. There was no other word for it. 'You can't! Verney's not offering nearly as much as Spence!'

'It's enough.'

'How can you say that? If we sell out to Verney, we'll hardly have enough to pay off the debts ... Then there's the winter to get through—an' what then?' Panic gripped her and she grabbed at Luke's arm. 'You can't do this, Luke, you can't! Don't you care about me an' Ellie?'

To her horror, Luke pushed her away and stood up. 'I've made up me mind, Rose. I'm sellin' to Jack Verney an' that's that.'

The slam of the wagon door behind him was like an iron gate crashing down between them.

CHAPTER 19

Luke knew he ought to feel happy, but the money in his hands felt like thirty pieces of silver.

'Come on, lad,' said Jack Verney, rolling up the sleeves of his work-shirt. 'Spence'll be in his office by now.'

Luke submitted to a pat on the back from a brawny hand. He contemplated the banknotes in his hand, and then the slowly-circling ride in the distance, which by the end of September would no longer be Barton's Famous TT Racer but Jack Verney's.

'Later.'

'No time like the present, eh?' Jack Verney's voice was insistent but not harsh. 'Get it over with, lad, you'll feel better when you've seen the look on Horace's face. I know I will.'

Luke let out a heavy sigh. 'I s'pose you're right.'

'I usually am, lad. I usually am.'

They walked side by side across the tober, almost deserted at this time on a Sunday evening, save for the odd showman setting up his stall for the morning. Seagulls circled overhead, occasionally swooping down to snatch a tasty morsel that had escaped the dust-cart, then soaring up into the cloud-flecked sky over Onchan Head. An easy life, thought Luke.

Easier, at any rate, than the life of a cheapjack showman.

Horace was not in his office. He was standing outside, one thumb hooked through his braces, the other hand jabbing at the air as he dispensed orders to his minions.

'Micky Kerruish ...'

'Yessir?'

'Do summat about them roller-coaster carriages. Oil 'em or summat—I'm sick of hearin' 'em squeak. Percy ...'

'Misther Spence?'

'Smarten up the pay booth—an' give it a bit of elbow grease this time. If I can't see me face in it, it's not clean enough.' He glanced aside at the sight of Luke Barton and Jack Verney descending on him, the one grim-faced, the other looking decidedly smug. 'Well well, what do you two want then?'

'A word,' said Luke. 'It's private.'

Horace's left eyebrow lifted a good half-inch, then descended.

'That so?' He jerked his thumb towards the middle distance. 'Gerron wi' it, then. What you lot waitin' for—Christmas? So, what's all this about, Barton? Don't tell me Verney's talked some sense into you at last.'

'You could say that,' said Verney. 'He's sellin' up.'

'It's all right, Jack, I can speak for meself,' Luke cut in. It was bad enough having to do this at all, without Jack Verney acting like he owned him as well as the ride.

'Sellin' up, eh?' Horace Spence beamed like

241

the rising sun. 'Well, you took your time but you got there in the end. Come inside an' we'll settle up.'

'Hang on a minute,' said Luke. 'I'm not sellin' to you, Spence, I'm sellin' to Verney.'

Horace Spence's face went through a rainbow of colours, from beetroot red to ashen white. 'You're ... *what?*'

'You heard.'

A thin trickle of perspiration ran down the side of Spence's face. He didn't even bother to wipe it off. ' 'Im? You're sellin' out to Verney? You're havin' me on, Luke Barton.'

Luke held out the banknotes Verney had given him.

'It's all there. Count it if you like. The loan plus the interest.'

'What's up, Horace?' enquired Verney gleefully. 'Something wrong?'

Spence's jaw clenched and his Adam's apple bobbed up and down as he swallowed hard. His pudgy fingers closed over the money. 'Right. So it's like that then, is it?' He looked Verney up and down. 'You're a slippery customer, Jack Verney.'

'Takes one to know one.'

'So.' Spence addressed himself to Luke again. 'That's the last we'll be seein' of the Bartons then, is it? Can't say I'll be sorry to see you go.'

Luke met Spence's small, pink-rimmed eyes with a steely gaze. 'Pity. 'Cause we're not goin'. We'll be stoppin' here next season, same as always.'

'Stoppin'!' Spence's rotund frame quivered with laughter. 'What with? You've just sold your rides to Verney.'

'Only the TT Racer,' replied Luke, with difficulty managing to control his anger. 'We've still got the Chairoplanes an' the sideshows. So if you don't like it you'll have to lump it.'

Spence laughed humourlessly. 'I give it six weeks,' he grunted.

'We'll get by, we always do.'

'Well, don't think you can come runnin' to me when you're down to your last farthing.'

Spence disappeared into the office, crashing the door shut behind him. Luke was left glaring after him, his chest rising and falling rapidly, hands clenching and unclenching with frustrated anger. 'Bastard,' he muttered under his breath.

Verney clapped an arm round Luke's shoulders. 'Don't worry about Horace, lad. He's just a bad loser.'

Luke shook himself free. 'I just wish ... I just wish I was sure.'

'Sure?'

'Sure I've done the right thing.'

'Course you have.' Verney reached into the breast pocket of his shirt, took out a roll of notes and peeled several off. 'There you go, lad.'

Luke peered at the notes. 'Where's the rest?'

'Half now, the balance in April, when you start riding for me, like we agreed.'

Riding. The word hit the pit of Luke's stomach like a sucker-punch. For the first time, as he looked at the money in Verney's hand, he really understood what all of this meant.

Verney must have noticed his hesitation in taking the money, because he asked, 'Not having second thoughts, are you, lad?'

'N-no. Course I'm not.' Luke snatched the notes and stuffed them into his trouser pocket.

'Glad to hear it. Wouldn't want my star rider backing out on me, now would I?'

Verney ambled off across the tober, whistling cheerfully to himself as he went. Luke recognised the tune. It was 'Buddy, Can You Spare a Dime?'. It was a warm day, but a dark chill of realisation surrounded him. He'd done it, he'd actually done it. Sold out to Verney and agreed to do the one thing he'd promised himself he'd never do. And not just himself: what about Rose? When and how and what was he going to tell her? For there was no avoiding the fact that he would have to tell her sometime. Sometime soon.

Just not now.

Rose sat on the grassy headland looking out over Douglas. Before her the bay swept round in a deep arc, the water greenish-blue and sparkling beneath her, the hills behind the town reaching up to meet a mackerel sky. On the promenade holidaymakers ebbed and flowed in a colourful tide. But Rose was too preoccupied to think about what a beautiful day it was, or how good it was to have a few hours to herself. She was too busy thinking about Luke.

She plucked thoughtfully at the grass in front of her, picking a daisy and turning it round and round in her fingers. Had she been wrong to bawl him out like that? Maybe. Whether she

244

was wrong or right scarcely mattered; Luke had made his decision and there'd be no going back on it now. What couldn't be cured would have to be endured. And maybe Luke would turn out to have been right after all—though she still couldn't understand for the life of her why he'd chosen to sell out to Mr Verney instead of Horace Spence.

Luke came up behind her so soundlessly that his voice made her jump. 'You should've said you was comin' here, I've been lookin' all over.'

'Oh! It's you.'

He dropped down to his haunches beside her. 'You still blazin' mad at me?'

Rose shook her head. The anger had gone now, to be replaced by a vague ache of resentment.

Luke sat down on the grass. 'It's done.'

His voice had a dull finality to it. Rose stole a look at his face and saw how upset he looked; deathly pale beneath the weathered tan.

'Verney gave you the money?'

He nodded. 'Most of it. We'll get the rest later.' He didn't say how much later. 'Oh, Rose ...'

The word tailed off in a long, slow, despairing exhalation of breath that stirred something deep inside Rose. She slid closer to him on the grass until their bodies were touching, and she could feel his warmth through the thin skirt of her dress.

'What is it, Luke?'

'Oh, Rose, what have I done?' His head

245

slumped forwards into his hands and he shook it slowly back and forth. 'What have I gone an' done?'

'But Luke, I thought ... I thought this was what you wanted.'

'It is, but ... Oh, Rose, I don't know any more. I don't know nothin'.'

She slipped her hand through his arm and drew him closer, knowing now that she had been wrong to be angry. It was obvious that the decision to sell the TT Racer to Verney had been made only at the cost of a great deal of heartache. And it couldn't have been easy, knowing he'd be selling in the face of his own mother's opposition. Whether Luke's choice turned out to be a right one or a wrong one, it was certainly a brave one; and it had been made from love.

'It's all right, Luke. Everything's all right.'

'You don't know that,' Luke said softly. But Rose snuggled her head against his shoulder.

'Yes I do. Look, you had no choice. We had to sell to someone, didn't we?'

'Well, yeah ...'

'If we didn't sell the Racer we'd go under, simple as that. Your mam'll understand, she's not daft.' Rose wasn't entirely sure this was true, but she was determined to make the best of things for Luke's sake. 'An' now it's done we can pay off all our debts, can't we? Eddie Kneale an' Sean Rourke an' all the rest of 'em.'

'I s'pose.' Luke managed a weak smile. 'I don't know how you do it, Rose.'

'Do what?'

'Keep goin' when for two pins I'd jack it all in tomorrer.'

'I don't do nothin',' she said firmly, kissing him on the cheek. 'It's you that's kept them rides goin'. We've survived, Luke, just like you said we would. There was times I didn't believe you. But we kept on goin'. An' now we can pay off the debts an' still have enough to run the Chairoplanes an' the sideshows next year. It'll be plain sailin' from now on, you'll see.'

'You reckon?'

'I reckon. An' you're a good man, Luke Barton, we could never have done it without you.'

They kissed, and Rose cradled Luke very tenderly in her arms.

'Mam, Dad!' An excited voice roused her and she drew back, blushing slightly. It was Ellie, skipping over the grass like a wood sprite, her feet bare, a necklace of threaded daisies round her neck.

'Ellie—what you doin' here? Is somethin' wrong?'

Ellie shook her plaits vigorously and giggled as she took the daisy chain from round her neck and put it over her mother's head. 'No, Mam. Look—I made this for you.' She gave Rose a sticky hug and plopped down on the grass between her and Luke. 'I was hungry, so Mister Christian gave me *two* toffee apples!'

'Two!' commented Luke. 'You won't want any dinner.'

'Yes I will,' retorted Ellie. 'I only ate one, I'm savin' the other one for Lola. Do you think Lola likes toffee apples, Mam?'

'Oh, I expect so,' smiled Rose. 'Everyone likes toffee apples.'

'Is it dinner time yet, Mam? I'm hungry.'

'Soon.' Rose slipped her arm round Ellie's waist and linked it with Luke's, and the three of them sat there on the headland, gazing out to sea. A steamer was coming over the horizon, steam billowing out of its red funnels.

Plain sailing, thought Rose. Or was it that simple?

Manfri picked up the letter from the doormat, recognising the handwriting instantly. 'It's a letter,' he called through the kitchen door. 'From Luke.'

He slid his thumb under the flap of the envelope, but before he'd had a chance to open it it was snatched out of his hand by Sofia.

'Give that to me!'

'*Dordy*, woman, no need to snatch like that. You can't even read.'

'Read!' Sofia blazed with righteous fury. 'Read *this?*' She spat on the envelope and, taking it in both hands, ripped it right down the middle.

Manfri pursued her down the passage, through the back kitchen and into the yard. 'What you do that for?' he demanded.

'See this? You see this?' Sofia scrunched the pieces of paper in her raised fist, took the lid off the bin and dropped them into the foul-smelling mess. 'That's what I think of your son an' his letters!'

'My letter!'

'If you want it, you can fetch it yourself!'

Crashing the lid back on to the bin, she stalked back into the kitchen; and would have slammed the door in Manfri's face if he hadn't got a shoulder to it just in time.

'For *Duvvel*'s sake, woman—'

She sneered at him. *'Nash avri.* Go away, leave me alone.'

She pushed him aside and stalked down the passage, turning left into the parlour. Gradually, in the weeks since Luke had first warned that he would have to sell the TT Racer, the parlour had become more and more like a shrine to Dan Barton. There were photos of him all over the place: silver-edged snapshots on the mantelpiece, a velvet-framed portrait sitting on the chenille tablecloth. Only one photograph of Luke remained in the room, and two seconds later even that had gone, torn into a confetti of little black and white squares.

Manfri's arthritic bones creaked as he stooped to gather up the pieces. 'You're crazy, woman! You can't do that!'

Sofia spun round and fixed him with her dark and murderous eyes.

'This Luke, he is a stranger. Why must I have his picture in my house?'

'A stranger? He's your *son!*'

'I have one son, Manfri, one son only. His name is not Luke.' The eyes caressed a picture of Dan, aged nineteen, arms folded and laughing as he leaned back against the TT Racer. They were filled with the fanatical, unquestioning devotion of a mother for her first-born. '*My* son, he does not steal from me.'

'You stupid woman! It's Dan who steals from you, not Luke!'

'Lies! Wicked lies.'

'Your Dan's a good-for-nothin' *dinilo*—but you'd rather see Luke an' Rose without a penny than admit it, wouldn't you? Well, wouldn't you?'

Eyeball to eyeball, they glared at each other. In the end it was Sofia who looked away first, but Manfri wasn't stupid enough to think he'd won. In the old days it wouldn't have been like this; a woman knew her place, and that included even headstrong Sofia Barton. But now ... now Manfri was ashamed to see how far he had fallen. So far that he couldn't even keep the respect and obedience of his own *monisha*.

'You will listen to me, you will *listen.*' He thumped the wall right next to her head and she didn't even flinch. And all at once Manfri felt exhausted by it all. His clenched fist swung away and swept all the dishes off the kitchen table in an avalanche of broken china. 'Right. If that's the way you want it I'm goin' out.'

'Beast!' she spat after him.

He didn't look back, just grabbed his jacket from the back of a chair and marched out of the kitchen, his heavy boots crunching on shards of broken teacup. He didn't even bother closing the yard door behind him, just trudged along, head down, not looking to left or right. It'll be all right in the end—that's what he kept telling himself. Sofia was fiery and stubborn, but not stupid. In the end she'd understand that Luke had done the only thing he could do. Just as Manfri had ...

He didn't stop till he came to the Ferry Arms. Pushing open the door, he went inside, picking his way across the floor, still wet from its morning mopping.

'We're not open yet.'

'Can I use your phone?'

The landlord shrugged. 'Help yourself. Mind you put the money in the box.'

Manfri went behind the bar counter and into the dingy hallway which led to the landlord's sitting room. Fumbling in his pocket, he took out the slip of paper with the telephone number on it, and dialled with shaking fingers.

'Woodside 2218.'

'Connecting you now, sir.'

It seemed to ring for ever; then, just as Manfri was about to give up, somebody picked up the receiver.

'Yes?'

'It's Barton.'

'What d'you want? This number's for emergencies.'

Manfri leant his hot, sweaty forehead against the cool paintwork of the doorframe. 'I ... I know. But I had to talk to you. It's about the ... our bit of business.'

'What about it?'

'I've had enough, I want out.'

He heard a sharp intake of breath on the other end of the line.

'Oh you do, do you?'

'I've made up my mind.'

'Well I'll 'ave to talk to the boss about that.'

'Talk to him all you like,' said Manfri, suddenly emboldened now that he had actually managed to get the words out. 'I'm not doin' any more.' He put the receiver back on the hook and dropped the pennies, one by one, into the honesty box. An immense wave of relief washed over him. It was done.

At last his conscience could be clean.

CHAPTER 20

Eddie Kneale frowned as Rose counted five-pound notes into his hand. 'You're sure you can afford this?'

Rose knew the question was kindly meant, but like Luke she had her pride. 'We sold the TT Racer to pay off our debts, an' that's what we're doin'.'

'Aye. Aye, I know. Well, tell him ... tell him thanks.' Eddie folded the notes carefully and slotted them into his overalls pocket, dodging to one side as he did so to avoid a mechanic who was wheeling the mangled remains of a motor bike across the forecourt of Kneale's yard. 'I can't say it won't come in handy.'

Rose scanned the yard. It was dotted with vehicles, the odd gleaming car-bonnet strangely at odds with the bikes damaged in the Grand

Prix a couple of weeks ago. For Eddie Kneale, at least, it seemed that business was booming.

'So,' he said, picking up a spanner and tinkering with a rusted-on petrol cap. 'What are you and Luke going to do, now you've sold out to Verney?'

'We're stoppin' on the Island,' said Rose. 'Leastways ...' She looked at Doreen, not knowing what to say to Eddie. Rose Barton wasn't accustomed to begging.

'Staying, eh?' Eddie's face remained impassive, but his voice registered mild surprise.

Doreen must have realised what Rose was trying to say, because she cut in. 'They want to stay, Dad,' Doreen said. 'But it all depends on Luke getting some work for the winter.'

'Ah.' Eddie nodded thoughtfully, tongue clenched between his teeth in concentration as he strained to free the petrol cap.

Doreen threw Rose a despairing look. She crouched down next to Eddie. 'Dad!'

'Mmm?'

'Dad, are you listening?'

'Course I'm listening. Luke's looking for work for the winter.'

'Well?'

'Well what?'

'Well, couldn't we offer him something? God knows, we've got enough mashed-up bikes here to keep us going till Christmas!'

The petrol cap freed itself with a grating noise and Eddie threw down his spanner. He looked up at Rose.

She was praying silently for Luke's sake, for

253

all their sakes, but she couldn't bear to let him see how desperate she was. 'I ... I just thought, if you had anythin' goin' ...' she began lamely.

'I see.'

'My Luke's a good mechanic.'

'One of the best,' agreed Doreen.

'So I've heard. But all my mechanics are good mechanics.'

That sounded very much like 'no' to Rose. She cushioned herself against the inevitable disappointment. 'Well, I just thought I'd ask.'

'Dad ...' appealed Doreen.

Eddie took off his cap, scratched his sparse, greying curls and put it back on.

'As it happens, I might have something for Luke.'

Rose hardly dared let her spirits soar too high. 'You really think so?'

'I can't promise, mind. We'll have to see—and it'd only be something casual.'

'Luke wouldn't mind. He'll do anythin'.'

'All right then, Rose, you tell him I'll definitely bear him in mind.'

'There!' said Doreen triumphantly as Eddie went off into the garage. 'Didn't I tell you?'

'He only said he'd think about it,' pointed out Rose.

'That's just Dad's way.' Doreen sprung up on to the bonnet of an elderly Austin and perched her bottom on it. 'You mark my words, he'll find something for Luke.'

'I hope so,' said Rose. 'I really do.' She hadn't meant Doreen to see how worried she was, but the words came out like a sigh.

'Oh, Rose, it'll all come right. At least now you've sold off the TT Racer you can make a fresh start. So you won't have Spence on your back any more.'

'No. You're right ... I s'pose that's one less thing to worry about.'

'Only there's about a thousand others, right?'

'You're tellin' me. For a start, there's all these other people Dan owes money to.'

'But I thought you were paying them off.'

'Oh, I am! Most of Dan's gamblin' mates were sniffin' round the vardo the minute they heard we'd got a few bob. But God knows where Sean Rourke's got to. He's left his lodgin's, see.'

'Sean?' Doreen looked concerned. 'Isn't he at the Albion?'

'Landlord says they've not seen him in weeks. So what do I do with his money?'

'Hmm. See what you mean.' Doreen swung her legs, her heels thudding against the radiator grille. 'Hope he's not gone back to Ireland ...'

'You're sweet on him, aren't you?' exclaimed Rose, rather amused by the thought.

'I am *not!*' retorted Doreen, but her cheeks were pink with embarrassment. 'He's not my type. Tell you what—I'll ask around, shall I?'

'Oh, Doreen, would you?' Bless you, Doreen Kneale, thought Rose; without you I'd be half-barmy by now.

'No problem.' Doreen rolled up the sleeves of her work-shirt. 'Chin up, Rose, no long faces round here, it's against the rules.'

'Oh yes? An' who makes the rules?'

'I do, of course!'

In spite of herself, Rose laughed.

'Besides, you *can't* go back to Birkenhead.'

'Oh no? Why not?'

'Because I'd have nobody to talk to all day but big hairy mechanics.'

'VERNEY'S FAMOUS TT RACER'. The words stood out in wet paint on the rounding boards, intricate red and gold against the plain yellow background. If Rose screwed up her eyes, she could just make out the faint outline of the word 'Barton's' underneath.

Standing by the perimeter fence, she hugged her cardigan round her shoulders and felt the dusk close in around her. The evenings were growing shorter and cooler now that they were well into September, the numbers of holidaymakers tailing off—and it was uncomfortably easy to remember that it would soon be winter.

Rose knew she ought really to go back to the vardo and check that Ellie wasn't reading by torchlight under the bedclothes, but something kept her rooted to the spot, unable to turn her eyes away until she'd seen the very last stroke of the paintbrush.

'That Jack Verney don't hang about, does he?' commented a voice beside her.

It was Charlie.

'What do you want?' she asked without bothering to turn and look at him. She spoke sharply, though she no longer felt any hostility towards him—only a peculiar, growing emptiness

256

that nothing seemed able to fill.

'I ... I was lookin' for Luke,' said Charlie, 'but I can't find him.'

'He's not here.' She didn't bother explaining that Luke had gone to Kneale's yard to see Eddie about winter work. That was none of Charlie's concern.

'Then I'll tell you instead.'

'Tell me what?' This time she did look at him, subconsciously anticipating the tiny electrical charge that would spark through her when their eyes met, and refusing to let herself acknowledge it.

'I need to ask you ...' Charlie, usually so smooth-tongued, was fighting for words. 'I've had this offer ... of a job.'

'So?' demanded Rose coldly. She'd long since told herself that she had no desire to punish Charlie, that she'd gone way, way past that stage, but somehow her words did it anyway.

'On a boat,' said Charlie. 'You know—a proper job, permanent like.'

'That's nice.' Rose stared ahead of her at the TT Racer, at Jack Verney's men swarming all over it like pirates boarding a ship. She ought to be glad to be rid of the thing, but there were tears misting her eyes and she was damned if she was going to let Charlie see them.

'The thing is ...' He clammed up. Rose looked at him sharply, and was struck by the awkwardness and confusion in his eyes. Part of her was pleased to see him squirm, but something deeper inside felt inexplicably sad.

When she spoke again, her voice was heavy with weariness.

'Whatever it is, Charlie, just get it out, will you?'

'This job. They want me to start right away. Course, I told 'em I couldn't 'cause I've said I'll work for you till the end of the month. But then I saw you'd let Verney take over the Racer a couple of weeks early, an' I wondered ...'

'Wondered what?'

'Well, with one ride less, you've got more men workin' for you than you need. No sense in payin' me if you don't need me, is there?' He paused, then began speaking again, this time with emphasis. 'I could go now, Rose, an' you'd be rid of me. For good.'

For a few seconds she found herself caught in the golden web of his eyes, then she broke free. 'I don't know, Charlie.'

'But you'll have a word with Luke?'

She nodded. Taking one last look at the TT Racer, she turned and walked back towards the line of vardos.

Charlie called after her. 'Rose ... I meant to say—'

'Not now, Charlie. It's been a long day, I want to go to bed.'

As September drew on, things began to wind down at Funland. One morning, Luke left Rose and Cec in charge at the fairground, borrowed Percy Sayle's pushbike and set off for Eddie Kneale's garage.

When he got there, he found Doreen half-way

up a ladder, nailing back a piece of the wooden hoarding.

'It blew off in the night,' she explained through a mouthful of nails. 'Looks like the summer's really over.'

'Don't I know it,' said Luke. 'Funland's half empty.' He craned his neck to look up at her, hammering away furiously. It didn't seem right somehow, her doing the hard work and him just standing there watching. 'I could do that if you want,' he ventured.

'No need, I'm done now. Here, catch.' Doreen threw down the hammer and jumped down after it. 'I'm not helpless, you know,' she teased, dropping the last of the nails into the pocket of her baggy overalls.

'I never said you was!' protested Luke. 'I just thought—'

'It was kind of you to offer,' said Doreen. Her sun-browned cheeks dimpled as she smiled at him; her eyes were smiling too. 'It's nice to be treated like a lady sometimes.' She took the hammer and dropped it into her toolbox. 'So—come to see Dad have you?'

'He said he might have a bit of work for me today.'

'Oh. Right. Well, he'll be out in a mo, he's just doing something out back. I can go and get him for you now if you like ...'

She made as if to go into the garage, but Luke touched her arm.

'No. Least, not yet. I ... er, wondered if I could have a quiet word. You know, just between you an' me an' the gatepost.'

'With me?' Doreen's eyes twinkled mischievously. She wriggled her hands into her overalls' pockets. 'Go on then, spit it out. Sounds fascinating.'

Luke looked into Doreen's happy, open face and wished this didn't feel so uncomfortably like a betrayal. 'You know the other week, when you let me have a go on your Norton?'

'Don't tell me you've caught the bug and you want to take her for another spin?'

'Sort of ... Not exactly.' Luke was finding this more difficult than he'd expected. 'I was sort of wonderin' ... if you could maybe let me have the lend of a bike now an' then.'

'Lend you a bike?'

'Nothin' special, not like your Norton. Just somethin' ... anythin' that goes, really.'

Doreen cocked her head on one side. Luke could almost see her thoughts ticking over. 'Luke ... *why* do you want to borrow a bike—all of a sudden?'

Luke stared into the distance over her shoulder, unable to look her straight in the eyes. 'Just ... you know, for a bit of practice.' That, at least, was true as far as it went.

'Well, I'm sure we've got something lying around the yard, an old BSA or something you could put back together. Dad wouldn't mind you borrowing it. I suppose you could keep it at the fairground and use it to get round the Island—'

'At Funland!' Panic gripped him. 'God, no.'

Doreen looked puzzled. 'Why not?'

'Doreen, you don't understand. Rose ... I sort of didn't ...'

'Ah.'

He could tell that Doreen thought she'd hit on the answer. 'You've not told Rose?'

'No.'

'But I thought ... I thought you weren't going to ride again, because of Rose.'

'I wasn't.' Shame weighed Luke down, and yet what else could he do? If he told Rose now, she'd refuse to let him ride for Verney, and then how in God's name would they scratch a living next season? Once it was too late for her to kick up a fuss, that's when he'd tell her. In the end, she'd be grateful to him. 'But somethin's come up. I've got me reasons, Doreen, I can't say more'n that.'

'Reasons. Oh.'

He could see that Doreen was disappointed he wouldn't tell her more. 'I can't tell you. I would if I could. But I'm doin' this for Rose's sake.'

'Well ...'

'Look, Doreen, I'd never do anythin' to hurt Rose, you know I wouldn't. What I'm doin', it's for her an' Ellie, I swear.'

'Still, you ought to tell her. If you made a promise—'

'I *will* tell her, when the time's right. I just need this one favour. Please, Doreen.'

For a moment he thought she was going to turn him down flat. Then her cheeks dimpled again.

'Well, I don't suppose it'll do any harm. I'll see what I can do.'

'Thanks, Doreen.' He would have hugged her if he'd dared. 'But, Doreen ...'

'Don't say it. You want me to keep my mouth shut and not blab to Rose, right?'

'Right. Just till I get round to tellin' her.'

'Don't fret, I can keep a secret. Just mind you don't crash that bike, all right? Or Rose'll have my guts for garters.'

You and me both, thought Luke.

From across the yard came a familiar voice. 'Doreen? Doreen, is Barton here yet?'

'He's here now, Dad,' she called back.

'Well send him over, I've got a job for him.'

Luke crossed the forecourt. The big double doors of the workshop were standing open, letting the low sunlight flood into the grimy interior. Eddie was standing over a shirt-sleeved youth who was dismantling the water-cooled engine of a DKW. The two men were so covered in muck and oil that they looked like a pair of Swanee Minstrels. Luke was more interested in the bike. It was a real beauty—a 1937 model unless he was very much mistaken. He could almost feel its power vibrating through him as he bent to take a better look at it.

'Glad you're here, Luke,' said Eddie. 'Just in time to get down to some work.'

'This what you want me to work on then, Mr Kneale?' Luke laid his hand on the chassis. If this was to be his first job, he'd have no complaints at all. It'd be a real pleasure working on this little lady.

Eddie chuckled. 'Not quite, lad. Wesley'll

manage the bike on his own. Won't you, son? Come with me, Luke, I'll show you what I've got in mind for you.'

Eddie led the way across the workshop, through the back door and out into a back yard. In the middle and almost filling it stood the biggest and ugliest lump of rusty iron Luke had ever seen.

'A *tractor?*'

He must have looked as miserable as he felt, because Eddie clapped him on the back and laughed. 'I don't normally take on agricultural work, but this fella belongs to a friend of mine, I said I'd sort it out as a favour.'

'Oh,' said Luke glumly. This was even worse than patching up the Chairoplanes.

'Come on, lad,' said Eddie. 'It may not be up to much, but a job's a job. And we've all got to start somewhere, haven't we?'

On most Saturday afternoons things would have been hectic at the fairground without Luke around; but with Verney running the TT Racer and there being so few late-summer visitors, Rose had plenty of time to notice that Ellie wasn't her usual self.

'Six balls, sir? That's fourpence. Ta very much.' Pocketing the money, she nudged Ellie in the ribs. 'Come on, Ellie love, you're supposed to be helpin'.'

Ellie slid grumpily off the barrel and dipped into it for six coloured balls. 'Here,' she sniffed, and promptly perched herself on the edge of the barrel again.

'You can't sit there.'

'Why not?'

' 'Cause you're in the way, that's why.'

'I'll go away an' play then,' pouted Ellie. 'I'm bored anyway.'

Rose looked at her, bemused. What on earth had got into the child? It wasn't like Ellie to be sulky and unhelpful. 'Oh no you won't. You'll stop here an' tell me what's the matter.'

'Nothin's the matter.'

'Don't give me that. Thanks miss. Nine balls—that's thrupence change.' She stepped aside and the balls whizzed past, flying satisfyingly wide of their target. Relenting, she crouched down so that she was on Ellie's level. 'You've been mardy with me all day. Come on, love,' she coaxed. 'Tell your mam what's up.'

Ellie's fingers twisted the patched skirt of her dress. 'You never said.'

'Said what?'

'You never said Lola was goin' away.'

So that was it. Rose felt a pang of guilt. 'Oh, Ellie.'

Ellie's golden eyes fixed on hers accusingly. 'You never said. You could've said.'

'I'm sorry, I was goin' to.' Sometime, she told herself. Sometime, when I've got used to the idea myself. 'Who told you?'

'Uncle Charlie. Why's he goin' away, Mam? I like Uncle Charlie.'

Uncle Charlie, thought Rose. The word was like a knife twisting in her heart. Thank God he was going away now, before Ellie got even closer to him and—God forbid—found out the truth. Go away, Charlie, she pleaded silently. Go, and take away this fear that you've put in my heart.

'He's got a job,' she said. 'There's no more work for him here, that's why he's goin'.'

'But Lola could stay here with us,' whined Ellie. 'She could, couldn't she?'

'No, Ellie, she couldn't. An' that's the last I want to hear about it. Sixpence, ninepence, an' that makes a shillin' ... Oh!' As she turned from giving the man his change she backed right into someone behind her—a sharply dressed young man with a thin face, reddish hair and a slender. pointed nose.

'Sorry,' he said, stepping smartly out of her way. 'Didn't mean to startle you. Only I heard you was lookin' for me.'

'Sean!' Rose nearly dropped the balls she was carrying. She fumbled with her money-pouch, took it off and thrust it at Ellie. 'Ellie love, you take over. Just for a few minutes.'

'But, Mam—'

'You heard. Your mam's got somethin' important to talk about with Mister Rourke. Come with me, Sean.' She led him out of the booth and round to the back, where there weren't quite so many folk to pry into her business. Behind her head, balls thudded against the other side of the plywood wall. 'Sean, I'm glad you've come. I never had a chance to say sorry. The way we treated you ... it was wrong.'

'I daresay you did what you thought was right,' said Sean. 'But I never lied to you, nor stole from you neither.'

'No. I know that now.' Rose's head teemed with words she wanted to say, but it was so difficult to arrange them into something that made sense, the words that would make things right again. 'We found out who'd done it in the end—it was Peg. Turned out she had a grudge against us 'cause of somethin' old Walleye did.'

Sean whistled. 'Peg, eh? Well, I'd not have thought it meself, my money was on that little tart Dot Matthews.'

Rose managed a wry smile. 'Yeah, well, we had to sack her an' all. But not for thievin'. Look, Sean ... I'm sorry, we both are. I just wish I could turn back the clock.'

'Forget it. What's done's done, Rose. I never did see the point of bearin' grudges. So.' He took off his hat and leaned back against the wall of the booth. 'What did you want to see me about then?'

'We've sold the TT Racer.'

'So I heard. But you'll be stayin' on next year?'

'To tell the truth we've not much choice. There's nothin' for us to go back to Birkenhead for. Besides, everyone reckons we're goin' to go under, an' I don't want to give 'em the satisfaction.'

'You're a plucky one, Rose Barton. God knows, any man'd be glad to have a wife like you.' Sean's eyes crinkled with good humour. 'Just as well I'm not the marryin' kind, eh?'

Sean Rourke was a rogue, thought Rose, with more twists and turns than the Wiggley-Waggley, but a charming rogue for all that.

266

Perhaps she'd been wrong to take such an instant, irrational dislike to him.

'The thing is, Sean,' she went on. 'I was ... We were hopin' that you might come back an' work for us next season. We'll need someone with experience, an' you've worked the fairgrounds all your life ...' Even before she'd finished speaking, Rose could tell that he was going to turn her down.

'I can't say I'm not tempted,' he conceded.

'But the answer's no?'

'There's too much bad blood, Rose. I couldn't work here again—and anyhow, I've lost the taste for it. There's plenty of other ways to earn an honest penny.' His eyes twinkled at the word 'honest', and Rose thought of all the petrol coupons and ration books that had passed through Sean Rourke's hands. Whatever his latest enterprise was, it must be a paying proposition, to judge from that sharp new suit. 'I reckon it's for the best.'

'Well, if you're sure.' She thought of the envelope in the secret drawer, the envelope with Sean Rourke's name on it. 'Ellie can manage for a few minutes, we'd better go now.'

'Where to?'

'Back to the wagon, to get your money.'

'Wait.' Sean blocked her way. 'I don't want it—at least not right away.'

'But it's your share—'

'Look, Rose. I've seen what's been happening here. People tell me things. An' you said it yourself: no one knows fairgrounds better'n I do. You wouldn't have sold that TT Racer if you didn't need the money. Keep it.'

This sounded just plain crazy to Rose. 'How can I keep it? It's yours.'

'Tell you what.' Sean jammed his hat back on his head. 'I trust you. You look after it for me, eh?' He winked. 'See you around, Rose. I hope it all works out for you, I really do.'

CHAPTER 21

Rose wasn't having a very good day.

She was peeling potatoes in the vardo when the first clap of thunder rumbled in the sky overhead. A few seconds later the rain came, gently at first, then harder and harder until it was drumming like impatient fingers on the vardo's leaky roof. Yet *more* rain to keep the punters away. Why couldn't the sun keep shining for just one more week, to get them safely to the end of the season?

She went on peeling, impatient to get the task done in time to take over from Gracie in the pay booth. But then came a hammering on the vardo door and Lissa Darwell stuck her head inside.

'Them shirts yours, are they?'

'What shirts?'

'Them blue ones on the line over there.'

Rose dropped her half-peeled potato with a curse. 'Oh no, me washin'! I'd forgot all about it, Luke's shirts'll be wet through!' Grabbing the laundry basket, she clattered down the vardo steps into the teeming rain. It was pelting on to the ground so hard that the drops were bouncing up again ankle-high, and the baked earth was already softening here and there to form slippery patches of mud.

The washing line stretched between two fence-posts behind the vardo, with the bigger items like sheets and trousers stretched out on the hedge. She spotted Luke's work-shirts, dangling limply from the line. If she didn't get them in quickly they'd take days to dry.

Rose's fingers were so wet they could hardly grip the pegs; the rain was sluicing down over her face as though someone had turned on a garden hose. She shook her damp fringe out of her eyes but it slipped back down again, sticking to her forehead, and as she reached up to unpeg another shirt the last one slipped off her arm and landed front-down in the mud.

'Stupid weather, stupid washin'!' She snatched up the shirt and tried to rub off the mud, but it was gritty and wet, and all she did was make things worse.

As she threw the muddy garment into the washing basket she saw a man tramping over the tober towards her, head down, his jacket held aloft to keep off the rain. Rose couldn't see his face but she didn't need to. It was Charlie. And that was all she needed right now.

Hastily unpegging the last shirt and grabbing at a pair of trousers, she flung them into the basket. Perhaps she could get back into the vardo without him seeing her. She tugged at a sheet, but it was snagged on the hedge, and the more she pulled the more it stuck fast.

'Damn an' bloody blast!'

'Here, let me help,' offered Charlie, tossing his jacket on to one of the fence-posts.

'I'm fine.' She wrestled with the sheet but it was so tangled up that if she pulled any harder it would tear. 'I don't need any help.'

'Look, it's easy. Just lift up this corner an' ...' Charlie unhooked the corner of the sheet, gave it a little twist and the whole thing came away as though it was the easiest thing in the world. 'There you are.'

Rose shook the water out of her eyes, snatched the sheet, bundled it up and dropped it into the basket with a glare. A voice called gleefully from the window of Lissa Darwell's living-wagon: 'Got yourself a new char, Rose? Send him over here, he can scrub my floor any time!'

Rose resisted the temptation to shout back something sarcastic. She bent down to pick up the washing basket but Charlie got there first.

'Let me.'

She shrugged, turned and stomped off towards her wagon, Charlie following with the wet washing, clumping up the steps and putting down the basket on one of the benches.

'Not there! We have to sit there!' She took the basket and dumped it pointedly in the middle of the floor.

'Oh. Sorry.' Charlie was so crestfallen that Rose couldn't help smiling. He looked like a big wet teddy bear, his blond hair plastered flat to his scalp and raindrops glistening on a two-day growth of beard.

'No, I'm sorry. I didn't mean to snap, it's just ... just been one o' them days, know what I mean?' Wearily, she pushed the sodden hair back from her forehead, knowing she must look a sight but past caring. She shivered in her wet, clinging frock, longing for a hot bath in a big, deep tub in front of a roaring fire. 'It's cold for September,' she said. It was the first thing that came into her head.

'Er ... yeah. Yeah, it is.'

'D'you want a cuppa?'

Charlie took a deep breath. 'I've spoken to Luke. He says I can finish up today.'

'Today!'

Rose didn't know why the news came as such a thunderbolt. She'd known for a couple of weeks now that Charlie might leave at any time. In any case, he'd not have stayed around any longer than the end of the season. Maybe it just hadn't seemed a reality until now.

'I'm startin' the new job tomorrow. You know, deckhand on a cargo boat?'

'Y-yeah. Yeah, you said.' Rose's head was spinning. Forgetting all about the tea, she lowered herself on to one of the benches. 'So ... you're goin' away then? Tomorrow?'

'I'm crewin' on the *Rose Marie*. She's a Manx boat but she works away most of the time—you know: Liverpool, Barrow, Belfast, Ardrossan ...' Charlie's voice petered out. 'Don't worry, Rose. I'll not be botherin' you again.'

Rose looked up at him. 'An' Lola? What about her?'

'There's this school I'm sendin' her to ... she'll be fine.'

'Oh.' The word seemed to echo in the emptiness, the fairground strangely silent, the only accompaniment the drumming of rain on the vardo roof. 'Right.'

Charlie picked up his jacket from the floor. 'I'll be on my way then. I ... I just wanted to thank you.'

'Thank me? What for?'

'When Luke offered me the job here—you could've said no.'

Rainwater dripped down Rose's neck and back from the rat's tails of her hair, but her skin felt so cold and clammy already that she hardly noticed it. 'You needed the money,' she said simply.

'But you could've said no,' Charlie repeated. 'An' I'd've gone, there an' then, no argument.'

She saw from the look in his eyes that he was sincere.

'I know it's not been easy for you, Rose ...'

Easy? she thought. Far from it. Sometimes it's been hell on earth being near you again, Charlie Cartwright, living from each day to the next in fear of something terrible happening, something that would hurt Luke terribly and turn all our lives upside-down.

But nothing terrible had happened, had it? Nothing at all. Charlie might have done wrong in the past, but this time he had kept his promise to her.

'What's done's done,' said Rose. 'There's no point draggin' it up again, is there?' She got up and placed the kettle on the hob. 'You want that cup of tea then?'

Charlie shook his head. 'Lola's waitin' for me.'

'Best go then.' Please go, Rose willed him. Leave, before this calm, dull emptiness inside me turns to something else, something I might not be able to control.

'Tell Luke ... thanks. An' ...' Charlie paused. 'You ... you'll say goodbye to Ellie for me? She's a good kid.'

That look said it all. He really does know everything, thought Rose; and yet he's kept his mouth shut—for her sake, or for mine, or for his own, who can say?

'I'll ... tell her.'

The wagon door thudded shut behind Charlie, and Rose heard his boots clumping down the steps. Then he was gone. Outside, the rain was pelting down more heavily than ever, and it was dripping on to the vardo floor through half a dozen tiny holes in the roof.

Rose sat very still and silent for a few minutes, the half-peeled potato lying forgotten on the table. Then the kettle sang on the stove, and she got up to drag it off the hob. But she didn't make the pot of tea she'd promised herself. Instead, she knelt down by the old oak chest, pulled out the bottom drawer filled with folded sheets and pillowcases, and set it to one side. She reached into the cavity where the drawer had been. Right at the back, so far back that she had to stretch to reach it, was a faded old matchbox.

At last she managed to get hold of it and pull it out. How many years was it since she'd looked inside that little box? The best part of a decade. So why open it now? Why keep it at all? And why hide it where no one else would think of looking? Her hands shook as she opened the lid and tipped the contents into the palm of her hand.

It was a cheap brooch. A bit of old tin plate, stamped into the shape of a bunch of flowers and inscribed with the words 'FORGET ME NOT'. A scrap of nothing, worthless and tawdry.

But as she touched it and remembered, the tears in her eyes brimmed over and trickled softly down her rain-washed cheeks. She knelt there for a long time, just staring at the trinket in her hands, not really knowing why.

She didn't even know why she was crying.

For the last day of the season at least, the sun decided to shine on Douglas. It blazed out of a cloudless sky, and nobody seemed to care much that a chill breeze was lashing Onchan Head, whipping the dead leaves and chip-wrappers into miniature tornadoes. Today was the last day of summer, the last chance for fun before everything closed down and the Island began the slow, grey decline towards winter.

Rose crossed the tober with a tray of tea-mugs, dodging a group of junior Red Indians as they raced by, pursued by a mongrel dog with a ruffle round its neck, and sidestepping a quartet of fisher-lads, well-oiled already at two in the afternoon. Horace Spence might not like throwing his money around, but today he had really pushed the boat out. Fancy-dress parades, clowns, acrobats, minstrel shows, the Douglas Town Band ... He'd turned Funland into a giant carnival. Spence had even persuaded those showmen who'd been planning to head back early to the mainland to stay right to the end. And it was paying off: the punters had turned out in force.

Rose stopped off at Knock the Lady out of Bed, and handed Terry two mugs of tea. 'One for you an' one for Gracie. How's it goin'?'

'It's going great, Mrs B,' enthused Terry. He patted his money-pouch. 'Had to ban a couple of lads, mind, for getting too good at it.' He grinned at Gracie, who was climbing back into the bed for the umpteenth time, and waved. 'Gracie's got bruises all over her backsi—'

'Shut your cakehole, Terry!' Gracie gave him the evil eye as she slid back under the bedspread. A couple of youths standing around winked and whistled.

'Come on, lads,' laughed Rose. 'Stop gawpin' an' put your hands in your pockets!'

She carried on, past stilt-walkers and the elephant that Spence had magicked up from somewhere, and ducked under a sagging banner that read: 'FUNLAND REOPENS EASTER 1947: SEE YOU NEXT YEAR!'

Ellie was with Mario on the coconut shy, handing out the balls while he counted the change. She thinks she's so grown up, thought Rose with a smile—bossing everyone around,

275

same as I did when I was her age. Poor Mario doesn't know if he's coming or going.

'You like to play, Signora?' Mario asked a passing girl. 'Is very good game, very nice prize ...'

'They're real pottery, them dogs,' piped up Ellie. 'Go on, missus, have a go.'

'Tea up, Mario,' Rose called, handing him a big tin mug. Ellie insisted on having hers in a pint mug too, though she'd hardly manage to drink half of it. It was the principle of the thing. 'How's business?'

'Is very good, very fine,' beamed Mario. 'I always do well with my Signorina Ellie, she plenty clever girl, no?'

'She's a good girl.' Rose nodded. 'Likes to help her mam an' dad. Don't you, love?'

Ellie beamed. There was nothing she liked better than being helpful. Rose was pleased for her. She'd thought Ellie might take it very badly, Lola going away like that, but she'd soon perked up and she and Billy Darwell were thick as thieves again.

There were just three mugs left: one for Cec, one for Rose and one for Luke. She carried the tray across to the Chairoplanes, waiting for Luke to jump down off the staging and Cec to take his place. She marvelled at the way such a big, burly bloke could jump up on to the moving platform with a mug of tea in his fist and never once spill a drop.

Luke drank half his tea down in a single massive gulp, wiping his hand across his mouth with a long gasp of satisfaction.

'Heck, Rose, I needed that.' He kissed the top of her head and gave her a quick hug. 'You're a mind-reader.' He surveyed the teeming fairground. 'Plenty in today.'

'That's 'cause it's stopped rainin'.'

'Yeah. Pity it chucked it down all last week, we'd've been quids in. Still, could be worse eh? How's the vardo?'

Rose pulled a face. The continuous rain had leaked right through the wagon's roof, and they'd had to borrow buckets and bowls to put under the drips. 'Dryin' out. No thanks to Percy's roofin' felt—I knew it was useless the minute I set eyes on it.'

'Still, he meant well.'

Rose laughed. 'Percy *always* means well.' She stretched in the sunshine, tipping back her head and closing her eyes to enjoy what might be summer's last swan-song. 'Anyhow, I can't wait till we get out of the vardo an' into a proper house for the winter.'

'A house?'

'Well, you know, a little cottage or somethin'. Now we've got Verney's money ... Did I tell you Doreen's seen one up for rent, in Onchan? It's ever so tiny, but ... Luke, are you listenin' to me?'

'What? Oh, yes, course I am.'

'Well? What do you think—about the cottage?'

To Rose's surprise, Luke didn't reply straight away. He just drained his mug and set it down on the tray.

'We'll see, Rose. Let's just wait an' see, eh?'

And Rose couldn't help thinking that there was

something Luke wasn't telling her. Something she really ought to know.

At last Manfri was beginning to relax. He hadn't heard a word from his contact since the telephone call, Luke had safely sold the TT Racer and settled Dan's debts, and as for Sofia ... Well, if Sofia still didn't agree with selling off the ride, at least she'd stopped locking him out of the bedroom.

He sat down at the kitchen table and watched Sofia bustling around. That rabbit he'd got off a *mush* in part payment for a new set of tyres smelt wonderful, particularly with a few carrots and a bit of onion and one of Sofia's inch-thick golden pie-crusts on the top. His mouth watered with anticipation as she dished up a portion and put it in front of him.

'Smells like a fine *drummer.*' He took a real big sniff, jabbed his fork into a chunk of meat and savoured it. It was soft as hedgehog and almost as tasty. Now he remembered what had made him fall for Sofia: her cooking. 'Aye, 'tis a fine pie all right. Sit yourself down, woman, take the weight off your feet.'

Sofia put an empty plate on the table, then sat down opposite Manfri. She wouldn't eat a morsel until he was finished; in her tribe it had been frowned on for the womenfolk to eat with the men, or even to use the same dishes. And since her daughters had married and moved away, she had grown accustomed to eating alone. To Sofia, the old ways would always be the best ways, even when they no longer made sense.

'Couple more tatties in that dish?' Manfri peered over his evening paper at the dish of potatoes. Dutifully but unsmilingly, Sofia picked up the serving fork. She was just spearing the second potato when a knock came at the front door. Manfri grunted through a mouthful of suet crust.

'If it's Jenkins about his van, tell him it'll be ready Friday.'

Sofia got up and went down the passage to the front door. The knocking came a second time, this time louder and more insistent.

'All right, all right, I'm comin', I'm comin'.'

The door opened. There were two men in raincoats standing on the doorstep, neither of them Tom Jenkins.

'Mrs Barton?' asked the older man, slipping his hand into his inside pocket.

'Who wants to know?'

Sofia looked from one to the other with the knowing suspicion of a true-born Romany. She didn't have to see what was written on the man's card to know what he was, she could smell it.

'Detective Sergeant Harrington, Birkenhead CID. This is DC Miles. Mr Barton home, is he?'

Sofia's mouth set in a thin, hard line, but her eyes were bright with alarm.

'Who is it?' called Manfri from the kitchen.

Sofia opened her mouth but didn't have a chance to say anything. The two policemen edged past her and headed straight for the sound of Manfri's voice. They found him still sitting at the kitchen table, a forkful of rabbit pie poised halfway between his plate and his mouth.

'Mister Barton?'

Sofia came marching into the kitchen, interposing her bulk between Manfri and the two detectives. 'It's the gavvers, Manfri! What you done, what you done?'

Manfri paled but calmly set down his fork.

'Quiet, woman. What you want with me?' he demanded.

The sergeant smiled with chilling politeness. 'Just a few questions, Mr Barton. To help us with our enquiries. You wouldn't mind coming down the police station with us, would you sir?'

Manfri looked at Sergeant Harrington's face and knew he was going, whether he minded or not.

CHAPTER 22

Rose stood at the top of the vardo steps and looked across the tober. It was only the second week of October, but to look at the barren emptiness of cracked concrete and trodden-down grass you'd never have believed it had been filled with noise and laughter such a short time ago.

Hardly any of the showmen and their families

remained. Some, like the Enfields and the Lees, had headed back across the Irish Sea to take up their old pitches at the charter fairs that filled the long gap between September and April: Pudsey Bonfire Fair, Wrexham Christmas Fair, Orrell Fair, Doncaster Gala Day ... The more affluent showmen, who could afford not to work over the winter, had gone off to comfortable winter quarters to enjoy the money they had made and paint up their rides for next season. The only ones who had chosen to sit the winter out on the Island were the locals, like Sid Christian and Percy Sayle, and those who couldn't afford to go back—like the Darwells and the Bartons.

Rose was beginning to feel very lonely and homesick, far more than she had done when they first came to the Island. Then, despite all the setbacks and disasters, there had been new things to discover and a long, busy summer to look forward to, a feeling that things could and would get better. It was only now, with Luke so often away at Kneale's yard and Ellie at school, that Rose was beginning to understand what it was to be alone. She was beginning to miss poor gormless Mario, and Gracie with her ridiculous hats and her mother's high-heeled shoes. At odd moments, she even found herself missing Charlie.

Still, there was plenty to keep her occupied— rounding boards to paint, canvas tilts to mend, tarpaulins to find. Everything must be ship-shape and weatherproof to get through the coming winter. Luke was doing his bit too, earning what money he could from Eddie

Kneale; she mustn't let him down.

Rose picked up the paint-pots, brush and an old scrap of rag, and walked across to the empty dukkering booth. Away to her left, Jack Verney's men were dismantling the TT Racer, shouts and crashes of metal on wood cutting through the air as they took down the swifts and quarterings. Some of the wood looked like it needed replacing. She turned aside, reminding herself that the TT Racer was Verney's concern now, not hers. Setting down the paint-pots, she dipped her brush into the red and started painting out the yellow and gold letters that read: 'MADAME PEG PETULENGRO—GYPSY FORTUNE TELLER'. It was high time they got rid of that last embarrassing reminder, thought Rose, irritated that Old Peg had got off scot-free. She had simply headed off to her old haunt on Douglas Head and set up another dukkering business in the heart of 'Little Egypt'.

'Hello, missus,' chirped Billy Darwell, passing by with Little Davey and his big sister Lalla, their arms piled high with sticks and old tin cans.

'Billy,' returned Rose, glancing warily at the boy.

'You missed a bit,' piped up Billy helpfully. He stuck a jammy index finger into the middle of the section Rose had just finished. 'There.'

Rose heaved an exasperated sigh and swiped the brush across Billy Darwell's fingerprints.

'Will you leave that!' snapped Lalla, taking a swipe at her brother's head with her free

282

hand. She's turning out just like her mam, thought Rose.

But Billy was wise to his sister's tricks—he just ducked and stuck out his tongue. 'I were only helpin'.' Several of the sticks he was carrying tumbled out of his arms and fell to the ground, one landing in the yellow paint and splashing it all over the red. Rose's patience finally snapped.

'Billy Darwell! Will you just get out of that paint an' stay out! An' why aren't you at school?'

The Darwell kids seemed to think this was the funniest thing they'd ever heard.

'School!' sniggered Billy.

'Don't go ter school,' echoed Little Davey, exploring the black paint with the toe of his shoe.

'Dad don't like us goin' to school,' explained fourteen-year-old Lalla, shifting her bundle of sticks so that it rested on her well-developed bosom. 'What's the point of school when you can go out an' earn money?'

Lissa Darwell came marching up like a stormtrooper, sleeves rolled up above her scaly red elbows and her lips pursed under a slash of crimson lipstick.

'This lot botherin' you are they, Rose?' she demanded, administering a swift cuff to Billy's ear before he had a chance to get out of the way.

'Well ...' Rose weighed up the consequences of saying yes. She knew what Ranty Darwell was like with the belt when he'd had a few down the Manx Arms.

'God help me, I've tried to knock some sense into the little blighters. I've tried an' tried an' tried, an' do they listen? Do they hell.' Lissa glared at her three offspring with a kind of self-righteous indignation that Rose found rather difficult to stomach. After all, everyone in Douglas must know by now that Lissa spent most evenings hanging round pubs in the inner harbour, picking up sailors. However much she might love her kids in her own way, she was hardly the model parent.

'Well, you know what kids are like,' said Rose. 'Always gettin' into trouble. No harm done, eh?'

Lissa sniffed. 'S'pose. If you say so.' She jerked her thumb towards the Darwells' trailer caravan. 'You lot. Move.'

The three kids trailed off towards the wagon, Billy and Davey leaving a straggly trail of sticks and bits of old iron.

'Bloody useless,' snorted Lissa, arms folded combatively over her chest.

Rose wiped a speck of paint off her nose and went on painting. 'So what're they up to with all them sticks an' stuff?'

'Collectin' stuff to make clothes pegs, aren't they?'

'What, out of old cans?'

'Your Luke a Romany, an' you don't know how to make a clothes peg?' Lissa laughed. 'You all right, are you?'

'Why?'

'Oh, nothin'. You just look down in the mouth, that's all.' Her voice, with its distinctively harsh rasp, softened slightly. 'Your Luke gone off again?'

'He's got a bit of work on.'

'All on yer own then.' It wasn't a question, and Lissa didn't wait for an answer. 'I gets down sometimes when my Ranty's off round the horse-fairs. He's a big, good-fer-nothin' lump, but I miss him. Tell you what'll cheer you up: a nice cuppa. You come over my van an' I'll put the *kavi* on the *saster*, like my old mam used to say.'

Surprised by this unexpected show of kindness, Rose found herself warming to Lissa Darwell. 'I ought to finish this first, so's it's ready when Luke gets back.'

'Five minutes won't do no harm.'

Rose was snapping the lid back on the paint tin when the car came in through the main gates—a big black saloon, shiny and important-looking. And on the roof, spelled out on a black and white sign, was the word 'POLICE'.

'Looks like the gavvers want a word with the Big Fella,' commented Lissa. ' 'Bout bloody time too.'

But the car didn't go down the track that led to Horace Spence's office. It took a left turn, swinging past the roller-coaster and heading towards the depleted line of vardos that cowered in the shelter of the hedge.

'Gawd help us.'

The wind had gone right out of Lissa Darwell's sails, and she shrank back against the booth, as if the police wouldn't make out her pink and blue dress against the red and yellow paintwork.

285

Rose saw her face sag, the skin wilting over the bones, as though this visitation was something inevitable that she had been dreading for too long. What on earth had Ranty Darwell been up to this time? The worst he'd been had up for in the past was brawling in Strand Street but Ranty was the sort of man who seemed to attract policemen like a magnet.

It was Rose's turn to be shocked as the police car slowed and came to a halt.

'That's not my vardo,' gasped Lissa. 'It's yours! Look, he's knockin' on your door!'

But Rose didn't need her to point it out. She was already hurrying across to the van, half-walking, half-running, the paintbrush still dripping threads of red paint as she ran. There were two men in dark raincoats, one standing by the car, the other on the steps, knocking on the vardo door. Plain-clothes policemen.

Dreadful imaginings raced through her mind, but none of them made any sense. There had to be some mistake.

'What is it?' she demanded. 'What d'you want?'

The man on the top step directed his attention to her.

'Mrs Barton?' The two words were enough to tell Rose that he wasn't Manx; if she wasn't very much mistaken he was from Birkenhead. 'Wife of Luke Barton?'

Her throat tightened. 'Y-yes. W-why?'

'Have you any idea where we can find Mister Barton?' The tone was courteous, respectful even, but the eyes were gimlet-hard. 'Only

286

we've got one or two questions we'd like to ask him.'

'Here y'are, mate. Room service an' all mod cons.' The warder's bunch of keys rattled ominously as he unlocked the cell door. Manfri hesitated on the threshold, his pathetic bundle of grey blanket and tin mug clutched before him, so the screw gave him an impatient nudge in the small of his back. 'Go on, get in, I haven't got all day.'

The door had clanged shut behind Manfri before he'd even realised where he was.

He was standing in a little square cell, just big enough to fit an iron-framed bunk bed in. Apart from a small wooden table, a chair and a chamber pot, there wasn't much else to look at except for row upon row of grey-green, cracked tiles. The overpowering smells of disinfectant and stale urine made his stomach heave, and sweat began to prickle on the nape of his neck as the feeling of claustrophobia began to close in upon him. This was the worst thing that could happen to a traveller: to be locked up in a tiny, windowless box, without so much as a glimpse of sky to remind him of the freedom behind the walls.

He stood in the middle of the cell, stupefied, his heart thumping. At first he thought he was alone, then the bundle of rags on the top bunk moved, rolled over and revealed a pus-laden face.

'Welcome to the Birkenhead Ritz.'

Manfri started. The bloke with the cropped

287

black hair and the skin disease leered down at him and burst out laughing.

'Not used to all this, are you? Well, you'd better get used to it, Barton—from what I've heard you're in for a long stretch.'

Manfri threw his blanket and mug on to the bottom bunk and sat down. 'How d'you know my name?'

'I just do. Pays not to ask too many questions in this place, know what I mean?' The bloke swung his legs over the side of the bunk and dropped down. 'Got any smokes?'

'No.'

'Get some. You'll need 'em to pay your way in here.'

Manfri shrank away from the stranger, his prison-issue uniform foul and stinking. 'I'm not stayin' in here, I'm only on remand. After the trial ... after the trial they'll let me go free. I'm innocent.'

'We're all bloody innocent, mate,' grinned the stranger. 'This place is crawlin' with the scum of the earth, but you'd reckon they were all fuckin' saints to 'ear 'em talk.'

'You've got me wrong,' protested Manfri, but it was no use lying, least of all to himself. He slumped forward, hands on knees, head hanging down. 'Oh God ...'

'You've bin a naughty boy, ain't you, Barton?' The stranger helped himself to Manfri's bar of soap and slipped it into his own pocket. 'By way of a fee for some friendly advice,' he grinned. 'Listen to me, Barton, there's things you ought to know. Ways of doin' things.'

'I've already decided what I'm goin' to do,' declared Manfri. 'Next time I talk to the police I'm goin' to tell the truth, tell them everythin'. When the judge hears what happened, why I did it, maybe I'll get off easy, he'll let me go home ...'

'Listen, mate.' This time the stranger's voice was harder, much harder. 'If you're smart you'll keep schtum, right? Take the blame an' do your time like a good boy.'

'But ...' Manfri gazed into his cellmate's face, suddenly very uneasy at the stranger's cold-eyed stare. 'But why should I take all the blame? All I did was ring a few motors. The boss, the man at the top, he should pay.'

The stranger shook his head and tutted. 'Not a quick learner are you, Barton? Listen. You got family on the outside, right?'

'A ... a wife. Two sons, couple of daughters.'

'You want 'em kept safe?'

A horrible chill crawled up the back of Manfri's neck. Now he understood what this man was saying, and he wasn't sure he wanted to understand.

'Please ...' he began. But the cell door was unlocking and the warder was back.

'You.' The warder beckoned to Manfri's cellmate. 'Get your things an' come. You're movin' cells.'

The stranger rolled his few bits and pieces into his blanket, picked it up and walked across to the door. Looking back over his shoulder he fixed Manfri with that same cold, hard look.

'Think about it, mate.'

289

'Get a move on,' grunted the warder, nudging him out of the cell with the toe of his boot.

'Think about it, Barton, it's the best advice you'll get.'

Then the cell door slammed shut again, and Manfri Barton was left alone with little else to do but think.

Luke was eating his sandwiches with Doreen and Wesley, Eddie's apprentice, when the police car rolled up the Peel road, gliding to a halt on the forecourt.

Having a police car outside his garage was enough of an event for Eddie Kneale to emerge from the office, pen stuck behind his ear, half-drunk mug of tea in his fist. He looked round the semicircle of faces. Luke could feel the question implicit in Eddie's expression; it said, 'I've done nothing to be ashamed of, the question is, have you?'

'What's all this then?' Eddie enquired calmly as the two policemen got out of the car. One was PC Deacon, the village copper, the other a stranger, a plain-clothes detective whose face had a weather-beaten, faintly lopsided quality that made him look more like a prizefighter.

'Eddie.' PC Deacon nodded an amiable greeting. 'Nothing for you to worry about. Sergeant Hawthorne just wants to ask a few questions.'

'Which one of you's Luke Barton?'

The Detective Sergeant's tone wasn't particularly hostile, but it chilled Luke to the bone. That old familiar feeling of guilt took hold of him, the irrational feeling that every Romany had because, although you might not have done anything wrong, you were a dirty gyppo and that was enough to pronounce you guilty in most gavvers' books.

'I am.' He stood up, crumbs falling from his overalls. Doreen looked up at him, concern showing on her face; Wesley just gawped like the fifteen-year-old boy he was, mouth hanging open and still chewing like a cement mixer.

'Right then, Mister Barton. Got somewhere private, have you? Where we could have a quiet word?'

Eddie Kneale nodded in the direction of the office. 'You can go in there if you want.'

Luke felt all eyes on him as he followed the detective and the PC into Eddie's office; and it wasn't a pleasant sensation. What were they thinking about him? What the hell was this all about?

The door closed, and Luke found himself face to face with the two policemen.

'Sergeant Hawthorne, Birkenhead CID.'

'Birkenhead?' Luke frowned. 'What are you doin' over here?'

'Mechanic are you, son?'

Wasn't it bloody obvious? Luke felt irritation burning inside him. Why did every question have to be answered by another question?

'Yes,' he said quietly.

'Know a bit about cars do you?'

Luke had to fight the revulsion he felt towards everything connected with the police. No sense in losing his temper and causing trouble—after

291

all, he'd done nothing wrong. 'I should do. I've been in the business long enough.'

'And where did you work before you came to the Island?'

Luke wished to hell he could see where this line of questioning was taking him; his innate suspicion warned him that they might be trying to trick him somehow, make him trap himself with a slip of the tongue. 'In Birkenhead, for me dad. He has this business repairin' cars. Look, I've answered enough questions. What's this all about?'

PC Deacon exchanged an edgy look with the sergeant, who nodded curtly.

'It's about your dad, son,' said the PC, in the sort of voice that could only presage bad news.

'What about him?' All of Luke's bad feelings melded together into one black, leaden ball in the pit of his stomach. 'What's happened to him? He's not ...?'

'He's been arrested,' said the PC, as gently as he could under the circumstances. 'For ringing cars.'

'What!' The impossibility of it hit Luke full-on, so hard he almost burst out laughing. It just couldn't be true.

'Gangs have been nicking cars and selling them on round Birkenhead for over a year,' said the sergeant, his voice tinged with a kind of clinical satisfaction. 'Unpleasant business. Seems your dad's got himself mixed up in it.'

'No!' exclaimed Luke, too stunned even to be angry at this moment. 'Dad? Dad ... he *wouldn't,* he just wouldn't.' He searched the two policemen's faces, appealing to their common sense, half-convinced that any moment now they would laugh and tell him it had all been some cruel practical joke. But they were almost expressionless.

'He's confessed,' said the sergeant. 'Insists he was working alone. Course, we know he couldn't have been. He's protecting someone.'

'You've got the wrong bloke,' Luke growled.

The sergeant smiled. 'No, Mr Barton, I don't think we have.'

The gimlet eyes bored into Luke's and, all of a sudden, it dawned on him. They weren't just accusing his dad, they were implying that he had something to do with it too.

As if that wasn't bad enough, over the sergeant's shoulder Luke could see Eddie Kneale, standing gazing towards the office door. And the look of suspicion on Eddie's face was the worst thing of all.

The warder ushered Manfri into a huge, cavernous room, empty except for a small square table and two chairs in the centre. 'Ready?'

Manfri nodded glumly. He wouldn't ever be ready, not to let Sofia see him like this, but she would have to see him sometime and there were things he had to explain to her.

The door opened and he saw her, her face red and puffy from crying, her dark eyes glittering dully from between swollen lids. The moment she spotted him she dissolved into tears, just as Manfri had known she would.

'Manfri! Manfri what they do to you? You're so thin ...'

'*Hush kacker,* Sofia, *hush kacker.*' He tried to put his arm round her but the warder shook his head.

'No touching. Hands on the table where I can see 'em.'

This seemed a terrible brutality to Manfri, but he sat down and Sofia subsided on to the chair opposite him, her occasional sniff the only sound in the room.

'When they lettin' you go, Manfri?'

The knife-blade of sorrow struck home. He felt as though all the guilt in the world rested on his shoulders.

'They're not lettin' me go home, they're puttin' me on trial.'

'But ... but you're innocent! They have a trial, *then* they send you home.'

Manfri let out a long, exhausted sigh. He forced himself to raise his head and look into his wife's eyes.

'I'm not innocent,' he said softly. 'I did it.'

Sofia's swollen eyes widened, the whites spidered with red veins. 'No!'

'Yes, Sofia, I did it. I'm guilty.' He paused, weighing up the best way to say it, finally deciding that there was no best way. 'I did it for Luke.'

The moment the words left his mouth he knew he could not have said a worse thing. The dullness of hurt in Sofia's eyes sharpened to the spark of anger.

'For Luke! You do this thing for *him*? For

this boy who is no longer my son?'

'Sofia—'

'For him!'

'It was the only way I could think of ... to get more money to help him an' Rose. He's our son, Sofia, I couldn't just let him go to the wall, could I?'

But he had lost her. That much was obvious. He had hoped he could win her over, make her understand, if he explained everything very calmly and slowly, repeated it over and over again until it sank in. But Sofia was already on her feet, screaming into his face.

'You bastard, you stupid *dinilo* bastard! You've ruined everythin', everythin' for *him!* This Luke is not my son, he is not my son, I hate him!'

Wrenching from her finger the heavy gold ring that had been passed down to brides through five generations of Manfri's tribe, she spat on it and threw it on the floor, grinding it into the tiles with the heel of her shoe.

'Take me out of here, I not stay.'

Then, without another word, she turned on her heel and stormed out.

CHAPTER 23

Manfri lay stretched out on the bed in his cell, staring up at the empty bunk above him, seeing nothing. A metallic swish and clunk startled him, and he turned his face towards the door.

'Two-three-one-seven-four?'

In the week since he had been here on remand, those numbers had engraved themselves in Manfri's mind. Automatically he responded, 'Yes, sir.'

'Smarten yourself up, you've got a visitor.'

A visitor? As Manfri got up and slid his feet into his laceless shoes, his flagging spirits rose a notch up the scale. Surely it couldn't be Sofia, not after the way she'd screamed at him on her last visit. Or could it? Was it possible that she'd relented and seen sense?

'Who is it?' he demanded as the warder clicked the cuffs round his wrists and locked the cell door behind him.

'How should I know? Just some woman—your old lady I 'spect.'

But it wasn't Sofia sitting at that square table in that big, empty, echoing room. It was a middle-aged woman with grey-streaked, red-brown hair, combed back from her face to reveal the strong, squarish contour of her jaw, the hazel eyes edged by fine lines that chronicled her hard-fought life. As the door opened she got to her feet and turned to face him, her fingers twisting the strap on her shapeless old handbag.

'Edie!' he gasped in astonishment. Knowing how Stan felt about Romanies in general and the Bartons in particular, just about the last people he expected to come anywhere near him were the Dobbses. You're a brave woman, Edie Dobbs, he thought to himself with more than a touch of respect.

'I had to come,' said Edie. 'For Rose's sake.'
She said the words awkwardly, as if she felt she
had to apologise for thinking only of her own.
Her eyes explored the room, lighting uneasily
on the stone-faced warder standing by the door.
'Does he ...?'

'He has to stay,' said Manfri, lowering himself
slowly and painfully on to one of the chairs. 'It's
rules.'

'Oh.' Edie sat down, her hands grasping the
top of her handbag as if it were the last relic
of normality in a crazy world. She took a
deep breath. 'There's things I need to know,
Manfri.'

'I've nothin' to hide,' replied Manfri. 'Not
any more.'

'My Rose ... I'm worried about her. All this
... it's a bad business, Manfri.' She fought for
the right words. 'I have to know. Is all this goin'
to hurt my Rose?'

Manfri shook his head. 'Nothin''ll touch her,
Edie.'

Edie's face looked grey and ill in the faint,
wintry light from the high window, the worry-
lines etched deep into her skin. 'You're sure?
How can you be sure?'

He had a curious impulse to take her hand
and hold it, just to make her see somehow that
he was sincere. But rules were rules, and he kept
his hands firmly to his own side of the table.

'This is all down to me. Luke never had
nothin' to do with the motors. I've kept him
an' Rose well out of it, Edie, I swear. Oh,
God, Edie, I'm sorry.' He rested his forehead on

297

his right hand, for the thousandth time asking himself why he had done this, why he had got himself into this mess and dragged these innocent people into it with him. 'I know it don't mean much, but ... but I only did it 'cause I wanted to help.'

'I know you did, it's just ...'

Manfri's eyes flicked up, surprised. Edie didn't exactly smile at him, but he recognised something in her expression—a softening, an understanding. Perhaps years of living with Stan Dobbs had taught her that things weren't always as black and white as you'd like them to be.

'If there'd been some other way ... I couldn't just let 'em go under, could I?'

Edie reached over and patted his hand. 'You did what you thought was best.'

'No touching, hands where I can see them,' barked the warder by the door. Edie drew back her hand quickly.

'But it weren't best,' sighed Manfri. 'That's the trouble. An' now look where I've got us all.'

'I'll not say what you've done was right,' said Edie slowly, 'but I'm grateful to you.'

'Grateful!'

'You've done what you could for Rose an' Luke; they'd have nothin' if you'd not helped 'em out.'

Manfri laughed humourlessly. 'Oh aye. An' they'd not have gone over there in the first place if it weren't for me. I wish to God I'd told Dan to sort out his own bloody mess.'

'We can't change what's done,' said Edie

simply. 'You tried to help, that's what matters.'

'Can't help 'em now though, can I? Stuck in 'ere, an' my Sofia refusin' to speak to me.'

'No, but maybe I can.' Edie got up, slipping her handbag over her arm. 'Your Luke'll be comin' over to see you, won't he?'

'I dare say, but Sofia won't have him in the house.'

'Well, I'll look out for him, see what I can do. He's family—it's only right.'

'You! What's your Stan goin' to say about that?'

Edie gave a grim smile. 'Nothin', if he knows what's good for him.'

Luke had only been away from Birkenhead for a few months, but he felt like a foreigner in his own town. Eyes followed him down the street whenever he set foot out of doors, curtains twitching, neighbours muttering comments under their breath but never saying anything to his face. But Luke didn't need to hear them to know that they were saying: 'There goes that gyppo lad; his dad's in jail, you know; bunch of crooks the lot of 'em.'

'Slept all right, did you, lad?' enquired Edie Dobbs, rolling up the blankets from the lumpy old sofa where Luke had spent the night. In places the ancient upholstery had worn clean away, revealing wiry tufts of horsehair and the odd rusty spring.

'Like a log, Mrs D,' he lied, not wanting to hurt Edie's feelings. She'd been kinder to him than he'd any right to expect, and he knew she

299

was sad not to have seen Rose and Ellie—but money was desperately tight; there was no way they could afford three boat fares.

'Wish we could do better for you,' remarked Edie regretfully.

'This is fine,' said Luke.

'Only the new lodger's got the spare room an' I can't really chuck him out, not with Stan sat on his backside day after day. We need the extra thirty bob a week. Fancy a bit of fried bread for your breakfast?'

Luke thought of Stan, who would already be sitting in the kitchen, glowering over the breakfast table like a malevolent gargoyle.

'No, ta. I'm not hungry.'

Edie started plumping up a cushion. 'If it's Stan, don't take no notice of him, he's just pig-bloody-ignorant that man.'

'It's not that, I'm just not hungry.' Luke pulled on his boots and started lacing them. 'Anyhow, I'm off out.'

'Goin' up to see your dad?'

'Later.' He picked up his jacket and put it on. 'Thanks, Edie. Be seein' you soon.'

He walked out through the back kitchen, forcing himself to say, 'Mornin', Stan,' as he passed. But Stan just grunted and went on listening to the wireless.

Out in the yard Luke began to breathe again. It might be ingratitude, but he could hardly bear to be inside the Dobbses' house, waiting for Stan to come out with yet another snide comment. Besides, there was something important he had to do, something that wanted sorting out once and for all. Head down, hands in pockets, he set off down the street.

Ferry Street hadn't changed much. The same kids were kicking a deflated football around, belting it at the space between two chalked goalposts on the side wall of the chapel; the milkman's skewbald horse was still ambling placidly along the kerb. But something *was* different. Maybe it was Luke himself—he'd learned some hard lessons these last few months.

Turning down the side entry he walked round to the back gate. It snicked open and he stepped into the yard, with all its familiar sights and smells. Dan's pushbike still stood propped up against the outside lavvy, kept exactly where he'd left it like a holy relic, and probably rusted to the spot by now. A line of hutches still stretched along the side wall, a couple of ferrets sticking their snouts through the mesh to look at Luke as he passed by.

Picking his way between the bits of old scrap iron, Luke headed for the back steps. But that was as far as he got. The door opened and a dark-haired woman in a blue pinafore stepped out, barring his way.

'Sara!' Luke's jaw dropped as he saw his younger sister. As kids, Sara had been Dan's favourite and Sofia's spoilt pet; there'd never been much love lost between her and Luke. 'What you doin' here?'

'Lookin' after Mam, what d'you think?' Sara tossed her long black hair. 'Don't know why you've turned up here.'

'I've come to see Mam.'

'She don't want to see you.'

'Then she can tell me that herself.' He tried to dodge past Sara but she wouldn't budge.

'It's no good, Luke, she won't have it. Why don't you just go?'

Luke stood his ground, determined not to be fobbed off this time. 'Tell her I'm here, Sara.'

Sara's mouth set in a hard line. 'No. I won't have you upsettin' her, you've upset her enough already.'

This was more than Luke could stomach.

'Me! What am *I* supposed to have done?' His voice rose to a shout, and the old gossip in the house next door peered over the wall to get a better view. 'It's Dad who's in prison, not me!'

'Enough!' Sofia Barton emerged from the back kitchen, her normally rosy cheeks haggard, the long braid of salt-and-pepper hair hanging in a ragged rope over one shoulder. Only her eyes were full of life, and it was a vicious, resentful life that glinted hard as a black diamond. Her lip curled. 'You.'

'Mam,' said Luke quietly, 'can I come in? I only want to talk to you.'

'You're not wanted here,' replied Sofia coldly. 'I won't talk to you.'

'But, Mam ...' The look of triumph on his sister's face only added to Luke's exasperation. 'Mam, this is stupid ... You're me mam, I only want to make sure you're all right.'

'You're no son of mine.' Sofia's whole body seemed rigid with cold fury. 'You understand? You steal from me, you sell my rides, my Dan's

302

inheritance!' Every word flew to the target like a well-aimed crossbow bolt. Anger and pain mingled in Luke's heart.

'I never stole from you, Dan stole from you! It's Dan who threw all his money away, Dan who got into debt, not me!'

'Liar!' Sofia spat like a cornered cat. Luke saw the pain behind the anger in her eyes; but why should he pity her when all she could offer him was hate?

'Me an' Rose have been workin' all year for pennies, just to save them rides. Dan'd have nothin' if it wasn't for us!'

'Liar, liar!'

'Mam, will you listen to me? Will you?'

Sofia raised her hand, trembling, her finger pointing at the gate. 'Go—get out! Your father, he is in prison, because of you!' Her voice grew dangerously quiet. 'Your twin brother, he died because of you—why didn't you die instead?'

There was a quarter-century of pain and resentment in Sofia's words. This question was almost a curse. The words vibrated through Luke's body and for the first time he realised the real depth of his mother's crazy loathing. All these years, perhaps from the very moment of his birth, she had blamed him for his elder twin's death, strangled by the umbilical cord about his throat.

'Go!' echoed his sister. 'Just go away an' leave your mother alone, you an' your *gorgio* woman. You're not one of us now.'

Luke hesitated for a few seconds, caught between the desire to get away and the burning need to get through to his mother. Then he turned on his heel and walked away without a word, leaving the back gate swinging on its one rusted hinge.

He walked aimlessly for half an hour, maybe longer, hardly aware of where he was or what he was doing. His mind was reeling, his body shaking with unresolved anger. Never in his whole life had he felt so alien, so cut off from everyone and everything, so powerless to make things go the way he wanted them to go. All this time he had done his duty, done what other people wanted him to do, and how did they repay him? With hatred.

When he finally came to his senses he found himself in the back lane leading to the bombsite where his father's garage stood. A terrible, sharp-toothed need gnawed at Luke's guts. Somewhere in that garage, safely stored because he had never had the heart to get rid of it, was his old motor bike. Without wanting to, without even trying, he could picture it in its every detail: black body work and shiny chrome, the engine waiting faithfully for its master to make it growl back into fierce life.

He had to get the bike out and ride. It was the only thing that could exorcise the rage and pain and frustration inside him. His footsteps quickened as the tension rose in his belly. Already he was anticipating the smell of old leather, the exhilaration, the speed so great that it left no room to think or feel anything else.

But even this was denied him. As he reached

the bomb-site, he saw that the police had been there before him. The wooden shed stood locked and boarded, a padlock and chain on the double doors, and a crudely painted sign hanging crookedly above: 'POLICE: KEEP OUT'.

'No!' In his impotent rage, Luke crashed his fist again and again against the door, making the chain rattle like dead men's bones. 'No, no, no!'

But it was no use, and finally he gave up, his chest heaving as he fell spreadeagled against the locked garage doors, one arm still outstretched in a clenched fist.

Oh, Rose, why can't you be here with me? he whispered soundlessly. Where are you when I need you to make the bad spirits go away? And it was almost as if he could feel the black *muladi* of his dead twin brother, perched on his shoulder, mocking him.

CHAPTER 24

October mists and November gales gave way to the fine, penetrating drizzle of early December. This had not been a good autumn for the Bartons, Rose mused, and winter didn't look like being any better. Only Luke's occasional work at Kneale's yard was keeping the wolf from the door. There'd be no cosy winter quarters this year, no little cottage for the Bartons, only Walleye's draughty old vardo.

The copy of the *Birkenhead News* Edie had sent lay in a crumpled ball on the floor of the vardo where Luke had thrown it. Rose stooped to retrieve it and as she did so the headline caught her eye again: 'GYPSY SENTENCED: 18 MONTHS' HARD LABOUR'. Above the words, a photograph of a hollow-eyed Manfri stared out. It was the look of a hunted animal. No wonder Luke had taken it so badly. It had hurt Rose, and it must have hurt him so much more. At night she felt him tossing and turning in the bed beside her, heard him mumbling in his sleep as the bad dreams returned to torment him. But her love seemed powerless to chase the dark shadows away, and Luke wouldn't even tell her how he felt any more. He just bottled everything up and pretended there was nothing wrong.

And there was plenty wrong, thought Rose, unfolding the greaseproof paper with the two meagre ounces of corned beef she'd queued for an hour to get. It wasn't just that Horace Spence seemed to take a particular delight in baiting Luke, or that people gossiped about them behind their backs; it was the drab, unremitting struggle just to get by.

A struggle that wasn't going to get any easier. All that money wasted on Luke's trip to Birkenhead—and it hadn't helped anyone or anything. In fact, things were worse than ever.

'Luke, love ...' she ventured.

Luke, stretched out on the bench, stirred and opened his eyes. 'Hmm?'

'Sorry to wake you love, there's somethin' ...'

She swallowed, a lump of trepidation rising in her throat. 'I've got somethin' to tell you.'

Luke yawned and shook himself awake, exhaustion sitting on his eyelid and dragging it down. Long days at the garage and sleepless nights were taking their toll on him, thought Rose. And now this ...

Luke raised himself on one elbow. Without his eyepatch, the left side of his face looked sunken and unnatural, like the face of a cracked and broken statue. 'Not now, eh? Later.'

Rose set the sandwich down on the table and perched on the edge of the bench. Her heart fluttered, caught somewhere between excitement and terror.

'Please love, it's important.' She caught her breath. 'I'd have told you before, only ... only I wasn't sure, see.'

'Sure? Of what?'

Rose fiddled with her apron, twisting it round her fingers. When the words finally came they rushed out all at once, more gabbled than spoken.

'I'm expectin', Luke. I'm havin' a baby.'

She saw his expression change to disbelief, and prayed that he wouldn't be angry. 'You're ...?'

'I know it's a bad time, but ... we'll manage, Luke, won't we? We'll manage somehow.'

Luke just stared at her. For a moment she thought he was going to explode with rage, tell her it was all her fault for being careless, that they couldn't possibly have the baby they'd always dreamed of—not now, when they had nothing, not even a proper roof over their heads. Then, quite suddenly, he reached out and grabbed her, wrapping his arms about her waist, burying his face in her hair.

'It's true? Really true?'

'That's why I waited so long, I had to be sure.'

'Oh, Rose.' Luke's voice was almost a sob. She felt the warmth of his breath on the nape of her neck, filtering through the softness of her hair. And as he held her there, very close, she could not tell if he was happy or sad.

The following afternoon, Luke lay under an old van in Eddie's workshop, listening to the rain falling steadily on the corrugated iron roof.

'You're early today,' commented Doreen, crouching down beside the van.

Luke slid out from underneath to grab a different wrench, his face peppered with flecks of rust. 'Thought I'd put in an extra hour,' he explained. 'Looks like we're goin' to need all the extra money we can get.'

'Spence hasn't put your rent up, has he?'

Luke laughed drily. 'Nothin' like that—leastways, not yet. No, Rose is expectin'.'

Doreen's eyes opened wide. 'Rose is having a baby? Oh, Luke, that's wonderful! I had no idea.'

'Yeah, well—'spect she'd have told you herself, only she weren't sure.' He wrenched off a rusty nut, slid back out and threw the spanner aside. 'God knows it's a bad time, but ...' He grinned. 'You know.'

'You'll manage, eh?' Doreen clapped him on the back. 'Give Rose my best, tell her I'll see her soon. And mind you take care of her, Luke Barton.'

Luke was about to slide back under the van when Eddie came across.

'Ah, Luke. Can I have a word?' The look he threw Doreen said 'Make yourself scarce'. 'Haven't you got things to do, Doreen?'

'Oh. All right. I'll ... go and change the oil on the Norton.'

She went out to the forecourt, where the Norton stood under the canopy, next to the BSA Luke used for his practising. Luke got out from under the van and stood up, wiping his hands on an oily rag.

'A word?'

Eddie nodded. 'It's about your work.'

Luke eyed him with instant suspicion. 'My work? Who's bin complainin' about my work?'

'Nobody. There's nothing wrong with it, that's not what I meant.' Eddie let out a long, weary exhalation of breath. 'Fact is, Luke boy, the supply of work here's been drying up these last couple of weeks. When this job's done I've nothing for you.'

'But you said—'

'I said I *might* have something for you—something casual.' Eddie shrugged. 'But I haven't. I'm sorry and that, I really am—but that's the way it goes.'

Luke's one good eye narrowed. He looked around him. The apprentice was hard at work on a farmer's truck, the other mechanic polishing up the chrome on a sports car.

'There's stacks of work here. What about that truck?'

'Wesley can manage that on his own—besides, he's apprenticed, I have to find something for him to do. Luke, I don't know what you're thinking ...'

'No? Well I'll tell you. I'm thinkin', funny how my dad gets sent down for ringin' cars, an' suddenly there's no more work for me. *That's* what I'm thinkin', Mister Kneale.'

'Look, I told you,' insisted Eddie. 'If I say I've got no work for you, that's the truth; your dad's got nothing to do with it. In a couple of weeks things could be completely different.'

'Oh yeah?'

'Whatever I've got, you'll be first in line. I'll let you know soon as I get something.'

Luke's face flushed with anger and he thew down the oily rag. 'Don't bloody bother. I'm goin'. I know when I'm not wanted here.' He swung round. Everyone was looking at him, Wesley blinking in owlish fascination through the open bonnet of the truck. 'That what you wanted, is it? To get rid of the thievin' gyppo?'

'Luke, don't be a fool!' shouted Eddie, but Luke was already striding out towards the forecourt and wrenching the BSA off its stand.

'Luke?' Doreen stepped in front of his bike as he swung his leg over it. 'Luke, what's this all about? What did Dad just say to you?'

'Out my way, Doreen.' Luke's face was a grim mask as he kick-started the bike, drew back the

310

throttle and powered out into the rain, not even bothering to buckle on his helmet.

'Luke ... Luke, come back!' Doreen swung round to look at her father, who had walked out onto the forecourt. 'Dad, what have you done?'

Eddie shrugged. 'All I did was explain we've no work for him for a week or two, and he flew off the handle.'

The drone of the BSA's engine was fading into the distance. On impulse, Doreen grabbed her helmet and jumped onto the Norton. 'Dad, you can be so ... Oh, hell, just leave this to me.'

She jumped hard on the kick-start and the Norton roared into life at the second attempt. A few moments later she was out on the open road and riding hell for leather.

The rain was really pelting down now. Rose peered out of the vardo window at the gathering gloom and shivered. The afternoon was so murky that you could hardly distinguish between ground, sea and sky. It wouldn't be much fun for Luke, coming all the way back from Union Mills on Percy's old pushbike.

'Mam?'

A wheezy cough from the bed brought Rose back from the window.

'It's all right, Ellie, Mam's here.' She sat down on the edge of the bed, repositioning the saucepans on the floor so that they caught the worst of the drips through the ceiling. No matter how many times Luke patched up the wagon

311

roof, it still had more holes than a sieve.

Ellie shook her head. 'Throat hurts,' she whispered croakily.

Rose passed her hand over the child's brow. She was burning up. Poor kid, she thought, stroking the hair back from her face; poor all of us if this weather gets any worse. 'Can't you sleep?'

'The rain's all noisy, Mam, it makes me head ache.'

As if in reply, the rain started coming down harder, making a noise like someone throwing gravel on to the wagon roof. Rose wished there was something she could do to make Ellie feel better, but what could she do? No wonder Ellie had a bad chest, with all this damp and cold. If only Luke had had the sense to take Spence's money instead of Verney's, maybe they'd have had enough money to move into a proper house for the winter. But it was no use thinking about what might have been. Life was so full of ifs and buts, and with the new baby on the way they must think about tomorrow.

She took the last blanket from her own bed and wrapped it round Ellie, cuddling her through the bedclothes, the little girl's head in the crook of her arm. And she began to hum, the way she used to hum to Ellie when she was a colicky baby. It was the first tune that came into her head, the folk song her Granny Hawkins had taught her:

'Johnny Todd he went a rovin',
For to cross the ocean wide,

312

An' he left his love behind him,
Weepin' by the Liverpool side ...'

Perhaps it was the song, perhaps just the sound of the rain on the roof and the distant swell of the sea breaking against the headland; but suddenly Rose found herself thinking of Charlie.

He could be out there on his boat, on that wild sea, huge, towering waves hurling it about like a child's toy. If so, she hoped he'd be safe. Funny how she could think about him now without sorrow or anger, as though all the bad feelings had worn themselves out, leaving just a trace of the warmth she'd once felt towards him.

She felt Ellie relax in her arms, and when she looked down she saw that she was asleep. Not daring to move away in case she woke the child, Rose stayed exactly where she was, listening to the rain drumming on the roof and waiting for Luke to come home.

The *Rose Marie* bucked on the waves like a wild steer, her squat hull groaning as she scaled each new peak, only to plummet down into the next watery trough.

Struggling along the deck to the wheelhouse, Charlie shook his head, trying to free his eyes from the stinging salt spray and torrential rain. This weather was worse than anything he'd had to face in the war, running guns from southern Spain across to the Free French in North Africa. The cargo of Irish eggs in the *Rose Marie*'s hold

313

must all be scrambled by now.

He wished to God he had not had to bring Lola on this trip, but at least she was safely bedded down below decks—and how could he have left her at that hell-hole prison that dared to call itself a school? The moment he had realised how they were treating her, he had had no option but to take her away. Whatever other way he found of bringing her up, it could only be better than what she had suffered at Brandsby Hall.

At last his wet, slippery fingers managed to heave open the wheelhouse door and he half-stepped, half-fell inside.

The mate was stooped over the wheel, only managing to keep it straight by sheer brute force. 'Charlie—take over while I plot a new course.' The December wind and rain were icy cold, but the mate's face was dripping sweat. 'This is more than the old girl can take. We'll have to put into Douglas and sit this one out.'

Doreen's intuition told her that Luke would be heading for Douglas. He was riding like a maniac and had a couple of minutes' start on her, but the Norton was a powerful machine and Luke didn't know the short-cuts like she did. Keep going steadily, and she'd catch him up before long.

The rain was torrential now, and a gusty wind was driving it right into Doreen's face, making it almost impossible to see through her goggles. In exasperation she pushed them up on to the top of her helmet, screwing up her eyes against the

314

lashing raindrops. She was used to bad weather, but this was bad even by Manx standards—and Luke wasn't familiar with the roads. Worse, he was angry and not thinking straight. One lapse of concentration and he could kill himself.

Doreen bumped along to the end of the narrow lane and came out onto the main road. There he was, head down, leaning over the handlebars of the BSA, just a couple of hundred yards ahead of her. She nosed the Norton out onto the carriageway and opened up the throttle.

'Luke!' The wind caught her voice and threw it away. 'Luke, stop!'

At the second attempt she managed to overtake him, turning to wave frantically at him; but Luke simply accelerated past her, taking the bend dangerously tightly and pulling away, only just in time to avoid a car travelling in the opposite direction.

Doreen moved up until she was almost abreast of him. 'Luke, for God's sake—stop!'

She knew Luke had heard her. But he shook his head and rode on. Doreen couldn't stick close to his tail, there were potholes around the next bend and she knew there wasn't room to ride two abreast. She would have to catch him up on the next straight.

But Luke didn't give her the chance. Rounding the bend, he hit a stretch of road that lay inches deep in water, the ruts and hollows hidden by the deceptively smooth grey of the surface. The front wheel dipped suddenly into a pothole, and there was no time for Luke to correct the error, the momentum was too great.

The BSA threw him like an unbroken mule, flinging him head-first onto the verge then collapsing sideways into the floodwater, its wheels still spinning.

CHAPTER 25

'Luke!' Doreen rushed across to where he was lying, face-down on the grass. 'Luke, are you all right?'

He groaned, rolled over and blinked, shaking rainwater and mud out of his eyes. 'Oh God.' He sat up slowly, a trickle of blood from his scalp turning into a pink river as it ran down his wet face. His fingers explored it gingerly. 'My head.' He shook it again, eyes struggling to focus. 'Feels like an elephant trod on it.'

'Can you stand up?'

'I dunno. Yeah, I think so.' He eased himself on to his feet, Doreen supporting his weight as he tried each limb in turn. 'Nothin' broken, just a bit ... dizzy, that's all.' He swayed slightly but Doreen steadied him.

'Dizzy? I'm not surprised, you must've been doing sixty coming round that corner. You're lucky your head's still joined to your neck.' Then her anxiety spilled out into anger. 'What were you trying to do, kill yourself?'

'Tell you the truth, Doreen, I was that steamed up I wasn't thinkin' straight. I was just tryin' to get away, take it out on the bike or somethin'.' Luke prodded the cut on his scalp and winced. 'God, that smarts.'

'Right,' said Doreen. 'That settles it, I'm getting you to a doctor.'

'I'm all right,' protested Luke. 'Don't fuss. I'll just ride back to the garage an' I'll be fine.'

'Ride back!' Doreen drew Luke's attention to the shipwrecked BSA, its front forks twisted, its front wheel sticking up at an unnatural angle. 'Have you seen the state of the bike?'

This brought Luke down to earth with a bump. 'The bike ... Oh, Doreen, I'm sorry. I'll pay for the damage ...' He walked unsteadily to the road and started trying to pull it out of the water, but Doreen pushed him back.

'Never mind the flipping bike, what about the state of you? You're not riding anywhere, Luke Barton. Get on the Norton.'

'The Norton?'

'Now, Luke.' Doreen meant business. 'I'm taking you home.'

Luke's face registered alarm.

'I can't. Doreen, I can't let Rose see me like this—she'll know I've been ridin'—'

'But she's bound to find out sooner or later,' reasoned Doreen, dragging the BSA out of the water and resting it against the hedge. 'Why don't you just own up and have done with it?'

Luke grabbed her by the hands, startling her with his sudden intensity. 'I can't. Not yet. Please, Doreen—you won't tell her?'

Doreen looked back at him, uncertain what

317

to do. 'I don't know, Luke ... I don't like lying to Rose, she's my friend.'

'Please?'

Doreen didn't reply, just got astride the Norton and started it. 'Get on, Luke. Now. I'm taking you home to Rose.'

Just after three the sky began to brighten and the rain let up, long enough for Rose to get across to Horace's office and pay him the winter retainer. It was money they could ill afford, but if they didn't pay up they'd be without a pitch for next season.

Rose felt better as she walked back across the empty tober, as though she'd just made a down payment on their future. Ellie would be better soon, the weather wouldn't always be cold and rainy, things would come right in the end. It was surprising what you could survive when you had to.

When she saw Doreen's Norton coasting in through the gates, with Luke perched on the pillion, she ran across to greet them, happy to see Doreen and glad that Luke hadn't had to cycle all that way back in the rain. It wasn't until the bike stopped and she got quite close that she realised there was something very wrong.

'Luke!' she gasped, her stomach turning over as she saw her husband's face, ashen beneath the reddish-pink streaks of blood, his hair plastered to his scalp. She clapped her hands to her mouth, so shocked she could not take a further step forward.

Doreen cut the engine and took off her

helmet. She turned to look at Luke and he got off the bike, dismounting slowly and rather painfully. Rose saw that the left sleeve of his shirt was ripped open, his shoulder grazed and bleeding. Panic rose like a storm tide inside her.

'Oh, God, no ... Luke, what's happened to you? Doreen, what's happened?'

'It's all right, Rose.' Doreen dismounted and put her arm round Rose's shoulders. 'It looks worse than it is. He's just had a bit of a knock, that's all.'

'A knock?' Rose shook free of Doreen's arm and rushed over to Luke. 'What kind of knock? Oh my God, look at all the blood, just look at it!' Rose ran her trembling hand down the side of Luke's face, all kinds of horrible imaginings racing round inside her head. 'Tell me, Luke. Tell me!'

Doreen spoke first. 'It ... he was just ...'

'Just an accident,' cut in Luke. 'At work. I'n't that right, Doreen?'

Almost as quickly as Rose caught the look that passed between them, it was gone. Maybe she'd imagined it.

'Y-yes,' said Doreen. 'An accident at the garage. A ... a ...'

'A car jack,' said Luke. 'I was fixin' this car an' it gave way, see, fell on me an' cut me head. It were nothin', love,' he reassured Rose, pulling her close against him. 'I'm fine, honest I am.'

Rose looked at Doreen. 'A car? A car fell on him?'

Doreen nodded. 'Yeah. That's right. A car,' she said quietly.

'But ...' Rose's fingers found the tear in Luke's shirt sleeve, and the long strip of grazed skin underneath. Something didn't quite ring true. 'But your shoulder ... If the car fell on top of you—'

'I did it gettin' out from underneath,' said Luke. He staggered a little and it was all Rose could do to keep him from slumping sideways.

'Luke—what's wrong?'

'Just a bit dizzy, love. If I could just ... just have a bit of a lie down ...'

Rose's mouth turned dry with fear. 'Oh, Doreen ...'

'Here, let me take his weight,' said Doreen, hastily slipping her shoulder underneath Luke's arm. 'You mustn't lift anything heavy.' She smiled. 'Luke told me. About the baby.'

Rose looked at her in surprise. She knew. Doreen knew all about the baby. And they hadn't even told Ellie yet.

Together they helped Luke to the vardo steps and up into the wagon. 'I've got to fetch the doctor,' said Rose. 'Will you wait with Luke an' Ellie?'

A small voice from the far end of the wagon murmured sleepily: 'Mam?'

Doreen touched Rose's hand. 'No, you stay here, it's you they want. I'll go and fetch the doctor.' Her gaze lingered on Luke for a long moment, long enough for Rose to wonder. 'After what's happened, it's the least I can do.'

The following day Ellie was much better and

Luke seemed back to his usual self, with nothing to show for his accident but a couple of stitches in his head and a torn shirt. A touch of concussion, that's what the doctor put it down to; just a nasty bump on the head that'd sort itself out with a bit of rest.

And it looked as if Luke might be getting more rest than he'd bargained for. Rose had lain awake for hours, wondering just how long it would be until Eddie had more work for him—if he ever did. Work was scarce, and there were plenty of other mechanics Eddie could employ: good honest Manxmen, men whose reputations hadn't been blemished by having a father in prison and a brother who owed money to everyone on the Island. Maybe Luke's suspicions weren't so crazy after all. Maybe Eddie really was looking for an excuse to get rid of him. Rose prayed that Doreen was right, and Luke had just jumped to the wrong conclusion.

One thing was for sure, though: if Luke wasn't working for Eddie Kneale, they'd have to get some money from somewhere else. But where? Local men like Percy Sayle could at least join one of the Government winter work schemes, mending roads, unblocking drains, planting trees. But there would be nothing for the Bartons: no hand-outs, no jobs to put food on the table and fuel in the stove. If things got really bad and their money ran out, they'd have nothing to keep them going but the soup kitchen in Douglas—and Rose was far too proud to contemplate charity. All those long years when Stan had been out on strike or nursing his famous 'bad back', Edie had always found an honest way to bring a few bob into the house and feed and clothe the family. Rose could do no less.

So there was no avoiding it. Pregnant or not, if Luke couldn't find work, Rose would just have to find some herself.

She didn't like leaving Ellie on her own, not when the child was still getting over bronchitis, but Lissa Darwell had sworn on her mother's grave that she would keep on eye on her while Rose went down to Douglas. It was funny how much friendlier the Darwells had been since Manfri was arrested—almost as if a brush with the law had sent the Bartons up in their estimation.

Rose trailed down Strand Street, a couple of potatoes and a quarter-pound of liver sitting forlornly at the bottom of her basket. A raw wind buffeted down Duke Street as she crossed, whipping salt spray off the sea and tugging at the decorations strung across the roadway. In the window of a grocer's shop a banner proclaimed 'SHOP EARLY FOR CHRISTMAS', above stacked cans of pre-war peaches labelled 'ONLY SEVEN POINTS'. 'EAT MANX MEAT', read the butcher's sign, propped between the horns of a china bull—but the queue ran half-way to the Strand Cinema and there was nothing to be had today but soup bones and offal. Even the iced cake in the window of Cannell's the bakers was a cardboard imitation.

This wasn't going to be the easiest of

Christmases for anyone, Rose thought, what with all the rationing and shortages to contend with, and so many families still divided by war. And it would be the toughest Rose had known, tougher even than those childhood Christmases when Christmas dinner had consisted of whatever Stan had pinched from the docks. But Ellie wasn't going to suffer, Rose had made up her mind about that. Somehow there would be presents and something nice to eat on Christmas Day, no matter how much Rose and Luke had to go without to pay for it.

A woman in a fur coat emerged from a hat shop on the corner of Victoria Road, carrying something in a large round box. If Rose hadn't turned to look at her she'd never have noticed the small, handwritten card in the window: 'Assistant Wanted, Apply Within'. Why not? thought Rose. They can only tell me to get lost. The shop bell jangled as she stepped inside. A tall, well-dressed woman with a crooked nose and bony fingers glided out from behind the counter, all smiles. If she noticed Rose's shabby old coat and holey shoes she was far too polite to mention them.

'Good morning, Madam, can I help you?'

'I ... hope so,' ventured Rose.

'A new hat, perhaps? Or a pair of gloves? Is it for yourself, or a Christmas gift?'

Rose swallowed. This must be the tenth shop she'd tried this morning—everything from ironmongers to cake shops and it didn't get any easier. 'I'm ... well, actually I've come about the job.'

The bony woman's smile scarcely slipped. 'The ... *job?*' Her eyes narrowed as they took in the tatty coat, the battered shoes, the thick, darned stockings.

'My husband's out of work, see, we need the money. I'll do anythin'—sell hats, scrub floors, anythin'.'

'I'm *so* sorry ...' began the manageress. She didn't sound it, thought Rose bitterly.

'But you've nothin' for me, right?'

'I'm afraid not.' The smile was a little frosty now.

'There's a card in the window,' Rose pointed out.

'I really am *very* sorry, madam.' The manageress was ushering her to the door, practically pushing her through it and out into the street. 'I'm afraid you wouldn't be quite ... suitable. But do call again, won't you?'

Not suitable. Out in the street, Rose told herself that next time she'd be lucky. Next time, there'd be something for her. But it still hurt, being told she wasn't good enough by someone who didn't even know her, just because she couldn't afford nice clothes.

She forgot all about her own troubles as she headed back up Strand Street and heard the hullaballoo. A small crowd had gathered outside the toyshop, angry faces and raised voices telling the story. Curious, Rose approached.

'Little thief!'

'Call a copper!'

'You listenin' to me, gel, are you? You'll

324

answer me when I'm talkin' to you, young lady!'

'You give that back right now, you hear?'

It wasn't until she was a few feet away that Rose saw who they were shouting at: a skinny, black-haired little girl with olive skin and huge dark eyes, blazing uncomprehendingly at her tormentors as she clasped her stolen treasure.

'Lola!' The word escaped from Rose's lips in a cry of astonishment. A middle-aged man in a shopkeeper's brown coat swung round, Lola pulling away from him as he held her firmly by the arm.

'You this little girl's mother?' he demanded. 'She's been pinching toys from my shop.'

'Ought to be ashamed of herself,' commented a young woman in a chequered coat. 'Letting the child run wild like that.'

'No,' said Rose, returning the woman's glare. 'I'm *not* her mother, but I do know it's no good shoutin' at her—she's deaf.'

This produced a sudden silence.

'Oh,' said the shopkeeper, scratching his head. 'Oh, I never knew.'

The moment that he relaxed his grip on Lola's arm she pulled free and flung herself forward, hurling herself into Rose's arms and hiding her face. Rose put her arm round the child. Her mind whirled. What on earth was Lola doing here? She was supposed to be safe in some special deaf children's school, miles away across the water. And whatever did Charlie think he was playing at, leaving her to roam the streets of Douglas in that thin little cardigan?

'Poor kid,' she said softly.

A man in a blue uniform pushed his way through the gaggle of sightseers. 'Now then, what's all this fuss about?'

'It's that little girl, officer,' piped up the woman in the chequered coat. 'She's been shoplifting.'

'That so, Mister Keig?' demanded the officer.

'Well ...' The shopkeeper looked embarrassed now. 'Look, I didn't realise the kid was deaf and dumb.'

'Deaf?' The policeman put his hand on Lola's shoulder and the little girl screwed her head round to look up at him, more curious than afraid. He mouthed his words very slowly and deliberately, as though addressing an imbecile. 'What's your name, littl'un?'

'Her name's Lola,' said Rose. 'Lola Cartwright. But she's deaf, not stupid.'

The constable got out his notebook, flipped it open and licked his pencil. 'So, Mrs Cartwright ...'

'I'm not Mrs Cartwright, I'm Mrs Barton. Lola's not my daughter.'

'So whose is she then?'

'Charlie's.' Rose felt a mounting sense of exasperation. 'Her dad's called Charlie Cartwright.'

'I see. So where will we find this ... Charlie Cartwright?'

'How should I know? I didn't even know he was on the Island!' Rose wished to goodness that she had never chosen this morning to walk down Strand Street, but she could hardly abandon

Lola now. 'Look, he's a deckhand on a cargo boat—the Rose something. *Rose Marie*—that's it, I think. That's all I know.'

'Hmm.' The constable slipped his notebook back into the top pocket of his uniform jacket. 'Well we'll have to have a few words with Mister Cartwright, won't we? Now then, Lola, are you going to give me that toy or what?'

'She can't understand a word you're sayin'!' Rose stroked Lola's hair and the little girl looked up at her. Rose smiled and pointed to the toy clasped tightly to Lola's chest, then to herself. Lola must have understood, because she slowly loosened her grip and held the toy out. The moment she saw it, Rose understood why Lola had wanted it so much: it was a little clockwork model of a fairground carousel.

Rose took it gently from her and handed it to Mr Keig. 'Here, this is yours. I'm sorry, I'm sure she won't do it again.'

'Aye, well ...' The shopkeeper looked at the toy and then at Lola. 'Look, officer, she's given it back. Can't we leave it at that?'

The policeman shook his head regretfully. ' 'Fraid not, Mister Keig. A complaint's been made and I have to investigate it. Besides, can't have deaf kiddies running riot all over Douglas, can we?'

'Kids like that ought to be put in a home,' sniffed the woman in the chequered coat.

Rose rounded on her. 'An' daft bitches like you ought to keep their flamin' mouths shut!' she snapped.

'No need for that, Mrs Barton,' said the

327

constable, reaching for Lola's hand. But Lola hung back, shrinking against Rose's coat. 'Come on, Lola, you're coming with me.'

'Now hang on,' said Rose. 'Where are you takin' her?'

'To the station, of course.'

Rose looked at Lola and knew she had no choice. 'Oh no you're not,' she declared. 'If you're takin' that kid anywhere you'll have to take me too.'

Charlie burst through the doors of the police station and ran up to the front desk, his chest heaving from the effort of running all the way. 'Charlie ... Charlie Cartwright,' he gasped. 'My daughter—you've got my daughter?'

The desk sergeant flicked through the pages of the day-book with maddening slowness. 'Ah, yes ... Lola Cartwright, aged seven years. So you're her father, are you, sir?'

'She's safe?'

'Safe as houses.' The sergeant nudged the police cadet standing by his side. 'Phelan, go and fetch the little deaf girl.'

'Yes, sir.'

Charlie slumped against the desk. 'Thank God. I thought I'd lost her. She was below decks, see. I only left her for a few minutes: I thought she was still there. Oh God, if anythin' had happened to her ...'

A door along the passageway opened and two figures emerged, the little girl holding on tightly to the woman's hand. But the minute she saw her father standing by the desk, Lola ran full-tilt down the passageway and into his arms, giggling with silent delight as he swung her up into the air.

Rose followed more slowly, her gaze meeting Charlie's as he set Lola down. There were tears in his eyes, tears of real love, and that made her start—she had never once seen Charlie cry—but she told herself that even tears were no excuse.

'Rose!' Charlie's mouth fell open. 'I ... What are you doin' here?'

'Doin' what you should be doin',' replied Rose. 'Takin' care of your daughter.'

'I never knew she'd even gone, Rose. I just turned round an' ... an' she wasn't there.'

'Do you know what she was doin', Charlie? She was wandering down the street in her cardi, in the middle of December ...'

'Rose—'

'An' that's not the worst of it. The coppers caught her nickin' from Keig's toyshop! Honest to God, Charlie.' She faced up to him with as much vehemence as if Lola had been her own daughter. 'I'm beginnin' to wonder if you're fit to look after a kid.'

CHAPTER 26

Sergeant Corrin came in through the door of the interview room with a young policewoman in tow. 'This is WPC Peters,' he said. 'She'll take care of Lola while we have a little chat.'

It all sounded so cosy, thought Rose, but the sergeant's tone of voice was deadly serious.

The WC went over to Lola and offered her hand. 'Hello.' She was kind-faced and smiling, but Lola just stared blankly at her, deep suspicion in her dark eyes. 'Come on, let's see if we can find you some sweeties, shall we?' Her hand closed around Lola's, and Lola started trying to tug herself free.

'No,' cut in Charlie, getting up from his chair. 'I don't want you takin' her nowhere.'

'It's just for a little while, Mr Cartwright,' replied the policewoman. 'You'll see her again soon.'

'She's my kid, an' if I say you're not takin' her, you're not.'

Rose knew Charlie had a lively temper, but she'd never seen him so agitated. 'Belt up, Charlie,' she pleaded. 'An' sit down, you're not makin' this any easier for anybody.'

Charlie's expression was murderous. 'If these coppers are lyin' to me—'

'Course they're not lyin',' hissed Rose. 'Just let it be, will you?' She grabbed his sleeve and pulled him slowly back down on to the hard wooden chair. 'Or do you want me to go home an' leave you to it?'

This shocked Charlie out of his rage. 'N-no. Course I don't. I'm glad you're here, Rose, I appreciate it.'

But even as he was speaking to Rose, his eyes were following Lola as WPC Peters towed her out of the interview room, the child straining to look back over her shoulder at her father as the door clicked shut between them.

'Right,' said the sergeant, plonking himself down on the other side of the table. 'There's one or two facts I need to get straight.' He beckoned to the constable who had brought Lola in. 'Maddrell.'

'Sarge?'

'Tell me where you found the little girl.'

'In Strand Street, Sarge. She'd pinched a toy from Ron Keig's shop.'

'I see. And was there an adult present when the alleged offence took place?'

Rose felt PC Maddrell's eyes light on her; it was an uncomfortable feeling, as though she were the one on trial.

'Only the lady there, sir. A Mrs ...'

'Barton,' said Rose flatly. 'Rose Barton. But I was only passin' by.'

'Quite,' said the sergeant, running his hands through his mop of iron-grey hair. 'So. Mr Cartwright, where were you when all this was happening?'

'On the *Rose Marie*. Like I told you, I only turned my back for a minute—she must've run off when I wasn't lookin'.' He looked terrible, thought Rose, his anger a cloak for real desperation.

'And what does her mother reckon to her living on a boat?'

Charlie's shoulders drooped. 'Her mother's dead. Lola's got nobody but me. I know it's not good, her livin' on the boat with me, but I've no choice.' It was Rose he looked at as he spoke, not the sergeant, and she had the curious feeling that it was her he wanted to forgive him.

'But, Charlie,' she said softly. 'I thought you'd found somewhere for Lola—a special deaf school or somethin' ...'

Charlie gave a sarcastic laugh. 'A school? Oh yeah, that was what they called it. Only it turns out it's not a proper school at all—just this horrible place where they lock up kids nobody wants. An' when I found out they'd been beltin' the livin' daylights out of her ...' He raised angry eyes to look at the sergeant. 'Look, mate, if it happened to your kid would you leave her there? Well, would you?'

The sergeant folded his hands and sat back. He didn't look unsympathetic, just beleaguered. 'We're not talking about me, Mr Cartwright, we're talking about you. And it's not right, is it? Keeping a young girl on a boat, letting her run wild, keeping her away from school—'

'I told you!' Charlie thumped the table in frustration. 'I couldn't find her a school, nobody wants to know!'

'Well,' reasoned the sergeant, 'she can't stay as she is. If you can't offer her a proper home she'll have to go back.'

'Back!' exclaimed Rose, horrified. 'You mean send her back to that home?'

'I can't see any other option, Mrs Barton,' said the sergeant. 'I wish I could.'

'Never. Never! I won't have it,' growled Charlie. 'Bring her here, I'm takin' her back to the boat.'

'I'm sorry, Mr Cartwright, I can't let you do that.'

Charlie stared, his golden eyes mad with fear in his weather-beaten face.

'I told you, Rose, I told you! They lied to me. They're tryin' to take my kid off me—'

'No, Charlie.' She soothed him, though she feared he might be right. 'Sergeant—that's not true is it? You don't want to take Lola away from Charlie?'

'It's not a question of what I want,' replied the sergeant. 'There's rules and regulations. I've got to think of the child. And if Mr Cartwright can't give his daughter a proper home, we shall have to find somebody who can.'

Alone with Charlie in the interview room, Rose watched him pace the length of the walls like a caged lion.

'Charlie, sit down,' she pleaded.

Charlie leant his forehead against the wall, his hands spread out like claws on the green distemper. His back to her, she saw his shoulders rise and fall as he fought to control his breathing. 'I'm goin' to lose her, Rose, I'm goin' to lose her.'

'You don't know that.'

He spun round. 'Course I know it! Didn't you hear that sergeant goin' on about how I wasn't providin' for me own daughter?'

'Yes, but—'

'An' d'you know what, Rose? He's right.' The last word was a shout that echoed round the room, bouncing off the walls. The tiny Christmas tree in the corner seemed to mock his despair. 'You're right an' all—I'm not fit to have a kid.'

'Oh, Charlie.' Rose watched him torment himself and pitied him; sympathised with him too, for she knew that in his place she would be just the same. What worse thing could there be than to face the loss of your own child? 'I know it seems bad ... but there must be a way, somethin' you can do.'

'You heard him. Unless Lola gets somewhere proper to stay, she goes straight back to Brandsby Hall. I can't let them do it to her, Rose. God help me, I never meant it to come to this—I just wanted to do the best for her. I can't let them send her back there! Not to that place.'

He flopped down on to one of the hard chairs and spread his hands on the table in front of him, staring at them as they shook. Rose could only guess at the horrible thoughts that were teeming through his mind. Was he remembering what he had gone through in that Spanish prison, the things he had seen and endured, too horrible for Rose even to imagine?

'You know somethin', Rose?'

'What?'

'All my life I've been runnin' away. I never could take responsibility, see, couldn't stand bein' tied down or told what to do. Even goin' off to Spain was a kind of runnin' away.' He glanced at her, then looked swiftly away again. 'Guess I was runnin' away from you. It took that hell of a war to make me grow up. God, but I was stupid. I should have stayed an' married you, Rose.'

'Don't talk like that, Charlie,' said Rose, her voice scarcely rising above a whisper. 'Don't dig it all up again.'

'I would've married you, you know,' said Charlie. 'I would've stayed, if I'd known.'

Their eyes met: Rose caught her breath, knowing instinctively what he was going to say next and praying that he wouldn't. 'Known?'

'About Ellie. She's mine, isn't she?'

In that moment Rose almost told Charlie not to flatter himself, the denial on the very tip of her tongue. She'd known this moment might come some day, and had rehearsed the words over and over again; but they wouldn't come out the way she'd planned them.

'Yes,' she said.

'Oh God.' Charlie stared unblinkingly down at the table-top. 'Oh God, Rose, I'm sorry.'

'It's a bit late for sorry, Charlie. Besides, I never knew I was expectin' till after you'd gone.' Rose said the one thing she knew she must make clear. 'Luke's Ellie's dad now, Charlie. Not you.'

Charlie nodded dumbly. 'I just ... wanted to know. To be sure.' He stood up, the legs of the chair scraping noisily across the tiled floor. 'What am I goin' to do, Rose? I've made a mess of bein' Ellie's dad, I can't let it happen to Lola an' all.'

'No.'

'But there's nothin' I can do. Nothin'. I've got no relatives, me mates are all dead or married, there's no one to help me, no one who could take Lola in.'

Rose felt the thought growing at the back of her mind and tried to kill it, but all it did was get bigger and more insistent. It was a thought she didn't want to accept, but each time she tried to suppress it she saw Lola in her mind's eye, the little girl torn once again from the only father she'd ever known.

'There might be,' she blurted out.

'Might be?'

'Someone to take her in. Only for a bit, mind. Till you've sorted yourself out, you know, found a proper place to live.'

'You!' Charlie's hands dropped to his sides. 'You'd do that—for me?'

'No,' said Rose firmly. 'But I might do it for Lola.'

Luke scrambled out from underneath the Chairoplanes, his face blackened with oil.

'You did *what?*'

'I said we'd take Lola in. Just for a week or two ...'

Rose had known Luke would not be pleased, but she hadn't bargained on him taking it so badly.

'Bloody hell, Rose, what did you think you were doin'? There's three of us in that vardo, an' another on the way, hardly enough money to keep us goin', let alone some *gorgio* stranger's kid—'

'Charlie's not a stranger,' protested Rose. 'He's a ... a friend,' she finished feebly, the word not sounding quite right. Over the last ten years she had adored Charlie, then grieved for him, then despised him; it seemed unimaginable that he could ever be anything as uncomplicated as a friend.

'Some friend!' Luke bashed irritably at a seized-up bolt. 'He neglects his own kid then expects you to take her in!'

'He didn't expect anythin'—I told you, I offered.'

'Well you shouldn't have,' growled Luke, stomping bad-temperedly round to the other side of the centre engine.

'What choice did I have?' demanded Rose, following him round. 'The coppers were talkin' about sendin' Lola back to this horrible place where they lock the kids up an' beat them?'

'Yeah, well, you've only got Charlie's word for that,' retorted Luke. 'He could've said it just to get round you.'

'He wouldn't!' insisted Rose, surprising herself with her own vehemence. 'Charlie's not like that.'

Luke looked at her oddly, in a way that made her feel profoundly uncomfortable.

'Really? You seem to know a lot about Charlie Cartwright.' Stuffing his tools back into his bag, he jumped down and set off back across the tober, Rose trailing behind him.

'Oh, Luke—Luke, don't be like that. I only did it for Lola's sake—poor kid doesn't know if she's comin' or goin'. An' it's only for a week or two, till Charlie sorts himself out ...'

Luke stopped. 'A week or two?'

'Yeah, I reckon. Not much longer than that.'

Luke reflected, then shook his head. 'It's no

337

good, Rose, it wouldn't work.' He looked at her again. 'An' you know what's worst about this?'

'What?'

'You never even bothered to ask me—you just went right out an' said you'd do it.'

Something old and not quite healed smarted inside Rose. 'Well hark at you talkin', Luke Barton!'

'What's that supposed to mean?'

'Well, you never bothered askin' me when you decided to sell the TT Racer to Verney, did you? Just went right out an' did it!'

'That was different.'

'Different? Oh, you mean *family?* So I'm not even family now, am I?'

'Don't be stupid, woman, I never said that.'

'You didn't have to.'

Rose and Luke stood glaring at each other, frost crackling underfoot.

'You'll have to go back an' tell him no,' said Luke, shouldering his toolbag and heading for the barn where the spare parts were kept in storage.

Rose watched him go, smouldering with resentment. 'I'm not doin' anythin' of the kind. I've told Charlie we're doin' it, and we're not lettin' him down now,' she shouted after him, at that moment not particularly caring if the whole of Douglas heard her.

Luke didn't reply, just trudged off towards the barn. Good riddance, thought Rose. It was only a few moments later, as she climbed up the wagon steps, that she began to wonder if she'd just made a very big mistake.

CHAPTER 27

January roared across the Island with a savage glee, sending slates scudding from roofs, snapping branches from the trees, whipping up the sea into waves so tall that they dwarfed the little Tower of Refuge in Douglas bay.

It had been a particularly bitter day, and as dusk fell there was no sign that the night would be any better. Vicious gales swept the tober, battering the scattering of vans huddled under the hedge, rattling the surviving panes of glass in their wooden frames. Inside the vardo Rose shivered as she cooked by the light of an oil-lamp, its beam swaying and guttering as the wagon rocked on its wheels with each new icy blast. Even the soup in the saucepan was sloshing about, the mutton bones rattling against the pan as if they were trying to climb out. It took an age to bring the soup to the boil with the few lumps of coal Rose had managed to scrounge to keep the stove going.

'Here y'are, love.' She managed to ladle a little of the broth into a bowl and handed it to Luke. 'Mind it doesn't spill.'

As the words left her lips the vardo gave a sickening lurch, teetering on two wheels before at last settling back down on the ground.

'God help us,' she whispered, praying the kids couldn't see how frightened she was. But Lola and Ellie were playing happily on the floor with bits of coloured paper and glue, so absorbed in their game that they seemed not to have noticed how perilously close the vardo was to toppling over.

'Luke ...'

Luke's face was set in a mask of grim determination. 'We'll be all right.'

'But ... these gales ...' She lowered her voice so that Ellie wouldn't hear. 'What's goin' to happen to the wagon?'

'She's built for worse than this.' Rose wondered if he believed what he was saying. 'Walleye drove this thing across Lake Windermere in a blizzard once, one year when it froze solid. Sit down an' eat somethin', will you?' he added irritably. 'It's gettin' on my nerves, you fidgetin' about like that.'

Reluctantly, Rose took her bowl of broth and sat down next to Luke, perching on the edge of the fold-out bed. She was grateful for his warmth on this wintry night, so cold that each of them was wearing every item of clothing they possessed. And still it wasn't enough to keep them all warm, with so little fuel left for the stove.

'I'll be glad when this is over,' muttered Luke, dipping his bread into his soup.

'I 'spect it'll blow over by mornin'.'

'Not just the storm.' Luke's eyes settled on the two little girls, laughing as they sat together on the rag-rug, managing to communicate in some silent way of their own devising. 'Charlie. I'll be glad when he comes an' ... you know.'

She knew. Luke meant he'd be glad when Charlie came and fetched Lola back. She'd been with them almost six weeks now, and it hadn't been easy for any of them. But things weren't as simple as Luke wanted them to be.

'Give him a chance,' she said, keeping her voice low. 'He's got to find a place to live on the Island first.'

'He's had over a month.'

'But it's got to be decent for a kid to live in. Or the welfare people won't let him have her back. An' besides ...'

Luke's spoon halted half-way to his mouth. 'Besides what?'

'When Charlie gets this place ... well, he's not goin' to be there more'n half the week, is he? Think about it, he's off with that boat—what—two, three nights a week? What's he goin' to do with her when he's not here?'

'I said two weeks, Rose.' Luke's voice had a hard edge to it, an edge Rose neither recognised nor liked. 'It's already been six.'

'I know, but ...'

'He's takin' you for a mug, Rose. What if he skips off to sea an' don't bother comin' back? What then?'

'Oh, Luke, you know Charlie's not like that,' pleaded Rose. 'That kid means the world to him.'

This disarmed Luke, but only a little. 'Yeah, yeah, I know. Charlie's a decent enough bloke, but this can't go on for ever can it?'

'It's not goin' to. But even when he's got this cottage or whatever, Charlie's still goin' to need help, isn't he? When he's off on the boat.' Rose appealed to Luke's soft heart. 'She's had a rotten life, Luke, we can't just—'

'All right, all right,' grumbled Luke. 'You don't need to go on.'

'I 'spect it'd only be for the odd night.'

'It'd better be.'

Ellie and Lola were kneeling on the floor together, heads pressed close and conspiratorially, as if they were hiding something. There was a great deal of rustling in the mess of scrunched-up paper. Outside, the wind howled above the rattling of timbers and the distant crash of surf. Cold air hissed and whistled into the vardo through every forgotten crack and cranny. The only other sound was the clink of spoons against the enamelled tin bowls.

Suddenly Ellie sprang up. 'Lola's got somethin' to show you.' She nudged Lola in the ribs and smiled, and the smaller girl smiled too. 'Go on,' she mouthed, nudging her again.

Lola scrambled to her feet, something red and green in her hands. It was more glue than paper, but whatever it was she was obviously proud of it.

'She made it herself,' said Ellie. 'I helped.'

The little Spanish girl came skipping up to the far end of the vardo, her hands outstretched. A strange child, thought Rose, and little wonder. Yet already she was different from the terrified creature who had first arrived on the Island, fearing and distrusting everyone. It brought a lump to Rose's throat to see her run up to Luke and present her gift to him.

'It's a pirate hat,' said Ellie helpfully. 'For Dad.'

Luke hesitated, then put down his bowl and reached out to take the paper hat.

'Go on, Dad, put it on,' urged Ellie, dancing from one foot to the other despite the wild rocking of the van.

The hat was several sizes too big, and only Luke's ears prevented it from slipping right down over his face; but Lola couldn't have looked more pleased if it had been a perfect fit. Delightedly, she jumped up on to the bed and wriggled her skinny body between Luke and Rose, grinning all over her impish face.

'It's lovely,' said Rose, squeezing Lola's hand and giving her a big smile. 'Isn't it, Luke?'

Luke put his arm round Lola's shoulders and gave her a big hug. But Rose could see from his face that he wasn't happy.

Early next morning Rose and Luke were awakened by a furious hammering on the vardo door. A greyish dawn was just crawling up over the horizon as Rose scrambled out of bed and fumbled her way to the door, dragging it open.

Horace Spence was standing outside, his normally slicked-back hair sticking up in ruffled wisps, his pyjamas visible underneath his vast cashmere overcoat, the stripy trouser legs tucked into the top of his Wellingtons. A storm lantern swung from his right hand, casting oddly shaped shadows on the frozen grass.

'Mister Spence!' exclaimed Rose, wondering

343

what on earth was going on. Horace Spence was not given to wandering around Funland in the small hours; still less calling on the Bartons just to pass the time of day.

'Where's Barton?' barked Spence.

'He's in bed.' She called back over her shoulder: 'Luke. Luke, get up, it's Mister Spence.'

'Who's there?' demanded a sleepy voice from inside the vardo.

'Spence. Mister Spence, he wants a word.'

She turned back to Horace. His teeth were chattering in the bitter cold, his blubbery body quivering as he hugged his coat to his belly. 'What's up?'

'Get that husband of yours out here right now, Rose,' said Horace ominously. 'There's summat he'd better see.'

Luke appeared behind Rose's shoulder, pulling on his boots.

'What time d'you call this, Spence?' he demanded. 'It's not even light yet.'

'Light enough to see by,' replied Horace. 'Get your coat on, Barton, you're comin' wi' me. Rose, put that kettle on. We'll all want a cup o' tea by an' by.'

Luke grabbed his donkey jacket and jumped down from the wagon, shoving his arms into the sleeves as he followed Horace into the gloom.

'Luke ...' called Rose, the kettle in her hand. She watched the two figures dwindling into the semi-darkness for a moment, then dumped the kettle back on to the hob and rushed out after them. 'Wait! Wait for me! What's goin' on?'

She didn't really need to ask. There was already enough light to see that the storm had done terrible damage to the fairground. Mercifully most of the rides had been dismantled and driven away on their lorries, to be stored for the winter, but some of the wooden booths had been literally lifted off their pitches and smashed down as if by a giant's fist, leaving buckled sheets of painted plywood flapping around the tober like the wings of wounded birds. The light from the lantern picked out the words 'SID CHRISTIAN' on one; on another, '... ONUT SHY'. Rose's heart sank. Sid's stall ruined, the coconut shy not much better—all that hard work destroyed in one night. Everything would have to be rebuilt and painted all over again.

'What a night,' groaned Spence, wheezing as his round body lumbered over the uneven ground. 'God knows how much it's cost me. The roller-coaster ...'

Rose struggled to keep up with Luke's long strides and Spence's wheezy trot. 'The roller-coaster? It got damaged in the storm?'

'Damaged? Half blown down, more like. There's bits of twisted metal all over the shop, pay booth blown right over the bloody cliff ...'

'What's this got to do with me?' demanded Luke. 'Where are we goin'?'

Horace Spence gave him a look that chilled Rose's blood. 'You'll see.'

He led them across the tober, past the billowing remains of a tattered canvas tilt, a pair of flattened palm trees, an upturned dodgem car, past the whitewashed office and

345

through the gate into the field beyond. Rose knew where they were going now—to the old Dutch barn where the rides were kept in winter storage—and she almost turned round and walked straight back to the vardo.

'Not ... the Chairoplanes,' said Luke faintly.

Spence raised the lantern and suddenly the barn came into focus. Or what was left of it. The uprights were still standing, but the roof had lifted off and come crashing back down, the corrugated iron and wood warping and splintering under the force. The north end had survived almost intact, its curved shell resting on the top of the TT Racer and the truck that carried the Waltzers. But the south end had turned into mangled scrap iron, with spars and splintered timbers lying everywhere. The rides stored at this end had suffered far worse than the others—the Devil's Disc, the dodgems, the Ghost Train, all lay battered and broken.

But none had fared as badly as the Chairoplanes.

'No.' Rose stared open-mouthed at the devastation, the mashed and mangled metal-work, the dented rounding-boards, the splintered staging. 'No, it can't be true.'

'It were a terrible storm.' For once in his life, Spence sounded genuinely sorry. 'Worst I've seen in years. Couldn't have done nowt about it. Just peeled the roof off the barn like icin' off a cake.'

Luke rounded on him. 'This is your doin', Spence. You *wanted* this to happen!'

'It were the storm,' Spence repeated.

346

'You've just been waitin' for your chance, haven't you? Ever since I sold out to Jack Verney. Just waitin' for a chance to put the knife in.'

'Don't talk rubbish,' scoffed Spence. 'I've more important things to do than put some gyppo lowlife out of business ...'

'What did you call me?' seethed Luke.

'You 'eard.'

'Luke, stop this.' Rose grabbed her husband's sleeve. 'It's not worth it.'

Spence met Luke's angry stare with equal force. 'For God's sake, Barton, I don't control the bloody weather. An' if you think I do, you're an even dafter bugger than I thought you were!'

'Oh, so I'm daft an' all, am I?' snarled Luke. 'A thick, thievin' gyppo?'

'You know what they say—like father like son.'

Men, thought Rose, anger adding to her despair. Stupid, boneheaded men; never happy unless there was somebody they could blame. Only men could take a misfortune and turn it into a disaster.

'Stop it!' she screamed, so suddenly that the two of them left off arguing to stare at her. 'Shut up, both of you! Are we goin' to put this mess right, or are you two just goin' to stand here all day bawlin' each other out?'

Charlie couldn't help noticing the mess as he came across the tober. The storms had hit the Island even worse than Barrow-in-Furness,

347

where the *Rose Marie* had sat out the worst of the squall. Spence's men were still clearing up barrow-loads of debris, and the roller-coaster looked as if God had reached down out of the sky and twisted it, making the final stretch bend sideways at a crazy angle.

At least the Bartons' vardo seemed relatively untouched, save for a broken window and a bit of torn roofing felt. And there was Lola, playing on the steps with her dolly. To see his daughter's eyes light up as she caught sight of him was ten times better than any pay-day—and the crew of the *Rose Marie* had done well out of this last trip.

Lola dropped the rag doll and came scampering across the fairfield, flinging herself at him like a delirious puppy. Laughing with pleasure, he swung her up and spun her round before setting her back down on her feet.

'My, you're gettin' heavy. Rose must be feedin' you up!'

Taking Lola's hand, he walked back with her to the Bartons' living-wagon.

Rose saw him coming and walked down the vardo steps to meet him, untying her apron as she went. She felt almost sad to see him, knowing that he had at last found a new place to live in Douglas, and today he'd come to take Lola away. She'd got used to having her around. Strange how one little deaf girl could build bridges between two people who had grown so very far apart.

'Must've been a heck of a storm,' commented Charlie, scanning the tober.

'Never known anythin' like it. Tell you the truth,' admitted Rose, 'once or twice I thought the vardo was goin' over.' She perched dolefully on the top step of the wagon. 'Guess Luke was right—it's stronger than it looks. More than you can say for the rides, though.'

'The rides? They got damaged?'

'The barn roof came down, didn't it? Made a right old mess. Luke's over there now, tryin' to put the Chairoplanes back together again.' She contemplated the toes of her battered old boots—a pair of Luke's, padded out with extra socks, and much more practical around the fairfield than any dainty shoes. Not that the Bartons had money for dainty shoes even if she'd wanted them. 'You've come to fetch Lola back then?'

Charlie cleared his throat. 'Rose, I wanted to say ... Oh heck, I'm not very good at this.'

She smiled at his awkwardness. 'Just spit it out, Charlie. It can't be that bad.'

'I just wanted to say thanks. For havin' Lola. If it wasn't for you, the Welfare would've took her off me. I owe you, Rose. You an' Luke.'

Rose tried to look nonchalant, but she couldn't quite deny the warm glow of pleasure that Charlie's words gave her. 'You needed a hand. We couldn't say no, could we?'

'Most would've done. Specially with what's gone between us.'

'Yeah, well ... me an' Luke understand. It's not goin' to be easy for you, not even with

349

this new place of yours, is it? I mean, what're you goin' to do with Lola when you're at sea? Till she gets a place at a proper deaf school?'

'I dunno yet,' confessed Charlie. 'But I'll manage. I guess there's John Gorry, if I'm really stuck ...'

Rose shook her head. 'No need. She can stay here.'

'Here? No, Rose. I couldn't, not after all you've done.'

She put her hand up. 'It's all right, I've talked to Luke, he's fine about it.' It would have been truer to say that Luke had given in to her nagging, but she didn't see why Charlie should feel guilty about it. After all, this was for Lola's sake, not his. 'She can stay here—long as it's only for a night or two at a time, mind. It's a bit cramped here, an' ...' Her hands smoothed over the barely-visible swell of her pregnant belly. Suddenly she felt quite embarrassed. 'An' with another baby on the way ...'

Charlie's eyes widened. It was obvious he hadn't guessed. 'You're ...?'

'Expectin', yeah. Luke's dead made up, we both are.'

'I ... I'm pleased for you.' It was Charlie's turn to look down at his feet. 'Well.'

'Well,' echoed Rose, equally tongue-tied.

'I s'pose I ought to be on me way ... Tell you what, though, you couldn't hang on to Lola for another hour or two?'

'If you like. Why?'

'Thought I'd go an' give Luke a hand clearin' up, if that's all right. Least I can do. An' I'd like to thank him—it's not always easy havin' Lola around.'

Charlie got Lola's attention and signed to her to go to Rose. She trotted back to the vardo, picked up her dolly and went back to playing as if nothing had happened.

'She likes it here,' he remarked.

'She'll like a proper house better,' promised Rose. Feeling a pin slipping from her hair, she pulled it out and fiddled it back in, suddenly acutely aware of how unglamorous she must look, and remembering the silly, vain hours she'd spent trying to make herself look nice for Charlie all those years ago. Funny how much things could change. 'So—where's this place you've got yourself then?'

'I was dead lucky,' replied Charlie. 'It's this tiny cottage Horace Spence offered me to rent. It's really cheap—he won it in a card game or somethin'. Up on the Douglas Head Road, it is.'

'A card game!' exclaimed Rose, shocked to the core.

No. No, it couldn't be. Not Dan's cottage, the one she and Luke and Ellie should have had. But she knew in her heart it couldn't be any other.

'Yeah. Nobody's lived in it for years. Needs a bit of paintin' an' fixin' up an' that, but me an' Lola'll be fine there.' He stroked the black hair off Lola's face. 'Won't we, kid?'

CHAPTER 28

As soon as the Kneales heard what had happened, Doreen drove Eddie over to Funland in the van.

'So you see the mess I'm in,' said Luke gloomily.

Eddie whistled as he looked up at the buckled remains of the barn roof. 'Good job nobody was in here when this happened. Wouldn't have stood a chance.'

Doreen picked her way carefully between the trucks to take a closer look at the Chairoplanes.

'Wrecked,' said Luke. 'Bloody wrecked.'

'They've taken a real pounding,' Doreen admitted, taking in the dented cars and smashed rounding boards.

'Couple of these cars have gone for a Burton,' said Eddie, easing one over on to its side to examine it.

'Some of them are all right though,' cut in Doreen, her eyes not on her father or the ride but on Luke's dejected expression. 'Aren't they, Dad? We could put them right if we worked on them ...'

'If,' grunted Luke, not giving Eddie the chance to reply. He kicked the grounded car and it protested with a tinny thunk. 'It's always if, i'n't it? *If* there'd been no storm, *if* we'd got pots of money to pay for all this, *if* the

Bartons wasn't cursed to buggery.' Each 'if' was accompanied by a miserable kick.

'Don't talk like that,' urged Doreen, scrambling over the ride, agile as an acrobat. 'Look, the centre truck's fine, not a mark on it, I'll bet the engine's got nothing wrong with it. The spindle's OK, the rods can be straightened out, the boards are only wood ... and there's plenty of time to replace them before April. Come on, Luke, it's not that bad.'

'Yeah?' Luke forced himself to calm down and look at the mess. 'Yeah, I s'pose you're right. But this is more'n I can do on my own, Eddie, you know that.'

'Aye,' nodded Eddie Kneale. 'You're right there.'

'But me and Dad'll help,' said Doreen eagerly. 'Won't we, Dad?'

'Well,' mused Eddie. 'What I can, I'll do. Same as before.'

Luke picked up a bit of broken board, aimed and threw it at the ground.

'I can't pay you, Eddie, you know I can't.' He saw Doreen open her mouth to say something but he got in first. 'An' before you say it don't matter, it does. I'll not have charity from nobody.'

'It's not charity,' countered Doreen. 'It's ... it's a loan. Just till you can pay us back.'

'Oh aye, an' when's that goin' to be? No, Doreen, I won't have it. I'll pay me way or not at all.'

Eddie rested his backside on the upturned Chairoplane car. 'Tell you what, Luke,' he said slowly, 'how about you pay me in kind?'

'How d'you mean?'

'I've got a bit more work on now; I was going to offer it to you anyway, like I said I would. How about you do up some cars and what have you for me, and in return I'll help you put the Chairoplanes to rights?'

Luke considered. 'Well ... sounds fair,' he conceded.

'Hang on, though,' cut in Doreen. 'If Luke works for you to pay you back, he'll not be earning any money, will he? What are he and Rose supposed to live on?'

Eddie raised his hands and let them fall to his sides. 'It's Luke's choice,' he said. 'If he won't take my work as a loan, what more can I do?'

'But surely,' pleaded Doreen. 'There's got to be some other way.'

'I'll do it, Eddie,' said Luke suddenly, as though he had to get the words out before he had time to think better of it. 'Just like you said. I'll work for you in return for you workin' on the Chairoplanes.'

'But what about Rose?' said Doreen, her mouth snapping shut again as she caught sight of Rose coming towards her, stepping gingerly over the bits of broken machinery.

'What about me?' demanded Rose, looking at the three guilt-ridden faces in front of her. It was obvious that something was going on and she'd turned up right in the middle of it. 'What is it I'm not supposed to know?'

'Oh ... nothing. We were just talking,' said

Doreen. 'You know, about the Chairoplanes.'

'An' what did you decide?' Rose looked to Luke for an answer, but he said nothing.

'Dad reckons it's OK, he can fix them,' said Doreen.

Rose looked at the damage and began to wonder. Clearly there was more to be fixed than Luke could possibly manage on his own; he needed skilled help and the use of a proper workshop. But if Eddie Kneale was offering to fix the ride, they couldn't expect him to do so out of the goodness of his heart. Eddie had a living to earn, same as everyone else.

'So.' She folded her arms and fixed Luke with a long, hard stare. 'If Mister Kneale's fixin' 'em, who's payin'?'

Luke squirmed. Doreen got down off the lorry and beckoned to her father.

'Come on, Dad, it's time we were going. I think Rose and Luke have got some things they want to sort out.' She led her father out.

Alone in the almost roofless barn, Rose and Luke perched side by side on the upturned Chairoplane car. The January weather was icy, but Rose felt colder still.

'You're goin' to work for him for no money!'

'What choice have I got?' demanded Luke.

'You could pay him back later. When the season starts.'

'No.' Luke's mouth set in a hard line. 'No more debts, no more charity.'

Rose understood how Luke felt, but fear and resentment were strong emotions, sometimes stronger than love and sympathy.

'Debts! Luke, what do you think we're goin' to have if you're not earnin' any money? All we'll have is the few bob Charlie pays us for havin' Lola, an' that's not enough to keep us in bread!'

'It's the only way,' said Luke firmly. 'I've told Eddie that's what I'll do.'

'Oh you have, have you? You never thought I might like to have a say in it?'

'What's the point of you havin' your six penn'orth? The answer's still goin' to be the same.'

Rose knew there was no point in arguing. When Luke was like this there'd be no going back, not even if he came to see that the choice he'd made was the wrong one. In any case, she had a horrible suspicion that this might indeed be the only way. 'Oh, Luke. Luke, what are we goin' to do?' Automatically she laid her hand on her stomach, frightened for the new life within.

'We'll just have to get by, won't we?'

A sudden thought came to Rose. Of course, why hadn't she thought of it before?

'Jack Verney!'

Luke stared at her. 'What about him?'

'He still owes you half the money, doesn't he?' A wave of relief washed over her. 'Do you think we can manage till he comes back to the Island? It'll only be another three weeks or so ...'

Luke got up off the Chairoplane car and walked over to the truck, hands thrust deep in his pockets and his back to her. 'It don't matter how many weeks it is,' he said dully.

'Course it matters! Soon as he comes back, we'll ask him to pay you the rest of what he owes you for the TT Racer.'

'It don't matter,' repeated Luke, slowly and deliberately, ' 'cause we'll not get another penny piece out of Verney till April.'

Rose's mouth dropped open. 'April! No, Luke, that can't be right.'

'End of April. That's what we agreed.'

Rose hardly knew whether to laugh or cry. This was ludicrous, it didn't make sense. 'But surely ... all you've got to do is tell him how hard-up we are, he'll not say no. Not Jack Verney. He's a good bloke, he'd not let us starve for the want of a few quid!'

Luke turned round slowly to face her. He looked utterly exhausted. 'It's not that simple, love,' he said quietly. 'There's ... conditions, see. I have to do somethin' for Jack or we don't get the rest of the money at all.'

'Do somethin'? For Verney? I don't understand.'

'I ... I did mean to tell you, honest I did. I would have too, only I knew you'd take it bad.'

Black foreboding roosted like a crow on Rose's shoulder. But surely, whatever this was, it couldn't be any worse than what had happened to them already? Surely not ... 'Take what bad, Luke? What've you been hidin' from me?'

'Verney's ditchin' the Wild Australia Show—he reckons it's all played out. Next season he's goin' for a TT spectacular, that's why he was so dead set on buyin' the TT Racer, see.'

Rose didn't see at all. What could this possibly have to do with them and their money?

'Go on,' she said. 'Whatever it is I want to hear it. All of it.'

'You remember that accident I had at Kneale's yard?'

'You were workin' on a car,' said Rose flatly. 'It fell on you.'

'Yeah.' Luke let out a gasp of breath. 'Only it didn't, did it? There wasn't no accident at work. There wasn't no car, it were a motorbike accident ...'

Rose felt her chest tighten. 'Oh, Luke, you didn't fall off the back of Doreen's bike?' She cursed him for his stupidity.

But Luke shook his head. 'I were ridin' this old BSA—'

'Ridin'!' She clenched her hands so tightly that the fingernails bit into her palms. 'You were ridin' a motor bike, after everythin' you promised me?'

He nodded wearily. 'Doreen lent it me.'

Four little words. Four burning arrows of betrayal.

'You borrowed a bike off Doreen? She knew all about this, an' she never said one word to me?'

'She wanted to ... I made her promise not to, you didn't need to know.'

'Didn't need ... But *why* did you do it, Luke? Why?' She willed him to make her understand. 'You swore you'd never get on another bike, you swore!'

There was a long pause before Luke replied.

'I've been practisin'. I never wanted to, Rose, but I had no choice. I knew we'd never last out another season with just the Chairoplanes. An' Verney offered me a job—trick-ridin' in the TT spectacular. It's good money. That's why I took his offer an' not Spence's.' He looked right into her eyes. 'I'm doin' it for you, Rose. For you an' Ellie.'

She wanted to believe him, wanted it more than anything. But there was a strange light in that dark eye, a wild defiance she hardly recognised. There was more to this than a simple desire to provide for her and Ellie—this wasn't just about them, it was about old desires never quite extinguished, old scores never settled. And all at once Rose felt very alone; alone and betrayed, not just by her husband but by Doreen too. Her friend.

'For us!' She searched wildly for the right words to express her anger and her pain. 'How can you say that!'

'It's true.'

'So goin' behind my back's supposed to help us, is it?'

'I knew you'd take it like this, that's why I never—'

She didn't let him finish. 'An' breakin' your neck on a bloody motor bike's for us an' all? I s'pose Doreen thought that was a good idea too, did she?'

'Don't talk rubbish,' retorted Luke. 'Doreen reckoned I ought to tell you straight off.'

'Oh, I see, you were scared of what I'd say, so you reckoned you'd talk it all over with

Doreen, did you? Nice an' cosy like?' Pain stabbed at Rose's heart. 'My God, Luke, that's pretty low—an' to think I thought she was my friend!'

'Will you just listen to me, you stupid cow!' snapped Luke. Hands on Rose's shoulders, he tried to shake her. 'Just listen!'

But Rose was past listening. Pushing him away from her, she screamed in his face. 'Bastard! You rotten, useless bastard!'

And as the tears cascaded down her cheeks she ran from the barn, sobbing as she fled across the field, determined not to let him see her cry.

Lissa Darwell looked startled to find Rose on her doorstep, her eyes swollen and her face blotchy from weeping.

'What's the matter, Rose?'

'Nothin'.' Rose gave a long noisy sniff. 'I just ... just w-want a word, that's all.' She tried to control the words, but every so often they turned into sobs; and as Lissa stood back to let her climb into the van, the tears started rolling down her cheeks again.

'Sit down,' ordered Lissa, pointing at a wobbly wooden chair. 'Now.' She produced a grubby handkerchief from her apron pocket and thrust it at Rose. 'Here, have a good blow. Nothin'? You're not much of a liar are you, Rose Barton?'

'Ta,' whispered Rose, a tear rolling down her nose and plopping into her lap. 'Ta very much.'

Lissa squeezed two more cups out of the interminable pot of stewed tea and settled herself comfortably on the other chair. Unbuttoning her blouse, she got on with breastfeeding the latest addition to the Darwell family, its tiny bald head almost lost in the vast pinkness of her bosom. 'Now. What's ailin' you then?'

For a big, rough woman she could be quite kindly in her own way, thought Rose. Normally she would have died rather than tell the Darwells her troubles, but today wasn't normal, not normal at all. 'It's me an' Luke,' she sniffed. 'We had this row ...'

'Don't tell me,' said Lissa. 'It were about money.'

Rose looked at her, surprised. 'How did you know?'

Lissa chuckled. 'Rows is always about money, ain't they? That or blokes!' She winked. 'You should come out wi' me sometime, let your hair down a bit.' Her grin subsided as she leant forward. 'Look, lovey, don't mind me. You keep it to yourself if you want, some things is private between man an' wife.'

'No, you're right, it *is* about money,' sighed Rose. 'We've got none.' She couldn't quite bring herself to tell Lissa about the motor bike riding, or the way Luke and Doreen had betrayed her with their secrets. She was too angry and too proud. 'If we're goin' to see the winter out I've got to earn some quick—an' I'm that desperate I don't care how.'

Lissa frowned. 'Earn some money? Now don't

361

you take this the wrong way, lovey, but you don't look the type.'

'The type?'

'To hang round back-streets lookin' for sailors.'

For a moment Rose didn't understand. Then she saw what Lissa was getting at and blushed crimson to the roots of her hair. 'No, no—I didn't mean *that!* I meant ... Oh, I don't know what I meant. I just thought you might know some way I can make some money.'

It seemed a stupid idea now. Especially seeing Lissa burst out laughing so loudly that Baby Darwell started grizzling and had to be soothed back onto the breast.

'Gawd help me, Rose, your face is a picture! Make some money, eh? Well, there's the pegs ...'

Somewhere at the back of her mind Rose could hear her father's angry warning, the day she'd announced that she was off to the Isle of Man with Luke: 'Bloody gyppo. He'll have you sellin' clothes pegs out of a basket, you mark my words.' She shut it out of her mind, just as she had done then; all that mattered now was putting food in her daughter's mouth.

'Anythin',' she said. 'I'll do anythin'.'

'Anythin' short of gettin' yourself arrested, eh?' chuckled Lissa, switching the baby to the other breast. 'Well, like I said, you could make clothes pegs like me an' the kids do, an' go out an' sell them. *Bikk'nin'*, we calls it.'

'But what'd Ranty say?'

'Ranty? He won't make no fuss. You'll have

to give him his cut, mind.'

'His cut? Why?'

'Look, lovey, the way it works is this: we all make the pegs an' paper flowers an' stuff, Ranty drives us out on the lorry an' drops us in different places. We go off an' sell, an' he comes back for us at night. Then you pays 'im his cut, an' the rest you can keep. Simple, see?' Lissa took a slurp of tea and scrutinised Rose's bump, just visible underneath her thick jumper and skirt. 'Expectin', eh? Far gone, are you?'

' 'Bout four months. Why?'

'Wear somethin' a bit tight when you go out—you know, show it off.' Lissa grinned. 'Folk always buy when they see you're pregnant; I've tried that one myself half a dozen times.'

'Tried it? How do you mean?'

'With a pillow up me front. Works every time.' Lissa winked. 'You'll make a fortune, Luke'll be well pleased. Just you wait an' see.'

But at this moment Rose couldn't have cared less what Luke thought; all she could think about was what she'd let herself in for.

CHAPTER 29

'Like this?' Rose held up the length of stick for Ranty Darwell's inspection.

Ranty, sitting cross-legged on a mat laid on the hard ground, rocked back and forth with mirth. Just to make Rose's discomfort complete, the Darwell kids joined in, giggling and pointing at her efforts.

'Like that? God help us, woman, try to use that on the line an' it'll split clean in two!'

'Shut it, Ranty,' warned Lissa. 'An' you lot, hush yer noise!' She silenced her brood with a swipe of one large red paw. 'Take no notice, Rose, yer doin' fine.'

'No I'm not.' Rose flung the stick into the brazier and watched it glow red as the flames licked round it. The only good thing about being taught how to make clothes pegs was getting to sit round the fire. Snow had fallen in the last few days, and the air was heavy with the threat of more. Rose was beginning to wonder if she would ever feel warm again. 'It's no good, I just can't do it.'

'Anybody can,' piped up Billy. 'Even girls, if they practise.'

'I told you to shut it,' said Lissa, raising her clenched fist just close enough to Billy's nose to put the fear of God into him. 'Now just you watch again, Rose. Take the stick ... That's right, that's a good dry 'un. Now measure it out.'

Rose did her best to copy Lissa, laying her stick against one that had already been cut, then marking off a five-inch length with the peg-knife. 'Like this?'

'That's right, gel,' nodded Ranty. 'Now stick 'er on top of the stake an' give 'er a good bash with the hammer.'

Conscious that six pairs of eyes were fixed on her, Rose balanced her stick on top of the stake which had been driven into the ground. It promptly fell off and she had to do it all over again.

'Go on,' urged Lissa. 'Hold it tight, but mind yer fingers.'

Rose picked up the hammer and gave the stick a light tap.

'That's no good!' exclaimed Lalla Darwell with a contemptuous pout. 'You've got to thump it real hard. Here.' She took the hammer and brought it crashing down on to the stick, which snapped neatly in two along the scored line. 'See? Now you do it.'

At the third attempt, Rose finally managed to produce a perfect peg-length of willow twig, provoking whistles and giggles of approbation from the Darwell tribe.

'Now what?' she asked.

'Now you give it to Ranty,' explained Lissa, passing it across to her husband, who sat armed with pliers and thin strips of metal cut from old cans and biscuit tins, begged or scavenged from local shops. 'He's a quick worker is my Ranty,' she added proudly.

It occurred to Rose that this was the first time she had ever seen Lissa express any kind of affection for her husband. Usually all they did was glare and shout, and Rose had always thought they loathed the sight of each other. Then again, she reminded herself with a twinge of resentment, love was not always what you expected it to be.

Ranty's fingers moved swiftly, binding the stick round with a strip of tin warmed and

365

softened in the fire, then passing it to Lalla, who stood it on its end and split it neatly down the middle. Billy sat next to her in the circle, waiting with his knife to shape the 'legs' of the peg with a few quick cuts before passing it to Jake, who neatened it by making the inside bevels. Little Davey and Rosanna were at the very end of the production line, gathering the pegs into bundles of a dozen and arranging them in Lissa's big hawking basket. And all of it happened so fast that Rose had difficulty keeping track of each step.

'There,' said Lissa, folding her arms and sitting back on her haunches. 'What d'you make of that then?'

'They're so quick!' exclaimed Rose.

'Quick!' laughed Ranty. 'That's slow. You'll have to learn fast, gel, three gross a day is what we make when we get goin'.'

'Three gross!'

'An' that's not countin' the wooden flowers,' cut in Lalla. 'Mam makes these lovely flowers out of elder wood ...'

'An' roses out of paper,' added Billy. 'Dipped in wax.'

'Don't worry, girl, I'll teach yer,' Lissa reassured her with a pat on the arm. 'Don't suppose you do lacework do yer?'

Rose shook her head. It was spinning. 'I can sew clothes ... but no, I can't do lace.'

'Pity. Always sell well, do lace doilies an' runners. You'll have to stick to the pegs an' the flowers. Still, you're bright enough, you'll earn plenty *bikk'nin'*.'

'Tell yer what,' said Ranty, binding another peg, 'Lissa can teach your Ellie an' all.'

'That's right,' beamed Lissa. 'An' that deaf kiddie too if yer like, give her somethin' to do. What d'you reckon?'

Rose was taken aback. 'What—teach them to make pegs?'

Lissa nodded vigorously. 'That an' the *bikk'nin'*. What with you expectin', an' two little kiddies in tow, folk are bound to buy plenty off yer.'

'But Ellie's got school to go to.'

Ranty clutched his sides and rolled about on the old rug, his tobacco-stained beard flecked with spittle.

'School! What yer want to send the *chavvi* to school for? What use is all them books if you've no food in yer mouth?'

Rose didn't reply; she knew they wouldn't understand that what she wanted more than anything else for Ellie was a chance: a chance to learn something, a chance to better herself, to do something really good with her life. A chance her mam had never had.

'No.' She shook her head. 'Not Ellie.'

'Well the deaf girl then. She ain't at school, is she?'

'No, but ...' Rose thought of Lola, cosy in Dan's old cottage with her father, and something ached very deep inside her. *They* could have been in that cottage if things had gone differently, she and Luke ... or did she really mean she and Charlie? Shocked, she swept the thought out of her mind. 'It's kind of you,

367

but I don't reckon her dad'd want her traipsin' round the Island in all weathers ...'

Rose's voice tailed off as she heard familiar voices approaching across the foggy tober. Letting fall her apron-full of sticks, she got to her feet and turned towards the voices just as two figures loomed out of the sea-mist.

'Still reckon you can patch it up, do you?'

'I told you, Horace, it'll be fixed up good as new.'

'Oh aye?' There was no mistaking the mocking quality in Horace Spence's voice. 'Still believe in Father Christmas an' all, do you, Barton?'

Luke didn't reply. He just trudged on, hands in pockets, while Horace puffed and panted in his wake, throwing taunts after him.

'Know what you ought to do, Barton? You ought to let that wife of yours talk a bit of sense into that thick skull—'

Luke's boots made the frozen grass crackle as he spun round. 'No! I'll tell *you* what I ought to do,' he growled. 'I ought to shut that fat mouth of yours ...'

He put up his fists like a bare-knuckle fighter, and all at once Rose was afraid he really was going to hit Spence. And no matter how much Spence might deserve it, that would be a disaster for the Bartons. Whatever had got into Luke these last few weeks? He had become so quick-tempered, almost frightening in his sudden changes of mood. What could have changed him so rapidly from the gentle, cheerful, easygoing man she had married?

She ran up to him and grabbed his arm. 'Luke, don't!'

But Luke lashed out at her with his free hand, making her stumble and almost fall.

'Get away, woman! This is none of your business.'

She stood her ground, more angry than she was upset. The Darwell kids were all watching, but they didn't turn a hair; they probably saw this kind of thing every day.

'If it's to do with the ride, it *is* to do with me.'

Luke lunged at Spence but Rose side-stepped, blocking his way. 'Leave him alone, Luke. For God's sake, calm down. What's got into you?'

Horace Spence sneered. 'Go on, hit me. That's all your sort can do, talk wi' your fists.'

'Don't push it, Spence.'

'You can't do it, can you? What are you, chicken or summat?'

Luke's face twisted into a grotesque mask of loathing. 'Right, if that's what you want ...'

Summoning up a strength she didn't know she possessed, Rose shoved Luke hard in the chest, catching him off-balance and forcing him to take a step backwards.

'I've had enough of this!' she shouted. 'You're like a pair of kids.'

Horace Spence chuckled delightedly. 'That woman's worth ten of you, lad. Sooner you realise that the better. Now get out my way. I've got more to do than stand here arguin' the toss wi' you.'

Luke stayed exactly where he was for a few moments, staring Spence out; then he caught the look on Rose's face and reluctantly moved aside, muttering a curse under his breath as Spence rolled off towards the site office.

Seconds later Luke turned on Rose. 'This is your doin'.'

'Mine!' Rose stared at him blankly.

'Tellin' all our business to strangers.'

'Me!' This was so ridiculous that Rose could think of nothing to say in her defence. But even if she had defended herself, she could see from the distracted look on his face that Luke was in no mood to be reasonable. Before she could ask him what was wrong, he'd turned his attention to the Darwells.

'See?' he hissed. 'Strangers.'

'Now hold on, Barton,' cautioned Ranty Darwell, getting to his feet. He was a head shorter than Luke but nigh on twice as broad, with arms so full of muscle they looked like twisted rope. 'Just you watch yer tongue.'

'Strangers?' laughed Lissa Darwell. 'There ain't no strangers here, boy, just Romanies doin' each other a favour.'

Luke looked sharply at Rose. 'Favours? What's she mean, Rose?'

'Nothin'. Well, all right ...' Luke had to know sooner or later; it might as well be now. And he might even be pleased. 'Lissa's teachin' me to make pegs, I'm goin' to go out *bikk'nin'* with her an Lalla—'

'*Bikk'nin'!*' Luke wasn't pleased; far from it. 'Forget it, Rose, I won't have it. I won't have

370

no wife of mine walkin' the streets sellin' clothes pegs.'

'But Luke—'

'I said no, an' I mean no!'

Perhaps if things had been better between them, and circumstances not so bad, Rose would have let Luke have his own way. But this was about survival, not some stupid notion Luke had got into his head.

'So what are we goin' to live on, Luke, fresh air?'

'We'll make ends meet. My way.'

'No, Luke, I've had enough of your way.'

'I'm the head of this family, what I say goes.'

Rose's temper quickened. 'Well if somebody don't do somethin' pretty quick, you'll be the head of nothin'.' She tried to reason with him. 'Look, I've always done everythin' you wanted, come over here to live like a pauper, given up the house we had, everythin'. An' what do you do? You go behind my back an' tell me lies.

'You've had your chance. I'm sorry, Luke, I really am. But this time we're doin' it *my* way.'

'Hello there!' A smiling face poked through the door of the Bartons' vardo. 'It's started snowing again, can I come in?'

Rose, sitting on one of the locker-seats tying pegs into bundles, did not even bother looking up at Doreen. 'Please yourself.' She went on winding string round the pegs, not really seeing what she was doing, conscious only of the

371

bruised heart pounding in her chest. Right now, Doreen Kneale was just about the last person she wanted to talk to.

'Nothing wrong, is there?' Doreen climbed inside the vardo in a cloud of swirling snowflakes, pulling the door securely shut behind her.

Rose tied a knot in the string and sliced through the ends with an impatient slash of the peg-knife. 'Why? Should there be?' She threw the bundle of pegs into the basket and picked up another dozen.

'I don't know.' Doreen sat down on the opposite bench. Rose could feel her looking her up and down. 'You tell me.'

Rose glanced up at Doreen's rosy, wind-whipped complexion, tousled curls and innocent expression, but it was more than she could bear. She lowered her eyes. 'There's nothin' to tell.'

Doreen shuffled her feet on the vardo floor. Snowflakes that had stuck to her motorcycle boots began to melt in the frugal warmth from the stove, forming little wet pools on the curled-up square of lino.

'I came over to see Luke,' said Doreen.

Rose felt the stab of betrayal all over again. She gave a sarcastic laugh. 'You're honest, I'll give you that.'

Doreen looked puzzled. She leaned forward, hands resting on her knees. 'I don't understand. Rose, what's this all about?'

Rose went on bundling pegs. 'Like I said, at least you're honest. Let's face it, you wouldn't bother comin' all this way to see me, would you?'

'Why not? Rose, why wouldn't I come to see you? You're my friend.'

Rose felt herself tense up inside, her heart contracting in her chest until she felt dizzy and sick and angry all at once.

'You've got a funny way of showin' it.'

'Rose ...?'

'Just leave it, Doreen.'

Doreen fell silent for a few moments. The only sounds in the vardo were the tick of the old clock on the shelf above the stove, and the thunk of bundles dropping into the hawking basket.

'Ellie at school, is she?'

'It's Monday,' pointed out Rose acidly. 'Where else would she be?'

'I just thought ... with the snow ... You're not minding Lola today then?'

'She's at home. With Charlie.'

'Oh.' Doreen paused. 'I've ... er, got a new part for the Chairoplanes on the truck. Where's Luke?'

So at last you've got round to what you came for, thought Rose, almost relieved that the charade of politeness could end. Her eyes snapped up. 'Don't you know?'

Doreen shook her head, a look of bafflement on her face. 'No—should I?'

'Well he seems to tell you everything else.'

Their eyes met, Doreen's expression infuriatingly blank.

'What ...?'

'Like his little garage accident. Bit careless

wasn't it, lettin' that car fall on him?'

Doreen coloured up. 'I ...'

Rage took over and Rose's fingers clenched into claws, cold and unresponsive as she tried to concentrate on tying string round yet another bundle of pegs.

'Don't come the innocent with me, Doreen Kneale, you know all about the bike ridin', don't you? An' the accident. If you'd not lent him that bike it'd never have happened!'

It was almost as though a pin had punctured Doreen. She sank down, head almost touching her knees, her body flaccid as a deflated balloon. 'The bike,' she murmured into the bubbly brown curtain of her hair.

'Yes. The bike.' Rose picked up the peg basket and hurled it to the floor, sending its contents skidding all over the vardo. 'Why did you do it, Doreen? Why? All the time pretendin' you were my friend.'

Doreen sat up, her face flushed. 'I *am* your friend.'

'Friends don't keep secrets. Not that kind of secret. Luke lost an eye trick-ridin', Doreen. He swore to me he'd never get on another motor bike—an' what do you do? You only go an' lend him one!'

Doreen raked her fingers back through her hair, shaking her head slowly as if trying to rid it of a guilty memory. 'I'm so sorry, Rose—'

'Sorry! You should be.'

'I really am.'

'Then why did you do it?'

Doreen sighed. 'He came to me one day and

said he wanted to borrow this old BSA we'd got lying around in the yard—just to practise on, he said. Well, I knew he'd promised you he wouldn't ride, so I said he should tell you, and he said ...'

'Go on.'

'He said he would ... when he was ready.'

'When he was good an' ready?' spat Rose. 'Oh, thanks, Doreen. Ta very much!'

'If I hadn't lent him a bike he'd have got one somewhere else,' Doreen pointed out gently. 'But I know I did wrong; I should've said no and come straight over and told you. I just ... Oh, I don't know, I just didn't think. There didn't seem any harm in it, I suppose. But then he had the accident ...'

Rose looked Doreen full in the face. 'He's not fit to ride, Doreen. He can't judge things like he used to. He could've got himself killed.'

'I really am sorry, Rose, please believe me.'

Despite her bitterness, Rose knew it was true. Doreen was white as a sheet and shaking; she didn't have it in her to be a hard-faced bitch. The worst she could ever be was thoughtless.

'I do believe you,' admitted Rose. 'But it's the way you an' Luke went behind my back ... an' then I only found out about this business with Verney by accident.'

'Verney?' Doreen frowned. 'What's Verney got to do with anything?'

Rose saw Doreen's puzzled expression, and it dawned on her that she wasn't the only one Luke had been keeping in the dark.

'You mean you don't know? About Luke

signin' up to do stunt-ridin' in Jack Verney's new TT show?'

Doreen's face blanched whiter still. 'Stunt-riding! Oh, Rose, I swear, I had no idea. Luke never said a word about stunt-riding. I thought he was just practising to try and get over his fear—you know, get his nerve back so he'd have something to make you proud of him. Oh, Rose ...'

The two women sat staring glumly at each other for many long moments.

'Maybe he'll change his mind,' said Doreen.

Rose shook her head. 'He can't. The stupid idiot did a deal with Verney—if he don't do the ridin' next season, Verney won't pay us the last of the money he owes us. An' without that ...' she spread her hands wide, 'we're finished.'

'You mustn't say that.'

'Why not? It's true. An' God knows how we're goin' to manage for money till April, what with the Chairoplanes the way they are. That's why I'm goin' sellin' clothes pegs with Lissa Darwell.'

'Clothes pegs!' Doreen looked horrified. 'What—walking miles in this weather?'

'I've no choice, Doreen. It's that or starve. Course, Luke don't like it, but to tell the truth I'm past carin' what Luke thinks. He goes behind my back, he bawls me out an' threatens Horace Spence, he's hardly got a good word to say for me or Ellie these days. The other day, I really thought he was goin' to hit me.'

'But he'd never do that, not Luke!'

376

'Not the Luke I married,' said Rose. 'But I'm tellin' you, he's changed. It's like livin' with a stranger.'

'Oh Rose,' said Doreen gently, 'don't say that. Luke loves you.'

'You really think so?' asked Rose doubtfully.

'I know so.'

'Well I'm beginnin' to wonder,' replied Rose. 'An' I'll tell you somethin' else. This can't go on.' She was so determined to be hard and cool and sensible, but even as she spoke she was struggling to stop tears springing to her eyes. 'Oh, Doreen. I can't take much more of this, I swear I can't.'

Doreen slid across and sat on the bench next to her friend, putting an arm about her shoulders, hugging her and sharing her troubles like only a true friend can.

'It'll be all right. Everything'll be all right.'

Rose blinked away her tears. 'Well if it isn't, I'm not standin' for it for ever,' she declared.

'What do you mean?'

Rose took a deep breath and wiped her face with the back of her arm. 'I managed without Luke before; I can manage without him again. If things get any worse I'll just take Ellie an' go.'

At least one part of Rose's life was turning out better than she'd expected—and that was the part that contained Charlie. Despite Luke's muttered insistence that it 'just wouldn't do', the arrangement that Rose would look after Lola when Charlie went to sea was working out fine.

Charlie arrived to collect Lola one bitterly cold February morning, whistling as he strode across the snowy tober, a brown paper package tucked under his arm.

Lissa Darwell hailed him as soon as he got within earshot. 'Mornin', Charlie. What you got there then?'

Charlie hugged the parcel to him and grinned. 'That's for me to know.'

Lissa nudged her eldest daughter. 'Bet it's more o' that Irish butter for Rose. I dunno, Charlie.' She winked broadly. 'People round here'll start talkin'!'

'They can talk all they like,' replied Charlie cheerfully, climbing the vardo steps and knocking on the door.

Rose was just putting the last of the breakfast pots away when she heard Charlie at the door. She hesitated for a moment, catching a glimpse of her reflection in one of the polished copper pans. Whatever would Charlie think of her, dressed like this, ready for the *bikk'ning?* With one of Lissa's shabbiest frocks, taken in at the waist to emphasise her bump, clumpy boots, an old patched coat and a shawl, she looked more like a bundle of rags than pretty Rosie Dobbs, who'd once sashayed down Grange Road on Charlie Cartwright's arm. Then again, what did it matter what Charlie thought? All they had to do was manage to be civil to one another.

A second knock jolted her into action. 'Come in,' she called, hanging the pan on its hook above the stove.

The wagon door opened and in stepped

378

Charlie, stooping to avoid hitting his head on the low doorframe.

'Cold out there,' he commented, kicking the heels of his seaboots against the doorframe to get rid of the snow. 'Brought you a bit of whey butter ...' As he straightened up he got his first proper look at Rose. 'What the ... what the heck have you done to yourself?'

Hands on hips, Rose pirouetted like a mannequin. 'What do you reckon? It's all the rage in Paris, you know.' She took in the expression on Charlie's face and burst out laughing. 'It's all right, Charlie, I've not gone barmy. This is Lissa's idea. I'm goin' *bikk'nin'*.'

'Bikk-what?'

'Hawkin'. You know, sellin' stuff door to door. Pegs, flowers, bits of heather, lucky charms ...' Picking up her basket, she tried to remember what Lissa had taught her. 'Buy a few pegs from a poor gypsy, lady? A shillin' to buy food for the littl'uns? Six at home an' another on the way ...'

Charlie's expression turned from amusement to disbelief. 'You're never goin' to do *that*?'

'Course I am.'

'But ... but dressed like that? Trampin' the streets?'

Rose offered a wry smile. Typical Charlie, she thought, always with his head in the clouds, no idea of reality. 'There's no shame in it. An' besides, I've no choice. Somebody's got to put food on the table, an' every penny Luke's earned is goin' on fixin' the Chairoplanes.'

Charlie's golden eyes narrowed. 'Is somethin' wrong—with you an' Luke?'

'Why would there be?' replied Rose briskly. 'Come on, let's go an' fetch Lola from Percy's.'

'What's she doin' there?'

Rose draped the shawl over her head and wrapped it tightly against the cold. 'Tell you the truth, I'm not sure. He's got somethin' in that yard of his, you know, locked in the big shed. Whatever it is, Lola thinks it's wonderful. She went off there first thing after breakfast.'

Charlie followed Rose down the steps on to the tober.

'Rose ...'

She looked back at him over her shoulder. 'What?'

'If you an' Luke ... I mean, if there's anythin' wrong ...'

'I told you, there isn't.' Rose willed him to drop it, but then Charlie never had been able to take a hint.

'But if there was ... an' if it was my fault. I wouldn't want to cause trouble.'

Rose gave a sigh: half weariness, half exasperation. 'Let it lie, Charlie.'

'But—'

'Just let it lie, all right?' She spoke quite sharply this time, and he looked almost wounded. 'Look, I know you mean well, but—'

'But it's none of my business, right?'

She met his steady gaze. 'Right.'

They trudged on together, Charlie quickly catching up so that they were walking side by side. Horace Spence was barking orders at the men repairing the roller-coaster, but he paused long enough to draw breath and take a good long stare at the two figures crossing the tober. Rose wondered what he was thinking.

'I'm grateful to you, Rose,' Charlie said suddenly.

She laughed awkwardly. 'I've told you already, you needn't be.'

'But I mean it, I really do. Lola's not an easy kid to look after. God knows plenty have tried, but you're the only one she'll stick with.'

Rose smiled. 'It's you she loves, though. You should see her face light up when you come to fetch her.'

'All the same, she's fond of you and Ellie ... an' Luke,' he added, almost as an afterthought. 'She loves it here.'

'Can't think why,' commented Rose, pulling her shawl around her and tensing against the salt-laden wind driving in off the sea. 'Anyhow, I don't mind lookin' after her, she's a good kid ... when you get to know her.'

'Nobody gets to know Lola if she don't want 'em to,' replied Charlie ruefully. 'She can be a right little devil.'

'Well she always behaves herself when Ellie's around. An' she was a real help when Ellie had that bronchitis. Wouldn't let anyone else look after her, you know. I'm glad to have her, Charlie, an' that's the truth.'

'An' what about Luke?' asked Charlie. 'Is he glad too?'

The silence that fell between them was more

eloquent than any words.

'Luke's been busy,' said Rose quietly. 'With the Chairoplanes. He hardly notices anythin' much.'

Percy Sayle's yard extended round the back of the ramshackle shed he leased from Horace Spence. Chickens, geese, rabbits and a pig called it home, and there were always three or four children swarming amid the mud and livestock.

'Percy?' called Rose as they walked round the side. 'Are you there?'

'Who is it?' asked a faint voice from the bottom of the yard.

'It's Rose—an' I've got Charlie with me.'

'Oh. You'd best come in then.'

A big old shed stood at the far end, its doors drooping on their hinges and the slatted wooden walls warped with age. This was Percy's 'workshop', a secret place which few people had ever seen inside, not that there could be anything worth stealing in there—even church mice were better off than the Sayles. Rose nudged open the door and stepped inside, blinking as her eyes accustomed themselves to the semi-darkness. A shaft of wintry sunlight slanted down from a high, square window whose cracked glass was half-covered by the fine tracery of a spider's web. She breathed in and sneezed in the dusty air, aromatic with the scents of creosote and well-rotted pig manure.

'Hello there, Missus Rose.' Percy straightened up from his workbench and touched his cap. 'Misther Charlie. You've come for the little lass then?'

Rose didn't reply immediately. She was too busy taking everything in. From all four corners of the workshop strange faces stared back at her—faces with long, curved beaks and red wattles and beady eyes that had once been black and gold. Cockerels. Giant wooden cockerels on barley-twisted poles, stacked up higgledy-piggledy against the walls or lying across broken tables and bits of rusty machinery.

One of them, freed from its pole, sat slightly askew but almost upright on the floor. And sitting astride one of its two leather saddles, her arms wrapped tightly round its neck and her cheek pressed against its peeling, painted flank, was Lola.

She smiled and laughed as she saw her father, but when he tried to prise her away from the wooden bird she clung on tighter and mouthed wordless sounds of protest.

Percy laughed. 'She loves them roosters an' no mistake, Misther Charlie. Loves 'em almost like I love 'em meself.'

He ran an affectionate hand over the carved crest of a fierce-looking bird, its beak half open and its pointed tongue protruding. It had seen better days—they all had—but even in its cracked and peeling state Rose could see the magnificence shining through.

'Where did you get them?' she exclaimed.

'Get 'em? Oh, I've had 'em years, Missus. Came off one of them old galloper roundabouts what got turned into Chairoplanes. Cryin' shame it were ...'

But Rose wasn't listening any more. And

383

all she could see were the painted cockerels looking back at her, amid the gilded poles and the bits of old steam organ. An idea was forming in her head, forming and spinning like an old-fashioned carousel.

'Rooster gallopers,' she whispered, and Charlie looked at her, puzzled.

'What?'

She laughed. 'Rooster gallopers, Charlie, don't you see? Barton's Rooster Gallopers.'

CHAPTER 30

'But Luke, it's the obvious thing to do!' pleaded Rose.

'Obvious!' Luke took off his jacket and threw it across the locker-seat. 'The obvious thing is to get them Chairoplanes mended. Where's my dinner, anyroad?' he demanded, hurling himself down onto the bench.

'Just dishin' up.' Rose ladled a dollop of potato stew on to a tin plate and tried again. Perhaps Luke would be in a better temper once he'd got some food inside him. 'You said the repairs weren't goin' well.'

'I said they were goin' a bit slow, that's all.' Luke picked up his spoon and started eating. 'There's nothin' in this but spuds.'

Rose resisted the temptation to tell Luke he was lucky to have spuds on the money that was coming in, but for Ellie's sake she said nothing.

'Here, love,' she said to the little girl. 'You go an' eat yours with Billy Darwell, eh? Your dad an' I have got things to talk about.'

'Why can't I eat at the table with Dad?' demanded Ellie. It wasn't like her to play up, but lately Luke's moods were so black that they were rubbing off on everyone.

' 'Cause I say so.'

'But Mam—'

'Do what your mother says,' snapped Luke. 'Go on, get out!'

Ellie's golden eyes filled with hurt and she shrank away, leaving her plate untouched on the table.

'Your dinner, love ...' said Rose, her heart going out to her daughter, too young to understand why her father was angry all the time.

'Not 'ungry,' muttered Ellie, and she turned tail and ran out of the van.

Rose saw her disappearing into the dusk as she headed for the Darwells' van. 'Now look what you've done,' she said. 'You didn't have to lose your temper like that.'

'Oh shut your mouth,' Luke growled back. 'That's all you ever do, whine on at me. Why can't you just leave me alone?'

'Oh, Luke.' Rose sank on to the bench opposite her husband. 'What's wrong?'

'Nothin' you can't mend by shuttin' up.'

'But Luke,' pleaded Rose, 'please listen. If the Chairoplanes can't be mended—'

'I said they can.'

'But if they can't ... we could use the stuff

in Percy's yard to turn the ride back into a carousel, the way it used to be when Walleye had it. Just think about it—it'd be lovely. Painted cockerels instead of horses, gilded poles, a proper steam organ ...'

Luke laughed sarcastically. 'Oh aye, an' all the punters in bloody top hats an' crinolines. Don't talk daft, Rose, nobody's interested in roundabouts any more. They want modern rides, not old fashioned rubbish.'

'Yes they do!' protested Rose, angry now because Luke wouldn't even listen. And for once, she truly believed she was right. 'Look at Lola—she loves those cockerels, you should see the way her eyes light up when she sees them ...'

'Lola!' snorted Luke. 'What is it with you an' that kid, Rose? It's Lola this an' Lola that, all the bleedin' day long. She's not even yours, she's just some *gorgio*'s kid—'

Rose seethed. 'Some *gorgio*'s kid? Like Ellie, you mean?'

Luke at least had the good grace to look uncomfortable. 'Ellie's different.'

'*Please*, Luke. Please just look at the gallopers.'

'Why should I waste my time lookin' at somethin' I'm not interested in?'

But Rose wasn't giving up. There was too much at stake. 'Nearly all the parts are there, Percy said so. It'd hardly cost anythin' ...'

Luke pushed his plate aside with an impatient shove. 'You don't give up, do you?'

'Not when I know I'm right. Please Luke.' She begged him with her eyes, laying her hand very gently on his. 'For me.'

But Luke snatched his hand away, grabbed his jacket from the seat and stood up.

'Where are you goin'?' demanded Rose.

'Somewhere I can get some peace an' quiet.'

'But you've not eaten your ...'

It was useless. Luke was already gone, leaving the vardo door standing open and Rose smarting from the sting of rejection.

That night the snow that had been hanging in heavy grey clouds over the Island came tumbling out of an off-white sky. By the time Rose left the wagon the next morning it was over a foot deep, and she had to hike up her skirts as she waded through the powdery softness. Deep down she knew there was truth in what Luke had said—this was no day to be out on the roads, hawking clothes pegs—but how else could she earn the money they so desperately needed?

Ranty and Lalla were already at the ancient truck they used to get about in, Lalla handing up the baskets to her father in the cab.

'Mornin',' Rose, cold enough for you yet?' enquired Ranty with a good-natured laugh.

Lalla handed up the last of the baskets, the wares covered with a teacloth to keep out the snow. 'It'll warm up a bit now,' she reassured Rose. 'Now it's snowin' proper.'

'I hope so.' Rose peered doubtfully at the whirling sky. The snow was so thick that she could only just make out the distant outlines of the vardos and the roller-coaster beyond. And

387

now the wind was getting up too, whipping the snow into eddies and drifts. 'We're still goin' out sellin' then?'

'Course we are,' declared Lalla, jumping up into the cab and making room for Lissa, who was clumping towards them through the snow. 'Wouldn't let a bit of snow stop us. Would we, Dad?'

'I shouldn't worry, love,' said Lissa, puffing and panting from her exertions as she flopped down next to her daughter. 'Snow never settles long on the island, does it Ranty?'

'Never.' Ranty nodded, jamming the stem of his pipe between his teeth. 'Not with all this sea roundabouts. Probably all be gone by tomorrer.'

Rose found that hard to believe. This was the harshest winter she could recall, in or out of a leaky vardo. She'd heard that some places on the mainland had got it so bad they were almost cut off.

'But Percy says—'

Lissa laughed. 'Percy? You don't want to bother about him, love, he's sixpence short of a shillin' that one. 'Course, you don't have to come out today if you don't want ...'

'It's all right,' said Rose hastily. 'I'm comin'.'

'Budge up then, Lalla.' Lissa jabbed her daughter in the ribs. 'Shift yer fat backside an' make room.'

Grudgingly Lalla shuffled sideways on the bench seat. Rose found a toe-hold on the top of the front wheel and managed to haul herself up with Lissa's help. It was a tight squeeze in the cab, but at least there was warmth in their clustering up together. Ranty was like a one-man furnace, the sleeves of his work shirt rolled up even in this weather.

The lorry's engine grumbled in the cold then at last growled into life, and they lumbered slowly off the tober, wheels skidding on the ice beneath the snow as they hit the downward slope. Rose held her breath and tried not to look scared as the road curved perilously close to the cliffs. It wasn't until they were on the main road, heading south, that she began to breathe again.

'Where are we goin' today?' she asked, peering into the whiteness ahead. The windscreen wipers struggled to scrape away the fat, white snowflakes as quickly as they piled up on the glass.

'South of the Island,' explained Lissa. 'Santon, Ballasalla, Ballakeeill.'

'Balla-where?' asked Rose, suddenly realising how little she knew about this Island. In all the months she'd lived here, she'd scarcely ventured outside Douglas.

'Villages,' said Ranty. 'Down Castletown way. Good earnin's there, ain't there Lalla?'

Lalla grinned and rubbed her thumb and forefinger together. 'Plenty of money, them farmers' wives. Like their palms read an' all.'

'Just tell 'em a load of old *hokibens*,' said Lissa. 'Like you do in the dukkerin' booth. An' make it good—there's always a bob or two extra for a good tale.'

The lorry rumbled slowly on down the old Castletown road past the Crogga estate, through

389

the steadily worsening weather, the sky turning gradually through shades of dirty grey to pure white. Few other vehicles had ventured out to clear a way, and within a few moments their tyre tracks were completely obliterated by fresh falling snow.

Face pressed against the cab window, Rose gazed into the distance, trying to make out her surroundings. Beyond the hedges, dark shapes that might be cows or sheep were huddled together in the snow. And over there, up on the hill, she could just distinguish the dark rectangle of a cottage or barn. But she could have been on the moon, for all she knew.

She shivered, but not with cold. Suddenly she felt very alone and very far from home.

'You know Rose is right, don't you, Luke?' Doreen hopped up on to her father's bench, next to Luke, and perched on the edge.

Luke didn't reply. He just went on gazing grimly ahead at the pieces of mechanism laid out on the floor of Eddie's workshop.

'Luke?'

His head sank down until it rested in his hands, the tips of his fingers pushing so hard against his temples that they left white indentations in the tanned flesh.

'Luke, what's wrong?'

'Nothin',' he said flatly.

'Don't give me that; I'm not blind, you know.' She swung her long legs thoughtfully back and forth. 'There's been something wrong ever since you had the accident, hasn't there?'

Luke's fingers trailed slowly down the sides of his face and fell into his lap. 'I'm all right. All it is ...'

'Go on, I'm listening.'

'I get these headaches sometimes. It's nothin' really.'

'Have you told Rose?'

Luke said nothing.

'Well have you seen a doctor then?'

The backlash was sudden. 'I told you, I'm all right! Just leave me be, I'm fine.' Luke got off the bench and walked across to the scattered assortment of twisted and broken metal. 'Us Bartons are finished, aren't we?'

'Don't be silly, of course you're not.' Doreen jumped down and came over to join him. 'But ... but I think Dad's right, we can't mend all these Chairoplane cars, it'd cost more than they'd ever earn you. You ought to listen to Rose, Luke, she's got a good idea.'

'What?' Luke's expression turned to a sneer. 'Take a load of old rubbish off Percy Sayle?'

'Those fittings aren't rubbish,' insisted Doreen. 'They're in pretty good condition; all they need is a bit of grease and paint. It wouldn't be difficult to convert the Chairoplanes back to an old-style carousel.'

'Old-style? Old hat more like.' Luke kicked a sheared-off bolt and it scudded noisily across the oily floor. 'People want new rides, American-style rides, the stuff only Verney an' Spence can afford.'

'They don't all want new stuff. They like the old rides too. Think about it: a carousel, all done up like it used to be—it'd be a real crowd-puller.'

Luke stood in contemplation for a few moments. 'You really think so, don't you?'

'I wouldn't say it if I didn't.'

'Maybe. Maybe ... I guess you could be right.'

'Not me, Luke,' said Doreen firmly, 'Rose. This is Rose's idea and it's Rose you should be talking to about it.' But Luke seized her hands, squeezing them so tightly that she gasped.

'It's not Rose I want to talk to, it's you,' he said softly.

Their eyes met, only for a moment but a moment was long enough. Speaking softly like that, standing in profile against the light so that his injured face was in shadow, Luke Barton looked so very much like Dan. And looking at him standing there, Doreen remembered not just the pain that Dan had caused her, but the love she had felt for him. A love that had never quite died.

'You don't mean that,' she said, pulling away.

'I know what I mean. You understand me, Doreen, you're the only one who does.'

Doreen opened her mouth to say something but the right words wouldn't come out. 'I don't think you should talk like that, Luke.' She walked over to the door and looked out. 'The weather's closing in. Time you were going.'

'I don't care about the weather, I—'

'Best go home, Luke.' She was smiling but

392

her tone was firm. 'To your wife. You don't want to be stranded here with me, do you?'

But from the look on his face, she knew that he did.

It was a hard job getting back to Douglas, even with a lift part of the way along the main Peel Road. By the time Luke reached Funland, gales had whipped the heavy snowfall into a blizzard and he could hardly see his hand in front of his face.

'Dad, Dad!' Ellie ran towards him as he stumbled through the gates, flinging herself into his arms.

'What's up?' he demanded, picking up on something in Ellie's voice. 'What's happened?'

'Mam's not back, Dad. I come home from school an' she's not here.'

'Not back?' Luke took Ellie's hand and marched, head down, through the snow towards the Darwells' wagon. 'Course she's back. Look, there's Ranty Darwell's motor.'

'She's not here, Dad, she's not,' insisted Ellie, having to trot through the snow to keep up with him.

Luke would have gone straight to the Darwells' vardo and fetched Rose home. But he spotted Ranty, Lissa and Lalla piling out of the lorry's cab, deep in a noisy argument.

'You should've stayed an' looked for her!'

'Looked? We looked everywhere, you stupid *monisha!* Any longer, an' we'd all have been stuck in the bleedin' snow.'

'What's Luke goin' to say when you tell him?'

Ranty Darwell's face was gaunt with horror as Luke surged up out of the snow.

'Where's my Rose?' he demanded.

Ranty, Lissa and Lalla exchanged looks but nobody said anything.

Luke raised his voice to a shout. 'I said, where's my bloody wife?'

'Now steady on,' said Ranty, looking nervous for all his muscle. 'She'll be all right. We've told the gavvers an' they're out lookin' for her now.'

'The gavvers? What the hell's the gavvers got to do with this?'

Only Lissa had the guts to come out and say it. 'Rose ... She wasn't there at the pick-up point when Ranty went to fetch her back. We looked everywhere, but the roads round Ballakeeill is all blocked, see—the weather's that bad we had to turn back.'

Luke roared with fury as he hurled himself at Ranty Darwell, throwing him back against the lorry and twisting his red neckerchief so tight that the man's eyes bulged.

'You left her there? You left her out there, in this? You bloody *pikie* bastard, you filthy bloody *diddikoi* ...'

Somebody hauled Luke off Ranty, but not before he'd spat every Romany curse he knew in his face. And even then he felt no release. For Rose was out there somewhere, lost in the snow, and there was not a damn thing he could do about it.

CHAPTER 31

Must keep going. So tired, but I must keep
going ...

Rose stumbled as she waded through the
drifting snow. Flakes drove hard as frozen
needles against her face and she screwed up
her eyes, trying desperately to focus on the
horizon. But there was no horizon any more,
no difference between sky and hills and hedges;
just whiteness everywhere.

She had lost her bearings hours back, taking
a wrong turn off a farm track and wandering
further and further from the road. There was
no sight of it now, no sight and no sound.
Everything was curiously muffled and distant,
nothing breaking the silence save the faraway,
high-pitched bleat of a lost lamb.

The wind whistled past her, cutting through
her wet clothes and stinging her skin; but she
hardly felt it any more. The cold had numbed
her brain and dulled her senses. She felt sleepy
and dazed, but forced herself to walk on, feeling
with her left hand for the line of the drystone wall.
Surely somewhere, at the end of it, there would be
a road or a house or, best of all, Ranty Darwell's
lorry, waiting to take her home. Would he be
angry—when he knew she had lost the basket and
most of the takings, scattered under the snow she
couldn't remember where or when?

So tired. But she must find shelter.

The drystone wall gave way to hawthorn hedging, with thorns that pricked and scratched her flesh as she leant against it. Her free hand curved over her stomach. Night was falling. For the child's sake, if not for her own, she must find somewhere safe and dry.

And so she trudged on, each step more leaden than the last, her whole body bent with fatigue and cold. The wind screamed and whirled about her, so strong that it threatened to lift her off her feet and plunge her into six feet of snow. If that happened she would be lost. No one would find her, not out here. For the first time her numbed brain began to feel real fear. She might even die ...

As she reached out to stop herself falling, something moved beneath her hand. Something soft and alive—another human being? A low bleat was joined by another, and then another. She had stumbled into a flock of sheep, crowding miserably together against the hedgerow in the feeble shelter of a gnarled hawthorn tree.

A tear started from Rose's eye but the wind dried it on her cheek. It was useless. She was hopelessly lost, she had no idea where she might be, Ranty would be long gone and she would never find her way back home to Luke and Ellie.

She might just as well give up now.

'Look, she's waking up.'
'Are you all right, dear?'
At first the voices made no sense to Rose.

And as she opened her eyes the faces swam in and out of focus.

'W-who ...?'

She tried to sit up and kind hands supported her, sliding a cushion behind her head.

'That's it, Sam, you hold her up. She's weak as a kitten, poor thing.'

'It's all right, gel, you're quite safe.' The man's voice was kind too, and so was his face: an honest, middle-aged, Manx face, ruddy from working out in all weathers, and topped by a countryman's greasy brown cap. His clothes were damp with melting snow. 'That tea on, is it, Cissie?'

'I'll put a drop of whiskey in it,' nodded Sam's wife, a neat woman in her fifties with pepper-and-salt hair tucked into a pleat and wearing a crisp apron over a sensible brown frock. 'That'll warm you up a bit,' she smiled at Rose.

Rose looked down at herself, suddenly realising that her clothes had gone and she was wearing a voluminous flannelette nightie and big woollen socks under a scratchy grey blanket, tucked in tight round her hips. Even stranger, she was sitting on a sofa in somebody's parlour, a fire roaring in the grate and a china shepherdess smiling down at her from the mantelpiece.

'What's your name, dear?' asked Cissie, pouring a cup of tea and adding a dash of Irish whiskey and three sugars.

'R-Rose.' Her lips felt numb and unresponsive, as though they had been almost frozen and hadn't quite thawed out yet. All she could remember was being lost and very, very sleepy—and then ... nothing. 'Rose Barton. Who ...?'

Cissie perched on the arm of the sofa and handed Rose the cup of tea. 'I'm Cissie Maddrell, and this big lump here is my Sam. Now drink that down. *All* of it, mind.'

The cup rattled against the saucer as Rose raised it to her lips. The tea was warm and sweet, and she was grateful for the slow burn of the whiskey, trickling down into her stomach and waking up her shivering body. But as her body awoke, so did her memory.

'Ellie ... I've got to go! Ellie'll be wantin' her tea!'

'Ellie?' Cissie looked at her, head cocked on one side. 'Who's Ellie?'

'My little girl. Please ... you've been very kind, but I've got to go.' She tried to get up but her legs wouldn't let her.

Sam eased her back down on to the sofa and tucked the blanket round her again. 'You're not going anywhere tonight, gel. Roads is all closed, snow's coming down fast. I'd not send a dog out in that.' He shook his head disbelievingly. 'Whatever were you doing, wandering about in the snow?'

'And you in your condition,' added Cissie, with a note of gentle reproach.

'I was out *bikk'nin'* ... with Lissa. Sellin',' she explained to the puzzled faces. 'You know, pegs an' stuff. I was in Ballakeeill ... then I got lost. How did I get here?'

'You were out cold under the hedge,' replied Sam.

'If Sam hadn't gone out to see to the beasts you'd be there still,' added Cissie. 'It was only the sheep kept you from freezing to death.'

'The sheep ...' murmured Rose, remembering a little more now. The huddle of bodies clustering round her as she'd swayed against the hedge. 'You're very kind.'

'Nonsense,' said Sam. 'Now drink up and then Cissie'll get you some soup.'

Part of Rose was so exhausted that all she wanted to do was drift back to sleep. But there was panic inside her too. What about Luke and Ellie, waiting for her back at Funland? They'd be frantic, wondering what had happened to her.

'My family,' she said. 'I've got to get home.'

'But you can't, Rose love, the roads are all blocked. Where do you live?'

'At Funland ... the fairground.'

Cissie shook her head. 'All that way? Heavens, no, dear, you'll have to stay here tonight. In the morning Sam'll go down to the school house and ask Mr Quilliam if he can use the telephone.'

The Maddrells had been so kind that Rose almost wept when the police finally came to take her back to Funland. Life had been so brutal and unforgiving of late that it hurt to be reminded that it wasn't like that for everyone. Some people managed to be happy no matter what—the way she and Luke had

399

been happy before they came to the island. How had everything gone so wrong?

It wasn't Luke who greeted her as she stepped out of the police car, still wearing the old-fashioned clothes Cissie Maddrell had lent her. It was Ranty and Lissa Darwell, Lissa rushing up to the car and giving her a hug as if she were part of the family.

'God help me, Rose, I thought we'd lost yer. Let me look at yer, girl. Oh, thank the Lord ... is the baby all right?'

'I'm fine, but where's Ellie?' demanded Rose, grateful for Lissa's concern but more than anything wanting to see her daughter again.

'At school,' said Lissa. 'Soon as Horace gets the phone call sayin' you're safe, I tells her, "You go to school fer yer mam, like a good girl." She'll be back come four o'clock.'

Ranty hung back, gruff in his embarrassment. 'I'm real sorry, Rose,' he said, his usual roar subdued to a mutter. 'Real sorry. It was the weather, see ... We looked everywhere.'

He was staring at his boots, and it wasn't until he looked up that Rose noticed the huge black eye and the split lip. It came as quite a shock to her—she'd never known Ranty to come out of any disagreement with a mark on him, he was that handy in a fight.

'Your face!' She clapped a hand to her mouth.

Ranty's expression darkened. 'It's nothin',' he said, shuffling his feet.

He threw a look at Lissa that said 'Shut up'—but Lissa wasn't one to let sleeping dogs lie. 'It were your Luke,' she said promptly, with more respect than malice.

Rose gaped. 'Luke!'

'Reckoned it was all my Ranty's fault, you gettin' lost like that. An' I don't know as it wasn't,' she added with a meaningful look at her husband. 'Leavin' her out there to fend for herself on a night like that.'

'I never had no choice, woman,' growled Ranty. 'I waited long as I could. An' I told you, I'm real sorry.'

'That's as maybe,' returned Lissa. 'Anyhow, your Luke went straight round an' put one on him.'

'No. No, not Luke, he wouldn't!'

Not the old Luke perhaps, whispered a voice inside Rose's head, but Luke's changed. He's not the man he used to be, you don't really know him any more.

Lissa shrugged. 'He's over in the vardo. Ask him yourself if you don't believe me.'

The vardo door was ajar and Rose didn't bother knocking. She ran right up the steps and found Luke sitting on one of the benches, stuffing newspaper into his wet boots.

'Rose!' He dropped the boot he was holding and leapt to his feet. 'Rose, are you all right?'

She dodged his outstretched arms, in no mood to beat about the bush. 'Why did you do it, Luke?'

'Do what?'

'Hit Ranty Darwell—what the hell did you go an' do that for?'

Luke's expression darkened to angry contempt. 'Darwell?' He spat on the floor. 'That's all that *dacker*'s worth. Him an' his whole stinkin' tribe of *diddikoi* brats.'

'The Darwells are the only friends we've got, you bloody fool!'

'Friends Luke's one good eye held a glitter of madness. 'That slime leaves you for dead an' you call him a friend?'

'He never did nothin' of the sort, he had no choice—'

'It was all his fault, woman, all his stinkin' fault.' Luke's right fist clenched and unclenched as though reliving the sadistic satisfaction of bone crunching against flesh. Rose edged away, sickened that her once gentle husband could derive such pleasure from violence. 'Every bloody thing that's happened to us, all his fault ...'

The ludicrousness of it stirred the anger festering deep inside Rose. *'His* fault, Luke? Ranty Darwell's?' She laughed in his face. 'You're crazy, d'you know that? It's *your* fault, Luke. Yours, do you hear?'

Luke stared at her, stony-faced and silent. She knew instinctively that she was overstepping the mark, that she ought to shut up right now, but this fury inside her had eaten away at her for so long that there was no stopping it.

'What's that you say, woman?' he hissed under his breath.

'You heard me. All of this, it's your fault. You an' your promises—I believed 'em all, d'you know that? You an' your stupid motor bikes, an' your pig-headedness an' your goin' behind my back.'

'Shut up, woman, shut up!' snarled Luke, his hands on her shoulders. But she just kept on at him, because somehow she had to make him feel her pain.

'We'd never have been brought this low if it wasn't for you. An' you know what?' Her fury reached its peak and she shouted right in his face. 'If I'd died out there, that'd have been your fault an' all!'

He hit her so savagely, and with such sudden ferocity, that she didn't even see it coming. His fist caught the side of her face and sent her spinning backwards.

'I'll shut your mouth for you, you bitch!'

The second blow hit her full in the stomach, and she cried out in pain and fear.

'No, Luke! Please, no! The baby ...'

She was standing very near the door, and as Luke struck her a third time she instinctively clawed at the frame to stop herself falling; but her fingers met empty air, and the next thing she knew she was falling backwards, rolling and tumbling down the vardo steps like a bundle of old rags.

Two seconds later Luke was standing over her in the snow, sobbing and begging her to forgive him as he raised her up in his arms. But as she looked up at him and tasted the blood in her mouth, Rose knew that things could never be the same again.

Charlie was making tea for himself and Lola

when he heard someone knocking at the door. He wasn't much of a housewife, and the cottage was in a perpetual mess, but over the years he'd learned to fend for himself. Given half a chance he'd learn how to fend for Lola too.

'Stay there,' he signed to Lola as he dried his hands on a tea-towel and headed for the door. Charlie wished he had eyes in the back of his head: snow fascinated Lola; turn his back on her for five seconds and she'd be out of the house and away.

The front door wasn't used very often, and after years of neglect it stuck in its frame. He had to use all his strength to heave it open, and when he managed it he could hardly believe his eyes.

'Rose? Oh sweet Jesus ... what's happened to you?'

Rose raised swollen, tear-stained eyes and he saw her bruised mouth tremble. Charlie had seen many terrible things, but none had hurt him more than the sight of Rose's beaten and bruised face and her eyes brimming with unshed tears. Or the child by her side, all the sunshine gone from her golden eyes.

'Please, Charlie, can we come in?' asked Rose, her voice barely more than a whisper.

'Of course you can.' He stood aside.

'Go on, Ellie. Go an' find Lola an' ... an' play.' There was a sob in Rose's voice but she fought it back.

'But Mam—'

'Go on, I'll be fine.'

Ellie disappeared into the kitchen with a

404

backward glance at her mother. Charlie closed the front door and he and Rose were left alone in the passage. He couldn't take his eyes off her face, counting the bluish indentations that could only be the marks of some bastard's knuckles.

'Who's done this to you, Rose?'

Rose was exhausted and desperate, long past caring what folk might think or say. She didn't lie to him, but looked him square in the face and gave it to him straight.

'I've left Luke, Charlie.'

Charlie caught her as she swayed and fell, his strong arms lowering her on to a chair. And through the mist of sorrow and pain, Rose knew her first instinct had guided her well. Here, she and Ellie would be safe.

'*Luke* did this?' Shock-waves coursed through Charlie.

'Me an' Ellie ... I wouldn't ask, but we've nowhere else to go.' Rose's eyes asked but they would never lower themselves to beg. 'Could we stay here? It'd only be for a little while. Just till ... just till things are sorted out.'

CHAPTER 32

Day after day snow kept falling on the Island, until it lay so deep and white that it seemed it might never end. The roads were blocked, villages cut off, and it took days for a train plough to edge its way between Douglas and

Port Erin, slowly clearing the railway lines.

When at last March came, it brought torrential rain that turned the earth to mud and the snow to floodwater. Summer had never seemed so far away.

Luke turned up the collar of his coat as he walked past E. B. Christian's garage and across the swing bridge that spanned the inner harbour. The town was dismal and grey on this wet, wintry day, the seagulls crying mournfully as they wheeled above Douglas Head. He blinked the rainwater out of his eyes and trudged on towards Fort Anne Road.

Before him was the Fort Anne Hotel, standing proud, like a white castle against the bare rocks and damp grass of the headland; to his left, the Battery Pier, and the lift which carried summer visitors up to the camera obscura and the top of Douglas Head. It was deserted now, the pierrot theatres and amusement booths boarded up for the winter; even the gypsy vardos had gone from Little Egypt, headed off to somewhere more sheltered to sit the winter out.

A steep flight of steps led up from Fort Anne Road to the Douglas Head road above it. As he reached the top, Luke found himself in a huddle of yards and workshops, and a coal merchant's with a sign chalked on the padlocked gates: 'SORRY NO COAL'. Next to it stood the little two-up, two-down cottage that had once been Dan's. Perched high on the hill, its only shelter the rock face that dripped wetness behind it, it was nothing very special, just one of a row of stone-built workmen's cottages, their painted rendering lashed and stained by the elements. But Luke had dreaded seeing it again.

Without realising, he walked more and more slowly as he approached the cottage, his feet dragging on the roadway. The gate squeaked on rusty hinges as he stepped through on to the steeply-sloping front path and made his way to the front door.

He knocked and waited. A thin grey cat mewed at him from a patch of gorse, and he shooed it away with a poorly-aimed kick. Cats were *mochardi*, no Romany would have one near his vardo.

The rain kept on falling, teeming down out of the grey sky, drumming on the tin roof of the porch. It seemed an age before the door opened, and even then it wasn't Rose who opened it. It was Charlie Cartwright.

'Oh.' There was a flicker of concern in the golden eyes. 'It's you.'

'I've come to fetch my wife home.'

Luke made to step inside the house but Charlie blocked his way.

'Hang on a minute, mate. What if she don't want to be fetched?'

Luke's jaw clenched. 'Let me see her, Charlie. This is nothin' to do with you.'

But Charlie stood his ground, forcing himself to control his anger. 'Rose has a mind of her own, Luke. She told me she didn't want to see you, I can't just—'

'Oh, I see. Keepin' me from my wife, are you?'

'Nobody's keepin' anybody from anybody.

407

I'm just doin' what Rose wants.'

Luke stepped forward until he and Charlie were practically nose to nose. 'What she wants—or what *you* want?'

'What's that supposed to mean?' demanded Charlie.

'You tell me. You're livin' here with another bloke's wife, Charlie. What d'you think that looks like?'

Charlie looked mystified. 'Livin' with ...? Come on, Luke, surely you don't think ... Me an' her?'

'Think? I don't know what to think. First you get round her to look after your kid—God knows what ideas you've been puttin' into her head—next thing I know she's left me.'

This was just about the limit as far as Charlie was concerned. His voice rose to a shout. 'She left you 'cause you knocked seven bells out of her, Luke, or have you forgotten? Well, have you?'

The rain had eased off and an eerie silence fell. A thin, bird-faced woman came out of one of the other cottages and started banging her doormat against the front wall, all the time watching Luke and Charlie with a gossip's eye.

'Mornin', Mister Cartwright.' The beady black eyes fixed on Luke. 'Everythin' all right, is it?'

Charlie replied with a curt nod, then turned back to Luke. He lowered his voice, reminding himself that his own feelings and opinions didn't matter. For better or worse, Rose and Luke were man and wife. And man and wife belonged together.

'Look, wait here. I'll go an' ask her, but I can't promise—'

'Hello, Luke,' said a voice behind him. It was Rose, hair scraped back, thin and white-faced, her eyes the only bright things in her face. 'You took your time.'

The range was warm in Charlie's back kitchen, fuelled by the bucket of dusty coal he'd begged from the coal merchant's yard. But Rose felt cold and shivered as she sat down at the table. Horribly conscious of the yellowing bruises on her neck and shoulder, her fingers plucked at her holey old cardigan, tugging it tight round her throat.

'I'll stay if you want,' said Charlie, his eyes on Luke, watchful and wary.

'It's all right, Charlie, you go. This is between me an' him.'

'I'll not be far. If you need me—'

Oh, how he wished she did. She'd only to say the word, and he'd lay down his life for her. Not that she ever would, not now. His love had come ten years too late.

'I'll call you. Just go.'

Charlie's eyes tracked back over his shoulder as he reluctantly closed the door on them; and Rose listened to his footsteps going back down the passage before she spoke.

'Why have you come, Luke?'

She knew why. She could see the remorse in his face and almost wished she couldn't. In some ways, things would be easier if he hated her. Her heart almost broke to see him brought to this.

409

'To ...' He swallowed, and she saw how difficult this was for him. Luke was a proud man, a *Romani rai,* not accustomed to admitting he was wrong. 'To say I'm sorry,' he said, all in a rush. There was a tremble in his voice and Rose knew that he was close to tears. 'Oh God, but I'm sorry, Rose. I ... I've come to take you home.'

To take you home. The words ran down her spine like droplets of icy water. 'Oh, Luke, I can't come home, I just can't. Not yet.'

She knew that every word was a stab in Luke's proud heart.

'Why? Why not?' There was an edge of anger in his voice now. 'You're my wife, you belong with me.'

'But you *hurt* me.' She turned her face towards him in profile, forcing him to remember what he had done. The bruises had turned to a dull yellow blotched with mauve; the cut lip had scabbed over, dragging it slightly down at one corner.

She heard the soft gasp of indrawn breath.

'I never meant to,' he said.

'I know.' Reaching across, she took his hand. With the old oak table between them, she could bear this one small gesture of intimacy. 'An' it's not all your fault. I made you angry, an' you belted me. I shouldn't have lost my temper an' neither should you.' She looked into his face and tried to make him understand. 'But that don't make it right.'

'Come home, Rose, it'll never happen again. I swear I'll never hit you again.'

410

'I can't,' she repeated, letting his hand fall from hers. 'I just ... can't.' I'm afraid of you, Luke Barton, whispered a voice inside her head. I look at you and it's the fear I remember, not the love. 'It's not just me, Luke. What if you hit Ellie?'

Luke looked shell-shocked. 'I'd never—'

'Or the baby! Think about it, Luke, what if you lost your temper an' hit me again, an' I lost the baby?' She hugged her bump with both hands, possessive in her love. 'I just can't,' she whispered. 'Not yet. Please understand.'

'When, Rose?' demanded Luke. 'When are you comin' home?'

'When ... when I know it's safe. When you've changed.'

'I *have* changed!' Luke banged the table with the flat of his hand and Rose flinched away from him.

'Have you?' she said quietly.

Luke did not reply. Suddenly he got up from his chair and started pacing the room. 'It's him, isn't it?'

'Him?'

'Charlie. Charlie bloody Cartwright. This is all his doin'.'

'No, Luke!' she protested. 'All Charlie's done is give me an' Ellie a place to stay. We had nowhere else to go ...'

Luke's face twisted with rage. 'Oh yeah, along comes Charlie, good old Charlie. Bet he was only too happy to let you stay here.'

'What you sayin', Luke?' demanded Rose.

'Well it's obvious, i'n't it? First he takes this

411

house off me, now he wants to take my wife an' all.'

Rose stared at him in horror. How could he believe such a thing of Charlie, who had shown her nothing but kindness? 'That's rubbish, Luke, you know it is. It's just not true!'

'No?' Luke seized her by the wrists and she winced with discomfort. 'Well he's not havin' you, Rose. I'm not havin' you livin' here with some other bloke. You're my wife an' you're comin' home with me.'

Somehow, Rose found the strength to face him down. 'You know what this is all about, Luke?' she demanded. 'Jealousy, stupid jealousy. An' you've got nothin' to be jealous about! Charlie's done nothin' wrong an' neither have I. How dare you come here, tellin' me you're sorry an' then losin' your temper all over again?' Her voice was quiet and calm and steady, though inside she was in turmoil. 'Let go of me, Luke, you're hurtin' me.'

He looked at his hands as though he were seeing them for the first time, and suddenly let go. 'I ... I'm sorry, Rose. I shouldn't have done that.'

'Just go, Luke. Please go.'

She watched his chest rise and fall as his breathing steadied.

'I love you, Rose,' he said. 'I just want you to come home. When are you comin' home?'

'Just give me time.'

Luke picked up his sodden jacket from the back of the chair. 'Rose ...'

412

The word tore at her heart. 'Please.'

He turned and found Charlie framed in the doorway.

'Go on, mate,' Charlie said quietly. 'Best go, eh?'

Luke poked a finger in his face. 'If you lay one finger on my missus ...' he growled, and pushed past him into the wintry morning, heavy with rain clouds.

It was late in the afternoon and all the other mechanics had downed tools for the day. Doreen put down her wrench and went across the workshop to where Luke was tinkering with a part off the Chairoplanes.

'Fancy a cup of tea?'

Luke squirted oil into a seized joint and jabbed at it dispiritedly. 'If you like.'

'What's wrong?' Doreen sat down on the floor next to him, ignoring the big patch of oily sawdust. 'Is it Rose?'

Luke shrugged and went on working.

'Oh, Luke, I'm so sorry. But things'll work out, I'm sure they will.'

On impulse, she drew closer to him and put her arms round him, trying to hug away the pain. Rain drummed steadily on the corrugated roof as she snuggled her face into his shoulder, breathing in the comforting scents of sweat and oil; and instead of pulling away she clung to him, comforted by the quickening thump of his heart.

He turned slowly towards her and she felt his arms curl round her.

'Oh, Doreen,' he whispered. And then they kissed.

A moment later, Doreen pulled away and scrambled to her feet.

'I'm sorry,' she whispered.

Luke frowned. *'You're* sorry?'

'It's Dan, see ... I thought ...' She started to cry, the tears spilling unhindered down her face. 'Oh, Luke, I really loved him. And ... and that two-faced bastard just kept on hurting me, again and again and again.' She turned her face towards him. 'You're a lot like Dan, did you know that?' The sleeve of her shirt smeared the tears off her face and she forced a smile. 'Like Dan but without the bad bits.'

Luke gave a humourless laugh. 'There's plenty bad in me, Doreen. What I did to Rose—'

'You never meant to hurt her. You're a good man.'

'Rose don't think so.'

'Then you've got to prove it to her.' Doreen sniffed back the last of the tears. 'It's her you want, Luke, not me.'

Luke got to his feet and came over to her, holding out his arms. 'But Doreen, I ...'

She shook her head. 'We've been selfish enough as it is. You've got a business to sort out and a family that needs you.'

'You mean a business that's dyin' on its feet an' a wife who thinks I'm the devil,' grunted Luke.

'Do you want your life back or not, Luke?' demanded Doreen.

The cold, stark question shook him out of his torpor.

'Course I do.'

'Then you've got to stop feeling sorry for yourself and *win* it back. I'll help you, but you've got to help yourself.'

Luke ran his hand through the dishevelled waves of his black mane. 'Win Rose back? But how?'

'Well,' declared Doreen, sliding off the bench, 'we can start by going to see Percy Sayle about those rooster gallopers.'

CHAPTER 33

The days passed and Charlie went back to sea, leaving Rose alone in the cottage with Lola and Ellie.

Watching the two little girls playing outside in the street, she wondered what was going to become of them all: Lola with no mother and no school to go to; Ellie with no father and no home. What a miserable mother I am, she thought as she ran a broom listlessly over the cracked tiled floor.

Rose knew she had to do something—but what? Could she really believe Luke when he said he'd changed? Could she risk taking Ellie back to the vardo? If only she knew. She'd asked Charlie for his advice but he wouldn't commit himself. 'This is your business, Rose,' was all that he would say. 'Yours an' Luke's. You're welcome to stay here as long as you want, but I'll not meddle between man an' wife.'

Of course, she could always swallow her pride and go home to Birkenhead. Mam and Dad wouldn't turn her away, though there was hardly any room what with the lodger, and of course Dad would be full of I-told-you-sos. But what would be the point of going back? Her parents couldn't afford to feed one extra mouth, let alone three, and what chance did Rose have of finding a job with so many men out of work? And it was wrong to go back, that was what she kept telling herself. When things were bad, you had to make yourself a new future, not try to live in the past.

Stooping to gather up the sweepings, she cursed her aching back. Her pregnancy with Ellie hadn't gone easily, and it was all more difficult the second time around. How much more difficult would it be if she had to bring this new baby into the world without its father? Guilt weighed heavily in the pit of her stomach, but that was the price she had to pay. She didn't care about the pointing fingers in the street or the whispers behind closed doors; all she wanted was to be sure she was doing the right thing.

She stood by the window, rubbing the small of her back. Lola and Ellie were playing with an old rubber ball they'd found, throwing it against the wall of the coal-yard and taking turns at catching it. There wasn't much bounce left in the perished rubber, and the wind gusting in off the sea was bitter, but they didn't seem to

416

care. Life was much easier when you were a kid; hardships just seemed to bounce right off you.

Even so, Rose knew that all this trouble with Luke had touched Ellie deeply. What was it she'd said last night, as they were sitting down to their tea?

'Mam, when are we goin' home?'

'Home?'

'Back to the vardo.'

Rose pushed a scrap of potato round and round her plate and tried not to look at her daughter. It was better to be honest, but less painful to lie.

'I ... don't know,' she said finally.

Ellie wiped her plate with a piece of bread and chewed it. 'Mam ...'

'Don't talk with your mouth full.'

Ellie gave a huge swallow, like a snake gulping down its dinner. 'Mam ... I like bein' here.'

This time, Rose did look at Ellie. 'You do?'

'I like havin' Lola to play with, an' I like livin' in a house again, an' I like Uncle Charlie. But ...' Her eyes focused on the cheap patterned plate. 'But I miss Dad, Mam. When can we see him again?'

'Soon,' Rose said, not knowing if it was true or not. Luke hadn't been near them since that last visit, when they'd ended up shouting at each other for the umpteenth time.

'Dad did a bad thing, didn't he, Mam?'

Rose nodded, a lump of grief in her throat. 'Yes.' She laid her fork across her plate, not hungry any more. 'But I don't think he meant to.'

'Why did he do it, Mam?'

Why indeed, thought Rose. Maybe it was all her fault, maybe she'd just provoked him beyond endurance, maybe it was no more than she'd deserved.

'He was angry,' she said after a moment's silence. 'Sometimes, when people get angry, they do things they're sorry for later.'

And I should know, she thought to herself. I of all people should know. As she stood at the window, watching the children and wondering how to sort out this mess of a life, she heard the sound of an engine roaring up Douglas Head Road. A motorbike engine, straining a little as it took the steep incline.

For a brief instant she thought it was Luke. But she could see Ellie and Lola waving, and a moment later a gleaming black Norton glided into view. The rider was wearing a flying-style helmet, an RAF-issue flying jacket, and goggles that covered half her face, but there was no mistaking her. There weren't two like her on the whole of the island.

Doreen took off her helmet and pushed her goggles back on to her head. Catching sight of Rose through the parlour window, she came striding up the front path. Despite all the trouble over Luke and the bike, Rose was glad to see a friendly face. It was impossible to stay angry with Doreen ... and if Rose had ever in her life needed a friend, it was now.

She opened the door before Doreen had time to knock. 'What are you doin' here?'

Doreen took her by the arm and propelled her

418

into the parlour, plonking her down in Walleye's very old and greasy armchair. Rose was so taken aback that she just blinked. Doreen plucked the duster out of Rose's fingers and chucked it on the floor. 'Put that away. You look worn out.'

'I've got things to do,' protested Rose.

'No you haven't; all you have to do is sit and listen.' Doreen pulled up the only other seat—a wobbly-jointed old dining chair—turned it back to front and sat astride it, resting her chin on the back. 'Luke won't come and talk to you, so I've come to do it for him.'

'Talk to me? What about? Look, Doreen, if it's about goin' back ...'

Doreen gave a patient sigh. 'Just listen. You love Luke, don't you?'

Rose felt a tiny tremor pass through her heart, like the tingle of a mild electric shock. 'I ... He's my husband; of course I love him ... But—'

'And Luke loves you. He's too pig-headed to tell you, but he does. You do know that, don't you?' Doreen's steady brown eyes defied her to deny it.

Wearily, Rose nodded. 'I s'pose. But he hurt me, Doreen; you saw what he did to me.'

Doreen's expression dulled as a shadow crossed her eyes. Her eager voice softened. 'I know. What he did ... it was stupid, and it was wrong. And in your place I'd have done exactly what you did. You had no choice.'

'I weren't goin' to stick around an' see if he did it again,' said Rose drily, 'if that's what you mean.'

'He won't,' said Doreen.

'How can you say that?'

'I just know he won't,' replied Doreen firmly. 'He's truly sorry, Rose.'

'Sorry.' There was a bitter taste in Rose's mouth. 'It's easy to be sorry. *Afterwards.*' And I'm sorry too, she thought to herself. So sorry that this ever happened. If only I could turn back the clock ...

'Luke never wanted to hurt you,' insisted Doreen. 'He's a good man, he really is. He wants you back.'

Rose shook her head. She wanted to put her hands over her ears and not listen.

'No.'

'Please listen. He knows he has to prove he's changed, that it's no good just saying it.' Doreen paused. 'I want you to come back with me now. To Funland.'

Rose shrank back into the chair. 'Go back? Doreen—'

'I don't mean to stay. There's just ...' She searched for the right words. 'There's something I think you ought to see.'

Rose's heart thumped in her chest. 'What is it?'

'Come and see for yourself.'

'I ... I don't know.' Rose's lips were dry, her throat constricted. 'I don't know if I can.'

'Of course you can, I'll be with you.'

'But what about Ellie an' Lola?'

'The woman next door'll keep an eye on them, won't she? They'll come to no harm. And I'll bring you straight back here if that's what you want.'

Rose searched Doreen's face, desperate for reassurance. 'Promise?'

Doreen smiled. 'Cross my heart and hope to die.' She bounced off the chair and presented Rose with a motor-cycle helmet. 'Here, kid, put this on.'

Despite herself, Rose giggled. *'Kid?'*

Doreen winked. 'You heard. Now jam on the bone-dome and let's get going.'

Funland had filled up again in the last few days, with showmen and their families returning to the Island to prepare for the coming summer season. One of them was Jack Verney, but Luke wasn't pleased to see him.

'Now look here.' Verney folded his arms and glowered from beneath his bushy brows. 'A deal's a deal and I want you riding for me in my TT spectacular.'

Luke stomped around picking up his tools and throwing them into their bag. 'Yeah, yeah, I know.'

'No ride, no money,' Verney reminded him.

'Get off me back, Verney. I've said I'll ride for you an' I will.'

'Not if you don't practise you won't,' replied Verney.

Luke threw him a look that said 'Idiot'. 'I don't need to practise. I'm the best; you said so yourself.'

'You *were* the best,' Verney corrected him. 'That was a long time ago, before ...'

'Before what?' demanded Luke, wrenching off his eye-patch to reveal the brutal ugliness of the scarred and sunken socket. 'Before this? Is that what you're tryin' to say? Pretty, i'n't it? But don't worry, I won't be showin' it off to the punters.' He put the patch back on, the elastic snapping back against his skin. 'An' I haven't lost me touch neither, if that's what you're worryin' about.'

Verney's voice was a low, emphatic growl. 'The only thing that's bothering me, Luke, is whether I'm going to have three stunt riders or two. And it's going to be two if you don't show up for practice with Ray and Tom.'

Luke stuffed the last of the tools back into the bag and straightened up. 'Are you threatenin' me?' he demanded.

'Not threatening. Telling. I don't care how good you are or how great you used to be, if you don't practise you're not in the show.'

Luke had no chance to reply, because at that moment he caught sight of Doreen's bike, bumping over the tober as it headed towards the line of living-wagons. And it wasn't just Doreen on the bike. There was someone riding pillion, a woman in a shabby red dress and a man's old working boots, her arms wrapped round Doreen's waist and her red-brown hair flying out behind her.

Rose! Luke dropped everything and ran, practically knocking Sid Christian flying as he headed for the vardo.

At last Rose had come back to him.

Rose eased off the motor-cycle helmet and shook out her hair. Doreen was a careful rider, but her head was spinning, her heart racing, and it took a moment to catch her breath.

Luke came pelting across the fairfield and then stopped, very suddenly, a few yards short, as though there were some invisible barrier between them that he dared not cross. 'Rose. Oh, Rose.' He twisted his cap in his hands like a guilty schoolboy. 'Oh God, I can't believe it.'

It was Doreen who broke the tension, giving Rose a deft shove that forced her forward a few steps. 'I told Rose you've got something to show her,' she said.

Rose looked around her. Even though she'd only been gone a couple of weeks it was such a peculiar feeling, being back here. All these new people, new wagons, half-built rides where before there had been nothing but mud and concrete ... and the familiar faces too. Faces that stared at her, fingers that pointed. And then there was Luke, her husband who had somehow turned into a stranger.

'What is it then?' she asked him. Her voice sounded flat and distant, without real meaning, just something to fill the emptiness.

Luke grabbed her hand, and she let him tow her across to a ride covered by a protective drape of canvas. She could tell from the rounding boards that it was the Chairoplanes.

'This,' he said. Rose felt his hand shake, and then he drew it away.

'The Chairoplanes? You've mended them?'

He shook his head. 'I ... I've been workin' on them. For you.'

The canvas swished aside, and through the

gap Rose saw gold and yellow and red, fresh paint flashing in the March sunshine, barley-twisted poles and painted feathers, picked out in vibrant colour.

It wasn't finished, but it was obvious what it was going to be.

Rose's mouth fell open. 'The roosters! Percy's roosters!'

'Barton's Rooster Gallopers,' Luke corrected her. 'You were right, Rose. I just ... I just couldn't admit it.'

She stepped up on to the staging and reached out to touch one of the roosters' beaks.

'Careful, the paint's still a bit tacky.' Luke's voice sounded shaky with nerves. 'What d'you reckon?'

She turned and smiled at him through a veil of tears. 'They're beautiful, really beautiful. Just like I imagined.'

'I'll have them finished, Rose, I swear I will. In time for the season.'

'I know you will,' she replied. '*We* will. Us together.'

Luke clattered about in the vardo, scrabbling to find mugs, tea, milk, spoons. Rose watched him struggle to make a cup of tea, knowing he didn't want her to help him, because he wanted to do this one small thing for her himself.

It made her feel guilty to see how untidy the vardo had got. Almost reflexively, she reached down and picked up a pile of dirty tin plates, stacking them neatly on the table.

'Are you ... all right?' she asked.

He looked up from spooning tea into the pot. 'Managin',' he replied. 'But it's not been right without you, Rose, not right at all.' He smiled at her. 'Still, you're back now an' that's all that matters.'

Her heart skipped a beat. Oh no—how could she have let him believe she was back for good? How could she break the truth to him now without pushing him over the edge?

'Luke ...' she began. But Luke was talking nineteen to the dozen, full of his plans for the future.

'The gallopers'll bring in the punters, an' then there's the sideshows ... an' Verney's offerin' good money. Maybe we can afford to pay Gracie a bit more an' you can put your feet up till the baby comes—'

'Luke—about me comin' back ...'

The smile froze on his face. 'You're here, that's all I care about.'

'I'm here, yeah, an' I'm glad Doreen made me come. We're goin' to work together, an' that's a start. But things aren't sorted out between us yet.'

The teapot rattled in Luke's shaking hand as he set it down on the table. 'Not ... sorted ... out?'

'Give it time, Luke.'

'What d'you mean, give it time?' There was a terrible intensity in his face and it frightened her.

'I can't move back here, not yet.' She could hardly bear to look at him, but she forced herself

425

to go on. 'Doreen's offered to take me back to the cottage tonight.'

'No ... Rose, no, please.'

The words were a howl of agony. Luke's arm swept aside the teapot and the cups and they fell jangling to the floor as he sank down, bent almost double, hands clenching the table-top so hard that his knuckles showed bone-white through the skin. He raised his face and she saw with a stab of pain that he was weeping.

'Luke, I'm sorry, I'm really sorry ...'

Tears dripped from his cheeks, falling in a warm rain on to the mess of milk and tea. 'You can't do this to me, Rose.'

He wasn't shouting; he was begging, pleading. It tore Rose apart to see her husband like this.

'It's just ... I've got to be sure, Luke, don't you understand? Really sure.'

'Understand? Oh, I understand all right. It's him, isn't it?'

Rose didn't need to ask who Luke meant. It was written all over his face. 'If you mean Charlie—'

'Who else would I mean? Tell me that. What kind of hold has that man got over you, Rose? Tell me. Tell me!' His voice rose to a shriek, but it was a sound of pain and despair, not blind fury, and Rose wasn't afraid of him any more, only *for* him.

'No hold, Luke. He's just a friend.'

She tried to put her arm round him, soothe him, make him understand. But he shook her off. And as his hand made contact with the roundness of her pregnant belly, the light of a

426

twisted understanding sparked in his eye.

'The baby,' he gasped.

She shrank away, a horrible anticipation creeping over her. 'Please, Luke—'

'It's his, isn't it?'

Rose's eyes widened to round circles of disbelief. Surely not even Luke could believe such a thing?

'No!'

But there was madness on his face now; he had gone beyond the point of reason. 'Come on, Rose, I want the truth.'

'I'm tellin' you the truth!'

'Are you? Come off it, I'm not blind. Ellie's his, that much is obvious.'

Sick with horror, Rose pressed herself back against the vardo wall, her eyes fixed on Luke's grief-stricken, tear-soaked face.

'Ellie? You *know* about Ellie?'

Luke gave a laugh that was more like a sob. 'Just 'cause I've only got one eye, don't mean I can't see what's in front of me face. That kid's the dead spittin' image of Charlie Cartwright.' His shoulders heaved, his breath coming in halting sobs, as he sank to his knees on the vardo floor.

'Oh, Luke.' Rose stared down at him, filled with sudden remorse. 'I never meant ... I would've told you. I just didn't want to hurt you.'

Luke seized her hand and forced her to look into his face. 'The baby, Rose.'

'It's yours, Luke, I swear it is!'

'Is it? Tell me the truth. Rose, I've got to

know. Is this baby mine or his?'

But Rose saw the depth of Luke's anguish and knew that it hardly mattered what she said. He would never believe her anyhow.

CHAPTER 34

By late March the Island had at last shaken off the snows and the floods; and everyone at Funland had their fingers crossed that 1947 would prove to be a bumper summer season. As the grand Easter reopening drew nearer Horace Spence became tetchier than ever, barking out orders right left and centre. He was investing a lot of money to make Funland a big success, and didn't let anyone forget it. Spending money made Horace nervous—unless it was someone else's.

The tober was buzzing with activity as Charlie walked in through the gates. Some of the showmen were building up their rides, others scrubbing down paintwork and putting the final touches to stalls and sideshows. Fresh concrete bases had been laid down for the rides, banishing the mud and duck-boards that had made life so intolerable through the terrible winter.

In the distance Charlie noticed the brand new Water Chute, and the Flying Machine with its whizzing cars like airship gondolas tethered to a tall ironwork tower; and just a little further on, the brilliantly painted wooden stockade enclosing Verney's TT Spectacular and the Globe of Death. It was only a few weeks since he'd been here, but already there was so much he didn't recognise.

Some things stayed the same, though. Ranty Darwell was giving the Wiggley-Waggley a trial run, and the Darwell kids were shrieking with laughter as the walkways jiggled them in a dozen different directions, defying them not to fall over. The empty Tubs were whirling round too, clattering as they spun, beneath gaudy old 'gag cards' that shouted 'Uncontrolled MIRTH!', 'Have a Nice Spoon by the light of the MOON on the TUBS!', and 'Only SIX COPPERS!'.

The Luxury Fish & Chip Saloon was parked on its usual pitch, and next to it Charlie saw Sid Christian, standing back to admire his rebuilt kiosk.

'Mornin', Charlie. Lovely one, isn't it?'

'Mornin', Sid.'

Sid was one of the few people to greet Charlie with a smile and a nod. Most were indifferent, a few pointed as he went past and gave him knowing looks—but frankly he was past caring. Let them talk.

He went across to the Gallopers. Luke's toolbag was lying on the ground next to the staging, but there was no sign of Luke. Heading back towards the vardo, he turned the corner of the coconut shy and almost walked straight into Gracie and Mario. The two of them sprang apart, scarlet-faced, but not before Charlie had seen them holding hands and gazing into each other's eyes.

'Mister Charlie!' gulped Mario. 'Me and Gracie, we only ...'

Gracie's cheeks dimpled as she smiled and held out her hand. The tiniest and cheapest of rings sparkled on her third finger. 'We're engaged, Mister Cartwright,' she blushed. 'Mario's asked me to marry him. Soon as I'm sixteen.'

'Congratulations,' said Charlie. 'But you'd better not let the gaffer see you skulkin' round here.'

Dot would have laughed in his face, but Gracie looked dismayed. 'You'll not tell him, will you? It was only five minutes.'

Charlie shook his head. 'Where is he, anyhow? I want a word with him.'

'He with Mister Verney,' said Mario. 'Practising for the motor bike, yes?'

Charlie headed off towards the TT Spectacular. As he got closer he could hear the motor-cycle engines buzz and whine like insects caught in a tin can; and as he came up to the pay box he saw them: three identical black Velocettes rocketing around the banked enclosure. One by one they sped up a ramp, hung in the air for what seemed like years, cleared a row of men lying face down on the ground and bounced safely down on to the grass on the other side.

As the lead machine rounded the end of the enclosure and headed back towards Charlie it slowed down, sliding to a halt in front of Jack Verney.

'Good lad, Barton. You'll do.' Verney clapped Luke on the back. 'Bit more throttle as you hit that ramp, though ...'

As Luke took off his helmet, he made eye-contact with Charlie and something in the set of his face seemed to harden. 'I'm takin' a break, Jack,' he said, cutting off Verney in mid-sentence.

'Now hang on—'

'I said I'm takin' a break. I'll be back in ten minutes.' Setting the Velocette on its stand, Luke turned and walked away from Charlie, heading for the riders' entrance at the other side of the oval enclosure. But Charlie had made up his mind, and he wasn't letting this chance pass by. He caught up with Luke just as he reached the tunnel, and put a hand on his arm.

'Luke ...'

Luke spun round, wrenching his arm away. The look on his face was pure venom. 'You've got a nerve comin' here.' He turned and started walking away again, into the riders' dressing room, but Charlie caught up with him a second time. Come on, Charlie, he told himself. You know this is for the best. For Rose.

'All I want is a word, Luke.'

'You've had a word. Now go away an' leave me alone.'

Charlie played his trump card. 'Rose asked me to talk to you.'

'Rose!'

'Just listen, will you? This won't take more'n a couple of minutes.'

Luke dumped his helmet on to a bench and dropped down after it, his leathers creaking as he sat and folded his arms. Aggression growled from every muscle in his body. 'You've got two minutes, Cartwright. Get on with it.'

Charlie felt awkward standing there, exposed, like a man on trial, though he had done nothing wrong.

'I'm sorry about you an' Rose ... It's none of my doin'.'

Luke's lip curled. 'You what?'

'I never wanted none of this, Luke,' insisted Charlie. 'But I could hardly let Rose walk the streets, could I?'

'No, course you couldn't,' replied Luke bitterly. 'Seein' as she was already carryin' your kid.'

'*My* kid! For God's sake, Luke—'

'Don't come the innocent with me. I'm not blind.'

Charlie's patience cracked. 'That's exactly what you bloody well are, if you think that baby's mine.'

'Come off it, Charlie. Just couldn't keep your hands off her, could you? You'd already got her pregnant an' dumped her once, but you just couldn't resist doin' it all over again ...'

Charlie counted to ten under his breath, telling himself that Luke had every right to feel this way towards him, especially now that he knew the truth about Ellie. But it was hard, so very hard, not to lose his temper with Luke's obstinate refusal to see reason. 'How many times do I have to tell you, Luke? Me an' Rose have

432

never done nothin'. *Nothin'*. She an' Ellie are stayin' at the cottage, *in their own room,* an' that's all there is to it. Half the time I'm not even there!'

Luke laughed. 'Yeah. Good at that, aren't you? Not bein' there.'

At that moment Charlie could cheerfully have hit him, but something deeper, something compassionate, seized hold of him, and suddenly he felt the terrible weight of sadness inside Luke.

'Look, mate. I swear to you on me mother's grave ... on me daughter's life.'

'Which one?' sneered Luke. 'The one you had by my wife, or the one you had by your Spanish tart?'

That stung, but Charlie kept on going, reminding himself that he wasn't here for his own sake, but for Rose. 'I'd never lay a finger on your wife—an' you know why?' The question hung, unanswered, for a few endless seconds. Outside, the motor bikes were revving up again. 'I'll tell you why. Not 'cause I don't want her, that's for sure. Any man in his right mind would want her. Not 'cause I don't love her, neither.' He saw the look of pain on Luke's face and it cut him to the bone. 'Yeah, it's true, I love her. I've loved her since I was a lad of eighteen, only I'd not the sense then to realise.'

Luke's wounded face stared up into his eyes with the forlorn hatred of a cornered animal. 'Then why?' he demanded. 'If that's what you want, why don't you just take it?'

'Why? 'Cause she's your wife, not mine. And

433

'cause she don't love me, Luke—it's *you* she loves, it's *you* she wants! An' the sooner you get that into your thick skull—'

'Why should I believe you?' Luke's voice was desperate, but there was a faint note of hope in it.

'Because I may be all the rotten, useless things you think I am, but I'm no liar.'

Luke considered this for a moment. 'If she loves me—'

'She does.'

'*If* she loves me like you say, why won't she come back home?'

Charlie sank down to his haunches, his voice softening. 'Rose loves you, Luke, she really does. She wants to come home to you. But you've hurt her deep. You can't expect her to come back till she's sure you'll never hurt her again. She's got Ellie an' the baby to think of, you know; it's not just herself she's frightened for.'

'Hurt her?' Luke stared down at his hands as though they were someone else's hands, a murderer's hands. 'I'd never hurt her ... I never meant to.'

'But you did.' Charlie couldn't keep the note of accusation out of his voice.

At this, anger flared inside Luke again. 'You smug *gorgio* bastard! Who d'you think you are anyhow?'

'I don't think anythin', Luke. I'm just tellin' you the truth. I can't make you listen to it if you don't want to. You know somethin'? Me and Rose an' Ellie—we've none of us done nothin' to be ashamed of.' Charlie straightened up. 'So

434

just who are you so angry at, Luke Barton?'

'You're a clever one, Rose,' commented Lissa Darwell, standing at the edge of the crowd with Rose and watching the Easter holidaymakers swarming round the Gallopers. 'Rescuin' them knackered old Chairoplanes.'

Rose couldn't help smiling as she watched Ellie and Lola, laughing and waving at them as the roundabout turned and the roosters rose and fell to the music of the old steam organ. Each day at Funland began with a free ride on the Gallopers for all the children. It was only the first week of the new season, but already Barton's Traditional Rooster Gallopers were proving to be one of the biggest attractions in Funland—bigger than the Tubs, bigger than the Wiggley-Waggley, even bigger than the Water Chute! Spence was so outraged he could hardly speak. But the children adored the old ride, caressing the gold and yellow cockerels, leaping astride and demanding, 'Again, Mam, again, again!'

'All I did was have the idea,' Rose protested. 'It's Luke what made it happen.'

There was a warmth inside her as she spoke Luke's name, and she realised how far she had travelled towards forgiving him, how much she respected him for the way he had taken a disaster and turned it round. If only he didn't frighten her so much with his jealousy.

Lissa nudged her in the ribs. 'Time you an' Luke sorted yourselves out,' she observed. 'Sure he done wrong, but let bygones be bygones,

435

that's what I say. 'Sides, you should be livin' back here with your husband; there's the baby to think of.'

'I know.' Rose gazed down at the roundness of her swollen belly, growing bigger by the moment underneath the long red gypsy dress she wore for dukkering.

'Talk to him,' urged Lissa.

'I know I should. But—'

'No buts, my girl. Just get on an' do it. You'll feel better, just see if you don't.'

Before Rose had thought of anything to say in reply, she noticed Percy Sayle weaving through the crowd towards them with his rubbish sack, his eyes fixed on the turning carousel as he picked up greasy chip-wrappers with his pointed stick.

'Hello there, Percy,' she hailed him. 'What d'you reckon?'

He beamed at Rose and Lissa and ambled over. 'Them gallopers is beautiful, Missus Rose. Just like they was when I was a boy.' He let out a long sigh and wiped the beginnings of a tear from his eye. 'Poor old Grandad Jimmy ...'

'Your grandad owned the gallopers?'

Percy nodded. 'His pride an' joy, they was. Worked the fairgrounds years ago, travelled all over the North West. Trouble was, he were no businessman, my grandad. Things went wrong an' he went bust, see. Then him an' his wife—that's my Grandma Ginny—they had this big row an' she left him, never saw her again. He didn't last long after that. Died a broken man, so he did, up the White Hoe.'

Rose watched the golden cockerels revolving on their glittering axis and had to close her eyes for a moment, dizzy from the thoughts tumbling round and round inside her head.

'Oh, Percy. Percy, that's so sad.'

Percy patted her hand. 'Never you mind that, Missus Rose. Them gallopers is a real picture. If it wasn't for you an' your Luke they'd just have sat in my shed an' rotted away.'

Me and my Luke, thought Rose; and Percy's story struck a shimmering chord. Jimmy and Ginny; Rose and Luke. Didn't she owe it to Luke to give this story a happy ending?

Life was busy for Luke now, what with working for Verney and running his own rides; though not busy enough to stop him thinking about Rose.

He thought about her every moment of every day. It wasn't right, her working at Funland but going home every night with another man. Especially not *that* man. Jealousy ate away at him like a cancer, destroying reason as it grew. They couldn't go on like this, something must be sorted out between them.

But what? All Luke knew was that he wanted her back.

He called up to Cec as the Gallopers wound down to a halt and children flooded off. 'I'll take over for half an hour. You go an' get a bite to eat.'

'Thanks, boss.' Cec jumped down and handed over the money-pouch. 'Good takin's again today.'

Luke nodded approvingly and tied on the apron. 'Mind you're back by quarter-to, I've got Verney's afternoon show to do.'

He was busy taking sticky sixpences from eager kids when a youngish woman came up to the front.

'Excuse me.'

He looked her up and down. She didn't look like a tripper; in fact she stuck out like a sore thumb in a place like this, with her neat tweedy swagger jacket and little hat. From her accent she was local but a bit posh. She might be official, somebody from the town commissioners, somebody causing trouble ... An inbuilt instinct made him cautious.

'What is it?'

The woman smiled. She was ordinary looking, with her button nose and unmemorable features, but her collar-length hair was a lustrous nut-brown, and she looked almost pretty when she smiled. She put out her hand, the fingers encased in spotless white cotton gloves.

'I'm sorry, I should have introduced myself. Josie, Josie James. And you're ...?'

Luke avoided replying. 'I'm a bit busy right now,' he said. 'If it's to do with the council or somethin'—'

'No, no, nothing like that. I'm just looking for someone.'

Luke's brows knitted.

'Who?'

'A lady with a little deaf girl. Rose, I think the lady's name is.' If she saw the shadow that passed across Luke's eyes she was far too polite to comment on it. 'Have you any idea where I might find her?'

Rose sat inside the dukkering tent and flopped back in relief as the curtain twitched, another punter going off happy. Her pregnancy was making her tired now, her back and legs aching almost non-stop, and she was glad that she didn't have to do the coconut shy any more. Terry was welcome to it. All that standing up and shouting was more than she could cope with.

The arrangement with Luke was working better than she could have hoped, but it was still awkward. They worked together, they exchanged words when they had to, and then she went home ... to Charlie's cottage. Not home at all. Did she really have a home any more?

Lost in thought, she didn't hear the curtain swish across. It wasn't until someone coughed, very politely, that she realised she was no longer alone.

'I'm sorry, am I disturbing you?' asked the woman with the neat hat and the snub nose.

Rose gave her best gypsy smile and passed her hands over the crystal ball. 'Come in, lady, come in. Cross my palm with silver an' I'll tell your future.'

The woman smiled and shook her head. 'I'm not here to have my fortune told. I'm here to see you.'

'Me? Why?'

'May I sit down?' Without waiting for a reply, she pulled out the other chair and sat, setting her handbag on the table in front of her.

In all her months as a fortune-teller Rose had learned quite a lot about reading character just from the look of a person. That handbag was good quality, but it was old and shabby; the collar on that cream blouse was frayed. True, most people were still a bit on the shabby side after the long, austere war years. But however respectable this lady might be, she certainly wasn't rich.

'My name's Josie. Josie James.' Seeing the blank expression on Rose's face, she explained, 'My mother and father are the Maddrells, they farm over Ballakeeill way.'

'Sam an' Cissie!' exclaimed Rose, suddenly remembering that terrible night when she'd got lost in the snow and almost died. 'How are they?'

'They're fine. They asked after you. In fact ...' Josie's fingers gripped the handle of her bag. 'It's Mum and Dad who told me about you. And Lola,' she added. 'That is her name, isn't it? The little deaf girl?'

'Lola? What about her?'

'Well, Mum and Dad told me about her being deaf, and not getting an education because there wasn't a place for her at a proper deaf school. I think they got rather mixed up though; they thought Lola was your daughter—'

'She's not,' cut in Rose hastily. 'I'm very fond of her an' that, but she's not mine. I look after her sometimes ... for a friend.'

'Oh, I see.'

'My little girl's called Ellie.'

Josie nodded. 'Your husband told me. The thing is,' she went on slowly, 'my little boy Andrew, he's deaf too. He wasn't born deaf, it happened in the war. A Doodlebug fell on the house we were staying in in London. He's almost six now.' Her gaze fell to the green chenille cloth on the table as she remembered, then she looked up again. 'My husband was killed in the same raid.'

'Oh ... I'm sorry,' said Rose. What else could you say to a woman who had lost her husband? She remembered how she'd felt when she thought Charlie had been killed. 'That's terrible.'

Josie took a deep breath and forced a smile. 'It was nearly four years ago. It's been hard, but we've managed. I'm a trained teacher and I've been taking in private pupils while I stay at home to look after Andrew. It's kept the wolf from the door, but money's very tight, and I've decided to come back to the Island to live with my parents.'

Rose wondered what this could have to do with her. 'What about your little boy?' she asked. 'Will he have to go away to a special school?'

Josie shook her head. 'I've been teaching him at home. He's already speaking quite well, and we're just starting reading.'

'He can speak!' exclaimed Rose, thinking of Lola's terrible frustration at trying to make herself understood with no more than a few simple signs and gestures. 'But I thought—'

'Deaf doesn't have to mean dumb,' said Josie.

441

'Andrew knows sign language, but I want him to be able to speak too. It would be so sad if he was cut off from other people. That's one reason why I want him to be taught with other children. And that's why I came to see you.'

'About ... about Lola you mean?'

'About Lola. I could teach her and Andrew together if you wanted me to. At the farm.'

'You mean ... she wouldn't have to go away to school?'

'Not if you didn't want her to. And you wouldn't have to pay me—it would be so lovely for my little boy to have the company.'

Rose's mind whirled. It all sounded so wonderful. Charlie had been dreading the moment when Lola would have to leave him, fearing what it would do to the child to be parted from the only proper home she had ever known. He would be thrilled ... For a moment Rose almost forgot that Lola wasn't her child. 'You'll have to speak to her dad,' she said at last. 'Charlie Cartwright. You see, Lola ... Lola isn't really anything to do with me.'

It was strange how painful it felt to say those words; and if she was honest, it frightened her to realise how much a part of her life Charlie and Lola Cartwright had become.

Engines buzzed and whined. Spectators clapped and shrieked and whistled. The air was smoky with the scent of fast-burning two-stroke oil. Rose could hardly believe that she was watching Luke riding in Verney's TT Spectacular. It had taken more courage than she thought she

442

possessed to walk through into the enclosure and take her place in the audience.

Her hands clutched the rail to steady her nerves as the loudspeaker announced: 'Ladies and gentlemen ... the famous Globe of Death!'

Rose's heart seemed to stop in its tracks, before starting up again with such a furious thudding that she felt dizzy and sick. The Globe of Death. It was the Globe of Death which had cost Luke his eye, all those years ago; the Globe of Death which had filled his sleep with nightmares that woke him up screaming. How could he bear to come back and do it all again? And how could she bear to watch him?

I must, she told herself. For his sake.

The Globe rose up twenty feet in the air, its sides made from criss-crossed strips of metal which allowed the spectators to watch the bikes whizzing round and round inside. Rose watched, heart in mouth, as the door clanged shut on the two black-clad riders and the sound of their engines crescendoed from a purr to a roar.

'Oh please God,' she whispered. 'Please don't let him die.'

Of course he wasn't going to die, she told herself. Luke was a fine rider; he'd already done this routine twice a day for the last fortnight without a hitch, and why should today be any different? But she felt the tension in the air, the electric crackle of excitement as the bikes began to move slowly round the base of the metal sphere, gradually picking up speed and climbing until they were chasing each other horizontally around the inner rim. And she knew that all these people were excited, not just by the skill and the speed, but by the faint, bloodthirsty hope that there would be a terrible accident.

With a sudden scream of power, the bikes hit top speed and began to shoot round the inside of the globe, upside down, side to side, missing each other by scant inches as they shot in opposite directions, plunging from top to bottom and back again. They were moving so fast that they were little more than blurs, one rider indistinguishable from the other.

Rose's fist was crammed into her mouth to stop herself crying out at each near-miss. She told herself that everything had been rehearsed again and again, that there could be no mistakes, but she knew the dangers too well to believe her own argument. Like parachutists, the riders were solely responsible for preparing and maintaining their own machines—at these speeds, one tiny error could prove fatal, and what mechanic would want another man's death on his conscience?

But the accident never happened. To the accompaniment of oohs, aahs and sighs, the bikes powered down and sank back down to the bottom of the sphere. Moments later, one of Verney's men unlocked the cage and out came the two bikers, grinning all over their faces as they rode a lap of honour.

'Ladies and gentlemen,' roared the voice on the tannoy, 'a big hand for Mister Tommy Vale ... and Mister Luuuke Baaarton!'

As applause erupted around her, relief washed

over Rose like a cooling tide. The thing she had feared more than any other hadn't happened. Luke was safe. As he looked across at her and their eyes met, she knew in that moment that she had made her decision.

She would go over and talk to him. Right now. But then she felt a tap on her shoulder. She swung round.

'Charlie! What are you doin' here?' She looked at him in puzzlement as Lola ran forward to give her a big hug around her middle.

'The *Rose Marie*'s puttin' to sea tonight.'

'Tonight? But I thought ...'

'So did I. But there's another load of butter to bring over from Eire. I couldn't leave Lola on her own ... You don't mind fetchin' her back to the cottage, do you?'

Rose looked back at Luke, his eyes still fixed on her. She knew he was willing her to go over. Perhaps it was cowardice that made her drag her feet, perhaps it was second thoughts. But if what she had to say had waited all this time, surely it could wait until tomorrow.

She took Lola's hand. 'I'll take her an' Ellie back now, I've finished for today.'

Luke finished his victory lap and took off his helmet, raising his face to the crowd to acknowledge the cheers.

But there was only one face in the crowd he noticed. Rose was standing there by the rail, watching him, the first and only time she had ever come to see him ride.

Verney gave him a hearty slap on the back. 'Good lad! There'll be a bit extra this week if you keep this up.'

Luke nodded, but his whole being was focused on Rose. There couldn't be more than twenty yards between them; all she had to do was step over the rail and walk across to him. If it was true and she really did love him, she would do that one small thing. But if it was all lies ...

Their eyes met. Any moment now she would come to him.

And then Luke saw him. Charlie Cartwright. He was standing right next to Rose, and suddenly Rose was smiling at him and the child was hugging her like she was its own mother. A stab of jealous rage seared through Luke as he saw Rose turn and walk away, with only the briefest backward glance, following Charlie and Lola through the crowd as if they were already one big happy family.

CHAPTER 35

She's happy now. Happy now she's free of you.

That was the thought that wouldn't leave Luke's mind as he sat alone in the vardo, the doors closed and the windows shuttered. It was dark outside too, but not so dark as Luke Barton's heart.

Her and Charlie. Her and that smug-faced

gorgio scum. The pictures in his head tormented him as he imagined the two of them together. Secret meetings ... How long had it been going on? Long enough for them to make the unborn baby that Luke had thought was his. He didn't care what Cartwright said or what Doreen said, he didn't even care what Rose said. Lies, all lies. All this time, carrying on behind his back, and they didn't even have the guts to tell him to his face.

The anger welled up inside him until it burst out in a spasm of uncontrollable rage. Roaring his jealous pain, he dashed the half-empty bottle of gut-rot whisky to the floor. Luke wasn't a drinking man, not like his brother; but tonight all he could think of was to drink and keep on drinking until oblivion drowned his senses.

Kicking over the table, he started prowling the vardo like Muldo Lee's toothless old caged lion, lashing out at anything and everything in reach. The mirrored shutter by the bed caught his image in the faint glimmer from the one smoky oil-lamp. He shattered it with a single blow, sending shards of glass tinkling to the floor. A second blow swept the china ornaments and the brass candlesticks from the mantelpiece above the stove. Wild with anger and grief, he snatched up the wedding photograph which hung above the chest of drawers. Three figures smiled back at him in the flickering lamplight: Luke, Rose, Ellie. A family. He flung it to the floor and ground his heel into the glass. No more family, no nothing. Only this leaking old vardo, freezing and empty. And he asked himself why Rose would ever want to come back to him. Why should she—what had he to offer her? Nothing but debts and hardship and other people's pity.

Although it was spring, the night was bitter. Luke shivered as he wrapped his arms around himself. The vardo was cold, so cold. His breath misted in front of his face, but all he saw was the icy breath of the black spirits who watched and tormented him from the shadows.

He remembered something. The cans of petrol Verney kept to refuel the stunt bikes. This place was so old and dead and empty. So very cold.

Well, maybe there was something he could do about that.

It was very late, but Rose sat alone in Charlie's kitchen, waiting for him to come home. What was the use of going to bed if she couldn't sleep?

The cup of tea sat in front of her, untouched. Her mind was racing. She glanced at the clock on the mantelpiece for the tenth time, but the hands seemed hardly to have moved. Sleepless and impatient, she could barely wait for morning to come. Now that she had made up her mind, all she wanted was to end the waiting.

A sound made her heart stop. Was that the gate opening? No, it was just the squeak of a loose floorboard, somewhere in the cottage. She called out, 'Ellie? Is that you?'

A small voice answered her from above. 'Mam, me an' Lola can't sleep.'

Rose got up and went into the hallway. Ellie and Lola were half-way down the stairs, hanging over the banister, their tousled heads pressed together like giggling conspirators.

'Go to bed, love,' said Rose. 'You'll see Uncle Charlie in the mornin'.'

'Lola wants a drink,' replied Ellie promptly, miming a drink to Lola who nodded.

'Go to bed an' I'll bring up a glass of water.'

Ellie's face fell. 'Aw, can't I have milk?'

Rose pursed her lips. 'I thought it was Lola that wanted a drink.'

'She does.' Ellie sat her ancient teddy bear on the banister and nodded its head.

'An' now you want one as well?'

'Only if it's milk. If it's water I'm not thirsty.'

The sound of the back door opening brought Ellie leaping down the stairs in two enormous bounds, dragging Lola behind her.

'Mam, it's Uncle Charlie, Uncle Charlie's home!'

The two kids bounced down the passage and into the kitchen, racing and tumbling like untrained puppies. Rose followed more sedately, a little afraid now that the moment had finally come.

Charlie was standing in the kitchen, his kitbag lying on the floor where he had thrown it, Lola clinging like a limpet to his neck and Ellie hugging him round his middle. 'Have you behaved yourselves for Rose?' he demanded, tickling Lola and making her wriggle.

449

'Mam says we're good as gold,' replied Ellie, tugging on Charlie's arm. 'Where's our presents, Uncle Charlie?'

'Ellie!' said Rose, but Charlie didn't seem to mind. He was so patient; never complaining, never judging. It pained her to recall how harshly she'd once judged him.

'Presents?' Setting Lola down, he patted his pockets thoughtfully, as if trying to remember where he'd put something. 'No, don't reckon I've got no presents.'

Rose smiled. They went through this panto-mime every time Charlie went to sea, and they all knew he never came back without bringing something for the kids.

'Uncle Charlie,' pleaded Ellie.

'Presents ... well, let's see.' Charlie slipped a hand into the inside pocket of his jacket and produced two red lollipops, like a conjurer magicking up a bunch of flowers. 'How about these, will they do?'

'Say thank you to Uncle Charlie,' scolded Rose as the lollipops vanished from Charlie's hand.

'Thank you Uncle Charlie,' chanted Ellie. The two girls planted wet kisses on Charlie's cheeks and scampered off upstairs with not so much as a 'good-night'.

'Cupboard love,' grinned Charlie, taking off his jacket and hanging it on a peg. He lifted the lid off the teapot and peered inside. 'Any bread left? Thought I might make myself a butty.'

Rose opened the pantry door and brought out a bottle of Okell's and a plate of fish-paste sandwiches. 'I made these. It's not much ...'

Charlie sat down at the table and flipped the cap off the beer. 'It's a feast.' He gave her a reproachful look as he bit into a sandwich. 'But you need your rest; you shouldn't be sittin' up waitin' on me.'

Rose fiddled with the cord on her dressing gown. Why was this so very difficult to say? Perhaps because she knew it wasn't what he'd wanted to hear.

'I couldn't sleep. I wanted ... There's somethin' I wanted to tell you.'

'Oh?' Charlie swallowed and wiped his mouth. 'Nothin' wrong, is there? Lola's not been playin' you up?'

'No, nothin' like that.' She sat down, resting her hands palm-down on the table. 'I've made my decision, Charlie. I'm goin' back to Luke.'

The golden eyes widened very slightly, but that was the only sign of surprise.

'When?'

'Tomorrow.' Now that she'd said it, Rose felt as if a huge weight of guilt had been lifted from her shoulders. 'There's no point in hangin' around, is there—not now I've made up my mind?'

'Does Luke know?' Charlie struggled not to let emotion show on his face.

Rose fiddled with her wedding ring. 'Not yet. I was goin' to tell him yesterday, then you had to go off on the boat an' there wasn't time ...'

'You're sure you're doin' the right thing?'

'I know how much he wants me back, an'—'

'But is it what *you* want, Rose?' Somewhere, deep in a selfish corner of his heart, Charlie prayed she would say no.

Rose took a deep breath and nodded. Butterflies fluttered in the pit of her stomach. 'Yes. Yes, it's what I want too.'

Charlie leant over and kissed her chastely on the cheek. 'Then I'm happy for you, Rose. Really happy.'

'You think I've made the right choice then?' She looked at him pleadingly, suddenly desperate for his approval. But Charlie's face remained expressionless.

'What does it matter what I think?'

'But you do?'

He squeezed her hand. 'For what it's worth, yes. But he'd better take proper care of you this time.'

'He will,' smiled Rose. 'This time I know he will.'

In the black of night there was no one to see what Luke was doing. No one to see the petrol slooshing out of the can as he shook it all over the vardo. Over the pot-cupboard, the chest of drawers, over the beds where Rose and Ellie had slept. Down the steps in a glistening waterfall; all over the roof and wheels, like deadly rain falling in dripping curtains down the vardo walls.

Fumbling in his pocket for the matches, he gazed back at the other vardos with their sleeping occupants, set well apart from the Barton wagon as if it wasn't good enough for them. Shunned. Just like Luke Barton.

The first match wouldn't light. The second sparked and fizzled out. Feverishly he struck the third and this time it flamed, yellow and bright. He flung it into the vardo through the open door and the petrol ignited with a soft whoosh. Two more matches took care of the exterior, and within seconds the flames possessed it.

An immense sense of release swept over Luke. He could almost imagine that the crackling flames were the screams of the bad, black spirits, the *muladi* who had pursued him all his life.

He laughed, and it felt good.

Someone shouted in the distance. 'Fire! Fire! Get Spence, get the fire brigade!'

But Luke didn't stay around to listen. He didn't even bother to put on his safety helmet, just jumped astride the Velocette and made it roar obediently into life. He almost ran down Percy Sayle as the bike screeched between the rides and out through the gates of Funland, but he scarcely noticed. All Luke could see was the darkened road ahead.

Head down, crouched over the handlebars, Luke opened up the throttle and the Velocette surged forward with a screech of whirling rubber.

Luke knew the TT course by heart, had ridden it to victory a thousand times in his dreams. Down Bray Hill in a desperate, stomach-churning swoop, accelerating so fast that the wind screamed in his ears. Riding out the bump as the machine leapt into the air and bounced back down again. Flat-out to Quarter Bridge, leaning to take the downhill corner and on to Braddan, swerving sharp left then right.

He tried to concentrate on the road, to think of nothing but the machine and the exhilarating freedom of speed. But all the time the voice was whispering in his ear: 'You're a burden to her, Luke Barton. Nothing but a burden.'

No. No. No. The pain in his head throbbed and pulsed, distorting everything, amplifying the hissing voices.

'She's better off without you. You know it's true, why fight it? You're nothing but a failure.'

Why couldn't he think straight any more? The bike cornered awkwardly as they shrieked through Ballacraine and headed north.

'If she comes back to you you'll only thump her again.'

His hands tightened on the handlebars. 'No, no—I'd never lay a finger on her, never again.'

'She doesn't love you, she's afraid of you.'

He didn't even touch the brake as he took the fast left-hand sweep past the junction to Doran's Bend, then the right-hand swing at Laurel Bank. Speed was the only thing that comforted him now, the only thing that dulled the voices and stilled the pains in his head.

Faster and faster and faster. He steamed up Creg-Willys Hill and even the steep gradient didn't slow him down. The throttle was wide open now and the engine was screaming, its heart fit to burst. At Handley's Cottage Luke almost came off on the fast S-bend but the

454

bike righted itself, the tyres scrubbing as they hugged the road and carried him on towards Baaregarroo and Kirk Michael.

Luke was doing eighty-five, maybe more, as the Velocette howled through Kirk Michael and on to Rhencullin.

'It's Charlie she wants. Charlie. Charlie. Charlie.'

He hit Birkin's Bend so fast that he wasn't aware of it till the bike's headlamp picked out the drystone wall. Even so, there was time for him to take control, to swing the bike sharp left and get out of trouble. But the ghost of Archie Birkin was beckoning to him and the wall was rising up faster and faster to meet him; and suddenly he didn't have the will to turn aside.

The bike's front wheel skidded as Luke squeezed out the last ounce of speed. But he clung on tight, and they hit the wall together.

And suddenly he was free.

CHAPTER 36

'Are we really goin' home, Mam?' Ellie asked the next morning, just after breakfast.

Rose turned from putting the last of Ellie's clothes into the suitcase. 'Yes, love. I told you.'

'Home to Dad?'

'Yes!'

Ellie sat down on the edge of the bed she'd been sharing, top-to-tail, with Lola and her mother. 'Mam ...'

'What now?' Rose squashed a pair of ankle socks into the suitcase and tried to fasten the lid.

'Dad won't hit you again, will he?'

That stopped Rose in her tracks for a second; then she clicked the locks shut and buckled the strap. She held her daughter close and ruffled her hair.

'Course he won't. Everythin's goin' to be fine, just you see.'

'What about Lola?' demanded Ellie. 'She's goin' to school at Missus James's now. What if I don't see her no more?'

Rose laughed, trying hard to be light-hearted for Ellie's sake. 'You'll see her. I promise. An' Uncle Charlie too,' she added, as Ellie's mouth opened to ask yet another question.

'Promise?'

'Promise. Now go an' put your coat on. We've got a bus to catch.'

Ellie went off down the stairs and Rose crossed the bedroom to the dressing-table to fetch her hairbrush. She sat down on the stool and looked at herself in the mirror, twirling one strand of unkempt hair around her finger. She'd been called pretty once, but now ...

'You look lovely,' said a voice behind her. Charlie's voice. He stepped into the room and Rose saw his face reflected in the mirror. She stiffened.

'Charlie, don't.'

'It's true. Luke's a lucky man.' He walked across to the bed and picked up the suitcase. 'I'll take this down for you, shall I?'

She swung round on the stool. 'No need, I can manage.' But Charlie clung on to the handle, as though it was more than he could bear to let go.

'I'm not havin' you carryin' this weight. Not all that way. I'll come as far as the Funland gates, it's the least I can do.'

'Well ... thanks.' She got up, stretching her coat over her bump to button it up. 'You've been a good friend to me an' Ellie.'

'Come off it, Rose—'

'No, I mean it, Charlie. All you've done for us, an' after the terrible things I said about you ...'

'They were all true.' Charlie shrugged. 'I deserved 'em.' He coughed edgily. 'Now, best get on, eh? The bus goes in fifteen minutes.'

But they never made it to the bus station. In fact they never made it out of the cottage, because just as Rose was coming down the stairs there was a knock at the front door.

'I'll go!' chirped Ellie, flying to the door and wrenching it open.

On the doorstep stood a tall, thin policeman, his helmet tucked under his arm.

'Mister Cartwright?'

Charlie nodded.

'I'm looking for a ...' The constable consulted his notebook. 'A Missus Barton.'

Rose's stomach turned over. Not more trouble with the police. What could have gone wrong now? She walked slowly down the stairs to the open door. 'Rose Barton? That's me.'

'I think I'd better come in, if that's all right.' The constable stooped to avoid banging his head on the low lintel. 'Somewhere quiet we can talk, is there?'

'In there,' said Charlie, pointing the way into the parlour. 'But what's this all about?'

'If you could just leave us for a few minutes, sir,' said the constable kindly. 'Take the kiddies and make us all a nice cup of tea, eh?'

Charlie looked from the policeman to Rose and back again, hesitated, then ushered the children out of the parlour. The door closed softly behind them, and Rose found herself alone with the constable.

'What's happened?' she demanded. 'If it's more trouble at the fairground ...'

'Best if you sit yourself down, eh?'

'I don't want to sit down,' protested Rose. 'I'm all right as I am.'

'Please, Missus Barton.' The policeman framed his words slowly and quietly. 'I've got some bad news for you.'

Rose felt her legs turn to jelly as she sank into Walleye's old armchair. 'B-bad news?' Horrible imaginings crawled over her skin like swarming insects.

'There's been an accident. Just past Kirk Michael. A motor-bike accident.'

Rose couldn't speak. All she could do was clutch the arms of the chair with fingers that were numb and trembling.

'Thing is, Missus Barton, we've found a body.

458

And we think it may be your husband.'

The distance between Douglas Head and Noble's Hospital couldn't have been much over a mile, but to Rose it felt like the longest journey of her life. All the way there she kept telling herself that the police had made a mistake, that it couldn't be Luke, that there were plenty of other young men on this motor-bike-mad Island who might have ridden out in the middle of the night and got themselves killed.

But what about the burned-out vardo, its carcass still smouldering on the tober? What about Percy Sayle, who'd told the police he'd seen Luke riding out through the gates in the middle of the night? In her heart Rose knew there was no mistake, even before the white-coated attendant took them down to the hospital mortuary.

'He's in here. If you could just follow me.'

The policewoman stood at Rose's side, supporting her elbow. 'You're quite sure about this? We could ask someone else.'

'No.'

'Really, Mrs Barton, if it distresses you—'

'I said no.' The word echoed off the blank, tiled walls. Rose searched the young policewoman's face, hoping to find understanding, but found only a mixture of compassion and bewilderment. The kid couldn't be more than nineteen. How could she understand? She'd hardly even lived yet.

'I've got to see him. I ... I've got to be sure. Can I see him now?'

'Of course. I'll come in with you.'

They went through into a green-tiled, antiseptic-smelling room where a harsh white light burned in the centre of the ceiling. It was very cold and clean and bright, reflections glancing off the polished tiles. Rose held her breath as the sheet twitched back, at once fearing what she might see and cherishing a tiny hope that this might be some other woman's husband.

The face beneath the sheet didn't look like Luke. Not like him at all. The eyelid closed, the lips parted, he didn't look angry any more, or sad, or anything very much at all. This wasn't the face that had shown rage and joy and passion; those weren't the lips that she had kissed and loved. They were cold and blue and lifeless. Luke's spirit had gone. This was a stranger.

'It's him,' she whispered hoarsely, her fingers stroking his brow, shocked to feel his skin so cold, startled to see no blemish on his face save a faint bruise on his left temple. A lump rose in her throat but she swallowed it down. 'How ...?'

The WPC's hand rested on her shoulder.

'It was very quick, his neck snapped when he hit the wall.'

'Then he ... he didn't suffer?'

'He wouldn't have known anything about it.'

The WPC nodded to the attendant to cover Luke's face, but Rose stopped him.

'Please, I want to be with him. Just for a few minutes.'

'Well ... all right. I'll be outside. Call me when you're ready.'

Alone in the antiseptic, airless room. Rose sat down beside Luke and stroked the hair off his face.

'Oh, Luke,' she murmured. 'Oh Luke, forgive me.'

Leaning forward, she rested her head upon his chest and tried to remember how it felt to lie together in their bed, his arms around her, listening to the rain pattering on the vardo roof. But all she could hear was the electric hum of the ceiling fan, casting swirling shadows as it turned above her head, and all she could feel was the coldness of Luke's hand beneath the warmth of her own.

Suddenly her strength crumbled and the grief hit her, squeezing all the breath from her body in one terrible, heart-wrenching sob.

'Noooo! Please God, no!'

Bad things had happened to her before in her life, but this ... this was more than she could bear.

Over the next few days Rose wept until it seemed there could be no more tears left in the world. But for Luke's sake, and for Ellie's, she knew she must find a way to carry on.

'The flowers ...' she murmured, her mind so dazed with grief that she couldn't even remember if she'd ordered any for the funeral.

Doreen sat beside her at Charlie's kitchen table and slid another cup of tea in front of

461

her. 'You ordered them yesterday, don't you remember?'

'I don't remember anythin' much, I can't think straight.' Panic churned inside her. 'I've got to do things proper, Doreen. I've got to—I owe him that at least.'

'You will,' soothed Doreen. 'And with Spence and Verney footing the bill.'

Spence and Verney. Was it guilt, or was it genuine concern that had sent them digging deep into their pockets to pay for Luke's funeral? In life they might have begrudged him a few extra shillings, but in death, it seemed, money was no object.

'Blood money,' she murmured, staring at the dark, brick-red tea. But she knew no one could feel more guilty than she did herself. Was this her punishment for not sticking with Luke through thick and thin, her penance for not going back to him when she had the chance?

'Drink up, Rose, it'll make you feel better.'

Rose stirred her spoon slowly round and round the cup, turning the tranquil surface into a miniature whirlpool. 'I don't want any tea.'

'Have something to eat then.'

'I'm not hungry, just leave me alone!' Rose startled herself with the sound of her own raised voice. She dropped the spoon and it tinkled into the saucer. 'I'm sorry, Doreen, I never meant—'

'It's all right,' Doreen reassured her. 'Shout at me as much as you like, that's what I'm here for.'

Rose pushed the teacup away from her. 'Why

462

do people always think tea makes everythin' better?'

Doreen shrugged. 'I expect it's because they can't think of anything else,' she said. 'I know I can't. I want to help, but I feel so useless.'

'You!' Rose looked at her, bemused. 'But you've done such a lot already. Honest to God, Doreen, I don't know what I'd have done without you here.'

'You've got Charlie too,' Doreen pointed out.

A dull ache pierced the numbness in Rose's chest. 'Oh, Doreen, I can't stay here,' she declared. 'Me an' Ellie, we've got to find somewhere else. What'll people think? My Luke not cold in the ground an' me stayin' here ...'

'But you can't go back to the vardo,' said Doreen gently.

Rose thought of the vardo, its blackened bones still sitting on the tober because nobody could bring themselves to have it taken away. Least of all her. She couldn't even summon up the courage to look at it.

'No,' she conceded, her fingertip following the tracery of cracks in the table-top.

'You could stay with us for a bit. Dad wouldn't mind,' suggested Doreen.

'But you haven't got room.'

'We'll make room. Wesley can move out ...'

'No. No, we'll have to stay here till we find a place of our own,' said Rose. 'If folk talk, it's no more than I deserve.'

Doreen looked horrified. 'Rose, you mustn't talk like that!'

'Why not?' demanded Rose. 'It's true. It's all my fault Luke's dead.'

'It was an accident, you heard what the police said.'

'Oh, an' it was an *accident* he burned down the vardo, was it? If I'd gone back to him like I was goin' to—'

'If you'd gone back he might have hit you again.'

'At least he'd not be dead!'

The two women sat in glum silence for a few minutes, Rose going over and over the same ground in her mind. If she'd gone back to Luke a day earlier ... If she hadn't provoked him into losing his temper ... If they'd never listened to Manfri and Sofia in the first place ... So many ifs, and all of them lost and gone.

'He wasn't himself, Rose,' said Doreen, getting up and pouring the untouched tea down the sink. 'Not after the accident. He changed. If this is anyone's fault it's mine.'

'Yours! How can it be yours?'

'I lent him that bike, remember? If I hadn't ... Look, Rose, you can't go on blaming yourself, it's not your fault. All you were doing was protecting yourself and Ellie. Luke knew that.'

'How can you say that?'

'He ... he told me.' Doreen dried her hands on a tea-towel and sat down again. 'He didn't blame you, Rose—he blamed himself.'

He blamed himself. The words echoed in

Rose's mind, and she remembered Luke's tormented face as he begged her to believe he would never lay another finger on her. Luke blamed himself. Could that be true? A cold clarity seemed to bring everything into painful focus.

'He wanted to kill himself, didn't he? He took that bike an' went out to kill himself.'

'Please, Rose,' begged Doreen. 'You don't know what you're saying.'

'Yes I do. He killed himself.' Rose felt the tears welling up again, and dabbed at her eyes with her sodden handkerchief. 'Because of me.'

'All I know is, he loved you. He really did.'

'I loved him too,' said Rose softly. 'Before ...' She straightened up. 'I've got to make things right, Doreen. The funeral—'

'I've told you, it'll be fine,' Doreen assured her. 'I'll stay here with you as long as you want me to. Then nobody can talk, can they?'

'It's not that ... not just that.' Rose scrunched her hanky into a sodden ball. 'It's all this bad blood. With Manfri an' Sofia ...'

An awful fear held her and wouldn't let her go. Whatever might have passed between her and Luke, it meant everything to bury him with dignity. But what if Sofia wouldn't let her do that? What if she made a scene and ruined everything?

'Surely Sofia wouldn't make trouble at her own son's funeral,' said Doreen.

But Rose wished she could be so sure.

CHAPTER 37

Rose stood in a corner of Onchan churchyard, looking down at the little wooden cross. In her mind's eyes she pictured the headstone which would soon stand there, and its simple inscription:

LUKE BARTON
ROMANY
1921–1947

Hazy sunshine warmed the fresh earth that rose over the grave in a smooth mound. It looked stark and bare now, but soon it would grow flowers and grass, and the fresh-hewn stone would soften with lichens and moss.

'Come on, love,' said Edie Dobbs, tenderly taking her daughter's arm. 'There's people want to pay their respects.'

In the distance, a straggly line of mourners was making its way from the church to the cars that Horace Spence had laid on to take them to the hotel. The number of people who had turned out for Luke's funeral astonished Rose; so many of them had no apparent reason to think kindly of a gypsy showman down on his luck. Sean Rourke, Dot, Percy Sayle and the Darwells, Sid Christian and Josie James. Even people they hardly knew.

'In a minute, Mam.'

Edie remained beside her, looking down at the grave. 'It was a good send-off,' she said. 'Pity your dad couldn't come.'

'*Couldn't,* Mam? Or wouldn't?'

With difficulty, Rose stooped to place her simple bunch of wild flowers on Luke's grave. Her pregnant body felt heavy and exhausted, and Edie had to help her back up, the feather on her old black straw hat swaying forlornly in the moist breeze.

'Your dad's a pig-headed old fool,' she said. 'He ought to be ashamed of himself. Now come on, the others are waitin'.'

As Rose turned she saw Sofia Barton standing by the church gates, her face grim, her eyes hard and bright as black marbles. Like an old black crow waiting for carrion.

'I can't, Mam,' she whispered.

'Come on,' repeated Edie, following Rose's gaze to where Sofia stood. 'There's no such word as can't, an' you've nothin' to be ashamed of.'

But Rose could feel a dozen pairs of eyes following her as she walked down the path with her mother, imagined she could hear whispers of condemnation: 'She's no better than she should be'; 'Living in another man's house, so they say'; 'Her husband did away with himself because of her ...'

At the gate, Edie and Sofia eyed each other up like familiar enemies.

'Missus Dobbs.'

'Sofia,' nodded Edie. She turned to Rose.

'You'll be all right now, I'll just go an' have a word with Charlie.'

'Mam ...' pleaded Rose, but Edie was gone and there was no escape.

'Charlie.' Sofia enunciated the word very precisely, very flatly, without an ounce of expression; but it felt like a knife twisting in Rose's heart.

'He ... he's ...' She was going to say 'a friend', but that sounded like an excuse for something shameful; and Edie was right: why should she make excuses to Sofia? 'His name's Charlie Cartwright. I'm stayin' in his house with Ellie. Just till I find a place for us to live.'

To her surprise, Sofia did not spit in her face or call her a *gorgio* whore. She just nodded as though this was what she had expected to hear. 'Death,' she said quietly. 'It change everything. My Luke ...' Sofia's face crumpled into a dry sob. 'I never told him I was sorry—I wanted to, but I am a proud woman. An' now he is gone. My son.'

Rose felt a stab of pity. Despite every vicious twist of Sofia's malevolence, every vengeful thing she had done to cause Rose and Luke pain, this was still an old woman who had lost a son. Yet she couldn't bring herself to comfort her. The pain had been too great.

Sofia looked towards the grave. 'This is not the Romany way.'

'I did what I thought was right,' said Rose defensively.

Sofia's long skirts fluttered in the breeze. The marble-black eyes fixed Rose with a basilisk stare. 'In the old time, when a man die, they make a ... a sacrifice, yes? They destroy everything—break the china, bury the clothes, burn the vardo ...' She cast down her eyes to the dusty earth. 'The sacrifice for Luke, it is done.'

The sacrifice. Rose imagined the vardo burning, and remembered how Luke had told her once that things had gone badly for them because they were living in a dead man's wagon with a dead man's spirit. She had never felt any warmth towards Sofia, and yet she could not fail to be moved by the terrible depth of her grief. What words of consolation could she offer when she had so little for herself?

'Luke's at peace now,' she ventured. 'He knows you loved him.'

But Sofia's expression darkened. 'At peace! He is dead, he is gone, he knows nothing.' She trapped Rose's gaze and would not let it go. 'He should not have married a *gorgio.*'

'He was a good man. I loved him,' said Rose. But could you still love him now? whispered a voice inside her head. In the beginning you loved him as your husband, in the end it was more like a mother's love for a child.

'Love,' scoffed Sofia. 'Love is not important. Only family is important.' Looking down at the swell of Rose's pregnant belly, she laid her hands upon it. 'This child. Is it my son's or this other man's?'

Rose knew what people were whispering in corners, she should have been well prepared for Sofia's question—but still it shocked her. She pushed Sofia's hands away. 'You don't own this baby, it's Luke's. Mine an' Luke's!'

Her anger seemed to please Sofia. 'It will be a boy,' she said.

'How—'

'He will not go hungry.'

And with that parting shot, Sofia turned on her heel and walked right out of Rose's life.

The next few days passed in a blur of unreality. Rose felt numb, as though her grief had worn itself out and she didn't know what to replace it with. The best she could do was take each day as it came, put on a brave face for Ellie, and try not to think about tomorrow.

The letter arrived the following week, in a brown envelope with a Birkenhead postmark. That evening, when Ellie and Lola were in bed, Rose showed it to Charlie.

'Looks official,' said Charlie.

'It's from Sofia's solicitor,' explained Rose as she washed the dishes. 'About the rides.'

'What—tellin' you she wants them back?' Charlie looked aghast. The sheer callousness of Rosie's in-laws never ceased to astonish him. 'That's a bit below the belt.'

'No. Not that. Read it. It says she's givin' me permission to go on runnin' them.' Permission! Rose thought sourly. After everything that had happened, this was the limit of Sofia's kindness. 'That must be what she meant about the baby not goin' hungry.'

'So.' Charlie folded the letter and tucked it back behind the clock on the mantelpiece. 'What are you goin' to do then?'

Rose scrubbed away at the inside of a pan. 'I've got no option, have I? Where else am I goin' to get any money?'

'But I told you, Rose, you don't need to worry about money, not now anyhow. You an' Ellie can stay here as long as you like.'

Rose banged the pan down on to the draining board. 'We're not charity cases, you know.' She knew it wasn't right to take it out on Charlie, but she couldn't help herself. She grabbed another pan from the pile of dirty dishes.

'I never said you were.' Charlie cursed his clumsiness with words. He wanted so badly to say the right thing.

'Soon as we've found somewhere we'll be out from under your feet.'

'Rose ...' Charlie tried to take the pan off her but she shooed him away and went on scrubbing. 'Rose, leave that. You're tired out ... why don't you sit down?'

'Give me them plates,' replied Rose, and Charlie reluctantly handed them over.

'How can you run the rides all on your own?'

'I'm not on my own.' Rose put every ounce of energy she had left into scouring the baked-on grease from a pie-plate. 'Sean was at the funeral. He said he'd come back an' work for me if I wanted. An' there's Cec an' Mario an' Gracie ...'

'Here, let me have that before you scrub the pattern off it.' Charlie prised the pie-plate from between her fingers and reluctantly she let it go.

'So is that what you're goin' to do then?'

Rose dabbled her fingers in the water, slimy with washing soda. Her heart was racing in her chest, the feeling of numbness giving way to a horrible crushing sensation of panic. She was utterly drained. The last thing she wanted to do was face the fairground again, with all its memories; yet to run back to Birkenhead was no solution either.

Right now, what she wanted more than anything else in the world was for Charlie to wrap his big, comforting arms round her and hug her, hold her like a child and tell her that this was all a bad dream, that she would wake up soon and everything would be sunshine and flowers.

Instead, she just stared down at her wedding ring and felt guilty for wanting to be happy.

'Can't see what else I can do,' she said. 'I need the money so's Ellie an' I can get a place of our own.'

Charlie patiently pulled her away from the sink, finding her a towel for her dripping hands. If only he dared hold her close, the only way he could think of to take away the pain. But he must not. And it tormented him to feel her so close, close enough to breathe in the warm, clean scent of her hair.

'Come an' sit down.'

'But I've got all these still to do—'

'Sit. We've got to talk.'

She lowered her heaviness on to a kitchen chair. 'What's the good of talkin'?'

Charlie perched on the edge of the table.

'Listen, Rose ... About you an' Ellie: how many times do I have to tell you, you can stay here till Doomsday if you want—in fact I *want* you to stay!'

Rose raised her stubborn chin. 'I can't stay, Charlie. You know damn well I can't!'

'Why? Because of some nasty-minded tittle-tattle? Not one word of it's true. An' when did you ever care about what people said?'

Rose turned the worn, dulled wedding band round and round her work-roughened finger. 'I just ... can't.'

Charlie got up and started walking round the kitchen, head down, hands in pockets. 'All right,' he said out of the blue. 'I'll move out.'

'What?'

'I'll go back to livin' on the boat, like before. Then nobody can say anythin', can they?'

Rose gaped at him. 'You'd do that? For me?'

As Charlie looked across and answered, Rose saw the depth of love in his eyes. It hit her like a thunderbolt, leaving her stunned and trembling. 'I'll do whatever it takes, Rose. Tell me to pack my bags an' get out of your life if that's what you want, tell me to take a runnin' jump off Douglas Head ...'

'Please, Charlie—'

'... but don't ask me to stop carin' about you, because that's the one thing I can't do.'

'Oh, Charlie.' A sob rose in her throat. 'Oh, Charlie not that, please don't say that.'

Charlie stared at the floor, wretched with remorse. 'I'm sorry, Rose, but it's the truth.

473

I had to say it once, I'll not say it again.'

A thought sprang, unbidden, into Rose's head; a question that had demanded an answer for so long. It hurt to voice it, but she had to know.

'Did you care about her too, Charlie? About Lola's mother?'

Charlie didn't answer. He went over to the dresser, slid open one of the drawers and took out a tin box. He brought it over to the table and opened it, tipping its contents on to the table-top. Foreign coins, photographs, a couple of medals spilled out on to the bleached and battered wood. A packet of letters too, weather-stained and tied with yellowed string.

Charlie saw Rose's eyes fall on them and nodded. 'I kept them all, Rose.'

'All my letters? Then why? Why did you stop writin', Charlie?'

Charlie picked through the jumble and selected a crumpled photograph. It showed two men and a girl in mud-spattered uniforms, their arms round each other's shoulders. 'That's John Gorry there. An' that's me.' He licked his lips. 'An' that there in the middle ... that's Consuela.'

Consuela. The name sounded so strange, so exotic. Rose took the photograph and made herself look at the girl's face. Why had Charlie preferred her? Was she rich, beautiful, brave, clever? But all she saw was an ordinary girl with her black hair cropped short like a boy's, her trim figure boyish in a man's uniform two sizes too big for her, and a pistol thrust through

474

her belt. The only thing that really struck Rose was how much she resembled Lola.

'This ... this is her?'

'Lola's mother. Yes.' Rose studied Charlie's face as he looked at the picture, but she saw no love there, only a kind of wistful sadness. 'She was a brave girl, fought like a man. An' it was hell out there, Rose, hell on earth. All mud an' blood an' shit. We ... It was the winter of thirty-eight, I was twenty an' she was twenty-five. I knew nothin' an' I thought I knew the lot. It was lonely out there an' I've never been more scared in me life. What happened that night with her ... well. it shouldn't have happened.'

Rose felt a pang of jealous pain as she imagined them together, Charlie and this dark-haired girl; then it was gone and Charlie took up his story.

'It only happened twice, but Consuela fell pregnant. It was only when she told me that I realised what I'd done. I couldn't write to you any more, Rose. I couldn't tell you I loved you when ... when all the time, me an' her ...' He swallowed. 'Lola was born in September. Three months later, the fascists rounded up Consuela an' executed her.'

The young face on the photograph smiled out at Rose, proud and serene, as though death was unimaginable.

'Executed,' repeated Rose.

'When I found out what had happened I took Lola to her grandparents in the south of Spain. She was just a tiny baby then ... I didn't even know she was deaf.'

'But did you love her, Charlie?' insisted Rose. 'Did you love Consuela?'

'No.' Charlie met her gaze without flinching, and she knew he was telling the truth. 'She meant a lot to me, but love her? No, never. She was my friend, she saved my life a dozen times.' He sorted through the mess of junk on the table, selecting and discarding each small memory. 'I was in prison for a year. Then I spent the war runnin' guns to the Free French in North Africa.'

He picked up the medal and dropped it on to the table with a tinny clunk. 'They gave me this,' he said with disgust. 'The Legion of Honour. A medal for gettin' people killed—doesn't seem right somehow. After the war I found out Lola'd been locked up in this horrible institution. I couldn't just leave her there ...'

Rose picked up the medal and turned it over in her hands. There was so much she'd never even guessed about Charlie, so much she was just beginning to learn.

'All those years,' Charlie went on. 'I thought about you a lot, you know, just wishin' an' wonderin' ... An' once I'd got Lola—'

Rose cut in, a twinge of the old bitterness resurfacing: 'You thought: I know, Rose is a soft touch, I'll sweet-talk her an' she's bound to take me back.'

'Yeah ... No. I dunno what I thought, not really.' Charlie ran his hand through his hair. 'I just wanted to see you again.'

He scraped everything back into the tin and

jammed the lid back on. 'I'm sorry, I shouldn't have shown you all that rubbish.'

'I'm glad you did,' replied Rose. And she meant it.

'Look,' said Charlie, putting the tin back into the dresser, 'you an' Ellie an' the new baby need somewhere to live—an' Lola needs someone to take care of her when I'm not here. Why shouldn't it be you?'

Rose looked down at her hands, folded across her belly. 'I don't know, Charlie ...'

'A place to live for as long as you need it, that's all I'm offerin'. No strings.'

From somewhere above, the sound of muffled sobs brought Rose struggling to her feet. 'That's Ellie cryin' again. I've got to go to her.' She got as far as the door and turned round. 'I'll think about it Charlie, I can't promise more than that.'

CHAPTER 38

In a strange way, it was too easy. Too easy to stay away from Funland and let Sean run the show. Too easy to hide behind the half-drawn curtains in Charlie's cottage. Too easy to pretend that the last ten years had never happened. But they *had* happened, and even as Rose struggled to make sense of the future, she couldn't shake off the past.

Doreen was kind, Charlie was kind; sometimes

Rose felt they were too kind. At eight months pregnant it was so tempting to give up, to let go, be swept along and cosseted, just be the helpless little woman for whom everything was too much. Well, she'd done that for a month, but it hadn't brought her any peace. She'd loved Luke too long and too fiercely to put the past behind her—and anyway she knew now that she didn't want to.

Besides, Luke still needed her. Needed her to carry on his rides. And she wasn't going to let him down now.

Charlie offered to go with her to Funland, but she turned him down flat. She knew what had to be done, and that she was strong enough to face up to it alone. All the same, a creeping dread slowed her steps as Doreen helped her out of the van and she walked the last few yards to the gates of the fairground.

'Shall I come in with you?' asked Doreen.

'No need. Just leave me here, I'll be fine.'

It was early morning, but Funland was a swarm of breathless activity, men shouting to each other, noise everywhere as boards were taken down and rides powered up for the coming day.

'To me, Fred.'

'Mind yer 'ead.'

'Got that, Sid? Don't drop it now ...'

At first no one noticed her in all the hustle and bustle. A tub of wet fish trundled past her on its way to the Luxury Fish & Chip Saloon. A semi-deflated football bumped past her legs, swiftly followed by a scurrying child. As the boy scooped up the ball, he saw Rose.

'Missus Rose!'

'Billy, love. How's your mam an' dad?'

'All right, s'pose.' He wiped his nose on his mud-encrusted sleeve. 'I'm sorry,' he added gruffly. 'About Mister Barton.'

'I know,' said Rose.

'Sorry I nicked that dog off him.'

Ranty Darwell came lumbering across the tober like a big grizzly bear. 'Billy Darwell, you little ...' Seeing Rose he stopped, suddenly struck dumb. 'Rose.'

'Hello, Ranty.' She smiled as best she could. It was their first meeting since Luke's funeral, and from the look on Ranty's face he felt even more uncomfortable than she did. 'How's Lissa?'

There wasn't time to listen to Ranty's reply, because all at once she was surrounded by familiar faces. Sid Christian clasped her hands and pecked her on the cheek. 'Rose, oh Rose, I don't know what to say ...'

'You should be at home puttin' your feet up, Missus,' scolded Percy Sayle. 'Not traipsin' round here ...'

'Just you come back to our vardo an' have a proper sit down,' interjected a woman Rose didn't even recognise, putting an arm round her shoulders. 'Nice cup o' tea with a bit of gin in it, that's what you need ...'

Rose looked around at the circle of faces. Some she had grown fond of since she and Luke had come to Funland; some had caused her nothing but trouble; others she scarcely knew. She had been terrified of coming back here, certain that there would be cruel remarks and meaningful stares, but all these faces showed nothing but sympathy and kindness.

She remembered something Manfri had said, long ago: 'Fairfield people don't have much, but treat 'em right an' they'll give you everythin'.' A lump rose in her throat. Where had they been, all these kind faces, when she and Luke were up against it and she'd felt so alone? Why couldn't they have helped her then? But that was a childish thought. They were here now, and she was grateful.

'Later,' she promised. 'When I've sorted things out.'

She walked on, acknowledging greetings as she went, observing changes here and there. But it was the red and yellow canvas tilt of the roundabout that drew her, the rounding boards proclaiming in red and gilt: 'BARTON'S TRADITIONAL ROOSTER GALLOPERS'.

As she walked past the Wiggley-Waggley, Rose saw that Sean and Cec were by the gallopers, having one of their famous arguments, fingers pointing, arms waving. And there was Gracie, darting about between them, ever the peacemaker, trying to get a word in edgeways.

'I tell you, I'm not doin' it,' growled Cec.

'An' I tell you, you are,' snapped back Sean.

'How come Mario gets to go in the pay booth, an' all I ever do is hump bleedin' coconuts about?'

'Come on, Cec,' pleaded Gracie, but she might as well have been talking to herself.

'Why?' enunciated Sean with venomous precision. 'Why? Because Mario can add up, an' you're just a stupid great lump of ...'

Typical, thought Rose, nothing changes. Sean might be a born spieler, but he didn't have the faintest idea how to handle Cec.

And that was the moment she found the courage to walk right up to the gallopers and take charge.

Now that she was back, it seemed to Rose that she had discovered a hidden resource of energy, a drive that made her keep on working even when she thought she could go no further: for the new baby's sake, and for Luke ... and for Ellie.

Poor Ellie, she thought to herself, watching the little girl push food around her plate. It's hit her hard, so hard that nothing I can say does any good.

First thing the next day, she went across to Horace Spence's office and demanded a better pitch for the Gallopers.

'They're makin' twice what the Chairoplanes were makin',' she told him when he protested.

'That's as mebbe, but—'

'No buts,' she said. 'I want a better pitch an' I'm not shiftin' from here till I get it.'

Horace squirmed as Rose settled herself comfortably in his leather armchair. Five minutes later, she had everything she wanted.

Jack Verney was sitting outside his luxurious living-wagon when Rose came to confront him, Ellie dragging disconsolately in her wake.

'Rose.' He looked her up and down. It wasn't like Jack Verney to look uncomfortable, but there were beads of sweat on his brow.

'I want a word, Jack.'

'Oh. Right. You'd ... er, better come inside then,' he said, getting up from his chair.

'Come on, love,' Rose urged as Ellie hung back.

'Don't want.'

'Please, love ...'

But Ellie pulled her hand free and ran off, pushing her way blindly through the milling crowds until she was lost from sight.

'She's took it bad,' observed Verney.

Rose rounded on him. 'Bad? You'd take it bad if someone gave your dad a motor bike to kill himself with!' As soon as the words were out of her mouth she regretted them. 'I'm sorry,' she said. 'I should've kept my big mouth shut.'

'No, I had it coming.' Verney knocked out his pipe and slipped it back into the top pocket of his shirt. 'Something I can do for you, Rose?'

'Spence is givin' me a better pitch for the Gallopers.'

Verney's bushy eyebrows lifted half an inch. A look of respect crossed his face. 'Is he now?'

'I need to get them moved, next Sunday. But Terry an' Cec won't be here, an' I can't manage with just Mario an' Sean.'

'So you want to borrow a couple of my men?' He looked doubtful. 'Next Sunday's difficult ... I'm short-handed. What about the week after?'

Rose didn't back down; this was one fight she wouldn't concede. 'You owe me, Jack,' she said.

He hesitated briefly, then nodded. 'Next Sunday it is.'

Rose didn't have to look far to find Ellie. She knew exactly where she'd be.

The little girl was sitting cross-legged on the ground, fingers plucking at the rectangle of blackened grass where the vardo had stood. Rose's heart went out to her, but what could she say that hadn't already been said a thousand times?

'Ellie, love ...'

Ellie didn't even look up. 'Go away,' she said dully. 'Leave me alone.'

Rose tried again, coming nearer and stroking her daughter's golden hair. 'Please, love, you can't stay here.'

Ellie shrugged her off and turned on her with blazing eyes. 'Why? You don't care, you don't care about anythin'!'

The words scythed into Rose's heart. 'Course I care, I love you.'

'You don't care about Dad. You don't even miss him. Nobody misses him but me.' And she burst into tears, her shoulders heaving with sobs as she curled forward into a tight ball of misery, hugging her scuffed knees.

'Oh, Ellie. Ellie, sweetheart, you mustn't think that.'

It wasn't easy to lower herself down on to the grass beside Ellie, but Rose managed it.

'Why not?' sobbed Ellie. 'It's true.'

'No,' said Rose. 'It's *not* true. I haven't forgotten Luke, I'll never forget him. An' I've not stopped lovin' him either, any more than I could stop lovin' you.'

Tentatively, she reached out a hand and laid it on Ellie's shoulders. The child didn't uncurl, but at least she didn't shy away at the touch. Rose prayed desperately for the right words: please God, this time let me say the right thing, for Ellie's sake.

'Sometimes ... people die,' she said, stroking the long smoothness of Ellie's hair. 'No matter how much you love them, no matter how much you want them to go on livin'.'

'Not Dad,' sobbed Ellie into the folds of her skirt. 'Not my Dad.'

'I know it's hard,' said Rose. 'It's hard for me too—I miss him every day. But we have to keep goin'; he wouldn't want us to just give up, would he?' She thought how very close she had come to giving up. 'Would he?'

Ellie raised her head a few inches to look at her mother. 'N-no,' she said doubtfully between sobs.

'The bad things that happen ... in the end they stop hurtin' so much. An' that's when we have to start puttin' them behind us.'

'But you can't!' wailed Ellie. 'You can't. You can't make me forget my daddy.'

Rose put her arms round her daughter and hugged her very tight, kissing her again and again. 'Oh, Ellie, I don't want you to forget him. That's the last thing I want. It's just ... we have to move on, see?'

Ellie sniffed and snuggled her face into her mother's hair.

Rose searched for a way to explain. 'It's like ... you know I told you you had another dad, a dad before Luke was your dad?'

Ellie nodded.

'Well, if I hadn't put him behind me, Luke would never have been your dad. An' you wouldn't've wanted that, would you?'

Ellie's face emerged, strands of hair stuck to her tear-stained cheeks. 'No, Mam.'

'Luke wants you to be happy, Ellie.' Rose stroked away the stray hairs, knowing that what she was saying was as much a comfort to herself as it was to Ellie. She wanted so much to believe it. She *had* to believe it. 'Why do you think he was out practisin' so late at night? To be a better rider, to give a better show.' She held Ellie very tight against her, feeling the new child kick against her belly. 'To make us proud of him.'

'Oh Mam,' said Ellie. 'We *are* proud of Dad, aren't we?'

'Very proud.' Rose struggled to her feet, extending a hand to Ellie. 'An' we want him to be proud of us, don't we?'

'Yes, Mam.'

'Come on then, love.'

Ellie took her hand and stood up. 'Where are we goin', Mam?'

'To give all these punters the best galloper ride they've ever had.'

The baby arrived in the middle of a sticky summer night, so swiftly and suddenly that there was no time to get Rose to the Jane Crookall maternity wing. And Rose was glad it had happened that way, as dawn broke on the second day and she and her new son lay together in the big feather bed, watching the seagulls swoop and wheel over Douglas Bay.

She must have fallen asleep, for the next thing she knew Doreen was hovering on the threshold, half-hidden behind a huge bunch of flowers.

'Can I ...? Is it all right?' She held out the flowers. 'I brought these.'

Rose struggled up in the bed, easing one of the pillows behind her back, and kissed her sleepy son on the forehead. 'Come in, sit down.'

Doreen perched on the edge of the basket chair and laid the flowers on the counterpane. 'Oh Rose. He's lovely.'

Rose eased the blanket off her baby's face and stroked the shock of blue-black hair. 'Just like his dad,' she whispered. 'Would you like to hold him?'

Doreen held out awkward arms and giggled nervously as Rose placed the baby in them.

'I hope I don't drop him!'

'You won't.'

'I can't tell one end from the other when it comes to babies.' Doreen made cooing noises at the baby and he peered up at her through tiny, unfocused eyes. 'I'm better with motor bikes. How about you ... are you all right?'

Rose nodded. 'I've got him to live for now,' she said, love welling up inside her like a warm spring. 'Him an' Ellie.' She watched Doreen, clumsily rocking the newborn child, looking just as she herself must have looked when she first had Ellie. ' 'Spect you'll have one of your own one day.'

'Doubt it!' Doreen scoffed. 'Dan put me right off men.'

'That Sean Rourke's a good man,' commented Rose. 'Thinks the world of you an' all.'

Doreen coloured up. 'Rose!'

'It's true.' Rose wriggled on to her side, easing her aching back, and took the child back from Doreen, soothing his waking cries. 'You shouldn't let chances pass you by. Should she, littl'un?'

'Where's Charlie?' asked Doreen, changing the subject.

'Off somewhere with the *Rose Marie*. He'll have a shock when he gets back an' there's four of us here.'

Doreen edged her chair nearer the bed. 'Is it true what I heard? That Spence is giving you this cottage?'

Rose nodded. It had come as a shock to her too. Then again, it wasn't costing the old skinflint much to show everybody how generous he was.

'He said it should've been Luke's by right, an' now it ought to be mine.'

'But what about Charlie an' Lola?'

'They're stayin'.'

Doreen looked surprised. 'But I thought—'

'I know. An' Charlie was all for movin' out. But he took me in when I had nowhere else to go; I'm not throwin' him out on the street, not with a kid to look after. There's room here for all of us.' Unbuttoning her nightdress, she put the baby to her breast and watched him latch on eagerly. 'There's somethin' I wanted to ask you.'

'What?'

'Will you be his godmother?'

Doreen's expression turned from astonishment to delight. 'Me? A godmother? I'm not very ... holy.'

Rose smiled. 'You've got your head screwed on right—you'll do.'

'Have you chosen a name yet?' asked Doreen.

'Yes,' replied Rose, a single tear budding at the corner of her eye. 'I'm callin' him Robert. Robert Luke.'

TWELVE YEARS LATER

Douglas, Isle of Man, 1959

The wind blew in bitter gusts through the cracks in the wooden shed, but Rob Barton hardly noticed. His nimble fingers worked quickly, rubbing off rust here, dabbing on oil there, putting the old steam organ to rights, the way Aunt Doreen had shown him. It looked like being a long, slow job but Rob knew he'd get it done, no matter how long it took. Once he'd set his mind to doing something, he never gave up.

The shed door rattled open and Rose came in, five-year-old Alice scampering in before her, running up to her brother and flinging her arms round his neck.

'Alice, no!' scolded Rose, half-laughing at the look of disgust on Rob's face as he wiped the kiss from his cheek. 'You'll get your nice frock all oily. Come on, Rob, time to go.'

Rob's face fell. 'Aw, Mam, can't I just ...?'

Rose shook her head, tidying a strand of her red-brown hair, streaked here and there with a few grey hairs. At thirty-nine she'd kept her figure and was still a handsome woman, smartly dressed too, in her Sunday best.

'Come on an' get yourself washed. If you don't get changed now, you'll miss the party.'

'I don't mind missin' the party,' Rob ventured

hopefully, but his mother gave him a playful cuff round the ear.

'Get in that house *now*. An' make sure you wash behind your ears,' she called after him as he slouched off towards the cottage, hands deep in the pockets of his oily trousers. 'You too,' she told Alice, and the little girl bounced off down the path, dancing rings round her brother in her pretty ballerina-style frock. Alice at least understood that this was a special day for Ellie and Lola. It wasn't every day your two sisters shared a twenty-first birthday party.

Rose lingered a little longer in the workshop, fingers running over the shabby old steam-organ, remembering ...

'Doreen an' Sean are here,' announced Charlie, sauntering in through the open door. 'What are you up to in here?'

'Oh, you know ...' The old, blistered paint felt rough but familiar under her fingertips.

'Not wishin' we'd kept it, are you?'

'Oh no. The new organ we've got on the Gallopers is much better. I was just rememberin'. You know, how Luke found this one in Percy's shed, an' now Rob's workin' on it too. When I came in just now, an' saw him kneelin' there ... he looked the spittin' image of his dad.'

Charlie slipped his arm round Rose's waist and drew her very close, planting a gentle kiss in her hair. 'Don't be sad, Rose, love.'

'I'm not sad, Charlie. That's just it.' She smiled up at him. 'It's like nothing ever really dies, not if you love it enough. If you love somethin' enough, it's for ever.'

This Large Print Book for the Partially sighted, who cannot read normal print, is published under the auspices of

THE ULVERSCROFT FOUNDATION

Other MAGNA Romance Titles
In Large Print

ROSE BOUCHERON
The Massinghams

VIRGINIA COFFMAN
The Royles

RUTH HAMILTON
Nest Of Sorrows

SHEILA JANSEN
Mary Maddison

NANCY LIVINGSTON
Never Were Such Times

GENEVIEVE LYONS
The Palucci Vendetta

MARY MINTON
Every Street